REBEL HEART

SAINT VIEW REBELS
BOOK 3

ELLE THORPE

ELLE THORPE PTY LTD

Copyright © 2023 by Elle Thorpe

All rights reserved.

No part of this book may be reproduced in any form or by any electronic or mechanical means, including information storage and retrieval systems, without written permission from the author, except for the use of brief quotations in a book review.

Editing by Studio ENP.

Proofreading by Barren Acres Editing.

Original cover by Elle Thorpe. Photo by Wander Aguiar.

Discreet cover by Emily Wittig Designs.

For Donna.
Not sure how I ever ran this business without you. Thank you for all your help.
Elle x

1

REBEL

"Don't shoot! Oh God, please. Don't shoot."

Adrenaline shook me from head to toe. My finger on the trigger trembled. I forced my outstretched arms to remain steady, though they tried so hard to wobble.

I held a gun on my sister.

But the bullet in the chamber was meant for the man she was protecting.

"Move, Kara!" I screamed again. "This needs to end. He needs to die!"

Caleb's laughter echoed back from behind his human shield. "She's not going to do that. I've got your niece and I'm the only one who knows where she is." His eyes glinted with the evil that came straight from his soul. "You kill me, her baby is dead too."

One quick glance at Kara's expression, and the desperate pleading in her eyes told me everything Caleb had said was true. She was broken. A shell of a woman. Torn apart with grief for the baby he'd taken from her.

He was a monster, responsible for all her pain. For mine. For Bliss's.

I wanted to pull the trigger. I craved the crack of the gun and the noise he'd make when the bullet hit him right in the chest.

Watching him slump down into the dirt, gasping and pleading for his life, would be the only thing that satisfied the anger inside me.

I couldn't do it.

I couldn't leave an innocent child to die.

My wrists went limp, the gun pointing harmlessly at the ground.

"That's what I thought." Caleb gave a smug smile, backing away to a car parked at the edge of the graveyard, dragging Kara with him by the scruff of her neck.

Tears poured down her cheeks, her eyes silently begging me to let her go.

Caleb reached the driver's-side door and got it open, his gaze only leaving mine to flick to Bliss's, his ex-fiancée. He eyed her swollen belly, and his lip curled. "My, my, my. Quite the whore you've been, haven't you?"

Behind me, Bliss's guys were held back only by her putting one hand up, signaling them to stay put. Vibrating anger rippled between them, their desperate need to launch across space and put their hands around Caleb's throat palpable.

But she was their queen, and they followed her lead without question.

"What happened to you, Caleb? Who hurt you enough to turn you into..." She looked him up and down with pity in her eye. "...this?" She took a step forward, her eyes blazing. "Did your mom not love you? Did she see through your fake smiles to the pathetic little boy you are at your core?"

Caleb's eyes narrowed at the woman who had once loved him. The full brunt of his hate focused on Bliss, but it was only Kara he could physically hurt. He yanked her hair so viciously, a wound tore open in her scalp. She let out a scream of pain, her head jerking.

Blood coated Caleb's fist.

Bliss cringed at the sight, but she didn't stop. "You don't have to be like this. Whatever your anger at me, or Rebel, it has nothing to do with her. Let her go. Give her back her baby and let her go."

Caleb laughed darkly. "I hear you talking, Bethany-Melissa. So. Much. Talk. All the fucking time. Do you not learn? You don't call the shots. You never did."

He shoved Kara away with a vicious push that sent the woman to the ground. She hit it hard, crying out in pain, clutching her head.

Caleb slammed his door shut. The engine kicked over with a deafening roar.

Despite her injury, Kara's eyes widened, and she shot to her feet, throwing herself toward the car. "No! No! Take me with you!" She pummeled the driver's-side window, leaving a bloody smear behind. "Caleb, please! Take me too!"

Caleb gunned the engine without glancing at her. He put his foot down on the accelerator, and the car sped away, rounding a corner to disappear out of sight.

For the longest moment, silence descended over all of us. Birds didn't chirp. Nobody breathed.

Then Kara dropped to her knees, a keening wail slipping from her lips.

Beside me, Bliss clapped a hand over her mouth, stifling a sob.

I made the mistake of looking down.

A body lie at the mouth of the open grave, an exit wound in his back from where my bullet had passed straight through him.

Hugh stared at me with unseeing eyes. The whites showed all around the irises, like he'd been surprised I'd actually had the guts to pull the trigger. Blood dribbled out of his mouth, down his chin, and onto the browning winter grass beneath him.

I'd done that.

I'd killed a man.

The impact hit me like a freight train now Caleb wasn't there to focus on. My knees gave out, too, and I stumbled forward a step, teetering on the edge of the grave meant for my mother's casket.

Panic crept in. There was an entire church full of mourners barely half a mile away. They would have heard the gunshot. Kara's screams. They might have called the cops.

Or worse, they hadn't, and they'd all be down here at any minute, ready to watch a casket be lowered into the cold, hard, unforgiving ground.

The world around me spun in dizzying circles, colors blurring, sounds distorting.

Fang caught me, steadying me with strong hands and a sharp shake. "Pix. Hey. We aren't done here. You can't check out."

I stared at him, the world coming back into focus when I concentrated on his icy-blue eyes.

I didn't want to check out. Not again.

There were people here who needed me.

But more than that, I was done being weak.

I pulled my shoulders back and glanced over at Scythe. "I need a favor."

He had Bliss wrapped in his arms, but his face lit up, like he already knew what I was about to ask him.

"Can you deal with that?" I nodded toward Hugh's body. "And quickly? I don't know how long we have until people come down from the church or the police show up. Either wouldn't be great."

He handed Bliss off to Nash then rolled his eyes at me, toeing the body with his heavy black boot. "Please. Easiest cleanup ever." He gave Hugh's body a solid kick. "Timberrrr!"

The dead man toppled over the edge, falling into the casket-shaped hole. Scythe whistled as he moved toward the dirt pile. "If only all the bodies I buried came with pre-dug graves. Damn, wouldn't that be sweet? Seriously, Rebel. You might be my new favorite killer. So considerate." He ruffled my hair affectionately, like I was a kid who'd just won a Little League game.

"Jesus fuck," Vaughn murmured, pressed tight to my side. "Why does he look like he's enjoying this?"

War followed Scythe's lead and kicked dirt into the grave to cover Hugh's body. "Because he is. You get used to his murderous delight if you hang out with him long enough."

I ignored Scythe's snort of amusement and edged my way around him to Kara, approaching her like I would a startled horse or a scared child. Her hair was a bloodied mess, and tears ran down her face as she lifted her eyes to meet mine.

There were differences between us. Her face was rounded. Her hair longer. But there was no doubt in my mind we were sisters. Her eyes were the same deep brown. Her lips had the same bow shape, and she even had a similar dusting of freckles across the bridge of her nose.

Even if I hadn't seen her photo in my father's house, I would have known.

Maybe I had from the very first moment I'd 'met' her, when we were both trapped in Caleb's basement. Something inside me had connected to her in that instant, and it hadn't stopped since.

"He has my daughter." Blood seeped down her neck from her ripped-up scalp, but she didn't seem to notice. "She's probably already dead, isn't she?"

My heart tore open at the complete and utter despair in her voice. Bile rose in my throat, just thinking of what Caleb would do with a helpless baby when he hadn't even tried to hide how deep his evil ran. I didn't want to tell her she was probably right.

Caleb had no reason to keep her baby alive. All he needed was for Kara to *think* she was. That was enough to keep Kara compliant.

Caring for an infant would be an effort that had no reward, and one I doubted he would bother to take.

Caleb never did anything that didn't have something in it for him.

Instead of uttering that bleak thought, I shrugged out of my jacket and wadded it up to press against her wound, trying to stem the bleeding.

Church bells rang at the top of the hill, a sharp, rhythmic clanging. Everyone paused, staring toward the sound through the branches of the weeping willow that surrounded us. It provided some cover, but it had lost its thick covering of leaves due to the cold, so we weren't completely obstructed from the view of anyone who might come wandering over the hill.

Vaughn's eyes met mine. "They ring the bells when a funeral is over. There'll be people down here any minute now. We need to leave."

The others nodded, picking up the pace, Bliss's guys and mine working together to cover up a murder.

A clump landed on the dead man's face, and I shuddered as it filled his eyes and gaping, bloodied mouth.

But I wasn't sad.

Hugh had raped me. Beaten me. Tortured me, and I wasn't the only one. He deserved to be put in the ground. Not a soul would miss him.

Soon enough, Caleb would join him. I didn't know how, I didn't know when, but if I'd killed one man, I could certainly kill another.

2

KARA

The throbbing in my head was nothing compared to the pain in my heart. I didn't know why I hadn't come to the realization sooner, but it was suddenly crystal clear now.

Caleb had killed my baby.

His own daughter.

He'd probably thrown her little body in a dumpster minutes after he'd ripped her from my arms. The thought was barely conceivable. But then, I wasn't born from Satan himself like he was.

"Kara," the woman said quietly. "We need to get you to a hospital. You're bleeding pretty badly, and it's not stopping."

I shook my head. "No. No hospital."

What was the point? I didn't want to be stitched up and sent on my way. I wanted to bleed. If I bled long enough, I'd get to join my daughter on the other side. That was the only thing I wanted now.

"Fine, no hospital. But you can't stay here either. This

place is about to be crawling with people. We need to move. Can you stand up?"

I pushed her hands away. "Leave me alone. I don't care who sees me. I don't care about anything anymore. None of it matters without her."

But she was persistent. She held something to my scalp to stop the bleeding and then moved to squat in front of me.

Had Caleb really said she was my sister?

She ducked her head until our eyes met. "I've been where you are. Broken. Wanting to die. He sent me to the lowest low I've ever experienced."

I stared into her eyes, knowing she was trying to help, but she knew nothing. All I felt was anger and a sorrow so deep I wanted to drown. "Unless he took your child and murdered her, then you don't have any idea what this feels like." The words came out bitter. Cold. Like I was already dead inside.

She nodded. "You're right. It's not the same. But we don't know she's dead. Not for sure. So until we do, then you don't get to give up, okay? Because what if you gave up and she is alive?"

I didn't think it possible, but if someone else did, maybe that was enough. Something glimmered inside me. Maybe not hope, but it might have been a sliver of doubt.

That was better than the absolute surety my daughter was gone forever.

Rebel must have seen it, because she put her hands beneath my arms and pulled me to my feet. "Come on. We need to do something about your head."

I trembled all over, but I let her guide me to a car. What else was I going to do? I had nowhere to go.

Rebel opened the back door and helped me onto the back seat. With cold fingers, she picked up my hand and pressed it to the jacket stemming my bleeding head. "Hold this, okay? Don't let it drop."

It was easier to agree than to fight her.

Satisfied I was listening, she shut the door and ran around the other side, getting in and then scooting over to sit in the middle seat.

A man got in on her other side and instantly put his hand on her thigh reassuringly.

I flinched at the contact, even though it wasn't me he was touching.

Not noticing my discomfort, he squeezed her leg possessively, but she didn't seem bothered. In fact, she put her hand over his and linked their fingers. With her other arm resting on the back of the driver's seat, she leaned forward, speaking to the two men in the front. "No hospital. But she needs medical treatment. That head wound is bad, it needs cleaning and stitches."

The big blond man in the passenger seat spoke up. "We can take her to Hawk. He's no doctor, but his stitches are the neatest out of all of us. We've got all the supplies there already. It won't be pretty, but it'll do the job."

Rebel sat back and nodded. "Okay, let's do that then." She turned to me. "We're going to get you some help, okay? And some food, a hot shower, and then we'll plan how to get your baby back."

I swallowed thickly. It all sounded so good.

Too good. There had to be a catch. There always was.

But I nodded anyway, unable to find the words to thank her.

She didn't seem to need it. She let me be, the car lapsing into silence as we turned off a main road, onto one that was lined with trees and thick woods. The sun sat high, shining brightly in a deep-blue sky that didn't fit the somber mood in the car.

Still, I stared out the window silently, numb from head to toe. A high fence with a barbed-wire coil on top edged the road, and I idly wondered if there was a prison on the other side. Maybe their friend, Hawk, worked at the prison infirmary. They'd said it was fully stocked, so that would make sense. Could they do that? Just walk me inside a prison for medical treatment? I wasn't sure I wanted to be around criminals, but I did need stitches. My hair, at least what was left of it, was coated in sticky blood.

I didn't trust anyone anymore, but if Rebel was my sister, surely, she wouldn't be leading me into danger. I had to believe she'd get me in and out of this prison safely.

My head pounded. It was a strange sensation to be numb everywhere, but in pain at the same time.

It was another ten or so minutes before Rebel pointed ahead, her voice full of worry. "We're here. Just hang in there, we'll get you some pain relief really soon."

I twisted to where she was indicating, searching for the prison signs.

There were none.

A set of thick black gates loomed ahead instead.

In the middle, crafted from metal, a hooded demon

wore a Saint View Slayers MC vest, a scythe clutched in his hand.

"No," I whispered, cringing away in fear. I snapped my head to the man in the passenger seat and his black leather vest.

When he turned to look back at me, the same emblem stared me in the face from the patch on his chest.

He was one of them.

They'd chased the ambulance Caleb had stolen.

He was one of the men who'd killed Hayden.

Panic spiked inside me, clutching at my chest. "No!" The gates slowly opened. I struggled with the door handle, trying to get out, but it was locked, and no amount of switching the locks seemed to do anything. "Let me out! Let me out!"

"Kara, it's okay. Shh—" Rebel tried to calm me, but I'd seen those men, following us in the dark, pouncing on Hayden when he'd sacrificed himself. They'd wanted him dead. Maybe me too.

There'd been rounds of gunfire as we'd escaped in the ambulance. My friends, the other women held captive with me, had been left behind to die at the hands of these men.

Rebel was the same. She'd killed a man right in front of me, and then they'd covered it up like it was something they did regularly.

Who were these people?

Fear spiked my adrenaline again, but there was no escape.

The man behind the wheel glanced at us in the rearview mirror. "What's going on?"

Rebel grabbed at my hands. "I don't know. Something's freaked her out. Kara, stop. It's okay. As soon as he stops driving, you'll be able to get out. The car has automatic locks when it's in motion."

Fear gripped my throat. They were just as bad as Caleb; I was sure of it. Did she hold women against their will as well? He lied all the time. She probably did too.

The moment the car stopped; I yanked on the door handle. It released the lock with a click, and then I was out, running, trying to put as much distance between me and those men, and Rebel, as I could.

"Kara!"

I ignored her shouts and put my head down, sprinting for the woods, easily outpacing her shorter legs.

"Shit, Fang! Go after her! Those woods are thick, she'll be lost in minutes."

I doubled my speed at the thought of the bearded, tattooed biker chasing after me.

I couldn't let him catch me. I wouldn't be held against my will again. Not by him. Not by a woman claiming to be my sister but who congregated with killers like them.

I stumbled through undergrowth, jumping over logs and avoiding trees. Branches scraped at my skin, scratching and tearing. My vision blurred, and my head ached. Running had never felt so difficult, but I pushed on, too scared to stop.

I couldn't hear anyone coming behind me, but my blood rushed in my ears so loudly I wasn't sure I could trust what I was hearing. When I hit a small clearing, I glanced over my shoulder, waiting for someone to come crashing through the trees after me.

There was no one there.

I slowed, trying to catch my breath, walking backward with my eyes glued to the spot where I thought my pursuers would emerge.

Without the noises of running, I could hear better. From a distance, they called my name, assuring me they weren't going to hurt me.

Caleb had tried that once too.

None of them could be trusted.

I spun, running again, no idea where I was going, but just that it needed to be away from these people. I put my head down, watching my footing so I didn't snap my ankle.

The boulder came out of nowhere. I hit it hard, bouncing off and stumbling back with my face aching as much as my head.

Strong arms kept me from toppling over. "Whoa. What the hell is this?"

I stared up at him in shock, the boulder not actually rock at all but the solid chest of a man.

One wearing that same leather vest with the demon on the emblem. This one wasn't quite as big or intimidating as the Fang guy, but he didn't exactly seem like a kindergarten teacher either. Medium-brown stubble coated his jawline, and tattoos crept from the collar of his shirt and disappeared into his hair. His sea-green eyes gave nothing away. They were completely blank, no way of me telling if he was friend or foe.

But judging by that MC vest and the demon on it, he wasn't going to help me. He was probably a cold-blooded killer, just like the rest of them.

I opened my mouth and screamed, "Let me go!"

He winced and dropped my hand but didn't let me pass. "No can do. You're trespassing on our land. But fuck, sugar. No need for shoutin'. I've got the hangover from hell, and you about busted my eardrum."

The woods spun around me; I was so woozy and exhausted and angry with myself for both. But I'd had a baby only days ago, and ever since I'd left Hayden's place, I'd barely eaten. I had no energy left to run. I stooped and grabbed a stick from the dirt at my feet, brandishing it as a weapon, creating a gap between me and the man. "Get back!"

He held his hands up. "I'm back, I'm back. But I don't know what you think you're gonna do with that twig."

I waved it at him some more. Just let him try.

He cocked his head to one side, studying me. "You don't look so good, sugar. Ballsy, I'll give you that. But that head of yours is bleeding pretty bad. Maybe you should let me take a peek at it."

I'd almost forgotten about my head. But now the pain came back in a rush. My vision flickered.

The ground suddenly rushed up toward me.

I was going down and there was nothing I could do to stop it.

"Well, fuck." The man scooped me up before I could hit the dirt.

He held me to his chest tightly, one arm beneath my shoulders, the other under my knees. I wasn't a small woman. I'd put on a lot of weight during my pregnancy and I hadn't been skinny to start with, but he lifted me like I weighed nothing.

I was completely powerless to stop him. I bashed my

twig at his arm but even I could tell how feeble my attempts were.

More people appeared in the little clearing. Rebel, as well as the other guys from the car. Her gaze fixated on me, and relief fueled her expression before she focused on the man holding me. She wrinkled her nose for the tiniest of seconds.

The man gripped me tighter. Like a dog with a bone he didn't want to give up.

I didn't have it in me to fight anymore. All I could do was concentrate on not passing out.

"You looking for this?" the man asked my sister.

This. Like I wasn't even a person. Just an item to be owned. I hated that. I found another burst of energy and struggled in his arms, but it didn't last long. The fuzziness clouding my brain made movement difficult.

Rebel nodded. "Thanks, Hawk. She's my sister."

"Why don't any of you people have normal names?" I asked groggily. "Hawk. Fang. Chaos."

They all looked sharply at me.

"Chaos?" Hawk asked. "As in Hayden 'Chaos' Whitling, leader of the Sinners?" He stared at Rebel; his eyes narrowed in suspicion. "What the fuck, short-ass? You brought us a Sinners's slut? She here fishing for club secrets?"

Rebel's eyes blazed as she stormed across the clearing to square off with him. "Don't you ever call my sister a slut again. If you weren't holding her, I'd punch you right in the nose."

He snorted, striding past her. "Like you could reach."

I could though. I was so sick of men calling me names. Throwing their weight around, making demands from me. I closed my fingers into a fist and used the last of my energy to connect it with Hawk's nose.

The last thing I heard before I passed out was a satisfying squawk of pain.

Hawk squawks.

Funny.

3

REBEL

Hawk carried my sister's limp body back to the clubhouse and put her down on one of the old brown couches that held many a memory for me. Ones that were a lot more fun than watching my unconscious sibling get her head laceration sewn up by an angry biker with tissues shoved up his nose because it wouldn't stop bleeding.

If I hadn't been so worried about her, I would have laughed at the sight.

When she woke up, I would high-five Kara for right-hooking Hawk. He was an arrogant asshole, and he'd deserved to get hit.

I would have never picked Kara as the type though.

I'd assumed she'd be as sweet and innocent as my other sisters had been. But Caleb had a way of sucking anything good out of anyone he touched. Losing her baby the way she had would change anyone.

I couldn't even imagine.

"Is she going to be okay?" I asked Hawk.

A lot of the other club members crowded around, watching him work, but Queenie shooed them back, keeping them at a distance. Hawk sewed neat stitches into my sister's scalp, War watching on with a frown, insisting Hawk do some over again if they weren't up to his standards. Kian stood off to one side, green from watching the needle pierce through Kara's skin.

Hawk scowled up at me. "Her head has been bleeding for fuck knows how long. That ain't good. She probably needs blood."

I bit my lip. Kara's skin was deathly pale, and she hadn't regained consciousness after passing out. "Can you do that here?"

He shrugged. "Maybe. But I used up all the blood stores we had the other day when..."

He glanced at War, who gave a slight shake of his head. "Yeah, anyway, we used up all the blood bags we had. So unless you're the same blood type she is..."

"I don't know hers. Shit. I'll call my dad." I pulled my phone from my pocket and hit his number. It rang a couple times before a woman answered, "Rebel? It's Sally-Ann. Torrence is out right now with Josiah—"

"What blood type is Kara?"

The woman paused. "Louisa Kara? Why do you ask?"

I hardened, remembering this was the woman who'd told my siblings their sister had died, just because she'd left the family farm to go out and find her own life. "Because I found her, and despite the rubbish you tried to tell your other children, she's actually very much alive."

The woman choked on a sob that sounded like one of relief. "Believe me, I never wanted to tell the other children that. But Louisa Kara went against God. She had a baby out of wedlock—"

I ground my teeth. "Like I fucking care, Sally-Ann. Your own husband had a baby out of wedlock too. Did you tell everyone he was dead as well?"

She swallowed thickly. "It's different for a man. It's built into their DNA to spread their seed. Louisa Kara refused to end her pregnancy. She'd never be accepted here as an unwed mother, so maybe she wasn't actually dead, but she was as good as."

I couldn't listen to this a second longer. "Unless you want your daughter to actually be as dead as you tell people, tell me her blood type."

Sally-Ann let out a sob. "A negative. Is she hurt?"

I screwed up my face and ended the call, not answering her question, even though it was cruel not to. That's just how mad I was. I'd call her back later, after I knew if Kara was going to be okay. "Shit. I'm not a match. Are any of you A negative?"

I looked around the room. Nobody raised their hands.

"Seriously?" I shouted, nausea swirling in my stomach. "One of you must be."

"I'm A negative," Kian said slowly and almost reluctantly, moving closer to the makeshift operating area.

I stared at him. "Really?"

"Yes." He eyed the needles laid out in front of Hawk. "Can you get it out of me and into her?"

Hawk glanced over at Kian's sickly face. "I can if you let me jab a needle in your vein. You going to be okay with that? 'Cause you're about as pale as she is." He nodded toward my sister whose cheeks were an unhealthy shade of white.

Vaughn cleared his throat. "I don't know if that's a good idea..."

"I'm not great with needles," Kian admitted, rolling up his sleeve. "Just be gentle, okay?"

Hawk raised an eyebrow and snorted. "Yeah, sure. Super gentle." He grabbed a fresh needle, studied Kian's arm for a moment to find a vein, then jabbed him.

Kian's eyes rolled back, and he passed out, crashing straight off his chair onto the floor.

"Oh my God!" I knelt at his side and slapped his face. "Kian!"

His eyes fluttered open, and he groaned. He looked past me to Vaughn. "Shit. Did I do it again?"

"Pass out? Yeah. You're fucking hopeless. You'd be the worst junkie, honestly."

He and Fang got beneath his arms and hauled him back onto the chair.

"Come on," Vaughn urged. "Get up. Blood doesn't flow uphill, you know."

Hawk taped down the needle so it couldn't fall out of Kian's arm. He chuckled. "You pussy."

Kian flipped him the bird, but I felt bad. I stood behind him and tilted his head back so he was staring up at me.

"Hey. Watch me instead, okay?"

He smiled weakly. "Sorry to be dramatic. I have a bad track record."

I dropped a kiss on his upturned mouth. "You're my hero."

Hawk scoffed. "I carry the girl back here, even after she punches me. I stitch her head up. Nurse her back to health, and yet the guy who passes out at your feet is your hero? You got your priorities messed up, girl."

I whacked the back of his head before I really thought about what I was doing. "Quit your bitching and get back to fixing my sister." It was a bold move, one that was totally out of line. A few gasps from the other club women watching on confirmed it.

Hawk was War's VP, and in this clubhouse, he commanded respect.

He slowly turned around to glare at me, a low growl deep in his chest.

Fang stepped between us; his blue eyes locked on Hawk's. "I love you, brother, but you fucking growl at her again, and VP or not, I'll end you."

I hid a smile.

Hawk shook his head slowly but stopped carrying on like a dog with a pulled tail.

Fang glanced over his shoulder at me. "Aren't you just the cat who got the cream. You just broke a club rule, disrespecting the VP like that. I'll deal with you later."

My little smile only grew. I'd been punished for breaking club rules before. But Fang's punishments were being publicly spanked until I was so wet and horny, I had arousal dripping down my thighs. Or tying me to his bed and edging me until I begged him to let me come.

I could handle another round of that.

Kara stirred on the couch, her eyes fluttering open. "What..." Her eyes widened as she looked up at all of us staring at her. "Where am I?" She noticed the needle in her arm delivering Kian's blood into her vein, and her mouth fell open. "What are you doing to me? Stop!"

Hawk wrapped his fingers around her wrists and

pinned her to the couch. He got in her face, hovering over her. "Settle down," he demanded. "You're going to undo all my work if you pull that out."

Kara took one look at him and slammed her forehead right into his nose.

The same one she'd already broken with her right hook an hour or so earlier.

Hawk sprang back like he'd been bitten by a cobra. "Jesus fuck! What the hell is wrong with you? I'm trying to help you! So you break my nose twice in one day?" He groaned, blood running down over his lips and chin, the tissues stuffed in his nose no longer able to cope with the renewed flow.

I jumped between him and my sister. "You scared her! What did you think was going to happen, holding her down like that?"

Hawk scowled at me and then shouted at Ratchet, one of the prospects, to get him some ice. He stormed away, leaving blood droplets on the floor.

Fang cringed and rubbed the back of his neck. He didn't need to tell me this wasn't good. Kara and I were probably about to be thrown out on our asses.

I spoke in the calmest voice I could muster. "Hey. Can we try this again? I know you're scared. But I promise, we really are just trying to take care of you."

Her gaze was firmly fixed on Hawk, who sat on the other side of the room with a packet of frozen peas on his face.

That seemed oddly out of place. "Who here eats peas?" I whispered to Fang curiously. Didn't really seem like big burly bikers would be getting their five servings of green vegetables a day.

He shook his head with a little grin. "You're so random. No one eats them. They're literally only in the freezer for when someone drinks too much and gets in a fight."

I shrugged, turning back to Kara. "You'd think they'd just invest in an ice pack, wouldn't you?"

She finally dragged her gaze back to me. "I'm sorry," she whispered. "He was in my face, and for a second I thought..." She swallowed thickly. "I thought he was someone else."

Anger vibrated through me again. Caleb had held me down too.

I hated the only thing my sister and I had in common was our rapist.

I slowly reached toward her, and when she didn't flinch away, I brushed her hair back off her face. She wasn't really that much younger than me. Maybe only five or six years. But that still made her my little sister. Everything inside me screamed she needed my protection.

"Lie here a bit longer, okay? Hawk got the bleeding stopped, and he's giving you some blood and fluids. Your color is already a lot better. I'd bet we can get you up for a shower and some food soon. If you want that?"

"I just want to leave. Please just let me."

I squeezed her cold fingers. "You can't, Kara. Where would you go?"

There was fear in her eyes. She didn't know any of us, and her first introduction had been me pointing a gun at her, then burying a body. I couldn't blame her for thinking we were bad people.

"We're the good guys, Kara. I promise you that. I

know they seem big and kinda terrifying, in a stupidly attractive way, but they won't hurt you. I won't hurt you. Ever."

Kara lowered her voice. "They killed Hayden."

I grimaced and glanced over at Fang and War, huddled together with their arms crossed over their chests while they watched us.

"Did you?" I asked them.

Fang didn't answer. He dropped his gaze to the floor. War just walked away.

Fuck.

"Hayden wasn't one of the good guys," I tried explaining to her.

Her reaction was instant. "He was! He's the only reason I'm alive right now. He cared for us when Caleb made him hold us hostage. Gave us beds. Clean clothes. He delivered my baby when Caleb wouldn't let me go to the hospital. He was the one who called the ambulance to get us out of there when your guys were shooting up the place trying to get at him."

"He put out a hit on War's dad, Kara. Hired a hit man. He knew what he was doing when he did that. Things like that don't go unpunished."

She dug her fingers into my hand. "No! That was all Caleb. He admitted it, right in front of me." She turned to War. "Hayden gave him the contact for the hit, but it was Caleb who wanted your father dead."

War's eyebrows furrowed together. "That's not true. One of Hayden's own men ratted him out."

Kara shook her head. "Caleb paid him off. It was never Hayden or the Sinners behind any of that. It was all Caleb."

War palmed the back of his neck. "That doesn't make any sense. Why would Caleb want my father dead?"

"You did steal his girl," I offered.

War smiled at just the mention of Bliss. "True, but it doesn't fit. My dad died before Bliss and I were anything. It can't have been retaliation for that."

Silence lapsed over us. It didn't make sense. Caleb was a businessman. He didn't run in the same circles as War's biker father. There should have been no reason for one to even be aware of the other.

"The women in the house," Kara said softly. "I was an afterthought, thrown in there only because Caleb needed someone to deal with me. But those other women had been held there for months. Picked up off the street, bound and gagged, taken against their will, or lured in with promises of more than their current lives. I think they were going to be sold."

I widened my eyes. "To who?"

"War's dad, maybe? Or maybe War's dad was supposed to move them on to someone else but he reneged on the deal. That would give Caleb the perfect motivation to kill him, wouldn't it? Caleb would kill someone just for going against his demands, but your dad would have known too much. He'd have known all of Caleb's dirty little secrets. It would be something he could hold over Caleb's head."

"Caleb would hate that," I murmured. "He doesn't deal well with feeling powerless."

War shook his head. "No. We aren't angels. We've always had a foot in with guns and drugs, but we don't run women."

Kara pinned him with a glare. "Can you say that for

sure? With complete and absolute certainty? Maybe you don't know as much about your own father as you think you do." She turned away. "I was blindsided by mine too, if it makes you feel any better."

I bit my lip, wanting to ask her what she meant by that, but now wasn't the time.

Kara struggled to sit up, and I helped by shoving cushions behind her back.

"It doesn't matter now anyway, does it? Your dad is dead. Hayden is dead. My friends are probably all dead, full of bullet holes courtesy of your men." She glared at War with fire in her eyes. "I hope you're proud of yourself. The only person who should be dead is still wandering around, free as a bird to do whatever he wants, leaving a trail of destruction in his wake."

Shit. Kara talking to War like that wouldn't go down well. I glanced up at him. "She's not—"

"She's not wrong," he interrupted, his voice weary. He sank down onto a couch and stared blankly at the wall above my head, his mind clearly ticking over everything Kara had said.

Silence fell over the rest of us, waiting for War to say something.

He slammed his fist down on the coffee table. "Fuck!"

There was a finality in his curse. A realization of pieces clicking together and unanswered questions coming full circle.

It was so loud, even Fang jumped. "What do you want to do, boss?"

War laughed bitterly. "Rewind the clock and kill Caleb back when I thought he was just a pussy who got off on controlling his fiancée. Or maybe go to my father and ask him why the hell he got us involved in something we swore we'd never touch." His head tipped back, and he stared at the ceiling. "You greedy fucking prick. You did it, didn't you? You didn't even bring it to us, so we could decide as a club if we were going to get involved. Because you know what I would have said. You cowardly fucking bastard."

A hush fell over the room. War never spoke about his father like that. No one did. Army, as a prez who had been killed, was an honored figure. No bad would have dared slip from a single member's tongue.

It was another one of their rules.

Respect of brothers who had gone out protecting the club.

War had just blown it to smithereens. "The women held at the Sinners' compound. How many were there?" he asked Kara solemnly.

"Four," she said quietly. "Winnie, Georgia, Nova, and Vivienne. That's their names. They had families and friends and jobs. Lives." Her tone turned bitter. "Now they're probably dead and rotting in that house."

War pushed to his feet. "Or the Sinners are still holding them, waiting for Caleb to make his next move."

A glimmer of hope lit up Kara's eyes. "You didn't go in and kill them after we left in the ambulance?"

Fang shook his head. "There were shots fired, on both sides. But a group of us went after the ambulance."

Hawk spoke up from his corner. "Those of us left behind were outnumbered. We had to fall back when the Sinners brought out semi-automatics."

Nausea roiled in my stomach at the thought of Fang out there in the darkness, being shot at by a rival gang. I knew this was his life and there was no other for him. But knowing the danger he put himself in was terrifying. I reached for him, taking his hand in mine, reminding myself he was still here.

Still mine.

Kara glanced between Hawk, with his eyes black from her double whammy nose breaks, to Fang who sat quietly like he always did, calmly stating the facts and holding my hand. "So there's a chance they're still alive?"

Hawk shrugged. "I'd say a pretty good one."

War pushed to his feet.

At some sort of silent signal from his boss, Fang squeezed my hand and leaned over and kissed my cheek. "Gotta go, Pix."

I still had the images of men with semi-automatic weapons aimed at him, burning through my brain. I grasped his hand. "Where are you going?"

War looked over at Kara. "I'm not too big a man to admit when I've made a mistake. And this, if everything you say is true, is a colossal fuckup. But I promise you, Kara. Either way, I'm not my father. If they're alive, I'll bring them home."

4

KIAN

Hawk and War bickered in much the same way Vaughn and I did, their longtime friendship showing through when Hawk tried to insist on riding with War over to the Sinners' clubhouse. War took one look at his banged-up bestie and told him to sit his ass down.

Hawk was still complaining about War pulling rank on him when War and Fang left to go stake out the Sinners's compound for any sign of the women they held captive.

"Fucking idiots," Hawk mumbled from beneath his probably now warm bag of peas. "We should all be on the road with them."

But Fang and War's plan seemed sensible to me. Two men in an unmarked vehicle drew a lot less attention than a dozen men on deafening Harleys. All they needed to do was find out if the women were still alive. An extraction would come later.

Rebel helped Kara up from the couch, and I stood quickly to get her other side.

Instantly, the room spun, and I crashed back down, the couch catching me.

Vaughn clapped me on the shoulder. "Easy. You've just given blood and you've probably got a concussion after hitting the decks earlier. I'll help them."

I scowled at him, but there wasn't really much I could do unless I wanted to embarrass myself again by trying to get vertical. He and Rebel took Kara to Fang's bedroom down the hall. A moment later, Vaughn reappeared and came to stand in front of me, a frown pulling at his mouth.

"Rebel is going to stay with Kara until Fang gets back. We agreed I'm taking you home before you pass out again."

I raised an eyebrow. "And by agreed, you mean she told you to take me home and put me to bed and you said, 'Yes, ma'am?'"

Vaughn held out a hand and hauled me to my feet. "I think I said, 'Yes, Roach,' actually, but same thing."

I sniggered but paused for a second, waiting to see if the world was going to spin again. When it didn't, I faked a bout of wooziness.

Vaughn grabbed my arm and slung it over his shoulders, the other coming around my waist. "Shit, are you going to pass out again, O'Malley?" The joking tone left his voice. "Did you actually hit your head earlier? Do I need to take you to a hospital? Fuck, if you have a brain bleed, I'm going to kick you in the balls."

I sniggered. "Nah, was just a ploy to get your arms around me."

Vaughn stopped and stared at me.

I flashed him my most charming grin.

He scowled back.

I loved when he scowled. It was so hot.

He shoved me away. "You jackass. Walk by yourself."

I slipped my fingers between his instead. "I'd rather do this."

Vaughn glanced around the club. He noticed Hawk watching and dropped my hand.

Right. It was like that then. Still. Same old shit, we were just older. Apparently, me sucking his dick on a road trip, and then a threesome with Rebel where he'd made me come with a vibrator, didn't count for shit.

Fucking typical, in-the-closet Vaughn.

"You two fucking now?" Hawk asked crudely around chewing on the end of a toothpick.

Vaughn's cheeks went pink, and his pace picked up slightly, until we were outside the clubhouse. He strode toward his car like a man on a mission, leaving me trailing behind.

With every step, I grew more and more annoyed. What was so wrong with me that he didn't want people knowing we were together? Was it just that I had a dick? Or maybe it was he was forever the millionaire's son, while I was just the gardener's kid.

Never fucking good enough.

Anger coursed through me until it had nowhere else to go. I quickened my pace until I was right behind Vaughn.

We drew closer and closer to the car, and I tried to reel in my anger so I could see it from his point of view.

Except I couldn't.

Because I'd never been ashamed of him.

He'd been the first person I'd ever fallen in love with. I would have told the entire fucking world about us, even back then, but at least when we were eighteen, he'd had an excuse. He'd had a girlfriend. Parents who maybe wouldn't understand. Harold Coker breathing down his neck about being straight and marrying to move the business forward.

None of that applied anymore. Vaughn was a full-grown man, not an impressionable little boy.

I shoved him so hard he went crashing into the side of his car. He let out a grunt as he connected with it, then spun around, eyes wide with surprise.

"What the fuck was that for?"

I kept moving, closing the distance between us until we were chest to chest. My voice was low. "Because you deserve it. God, Vaughn, you are such a prick."

"What did I do now?"

Behind me, at the doorway of the clubhouse, the jeering laughter of a couple of the guys floated back to us. "No fights on the TV today so Vaughn and Kian are filling in! Money on Kian."

I ignored them, but Vaughn's gaze drifted in that direction.

I shook my head. "That, Vaughn. You're always so worried about what other people think. How about you look at me instead?"

He dragged his eyes back to mine. "I don't care what they think."

"Bullshit," I threw back at him. "Them. Your dad's business partner. Your parents. Rebel. Everyone but me."

The words, even though they'd come from my own mouth, hit me hard.

They were laced with hurt.

The pain of being the one left behind while he went off and married someone else.

I couldn't do this with him again. Fool me once, shame on you. Fool me twice, I was just a dumb idiot.

I pushed away and went for the passenger side of the car. "Forget it. Let's just go."

"Kian."

I lifted the door handle, but it didn't open.

I waited for him to unlock the door, steadfastly ignoring him standing there, not making any attempt to do so. He just watched me.

I sighed. "What?"

His eyes burned through me. "Undo your fly."

I turned around and tried the door again, which was as useless as the first time I'd done it, since Vaughn hadn't even made a move toward his keys. "Fuck off, Vaughn. Let's just go."

"Undo your fly."

I glanced over at him. "Why?"

He slowly dropped to his knees in front of me.

Up by the clubhouse, a whoop of cheers went up.

I snorted, glancing up at them gathered in their folding chairs, now all pointed in our direction. Aloha was there with Ice and Ratchet. Hawk stood off to one side with his arms crossed. Queenie and Kiki giggled together.

"There's an entire clubhouse full of people up there. Get up."

He did. He pushed to his feet, while the others booed.

But he never stopped looking at me, his eyes burning. Not for a second did he turn away, and eventually, neither could I. Everyone else faded away, and all that was left was me, Vaughn, and the heat in his eyes.

A deep rumble rose through his chest. "I'm looking at you and telling you I don't care what they think. Maybe I didn't want to hold hands, but I just got down on my knees in front of all of them, and you rejected me." He leaned in close so his lips barely hovered over mine. "You rejected me, Kian. I'm well aware I'm not perfect. I'm not into public displays of affection like you are. And yeah, sure, maybe I don't need everyone knowing we're fucking. But if you do? If you fucking care that much, then tell me to get down on my knees and suck your cock. Because there's nothing I'd rather do right now than make you come, all those people up there be fucking damned."

He was full of shit. Playing me. But my dick kicked at the thought of him doing that with an audience. And fuck him. Two could play at that game.

I inched in closer, lips scraping his. I trailed them up his stubbled jaw and licked a path along his neck until I got to his ear. He was groaning when I whispered, "Get on your knees and take my cock, Vaughn."

To my surprise, he dropped down instantly. The second his knees hit the ground, he reached for my belt, pulling it tight to release the buckle then yanking it out from beneath the belt loops on my jeans with a sharp tug.

Hoots and hollers started up again. I smirked down at Vaughn, knowing he wouldn't follow through.

He twisted the button on my fly. Then lowered the zipper.

My pulse picked up when he reached inside my underwear and put his fingers around my erection.

Even as far as he'd gone, a big part of me still didn't think he'd actually do it. Not here. Not with an audience.

With one hand, he ripped down my jeans and underwear.

His mouth was over me in the next instant, and he sucked me in deep, hollowing out his cheeks and licking the underside of my cock.

I hissed through gritted teeth at the contact, but guilt instantly seeped in. I'd made him do this. It was as good as forcing him, and that wasn't who I was. If he'd done this to Rebel, I would have throat punched him.

"Get it, boys!" Queenie called happily.

Jesus fuck. I twisted, so they all had a perfect view of my bare ass, but Vaughn was blocked from their nosy eyes.

He withdrew his hot, warm mouth, then pushed forward, taking me deep until I hit the back of his throat.

I grabbed his head. It was involuntary; I had his hair wrapped through my fingers before I even realized I was thrusting into his mouth.

He took my dick so fucking sweetly my balls drew up, already thinking about coming.

He pulled off to jerk my shaft with his hand, while staring up at me. "Who's hiding now?"

He shifted, twisting us so everyone could see again. This time, I let him.

If it was even possible, I'd swear I got harder, knowing people were watching. None of them were strangers to public sex, I was sure. They all went to Psychos. I'd heard the parties here were more of the same. I knew exactly what Vaughn and Rebel and Fang had done in the common room, this just felt like evening the score.

Vaugh put a hand between my legs and squeezed my balls, not hard enough to hurt but with the experience of someone who knew exactly how far they could be pushed before pleasure turned into pain.

Vaughn's touch was all pleasure. He sucked me until my head spun, and I had to count backward from a thousand in my head to keep myself from coming down his throat. It was too soon. Fuck, I hadn't thought this through. It had been so long since we'd done this, I just wanted to come. If it had only been him and me, somewhere private, I probably would have by now.

But with an audience, I would never live that down. Fucking hell, if I came too quickly, they'd probably give me a road name like Two Tug Tony.

Vaughn seemed hell-bent on making that happen though. Fuck, when had he gotten this good? I yanked his hair back sharply, and he groaned, rubbing his cock through his pants.

"Whose dick have you been sucking in the last ten years?"

He opened his eyes. "Why? The thought of me doing this with someone else bother you?"

It really fucking did.

I realized I didn't even want to know the answer. If he'd been with someone else, I had no leg to stand on. I'd fucked my way through half the population of Saint View after he'd left. I'd tried to replace him with every good-looking brunette I came across.

But none of them had ever come close. Not until

Rebel had pranced her way into my house, with Vaughn following close behind.

I'd fallen hard and fast, for both of them. But that was the story of my life. I was the stereotypical stage-five clinger, the one who felt too much, too soon, and couldn't play it cool. I'd never stopped loving Vaughn. That feeling had only expanded to include Rebel too.

Vaughn would run for the fucking hills if I mentioned any of that though. So I didn't. I bit my lip, held his head, and fucked his face.

I could do sex without feelings. I could.

Maybe.

Fuck.

I didn't know if he was aware of my distraction, but he used it to sneak his index finger between my cheeks and prod at my ass. I wasn't lubed up enough to take him there, but fuck, the friction at my entrance was enough to drive me wild. I drove into the deep, wet heat of his mouth, desperately needing more.

I pulled out and dragged him to his feet.

He stared at me, eyes hazy with lust, before our lips collided. I reached for his jeans, fumbling to get them undone, walking him backward into the thicket of trees surrounding the club while the others booed that I was taking him out of view.

I didn't want anyone watching what I wanted to do to him.

This was just between him and me.

We stumbled into the trees, a mess of hot mouths and wet tongues and half-removed jeans. Our cocks rubbed on each other, slippery with precum. I pushed him up against a tree and kissed him deep, jerking his cock.

"I want you," I said gruffly into his neck. "Fucking hell, that was hot."

He grabbed at me, hauling me closer, tugging at my hair, my clothes, groaning into my mouth as I handled his dick.

"I want you to fuck me," he whispered on my lips. "I need it, Kian. This isn't enough."

For once, we were on the same train of thought.

"You need to come first. You won't take me without something to lube you up."

He thrust into my hand, moaning my name. A second later, his balls tightened, and he spilled over, his cum filling my hand. He bit down on my lip, shoving his tongue into my mouth and convulsing beneath my fingers.

With my eyes burning through his, I stroked my cock, coating it. "Turn around."

He did. He gripped the tree, and I steadied him with one hand, exploring him with the other.

"Fuck, Kian," he moaned when I touched a finger to his asshole.

I covered it in his slippery lube, rimming his ass until he could take my finger.

His moans became desperate as he held on, taking everything I gave him. I wanted to fuck him so bad. I rubbed my dick between his cheeks, not thrusting inside him but nudging at the place I wanted to be.

"Take it," he groaned. "Fuck, please, I need it. I'm hard again."

He stroked his cock with one hand while I fought back every urge to push forward, to claim him, mark him in a way that would make him mine.

"I don't want to hurt you."

He shook his head. "Do I have to fucking beg?"

This was going to be torture. I wasn't one-hundred-percent sure, but I had an inkling he'd never done this before. The two of us never had anyway. We'd come close a couple of times but had backed out at the last minute, switching to hand jobs or oral.

But neither of us were kids anymore.

He wanted this as badly as I did.

I reached around him, taking his cock in my hand again and working it so he could brace himself on the tree.

I kissed his neck from behind, sucking and licking him, then slowly edged inside his tight hole.

His head dropped back onto my shoulder, exposing his throat. "Fuck, yes."

It was all the encouragement I needed to edge farther in. To push through the tight canal until I bottomed out, fully seated inside him.

His breaths came in short pants, warm when he turned his head so our lips could meet. I dropped his cock and let him kiss me. It was blistering, filled with need and vulnerability, and trust. I thrust slowly, refusing to hurt him, even though he'd given me free rein to take him however I needed.

I withdrew then moved inside again, over and over, giving him time to breathe and adjust between each one.

"Fuck, you feel good," I encouraged him, picking up the pace a little. "I want you so bad." I kissed and sucked the sensitive skin at the side of his neck while I ground inside him.

"I need to come," I said into his flesh. "I don't want to, but I can't help it."

"Me too."

I paused, looking over his shoulder and down his body at his dick clutched firmly in his grip. It was slick with his arousal, the head popping through his fingers, then disappearing into his fist as he stroked himself in time with the way I pumped in and out of his body.

I loved he was getting off on what I was doing. Loved watching him pleasure himself and me all just by being him. I moved faster, my orgasm building from deep within my balls and low in my stomach, the sensation spreading between the two to combine until there was nothing else to do but demand, "Come with me."

"Fuck," he ground out, jerking his cock harder. He came with a groan, his cum spilling from the tip of his dick, over his hand and dripping onto the grass and dirt beneath our feet.

The sounds he made spurred me on, and a second later, I came with him, my balls drawing up and filling him with everything I had.

I couldn't breathe, his ass was so tight around my swollen cock. I came hard, connected with him in a way we hadn't before, but knowing it wouldn't be the last time.

It couldn't be. We were too good together.

When we were both done, neither of us moved. We just stood there. I reveled in the touch and feel of him, imprinting it all to memory in case he did flip around and deny this thing between us. But when he turned, his eyes were still hot, full of lust.

He pressed his lips to mine softly. "I'm a mess."

He was. He had cum everywhere. His. Mine.

He was a beautiful mess I wanted to clean up just so I could do it all over again. "Put your jeans on. Round two in the shower at home."

A small smile played at Vaughn's mouth. "You have a lot of faith in my ability to get it up again in such a short space of time after coming twice right now. It's only a ten-minute drive from here to our place."

I tugged up my jeans and winked at him. "Actually, I'm going to blow you in the car while you drive so you've got like, five minutes, tops."

Despite his complaints, Vaughn's pace quickened.

I laughed, trailing after him to the edge of the woods and back to his car.

From the clubhouse, cheers erupted, the club members all stamping their feet and clapping.

We both ignored them, too fixated on each other and getting ourselves inside the car so we could start all over again.

True to my word, while Vaughn drove, I coaxed his dick into a third orgasm in under an hour. His cock was still wet with my saliva when he turned into our driveway and hit the brakes hard.

A figure stood in the middle of it, her curly dark hair wild around her face. Sasha banged her hand on the hood and ran around to the driver's-side door.

Vaughn yelped and tried to shove his dick inside his pants, simultaneously rolling down the window so we could hear her.

If she'd noticed what we were doing, she didn't comment on it. Her eyes were big when she stuck her head in the window and looked frantically between me and Vaughn and then to the empty back seat. "Where's Rebel?"

I leaned forward. "Still at the Slayers' clubhouse. Why?"

"Shit!" She whirled away and ran back toward her house on the other side of a row of trees.

Vaughn and I stared after her, completely dumbfounded.

I cocked my head to one side. "What do you think that was about?"

Vaughn shrugged. "Maybe a period thing?"

"You're probably right. If it were anything else, she would have told me. I've known that girl since she was a baby. I'm like her big brother."

Vaughn finished parking the car and scoffed, "That girl has the biggest crush on you. She does not think of you as a brother."

I blinked at him in surprise. "Really? I don't see it."

He leaned over, pressing his lips against mine. "You never do. You have zero idea how attractive you are, Kian. How good. How fucking kind and sweet. You have no idea how many people think about being with you."

"Can I have 'excellent at blowjobs' also added to my list of achievements, please?"

Vaughn shook his head. "How about we go upstairs and have that shower? Maybe you can teach me some of your moves."

Dismissing Sasha's dramatics, I took Vaughn upstairs and let him prove that maybe I wasn't the only one good at getting down on their knees.

5

REBEL

Vaughn had once sat in a dark corner of my bedroom, watching me sleep after I'd nearly drowned. At the time, I'd thought it a bit weird and creepy.

But I sat beside Kara's bed in exactly the same way, watching her chest rise and fall and checking that her cheeks remained pink.

I got it now. That feeling of needing to protect someone. Of loving them wholeheartedly, even if you didn't know them that well yet. It didn't matter. All that mattered was the bond and the desire to be around them.

She slept most of the afternoon, tucked up in Fang's bed, her skin pale in a sea of navy-blue comforters and pillows. But she seemed okay, if you ignored the white bandage wrapped around her head and the bruises on her arms both from Caleb, as well as where Hawk had been forced to jab her with a needle.

The clubhouse was never super quiet, so noises floated

back from the common rooms where people were probably hanging out, eating and drinking. As well as from farther down the hall where some of the guys lived. I liked it. It was like white noise, not loud enough to be really disruptive but so much better than a completely silent room that would have given me way too much time to think.

Nobody needed time to think when they'd just brutally shot and killed a man.

Even if he did deserve it.

Silence let doubts creep in, and right now, I didn't have time for that. I needed to take care of my sister. Not that I really knew how. I had to rely on Hawk for that. Google said she should have her vitals checked every two hours, and she'd been in here, sleeping for at least that long. I needed to go get Hawk because I had no idea what 'vitals' were, or how to monitor them.

I pushed to my feet and wandered down the hallway toward the common room, where Hawk sat on one of the couches, both eyes black from his broken nose, and a beer bottle in one hand. A walkie-talkie sat on the coffee table in front of him, along with a host of medical supplies, many of which were bloodied.

I sat across from him. "Ouch."

He glared at me. "You don't fucking say. Your sister is a psychopath."

I scoffed, "Have you met Vincent and Scythe? Kara is hardly in the same league, and you know it. She was just scared."

"Yeah, well, so am I. Scared my nose is never gonna be right again."

"Scared you won't get laid with a crooked schnoz?"

"I might look like something out of *The Walking Dead*, but you'd still want me."

I couldn't help but laugh. Hawk was one of the prettiest men I'd ever met, with a mane of perfect hair and a sharp jawline. He was model-level hot, no doubt, but he also had the biggest ego.

"No, sir, I most definitely do not. Straight nose or not, I've got enough men to last me a lifetime. I need a favor though. Can you check on Kara?"

He glanced up, a frown creasing his forehead. "Why? What's wrong with her?"

"Nothing that I can see. But I'm just worried."

He opened his mouth to answer, but the walkie-talkie on the table crackled to life. "Hawk. We got a problem at the gate."

He sighed heavily and picked up the communication device, pressing in the button on the side so he could relay his message. "What sort of problem?"

"There's a woman here. Says her name is Sasha and she wants to talk to Rebel."

I did a double take. "Did he say Sasha?"

Hawk studied me. "That mean something to you, short-ass?"

"She's my neighbor." I grabbed the walkie-talkie from Hawk's hand. "Ice? Let her in, I know her."

Hawk just rolled his eyes. "How many club rules you trying to get Fang to punish you for?"

I winked at him, put the walkie-talkie down, and stood. "As many as I possibly can." I slipped out the door before he could chastise me anymore for bossing his men around.

Outside, I passed a group of club members with their

chosen women for the night, a grill fired up and lightly smoking with some steaks slapped on top.

Queenie gave me a wink. "You're a lucky, lucky girl, Rebel Kemp."

I spun around and grinned at her as I walked backward. "Why's that?"

She let out a low whistle. "Lordy, Lordy, those roommates of yours... They fine, girl. So freaking fine I about needed a cold shower."

I frowned at her. "What do you mean?"

Kiki interrupted, all too eager to spill the beans. "Vaughn sucked Kian's dick in front of all of us."

Aloha leaned backward on his chair, balancing it on two legs with his hands clasped behind his neck. "Then Kian dragged him into the woods, and when they came out, they were looking pretty damn satisfied."

I hid a smile. "Did they just?"

Queenie cocked her head. "You ain't jealous 'bout the two of them?"

I laughed. "You saw them, right? How hot they are together?"

She nodded.

I winked back at her. "I get to be in the middle of that."

Her mouth dropped open, but she put her hands together and gave me a slow clap while shaking her head. "Girl, I knew I liked you."

I blew her a kiss because I really liked her too. Then turned and went back to jogging down the gravel-lined drive to the big set of gates. Surely Ice was wrong, and Sasha wasn't really down here.

But halfway there, a woman emerged around a bend,

walking uncertainly in the middle of the path. I recognized her instantly and jogged the rest of the way to meet her.

"Sasha!"

Relief flooded the younger woman's face, and she doubled the pace, tripping over her own feet in her haste to get to me. She tumbled into my arms, throwing hers around me and squeezing me tight. "Oh my God! It's really you and not a mirage! I thought for sure I was lost somewhere, driving through those woods, and then when I finally found the gates, it dawned on me exactly who the Slayers are and what they do, but by then they'd already spotted me. Also, that guy on the gate? He's hot. Does he have a girlfriend?"

I frowned at her, and maybe it was leftover big-sister vibes I'd been pouring onto Kara, but I kinda felt the same way about Sasha. "Stay away from the sexy bikers, Sash."

She elbowed me. "You don't."

"Do as I say, not as I do. And right now, I demand you to say exactly what you're doing out here at an MC compound in the middle of nowhere. How did you even get out here?"

Her face sobered. "I drove, but the hottie on the gate wouldn't let me drive the car in. Bit ridiculous if you ask me. Not like I was trying to smuggle in bombs or something. I had to sweet-talk him into even calling down to you all on the walkie-talkie, because I needed to show you this, and you haven't been home in days."

She pulled a piece of paper from her back pocket and very dramatically unfolded it to thrust it into my face.

I batted it away and then took it from her, eyeing her with a frown. "What is it?"

"Your mom's autopsy report."

I glanced up and thrust it back at her. "Sorry for the wasted trip, but I already have a copy of this at home. The cops sent me one."

She shoved it right back at me. "Nuh-uh. Not this version. This one only just came up on my searches. I don't know where the cops have been hiding it, but I have an idea of why."

I peered at her, slowly taking back the sheets of paper, filled with small, black type. "What do you mean?"

"Turn to section forty-five."

I turned the pages, following the numbers printed down the left-hand side. "Why is this so much longer than the one I saw? It was only a double-sided page."

Sasha jabbed one of her manicured fingernails into the page so hard it almost tore. "Exactly! The one I saw wasn't nearly this long either. But you know how I follow those true crime groups? The buzz about your mom and Bart died down for a minute there, and I don't know what happened, might be because the funerals were this morning, but two days ago, someone anonymously posted this version of your mom's autopsy. And section forty-five..."

My gaze landed on the number and the words next to it. My head snapped up. "Pregnant? She was pregnant?"

Sasha nodded. "But hey, listen, hold my hand for a second, because section forty-six is the analysis they did on the fetus..."

Wide eyed, I scanned the text beneath a heading called 'Genetic Findings' and then read it out loud. "Fetus

DNA is not compatible with that of the mother's partner, Bartholomew Weston. Father unknown."

Sasha cringed. "Should I have not told you? Are you mad? I don't know what this means exactly..."

My fingers crumpled in the paper. "It means my mother was sleeping with someone other than Bart. And recently, if this report is to be believed. She probably didn't even know she was pregnant."

Grief crushed in. It was weird. I'd gone from having no siblings my entire life, to having four sisters, then five when Kara had come along.

Then in one fell swoop, I'd lost one I didn't even know about.

It shouldn't have hurt.

But it did. It hurt just as much as if I'd held that baby in my arms, stared down at her little face, and promised to look out for her always. My heart felt crushed and robbed of the fact I'd never get to do that.

It didn't matter to me that my mom had slept with someone else. I didn't think any less of her for cheating on her husband, though it did surprise me. She'd seemed so in love with him.

"Maybe this isn't true," I said to Sasha. "Maybe the original autopsy was the right one."

Sasha nodded, taking the piece of paper and folding it again before putting it back in her pocket. She looked up at me slowly. "But what if it is? Whoever killed your mother might have been her lover..."

I swallowed thickly. "Why do I feel like you've already played out this entire scenario in your head?"

Her shiny teeth dug into her pink bottom lip. "You being away for a few days after I found this gave me a lot of time to come up with different scenarios. I considered a lot of different people. Everyone I'd ever met at their place. Then I went further, digging into their pasts..."

"So you're saying you have a new list of suspects?"

"Actually, I'm saying it all came back to just one."

"Who?"

She cringed. "Kian."

I breathed out sharply. "He swears he had nothing to do with her death."

"Men lie, Rebel," Sasha said. "I think we both know that. I heard screams in that house nights before they died. Has he ever explained those?"

I shook my head slowly. She'd brought this to me before, but I'd let it die, unable to believe Kian had anything to do with it.

He'd promised me.

"He lived with them, Rebel. He was there every night Bart worked late. He's never mentioned your mom having a lover, right? Surely, if she had, he'd be the one to know about it. He lived there! He would have known!"

My stomach twisted painfully. "Unless it was him. Unless he was her lover."

She nodded.

"People are usually murdered by those closest to them." I'd heard that somewhere, and it had stuck with me.

Sasha grabbed my hand. "Ninety-nine-percent of the time, yes."

"What are the odds my mom and Bart are the one percent?"

She didn't answer. Neither did I.

We just stood there in silence as everything sank in.

Finally, I took a deep breath. "My sister is in the clubhouse, recovering from a pretty harrowing morning. I don't want her to wake up and be surrounded by men. Could you go sit with her?"

Sasha nodded, looking at me with big, worried eyes. "Sure. Whatever you need. But what are you going to do?"

I moved around her and strode toward the gates. "I need to borrow your car. I'm going to see Kian. And this time I'm not leaving until he tells me the truth. All of it. Every last detail."

6

FANG

The diner's cracked leather booths creaked and protested beneath mine and War's weight. I shifted uncomfortably, the table too tight against my abs, but I didn't say a word.

"We should have sat somewhere else," War admitted, eyeing the busy restaurant around us. "This table is tiny."

I nodded.

He wriggled around some more, trying to get comfortable, but stopped when a waitress brought over our order. The fries sparkled with oil fresh out of the fryer, and a thick burger called my name, but War didn't touch his food, so neither did I.

The smell wafted around my nose tantalizingly. I really wanted to eat those fries. "You good, boss?"

He sighed heavily. "Not really. Fuck, man. You believed her, didn't you? Kara? When she said it was Caleb behind my dad's murder?"

I poked at a fry with my fingertip, edging it toward a few stray granules of salt. "She sounded pretty sure."

War shook his head. "Why would Army get involved in that shit? Guns, drugs, whatever. We all know that stuff like the backs of our hands. But he was always so adamant we never get in with women. My mom has a history, you know? Shit that went down in her past, and Army swore to her he'd never get involved in anything like that. And yet…"

"Club's been low on money for a while now."

He raised his eyebrows. "It has?"

I nodded. "We lost that shipment of drugs last year… that wasn't easy to recoup."

"We what?"

I just looked at him.

"Seriously? We lost a shipment? How the fuck did that happen?"

I shook my head, trying to remember everything Army had confided in me. "I don't really know. I don't think Army did either. Gus, Army, and I took possession of them. The next day, they were gone."

War ran a hand through his hair. "Why didn't I know about any of this?"

I didn't say anything. What was there to say? War had been VP at the time. He should have known what was going on better than I did. But the man seemed truly baffled.

I didn't want to make it any worse. "I think your dad kept it from you because he didn't want to appear weak."

War's grip on his knife tightened. "I was his VP. Not to mention his son!" He slammed the blunt end of the knife down onto the table. "Fucking Army. He never thought I was good enough. Why the fuck he made me VP in the first place I'll never understand. He clearly didn't trust me with the position."

I reached over and took the knife from his fingers before he mangled the utensil. "You had to be VP. You were his son. It would have looked bad if he hadn't given you the position. But you're a fucking good prez, War. Better than he ever was. If he kept you out of the loop, it was probably more because he didn't want the weight of the club on your shoulders before you were ready for it. You know now it's not exactly an easy burden to bear."

He slumped back against the booth and eyed me. "That's some poetic bullshit, Fang. You're a good friend, even though he's six feet under. But I doubt Army ever cared that much about me."

I shook my head. "You'd be surprised."

He mulled on that for a moment. "Fuck, man, I don't want my kid growing up like I did. What if Bliss has a boy?" He groaned. "Fuck, worse, what if she has a girl? Bliss already has me wrapped around her little finger. How much worse will I be with a daughter?"

I couldn't help the smile. "She'd be a hell-raiser. Especially with Scythe and Vincent and Nash around to influence her. Give her twenty years and she can be your VP, just like you were for Army."

He smiled at the thought. "I kinda fucking want that, you know? A biker princess."

I grinned. "That would be sweet."

War jerked his head toward me. "What about you?"

I frowned. "What about me?"

War finally tossed a fry in his mouth while raising his eyebrow at me suggestively. "You gonna knock your little pixie up anytime soon?"

I flushed hot at the thought of Rebel's taut belly rounding with my baby. My balls tightened at the idea of wrapping my arms around her from behind and feeling our child move beneath her skin. Shit. The rush of longing hit me so hard I could barely breathe.

War raised an eyebrow. "Damn, Fang. Quit staring at me like that before I get pregnant."

I rolled my eyes at him. "Fuck off."

But the image wouldn't go away.

I wanted her pregnant. I wanted a family.

I tried in vain to push the desire away, because if I knew Rebel at all, it was that she would despise the idea of settling down and having a kid. Sure, she was thirty, and excited for Bliss's baby, but that was one she could give back.

Rebel was never going to be a woman I could tie down with a house and rugrats. Her size wasn't the only reason I called her Pix. She was wild and free and magical. Just like pixies.

It didn't matter what I wanted. All that mattered was her.

She would always be enough. She always had been everything I ever wanted. I was only getting all up in my head because War had put stupid ideas there. I shoved food in my mouth to avoid talking about it anymore.

War did the same, both of us eating in silence, lost in our own thoughts.

Eventually, when there was nothing left between us but crumbs, War glanced outside. "Sun's just about gone. You ready to do this?"

I scrunched up my napkin and threw it onto the table. "When you are."

War jerked his head toward the door, signaling to get going. We both tossed a few bills onto the table, then scooted out from beneath the table.

In the parking lot, we got into the white, unmarked club van, and headed for the Sinners' house.

War gave nothing away, staring straight ahead, eyes on the road in front of us.

I did the same. My pinkie finger twitched, though.

I wasn't sure if it was because I was on edge about coming back here. Things hadn't exactly gone well last time.

Or if I was jumpy because all I could think about was my woman holding a baby whose eyes were the same color as mine.

Fucking War. Corrupting me with his sappy family life bullshit. That wasn't in the cards for me, no matter how sweet it seemed.

War pulled up at the end of the desolate street in the shittiest part of Saint View. Most of the houses around here were abandoned, too old and run-down for anyone to live in, apart from guys like the Sinners who had nowhere else to go while they tried to etch out a place for themselves in this world.

Broken glass glittered in the moonlight, and piles of rubble lay between the houses that were left standing. Danger whispered from deep shadows.

We were one of them.

War looked up ahead to where the Sinners' house sat, dark but with the tiniest scraps of light peeking around heavy curtains. It was clear to me there was still someone there, but they didn't want anyone seeing in.

War tapped his fingertips on the steering wheel.

"What do you think? Drive past? Go check it out on foot? Or sit here and wait?"

I ran my tongue along the backs of my teeth, considering the options. "Driving past doesn't seem smart. Even though we aren't on our bikes, we'd be drawing attention."

"I want those women out," War muttered, his leg bouncing impatiently. "Last time we didn't know who they were or why they were there. All we knew was Caleb had that one girl. But fuck, all I can think about was when Bliss was taken and how her stepdad was going to put her to work on the streets..." He gripped the steering wheel so tightly his knuckles turned white. "I'm gonna have a kid soon, and dammit, I need to be able to look her in the eye and know I'm not a piece of shit who enables men to sell women. I can't fucking do it, Fang. After what my mom went through... I don't know how Army got himself messed up in this shit, but I won't be."

He opened the car door, and the interior light came on, washing over his face.

I'd never seen him so determined.

This was what made him a better prez than Army ever was. War cared. He'd grown up in this life. He'd seen death. Murders. As many horrific sights as I had. And yet, while those things made other men hard and me silent, it made War honorable.

He was a good man.

I was determined to be the same. I pulled the door handle. "Let's go get them then."

War grinned. "This is why I brought you, brother. No fucking arguments. Just action."

He leaned across the center console with his fist held

out for me to bump. I connected with him, nothing but respect for the man across from me. I felt it right back in return.

The windshield shattering wasn't what I noticed first.

Nor the glass that sprayed in, showering the two of us in deadly sharp shards.

No. The first thing I noticed was blood seeping through War's shirt.

And the bullet-shaped hole that had caused it.

7

REBEL

With trembling fingers, I drove Sasha's car into the driveway of my home. My head was a mess of confusion over that autopsy report, my sister, and I was still reeling from the fact I'd put Hugh in the ground. But one thing was clear.

Kian wasn't telling me the full truth.

That somehow hurt more than the idea he might have killed my mother.

I had feelings for him.

Stupid fucking feelings that felt a lot like love.

Feelings I didn't want to have, because obviously they were misplaced.

He'd lied when he'd said he'd had nothing to do with my mother's murder, and I'd stupidly believed him. Because he was Kian. Sweet and cute and protective.

I'd let myself believe that wasn't all just an act.

That made me stupid.

I wouldn't be stupid tonight. I couldn't be. There was no room left for fuck-ups. Only the truth.

My gaze snagged on Vaughn's car. I got out of Sasha's and peered through his windows, spotting my purse still sitting on the back seat. I'd left it there when we'd abandoned the car to go chasing after Kara as she'd tried to escape through the woods.

My gun was still inside, and though it caused me physical pain to think about pointing it at a man I loved, I couldn't go and confront him unprotected either.

The biggest percentage of murder victims died at the hands of someone they loved.

That wouldn't be me.

I tried the door handle, but it was locked. My gaze narrowed in on the heavy round rocks that bordered a garden bed, and stooped to pick one up. I struggled beneath its weight but found enough strength from somewhere inside me to hurl it through the back window.

Glass went everywhere, and the car alarm went off, blaring in my ear, but I just knocked shards out of the way and reached through to open the door.

Kian and Vaughn came crashing through the front door of the house as my fingers closed around the pistol grip.

"Rebel?" Vaughn was shirtless, a pair of gray sweatpants low on his hips. He folded his arms across his chest and rubbed at them, goosebumps dotting his skin in the cold night air. "What the hell?"

Kian jogged down the steps, rounding the car to my side. He surveyed the damage I'd caused and his eyes went wide. "Shit! Are you okay? There's glass everywhere. What happened?"

He was too close. If I didn't do something, in the next

minute he'd have his arms around me, and then this wouldn't happen. He'd hold me, and I'd inhale his familiar scent and then I'd let him sweet-talk me into believing more of his lies.

I raised the gun, pointing it directly at his chest.

He froze.

So did I.

"Rebel!" Vaughn's voice was sharp at the sight of the gun.

He took a step toward me, but I held one hand out to him in a stop motion.

"Don't. Just stay there, Vaughn."

Kian slowly raised his hands, his gaze burning through me, a mixture of hurt and surprise behind the green depths. "Talk to me. What's going on?"

"Were you having an affair with my mom? The truth this time, Kian. Don't fucking lie to me."

He shook his head.

Anger burned through me. "You're lying."

"I swear I'm not."

He took half a step forward, but I matched him, pressing the gun directly into his chest.

"Don't," I warned, but my voice cracked. Which only made me angrier, because damn him, I didn't want to be doing this. I wanted to believe him when he said he wasn't sleeping with her, but I just knew there was more to the story.

I'd known all along, ever since I'd found those magazines with my mother's handwriting on them.

I just hadn't wanted to believe it.

"Did you know my mom was pregnant?" I choked out.

He blinked. Then oddly, smiled. "She was? That's so

great." Then his smile dropped, and his shoulders slumped. "Would have been great," he corrected himself.

I stared at him, watching his face intensely for any little sign that might give me some sort of clue as to what the hell had happened inside this house when it was just my mom, Bart, and Kian living in it. "Sasha found the full autopsy report, and it had a workup on the baby." My gaze slid to Vaughn's for a second. "Bart wasn't the father. He wasn't a genetic match."

He didn't react.

But Kian did. "No. He wouldn't have been. He couldn't have kids. It was a miracle he and Riva even had Vaughn."

Vaughn's gaze slid to Kian's. "How did you know that?"

Kian sighed, focusing on me. "Can you put the gun down before I say this?"

I shook my head. "Nope."

He wasn't happy. But he said what I knew to be true anyway. "Bart wasn't the father. I was. Are those the words you wanted to hear?"

I shook my head, tears pricking at the backs of my eyes. I was so fucking stupid falling for this man. Had he ever truly wanted me? Or had I just been a substitute for her? Nausea twirled around my stomach at the idea of the two of them rolling around in bed, kissing and touching, his narrow hips pushing her legs apart while he thrust inside her.

"What the fuck, Kian?" Vaughn spat out, storming down the steps. "Are you serious? After everything my father did for you?"

Kian shook his head sadly, his eyes full of hurt. "Good to know what the two of you really think of me."

Before I could even blink, he grabbed the gun by the barrel, wrenched it from my hand, and switched our positions so the gun was pointing at me.

I gasped.

"Kian!" Vaughn's shout was desperate.

Kian tossed the gun into the garden and closed the gap between us. "I never slept with your mom. I never even thought about it because"—he turned to Vaughn—"because she was your dad's woman. I loved your dad. Like you said, he was good to me from the day we moved into the house. He never looked down on me as some poor kid from Saint View who didn't deserve a chance. You know he used to help me with my homework? He threw the ball with me while my dad worked and you were off at your swim practices. I loved your dad as much as I loved mine. I never would have betrayed him by sleeping with his fiancée. I'm fucking insulted that you thought I would."

It didn't make sense. If he'd never slept with her, how had he fathered her baby?

Kian's gaze drifted back to mine. "It was because I loved him, and her too, that I said yes when they asked if I'd donate sperm so they could have a baby."

My mouth dropped open. "What?"

"Your mom wanted a baby, Rebel. They both did, and your mom was only in her early forties. The doctors said it was possible, but they didn't have time to spare, and with dodgy sperm and your mom being older and therefore a high-risk pregnancy, the doctor said using Bart's sperm wasn't advisable." He shrugged. "They needed swimmers. I had them to give."

I tried to make sense of that in my head. He seemed

sincere, but I'd been fooled by him before. I played my ace card. "Sasha said she heard screaming in the nights before they were murdered."

Kian scrunched up his face. "I don't know anything about that..." He rubbed his arms, fighting off the cold. His hand traveled over the Band-Aid at the crook of his arm, covering up the wound from where Hawk had taken his blood. He paused, staring down at it. "A couple nights before the wedding, I walked into their room while Miranda was injecting herself with fertility drugs."

Vaughn groaned. "Let me guess. You passed out."

Kian scowled at him. "I can't actually help it, you know that, right? It's not like I choose to crash down on the floor every time someone whips one out. It's not exactly fun. Miranda was screaming when I came to, slapping my face. She didn't know about my needle phobia. Apparently, she thought I'd had a heart attack and died."

I bit my lip. "She would have already been pregnant then. She mustn't have known..." I wandered to the front steps and sat down heavily, my heart hurting. "I don't know why, but that's so much worse. She didn't even know she was going to be a mom again."

Her murderer had taken so much more than just two lives. They'd taken three. As well as the happiness of so many people around them. I would have loved that little baby. Judging by the expression on Vaughn's and Kian's faces, they would have too.

That baby would have connected the three of us. But now I just felt lost.

A tear dripped down my face before I lifted my head to meet Kian's gaze. "Why didn't you tell me?"

He lifted one shoulder. "They didn't want anyone to know. Bart's business partners are pretty big on family, and he didn't want Harold knowing he couldn't father any more children when Harold was still popping out offspring with his new wife, despite him being ten years older than Bart."

Vaughn swore low beneath his breath. "Sounds about right. Harold is still on at me to stay married to Brooke and hold up our image as strong, virile, powerful businessmen. It's his whole brand. Happily settled, straight white men with children at home and a loving wife to take care of them. They make for more trustworthy business partners than men like me, in love with both a woman and a man."

He took my fingers, threading them through his, and then stared up at Kian. "I love you," he admitted. "I never fucking stopped."

I squeezed his hand, warmth settling over me.

I'd seen this all along. The feelings between them. How deep they ran, and how neither could deny them.

But Kian didn't move. His face was still too filled with hurt. "I've waited so long for you to say that. Years, you know that, right? While you went off and married someone else, I hung around waiting, trying to find that feeling with someone else, and I never did." He looked at me. "Not until you came a long."

I drew in a breath. "Kian, I—"

He held up a hand, his features hardening. "Honestly, I don't want to hear it. Not from either of you. I'm always the nice guy, Rebel. Always. I put up with so much fucking shit because I learned young that being nice and sweet and funny and helpful was the way to fit in when the kids in Saint View teased me about living in this mansion, or the kids in Providence teased me about being from the ghetto. None of that mattered if I was good and funny and *nice* enough that they forgot all that and just saw me."

He shook his head sadly. "But where did that get me? With the two of you assuming I had such low morals I'd steal a man's wife. Or that I was capable of murdering innocent people. Hell, Rebel, you just turned a gun on me like you were afraid I would hurt you. So excuse me if your 'I love yous' now seem a little farfetched. And if you honestly do love someone who you think capable of that sort of behavior, then you aren't the people I thought you were."

Vaughn pushed to his feet and reached for him. "Kian, come on. That's not what this is."

I followed, hating the hurt in his eyes, and just wanting to reach out and touch him.

But he was right.

I'd made accusations. Ones that had hurt him.

"I'm sorry," I murmured. "But you lied…"

He shook his head. "I never lied. I just didn't tell you other people's business. I protected the privacy of people I cared about. People who the two of you were supposed to care about too, for the record. But do the two of you actually care about anyone other than yourselves?"

I opened my mouth to answer, but nothing came out. Vaughn was equally silent.

I'd been so caught up in my revenge plans. I'd dragged Kian into all of it without a second thought, just because he'd been willing. Nice. Kind.

The complete opposite of Caleb.

Had I ever really even asked what was going on in his life?

The clear answer was no.

When Kian brushed past us and went upstairs to his room, neither Vaughn nor I stopped him.

I was too clouded in my own regrets to move.

Kian deserved better.

8

WINNIE

I flinched at every sound now. Every little noise was as loud as gunshots, each one echoing around my head and rattling my brain until it ached.

Everything hurt, especially my stomach. It growled with hunger pains like I'd never known before. Back in the day, when I'd come home from school and complained to Mama I was starving because I hadn't eaten since lunch, I'd had no idea what I was talking about.

I knew what true starvation felt like now.

I'd barely eaten in days.

We'd had nothing more than scraps since Caleb had shot those paramedics right in front of us and then forced Hayden and Kara into an ambulance with him. Not since the cruel, angry men they'd left behind had dragged the paramedics' bodies out by their feet, leaving a thick, wide smear of blood behind.

It was still there now. They hadn't bothered to come back in and clean it up.

They hadn't bothered to feed us anything other than their stale pizza crusts, which didn't go far between the four of us. We survived only by drinking the water from the bathroom faucet.

They'd only opened the door one other time, throwing in a blanket-wrapped bundle, but just as quickly they'd locked the doors and boarded the windows so we couldn't even see out.

We were as good as caged rats.

Kept in the dark.

Ignored.

Forgotten.

Nova shifted on her dirty mattress to peer over at the door. "Something's happening out there."

Georgia and Vivienne sat up and looked in the same direction.

Georgia cocked her head. "I don't hear anything."

Nova shushed her, waving her hands at her to be quiet. "Just listen."

We fell into silence again, all of us straining our ears to hear whatever it was Nova had.

Maybe she was imagining it. She'd had the longest seizure that night Caleb had stormed into our room and destroyed any semblance of peace we'd found here. She'd seemed better after a day or two of sleep, but maybe it had damaged her hearing.

Maybe she heard noises that were only in her head, the same way I did.

"There's someone out there," one of the men said in a hushed whisper.

"There's not. You're paranoid."

"Nah, bro. I fucking heard the engine on their vehicle.

It turned onto the street but never came past the house. Something is up."

There was a pause for a moment, while the four of us women stared at each other, none of us daring to speak.

A groan came from one man. "You fucking kill me, Frank. Now I won't be able to sleep until we go and see."

"We'll go out the back door and stick to the shadows. If they're watching the house, we don't need to make it obvious we're aware."

"You're so fucking dramatic."

"Chaos never came back. He's fucking dead, and you know it. You want to be the same? Rotting six feet under, with worms chomping on your flesh?"

There was a huffed-out sigh. "Like I said, you're dramatic. Get your gun. Let's go check it out."

The back door closed with a snick.

Nova stared at me wide-eyed, hope shining there for the first time since the Slayers had circled their bikes outside. "We're alone. There's only two of them here tonight, and if they're both out, we can escape."

Last time, we'd talked her out of trying to get help. But last time, we'd had Chaos looking after us, making sure we were fed. We were still his prisoners, but he'd provided us with everything we'd asked for.

It had been a case of better the devil you know. We didn't know anything about the Slayers, other than they were an outlaw motorcycle club. Chaos had treated us well. Life with the Slayers could have been so much worse.

But things had changed now.

We were going to die in here if we didn't do something.

I ran for the door to our prison bedroom, barging it with my shoulder. Nova blinked at me in surprise, but this was it. The only chance we were going to get, and I wasn't going to waste it. Not again.

"Are you going to help me or what?" I ran at the door again, pain splintering through my arm when it connected.

But the fact nobody came to yell at us from the other side meant Nova had been right. There was no one else out there.

Hope sparked inside me, drowning out the pain. The other women joined in, each of us taking it in turns to run at the door, kick at it, all while praying the men who held us hostage wouldn't return.

The door splintered.

Nova's eyes went huge. "Oh my God, it's working. Don't give up!" With giddy laughter, she ran at the door again.

The locks gave, and the door sprang open.

For the longest of seconds, all four of us just stood there, staring at the gaping hole that offered us freedom.

It was right there.

We just had to take it.

A gunshot cracked through the still night air.

I flinched, a whole-body tremble picking up and coursing through me.

I couldn't do this.

I wasn't brave or strong like Nova, or beautiful like Vivienne or smart like Georgia. I was just little Winnie Russel, a nobody from Hicksville.

I doubted anyone had even noticed I was missing. I

certainly wasn't the sort of person whose face would be plastered all over newspapers and milk cartons.

"Winnie!" Nova hissed, grabbing her meager belongings from her bed. "Move! We've got to go before they get back here with that gun!"

But I couldn't. The fear had me in its grips again, and I just wanted to check out so I didn't have to feel it.

She slapped me, her palm sharp and stinging across my cheek, but I still couldn't move. I wanted to, but my legs were cement blocks, and any attempts at moving them seemed futile.

"Just go without me," I murmured. "I can't do it."

Nova got in my face and pushed a bundle of blankets into my arms. "No way. You saved me when I had that seizure. Now I'm saving you."

She hauled me toward the door, my feet shuffling for the first few steps while I clutched the blanket-wrapped parcel, but slowly, the movement felt more natural. One step turned into two and then ten until I was running, following the other women out the back door, down the steps, and across a darkened field.

We ran by the light of the moon with fear in our hearts but fresh night air on our faces for the first time in weeks. I wanted to stop, look around, take it all in because everything felt so new. We got to the edge of some woods, and I slowed, breathing heavily, my tiny bit of energy all spent.

Another gunshot cracked through the night, a bullet whizzing just by our heads.

I stifled a hysterical scream.

I wanted to drop to the ground and curl up in a ball

and weep. I wanted to give myself up, fall at our captors' knees and beg their forgiveness.

A tiny sound, one I'd almost forgotten, came from beneath the blankets in my arms.

I pulled them back an inch, gazing down at the tiny baby in awe.

She'd made a noise.

In the last few days, since Caleb had tossed her in here again, she hadn't made a sound. It was like without Kara, she'd given up as much as the rest of us had.

We'd all just been waiting to die.

But that noise. That tiny cooing sound broke through all my defenses. All my fears.

If Kara's baby could find her voice again, then I could do this. I could run. I could fight. I could survive.

I forced my feet forward, carrying the little baby with me.

9

FANG

I stared at the blood dripping down War's shirt and his pale, wide-eyed face.

His head dropped, and he groaned, clutching the bullet wound. "Fucking hell, and here I was, thinking we were so quiet—"

Another bullet pinged off the metal hood, and I ducked on instinct, sinking down on my seat and dragging War off his as well.

"Fuck," he moaned as he hit the floor. "That doesn't tickle."

The van had only two front seats, with a gap in between to access the rear. I shoved War into the gap, half lying on top of him, and tried to get my gun out of the waistband of my jeans.

"How bad is that wound? Flesh, or you gonna bleed out on me?" I raised my head, peeping over the dashboard through the broken windshield. I thought I saw some human-shaped shadows, so I popped off two shots then ducked again.

War's face contorted in pain. "It's high. Maybe more shoulder than anything else. Might have got my collarbone. Fuck. I don't know."

I reached over and turned the key that was still hanging from the ignition, and the engine came to life. Another round of bullets flew my way, but I returned them quickly, using the shots to cover me so I could get behind the wheel. "Hospital or clubhouse?"

War glared at me.

I shook my head. "You better not die if I take you there. I swear to God, boss. I'll resurrect you and then kill you all over again if you're downplaying how bad this is." I spun the steering wheel and put my foot down on the gas while bullets flew around us. "Put some pressure on it."

If the Sinners had a vehicle, they didn't chase us. I checked the rearview and side mirrors in between checking on War, who had pulled himself up into a half-seated position but didn't seem willing to try to get himself up off the van floor.

Red seeped from beneath his fingers as he tried to stem the bleeding.

I swore and got my phone out of my jacket pocket to call Hawk.

It rang too many times before he finally answered, his voice coming through the speakerphone. "What's up, big dog? You and War miss me already?"

"Prez has been shot," I bit out into the phone.

Hawk's tone changed instantly. "How bad?"

"Flesh," War called out from the floor. "You got this."

Hawk had about as much faith in War's diagnosis as I did. "Fang, is he lying?"

War gave me a look that said I'd better not rat him out.

I grit my teeth. "You should be able to handle it. Get everything ready and into the infirmary. Tell Ice to get the gates open 'cause otherwise I'm driving right through 'em. Don't need no prez dying on my watch."

Hawk scoffed down the phone line, "Oh, but he can die on mine? Thanks, Fang. Awesome. War, you're an asshole. Just in case you die before you get here, I just need to be sure you know that. You fucking suck."

War chuckled. "Just get your needle ready, would ya? I ain't dying. Not when I got a baby on the way. Speaking of, don't tell Bliss."

I flew up the dirt road that led through the woods to the clubhouse gates with one eyebrow raised at him. "Seriously? I think she's gonna notice her man has an extra hole. And I ain't lying to Rebel. She'd destroy me if she found out."

He grinned at me, though it was tinged with pain. "You're so pussy-whipped."

I grumbled at him. "Like you can talk."

As requested, Ice had the gates open when we arrived, and he stood beside them, his hands gripped at the back of his neck, his expression full of worry. But I couldn't be concerned with him. I blew through the entryway and stopped with a cloud of gravel and dust that filled the car, thanks to the lack of windshield.

Aloha and Hawk were on standby to open the sliding door, and Hawk swore loudly as he took in the sight in front of him.

"I don't know why you assholes keep doing this to me. I don't have a fucking medical degree, you know?"

"Nah, but you'd be real pretty in a nurse's uniform." War grinned weakly at him. "Gimme the good drugs, man. Don't be stingy with 'em, okay?"

Hawk grumbled something, but he was already striding away, letting me and Aloha grab War and get him out of the van. We got his arms over our shoulders and put one arm around his back, the other underneath a knee each.

"I can fucking walk," War complained.

We both ignored him, rushing through the crowd of people who watched on with shocked expressions, through the common rooms, and down the long hall that housed my bedroom. At the very end, Hawk held open a door, and on the other side, stairs led down to the basement.

Otherwise known as the infirmary.

Hawk flicked a switch, and light flooded the room. "Put him over there, on the bed right beneath the light. Gonna need it to sew up that mess. You better hope that bullet didn't hit anything vital. Fang, get me some antiseptic, will you?"

I deposited the patient on the bed and then spun around, eyeing the wall full of medical supplies, most of which we'd bought on the black market to create a pretty decent first-aid room.

More than one gunshot wound had been fixed up here. But normally they were arm or leg wounds. I didn't like that this was through his chest, even if he did swear it was more of a shoulder wound.

I finally found what I was searching for, plucked it from a shelf, and tossed it to Hawk.

He grinned at War. "This is gonna hurt."

"Then give me some painkillers first!"

Hawk shook his head. "Nah. Serves you right for being a dumbass and going down there without backup. What were you thinking, you idiot?"

If anyone else had spoken to the prez like that, there would have been consequences. And not the sexy kind I liked to punish Rebel with.

But Hawk and War had been best friends since birth, so if anyone was going to get away with talking to him like that, it was him.

He checked War's back for an exit wound, then poured the entire bottle of antiseptic onto the bullet hole.

War's eyes rolled back.

"Shit, Hawk, he's out cold." I slapped War's face.

"Good. It'll hurt less when I shove this needle through his skin if he's not conscious. Get me one of those fluid bags, he'll need that too. But I think he was right. This isn't bleeding enough to have hit anything vital. Prick will live to see another day if we keep it clean and he lies here to rest for a bit."

Relief flushed through me. "He won't like that."

Hawk looked over at me with a grin, his smile slightly evil. "I know. So go call Bliss and tell her what the dumbass did. She'll be down here in no time and if she tells him to keep his ass in bed, he will." He shook his head. "Pussy-whipped fool."

I didn't say anything because I was the same for Rebel.

Hawk didn't have someone he loved the way I loved Rebel or War loved Bliss. If he ever did, he'd understand the deep-set urge to never upset them.

But Hawk was cold and arrogant and self-centered.

Pigs would probably fly before he ever opened up to a woman in any way other than getting his dick wet.

Hawk jerked his head toward the door. "Go. I got this. He'll be awake by the time you get Bliss down here, but can you go check on Rebel's spitfire of a sister while you're up there? I wasn't expecting to have to do this much doctoring today and I can't clone myself."

I watched him for a second, making his second set of neat stitches for the day. "You're good at that."

"Yeah, I know."

Typical Hawk. I shook my head and walked away, searching for somewhere quiet to call Bliss, but first I needed to get all this blood off my hands. My fingers were sticky with it. I went to the little sink in the corner and turned on the faucet. I wet my hands, added a few pumps of antibacterial soap Hawk had insisted we buy, and lathered up.

A groan came from a curtained-off partition beside the one Hawk was working on. Hawk didn't seem to notice, but I rinsed off my hands and pulled aside the curtain.

The man on the bed was covered in bandages, so many I could barely see any of his skin.

"Leave War his gun," I called to Hawk. "Just in case this asshole wakes up. How is he anyway?"

"War? Or the Sinners' prez over there, who's probably going to die at any minute?"

I guess that answered my question.

"Don't fucking let him die," War gritted out. "I want to know everything he knows about Caleb Black. And everything he knows about my father and his involvement with any women they're keeping at that house."

We'd scraped Hayden 'Chaos' Whitling off the side of the road after he'd fallen out of the ambulance and been left for dead by Caleb. Kara had asked if he was still alive, and I hadn't dared say yes, because there was no point in getting her hopes up.

Fact was, Hayden probably wasn't walking out of here breathing, even if he did survive his injuries.

Sins didn't go unpunished in this world.

Neither did Sinners.

10

VAUGHN

Rebel and I sat in silence at the kitchen table, both of us chewing mouthfuls of cereal, lost in our own thoughts.

I was still trying to work out how Kian and I had gone from what we'd done in the woods, and then later in the shower, and then in his bed, to whatever the hell we were now.

Which felt like a whole lot of nothing.

I'd walked away from us once, and it had nearly killed me.

If I tried to do it again now, I was sure it would be the end.

"We fucked up, Roach."

She gradually lifted her eyes from her cereal bowl to meet mine. "I know. I hate myself so much right now."

"Me too."

"We don't deserve him."

"No, we don't. We're assholes."

She sighed heavily. "Like brother, like sister. How do we make it up to him?"

"I've been thinking about that all morning. I don't think a blow job is gonna cut it."

"Not even close."

We both lapsed into silence again.

Rebel played with her cereal, nudging it around her bowl with her spoon. "I'm in love with him."

I wasn't surprised. He was easy to love. "I am too."

She reached across the table and threaded her fingers between mine. "I love you too, you know? I haven't even had a chance to say it, with everything that happened..."

I nudged my cereal bowl out of the way and leaned over the table to take her lips with mine. The kiss was soft and sad. Not how an 'I love you' kiss should have felt, but with everything that had happened the day before, it didn't feel like a thing to celebrate. It felt like something was missing. Like she and I didn't quite work without him.

She pressed up to her feet. "I should go have a shower and get back over to the clubhouse. When I talked to Fang last night, he said he was keeping an eye on Kara and he wouldn't let any of the prospects drag Sasha off to their rooms, but I saw the way she checked out Ice, so I think I better get her out of there before she falls in love with him."

A door opened at the top of the stairs, and Rebel and I jumped up eagerly.

Kian walked down slowly, not looking at either of us.

Rebel's shoulder slumped, but she called out a greeting anyway. "Do you want some breakfast? There's cereal. Or toast. Fruit. I could make bacon or eggs or pancakes..."

Kian shook his head. "Can't. Got another job interview. Gotta go."

He opened the front door without even glancing in my direction.

Rebel ran after him, grabbing his arm. "Kian, wait— Oh my God." She clapped a hand over her mouth and stumbled back. "Is that...I'm going to be sick."

Kian just stood there staring at the front porch. He stood there so long without saying anything that I stood slowly and walked over to them.

With every step, my heart sank.

After receiving an envelope full of Brooke's hair, with promises there'd be worse if I didn't come up with the money she owed, I was almost sure I wasn't going to like this.

I caught Rebel around the waist, pulling her close against my chest while she gagged.

She was plenty short enough I could see easily over her head at the severed, bloody finger that lay on my porch.

A string was tied around it with a white card attached. In simple black type, it read: *Last warning. Next time it's your wife in a body bag.*

Kian glanced over at me. "I'm going to be late." He stepped over the severed finger like it was a couple of stray leaves the breeze had dragged in. He got in the driver's side of his truck, gunned the engine, and disappeared down the driveway.

Rebel watched him go, then stared up at me with big

eyes. "What the hell? Is that finger Brooke's? What are we going to do with it? Should we call the cops?"

We were already in enough trouble with them, all of us suspects in my dad and Miranda's murders. I wasn't sure calling up Detective Dickhead and telling him we had random body parts delivered to us was the smartest idea.

But this couldn't keep happening. Anger boiled up inside me. At Brooke for getting herself in this predicament in the first place. At Harold for not telling me sooner that the company wasn't as profitable as I'd always believed.

At myself for being a stubborn jackass, so caught up in his own shit that I'd left Brooke to deal with this herself.

I'd loved her once. At least a little bit.

If it had been Kian, he wouldn't have hesitated. He would have done whatever needed doing because that's the kind of guy he was. He might have thought being good was a flaw, and that being nice meant he got walked all over.

But the world needed more people like him.

I needed people to remind me to pull my fucking head out of my ass and be a decent human being.

I grabbed my keys from the hook by the door. "I'm going to my mom's place to see if Brooke is still there. If these guys have taken to hand-delivering body parts, they must be in town, which means she is too."

Rebel trembled in my arms. "Did I do this?"

I spun her around so we were facing each other. "What? This has nothing to do with you."

But she shook her head. "I've been so hell-bent on getting revenge. On hurting the people who hurt me. I've spent all this time putting out this negative energy, but instead of releasing it, it just feels like I'm drawing more and more in. Kara's lost her baby. Kian's hurt." She gestured down at the porch. "Brooke is apparently missing a digit!"

I squeezed her arms. "This is Brooke's problem. My problem. This isn't the universe punishing you, Roach. You did nothing wrong."

But if she was listening, it didn't get through. "This has to end. The murders. The threats. The revenge." Her eyes were glassy with tears. "I'm hurting people who I'm supposed to love."

I didn't know how to make her feel better, because I was doing the same thing.

I straightened my shoulders. "We start with Brooke then. Come on, I'm not leaving you here alone. Let's go see if we can find her. Maybe it isn't her finger at all."

Rebel nodded and put her shoes on while I gingerly picked up the severed body part and deposited it into the trash so she didn't have to see it. The blood we'd have to deal with later.

Brooke's car sat in the driveway at my mom's place, just down the road from mine. I let myself into the house, calling out for my mom.

She stuck her head out of her bedroom down the hall. "Vaughn? What's going on?"

"Is Brooke here?"

Mom's eyebrows furrowed together. "No, I don't think so. She went to meet up with some old friends from college in the city last night. I didn't hear her come back in."

She walked a few steps down the hall to the guest bedroom and peered inside. "Her bed hasn't been slept in."

"Shit."

Mom took Rebel's arm, squeezing it in greeting. "Is there a problem?"

"Maybe," Rebel said quietly. "Vaughn, we should call around to the hospitals. I'll check the city hospital and you call Saint View."

Karmichael padded down the hallway, wearing one of his brother's pool cleaning company's branded work shirts. He had his boots in his hand and was obviously on his way out to work. "Who's in the hospital?"

"Hopefully no one," I mumbled, phone already to my ear. When it connected to the hospital's switchboard, and a pleasant-sounding receptionist greeted me, I asked if they had a patient by the name of Brooke Weston.

"Oh yes, I remember that patient, she came in while I was on duty. She's in room two-oh-three. Would you like me to put you through?"

"Can you give me an update on her condition?"

"Are you family?"

"I'm Vaughn Weston. Her husband."

I glanced down at Rebel, hating I'd even had to utter the word in front of her. I wasn't Brooke's husband anymore. Not in anything but name.

But Rebel shook her head. "It's fine. What are they saying?"

"Oh, yes. I believe we met this morning. Hello again." The receptionist hummed under her breath as she clicked keys on her mouse or keyboard. "She did list you as her next of kin. Her notes say she was admitted at two this morning, and she's had surgery on her index finger, but the finger was never found in order to attempt reattachment. It's good you brought her in when you did. She's being held for observation but should be ready to be picked up in a couple of hours if you want to come down soon."

A lump rose in my throat. "Could you put me through to her now, please?"

"Most certainly. It's good you brought her down when you did."

That was twice now she'd said that. The first I'd ignored as a slip of the tongue but now I was curious. "I didn't bring her in this morning."

The woman paused. "Oh, you weren't the gentleman in the suit? I could have sworn he said he was her husband, but we were very busy this morning. I must have her confused with another patient. Apologies. I'll connect you now."

"That's fine, thank you." I waited, and eventually, Brooke's groggy voice came down the line. "Hello."

"It's me."

Brooke burst into tears. "They cut my finger off, Vaughn! I told you this was going to happen if you didn't pay!"

I swallowed thickly through my guilt. I might not love her anymore, but it still hurt to know she'd been injured because I hadn't been able to help her. "Who the hell are these guys? Who's the guy in the suit? They cut your finger off but then take you to the hospital?"

"Why do you act like you're surprised? They can't blackmail you if I'm dead, can they! They're just going to keep torturing me until it eventually goes too far."

"There's no money," I confessed. "I went to my father's business partner, but the business hasn't been doing that well. He can't get me the money you need."

My mom frowned at me.

Her disappointment wasn't going to help the situation.

Brooke's response was only to wail louder. "My finger, Vaughn! It's completely gone! Forever!"

I sighed. "Your father needs to know what's going on. He has the money, and this has gone way further than I ever thought it would. Lopping off your hair is one thing, but a finger is a whole different level of messed up. He's not going to let them keep chopping you up into pieces."

Rebel slapped my arm, her mouth open in horror. "Don't say that!" she whispered at me.

"It's true," I whispered back.

Brooke just cried down the line, her voice finally going soft and resigned. "They won't stop at killing me, Vaughn. You know that. Once I'm dead, they'll just find someone new to blackmail you with. My dad is a cold bastard who doesn't care about anyone. If I had to guess, I'd say they already tried with him, and he told them to have at me."

It should have been a shocking statement; except I knew it was probably true. Brooke's father was no different than Harold Coker and the other men who ran in their circles. They didn't care about anyone but themselves.

I had to try though.

I didn't want to be like them. "I'll go see your dad. I'll make him listen."

"You're wasting your time. Tell Rebel to watch her back. She'll be next after I'm gone."

The line went dead.

"What did she say?" Rebel asked.

Fear choked me with its grip. I was beginning to see all too clearly she wasn't exaggerating. The proof was right there in our kitchen bin.

I had to get Brooke's father to pay up.

I'd already lost Kian.

I wasn't losing Rebel too.

11

KIAN

I hadn't been out of the construction manager's office for longer than an hour before he called my phone and offered me the job.

A big part of me wanted to say no. I'd worked at Bart's house for years. I liked running it. I was good at keeping the creaky old mansion from falling into complete disrepair.

But it was hardly a career.

I'd needed to move on for a long time. I'd only stuck around because I hadn't wanted to disappoint Bart and Miranda.

Same old shit, different day. I was always more worried about everyone else than I ever was about myself. If I'd put myself first, maybe I would have stayed away at college when my dad got sick. I could have had a professional career in sports, instead of dropping out to come back here and watch him wither away slowly and painfully as cancer racked his body.

If I'd put myself first, maybe I wouldn't have spent a decade lusting over a man who left me to marry someone else. I could have found someone, fallen in love, started a family. Instead of sitting in the parking lot at the gym, desperate to take my frustrations out on a punching bag.

I sighed and dragged myself out of my truck. I'd just yesterday accused Vaughn and Rebel of being assholes for only ever thinking of themselves, but it had been unfair. Life hadn't been kind to Rebel, and making out she wasn't a good person made me feel sick with regret. She was just trying to understand what had happened to her mom while trying not to let the grief pull her under.

I'd been too hard on Vaughn too. If I was being honest, a little of my problem with him was that Rebel loved him.

I was so stupidly in love with both of them and spiraling because neither of them seemed to feel the same.

I was so fucking pathetic. It was the story of my life. Big and good at sports. Reasonably attractive. Dumb as a doornail.

I really needed to hit something.

I stormed the gym, grunting a hello at Gino, sitting behind the front desk watching YouTube on his phone. He waved distractedly as I passed, but I didn't stop to chat.

I wasn't good company for anyone in the mood I was in. There were two rings in the gym, and my favorite was the one in the back right-hand corner. I made a beeline for it, hoping it would be empty.

It wasn't.

A teenage fighter danced around the ring, hands up, protecting his face.

Another man held a set of pads for the kid to punch.

Luca Guerra.

I would have recognized him, even if he hadn't been wearing fitted business pants and a collared shirt with the sleeves rolled to his elbows, which made him as out of place in this gym as the last time I'd seen him here. His tanned skin rippled with muscles hidden beneath, and his pants pulled tight across his ass. He caught my eye and jerked his head in acknowledgement.

I returned the nod but went to the boxing bags hanging from the ceiling. I could wait until they were finished. I needed to warm up anyway.

I sat, watching him train the younger fighter while I took off my work boots and socks. I wrapped my hands and then pulled off my T-shirt. I only had one with me, and I didn't need it getting all sweaty when I was going to have to wear it home.

I didn't miss Luca's interest in my direction, my shirt falling in a clump on top of my bag.

I warmed up slowly, jogging on the spot, shifting my weight from foot to foot and striking the bag with quick, smooth, strong punches.

"Done for the night, Scott. See you later." Luca's voice was deep and smooth like fucking butter as he dismissed his fighter.

The younger guy fist bumped me, headed for the locker rooms.

Luca gathered up all their equipment, eyeing me while he picked up gloves and pads. "O'Malley. Good to see you again. Been hoping I'd run into you here."

I paused my workout and glanced over at him. "Yeah? Why's that?"

His gaze ran over my body slowly, before returning to my face. He grinned, not even remotely ashamed about checking me out. "Been hoping for a chance to get you in the ring."

"You've seen me fight before."

He waved his hand toward the ropes. "I've seen you fight men who aren't half as good as you are. I haven't seen you fight someone better."

I raised an eyebrow at the cocky son of a bitch. "You're better, huh?"

Luca lifted a shoulder. "Care to find out?"

I wasn't sure if he was calling my bluff or what. But I was keen to get in the ring. I needed to fight. I needed somewhere for my frustration to go.

I grinned. "You're on."

Parting the ropes with one hand, I pulled myself up with the other and climbed through. On the other side of the ring, Luca stripped his shirt, revealing a washboard stomach and a host of tattoos across his back and shoulders. Muscles rippled when he bent to slip his expensive shoes off, leaving him in nothing but business pants.

I eyed him.

Luca was exactly my type. Dark-haired. Dark-eyed. Asshole smirk that would have normally done things to my insides.

But it only reminded me of Vaughn. And thinking of Vaughn reminded me of Rebel.

"Fuck," I muttered.

Luca chuckled, taking my curse the wrong way, I was sure. "You ready?"

I nodded, raising my fists.

Luca was quick off the mark, reaching out with a right hook I ducked, then following with a low left that caught me in the side.

I flinched at the pain that speared through my ribs.

Luca grinned. "Got ya."

It only fueled my determination. I landed a quick flurry of punches, followed by a kick that forced a grunt from between Luca's perfect pink lips.

It was my turn to smile. "Got ya right back."

Before I could even comprehend what was happening, he took my feet out from beneath me with a sweeping kick I didn't even see coming. I landed hard on the mats, and he followed up with punches and kicks until I caught his foot and brought him down into a sprawling heap with me. In a moment, I had him pinned to the mats, my body over his, our arms and legs locked around each other so neither of us could move.

"Tap out," I murmured, breathing hard.

He winked. "I kinda like it here, actually."

My face hovered over his. Our lips were mere inches apart. It would have been so easy to erase the space and kiss him.

Except I didn't want to.

Kissing him would fuck everything up with Vaughn and Rebel. If I hadn't already done that with my stupid tantrum yesterday.

I let Luca go and got up.

He watched me carefully, his head cocked to one side. "You're not into guys? Did I read the room wrong?"

I shook my head. "Just into one guy in particular."

Luca grinned. "Ah. I see. Monogamy man."

I chuckled. "Not sure I'd call it that. But I am seeing… people? I don't know how to explain it."

He cocked his head to one side. "Try. Sounds interesting."

I shrugged. "Vaughn is my ex, if you can really call him that. We were never officially out as a couple, but we fooled around in our teens. And Rebel…"

"The cute little dark-haired woman I've seen you hanging around with at fights, I presume?"

Just the thought of her name spread a smile across my face. "She's unmissable."

Luca nodded, leaning on the ropes. "So Vaughn is the big blond biker?"

"Nah, that's Fang. Don't even ask how he fits in. It's complicated."

Luca laughed. "I see. You've got your hands full; I get it. Shame. You're hot."

I flushed. "So are you." But there was nothing behind it. He wasn't Vaughn.

Luca stood slowly. "Can I ask you something personal?"

I jerked my head at the pads he'd been holding up while training the other fighter. "If you hold those up for me, you can."

He slipped his hands into the straps on the backs and then clapped them together before holding them up. "I heard you talking with Gino about your money troubles. You fixed that up?"

I shrugged, thumping the pads a couple of times. "Maybe. Got a job on a construction site. Starts tomorrow."

"What's the pay like?"

I snorted. "Lousy. But a job is a job."

"I've got better ones going at my club. Come join us."

I shook my head. "Not doing the match-fixing thing. I thought about it for a hot minute, but it's not for me. I'm too..."

Nice.

Decent.

Honest.

This time it actually felt like a good thing.

Luca snorted. "Is that the shit they're trying to get you into here? We got way bigger fish to fry over at my club. Way bigger paydays too. I've had my eye on you for a while."

I paused and raised an eyebrow. "You talk a lotta talk. But I don't actually hear a real offer. Gonna have to give me more details than that."

He chuckled. "You think I'm just gonna lay my cards out flat on the table without so much as you buying me dinner?"

"Don't think my partners would appreciate that too much." The door opening caught my eye, and I did a double take at the people in the doorway.

Luca followed my line of sight. "Looks like their ears were burning." He clapped me on the back of the shoulder as he left the ring. "Think about it, okay? I'll promise not to flirt with you anymore, since that's clearly not gonna get you on board, but I think you'd be good at what we've got going on over there. You've got that 'puppy-dog eyes, trust me' sort of face. Exactly what women like."

I frowned, no idea why that would be needed in a

boxing gym, but with Rebel, Fang, and Vaughn standing in the doorway, I just wanted Luca to go.

I needed to fix what I'd broken yesterday. Because it was clear to me now that nothing was ever going to compare to what I'd found.

12

REBEL

"We're closed," the man in the little office called out. "Open again at six in the morning."

That might be so, but I could see Kian across the other side of the gym, and I was pretty sure he could see me.

"Let 'em in, Gino."

Gino leaned over the counter to scowl at Kian. "I got a missus at home, Kian. It's already late. I gotta close up."

"Go home to Grace. I'll close for you."

Gino didn't need telling twice. He was gone quicker than you could blink. Another man pulled on a business shirt and smart, Italian leather shoes. He gave Kian a meaningful look.

A little seed of jealousy kernelled inside me.

The man picked up a gym bag from a bench and then walked toward us, his gaze landing on Vaughn. He paused. "Vaughn, right? Luca Guerra."

Vaughn frowned. "Sorry, have we met?"

The other man shook his head. "No. See you around."

He slipped out behind Fang so Vaughn couldn't question him any further.

"That was weird," he mumbled.

But with the gym to ourselves, I didn't want to waste any more time. I strode across the space to where Kian stood, quietly packing his bag.

Sweat glistened across his shoulders, and his biceps bulged from his workout. "Why are you all in my gym?"

I gave him a half-smile. "I wanted to do some cardio?"

The corner of his mouth flickered then flattened out again. "You're wearing a skirt and combat boots, and I think your earrings are nearly as big as your head. Nice try, what else you got?"

I swallowed thickly and pulled a sheet of paper out from my back pocket. "Okay, so don't laugh, but I wrote you a poem."

Kian blinked. "Sorry, what?"

I waved it toward him. "A poem. So you'd forgive me."

He scrunched his face up. "I've got a lot of questions, but maybe I'll save them for after this little impromptu poetry reading." He motioned to the ring. "Stage is yours, Rebel."

My heart fell. He hadn't called me Little Demon. I didn't like the way Rebel sounded on his tongue. Not when it didn't sound all warm and sweet like it normally did. But I needed to push on because I had things to say.

I cleared my throat and gazed down at the page, reading the words I'd scrawled across it earlier. "I wrote a poem to say I'm sorry. For all the things I said, good golly."

Vaughn let out a snort of laughter.

Fang kicked him in the shin, and that shut him up. He hobbled over to sit on the bench seat beside Kian.

I gave him a dirty look before continuing. "I made you feel bad, and for that, I'm sad. You are so kind and nice, and you keep away the mice."

Vaughn howled with laughter.

Oh, fuck him, asshole. "What? He does! I don't see you setting any mousetraps at home, Vaughn!"

He doubled over on the seat, laughing so hard tears rolled down his cheeks. "I can't breathe," he wheezed. "I seriously can't breathe." He looked at Fang through watery eyes. "Don't kick me again. I bruise like a peach."

Fang pulled out a gun from the waistband of his jeans and cocked it in his direction. "Could shoot you instead if you don't shut up and let her finish."

Vaughn didn't seem the least bit scared. But his laughter did die down enough for Fang to grudgingly put away his weapon.

I stared at Kian, who hadn't said a word. "The last line doesn't rhyme," I admitted.

"Thank God," Vaughn muttered. "I couldn't take any more of that. It's like you've been saving this up since tenth grade English class. I have a severe case of second-hand embarrassment."

I ignored him, well used to him by now, and waited for Kian to say something. My fingers shook. I was suddenly so nervous I could vomit.

Maybe Kian noticed the trembling page, or he sensed the nerves coming off me, but his voice softened. "Read it, Little Demon. I'm not going to laugh at you."

I nodded, putting all my focus on him. "You made me laugh when everything else around me felt dark and cold. You made me feel safe when I was scared and weak." I swallowed hard and put the paper down, no longer needing it. "I know I don't deserve your forgiveness, but I won't stop trying to earn it. Because I love you. I love you so freaking much, Kian. The thought of losing you makes me so sick to my stomach I can't even bear it."

Vaughn was finally silent. The entire gym was.

Kian just looked at me.

Heat flushed my cheeks. I was making a fool out of myself, and I knew it, but I didn't care. Even if he didn't feel it back, I wanted him to know someone loved him enough to fight for him.

He needed to know there was room in my heart for one more. That a third of my heart was always meant for him, and I would love him like he owned it completely.

Vaughn elbowed him. "You gonna say something?"

I hated that Vaughn was having to prompt a response from him. I held my hands up. "No, it's fine, you don't have to say anything, but I wanted you to know—"

Kian closed the gap between us.

The words died on my lips as a little smile lifted his mouth. "You love me, huh?"

I nodded so fast it was surprising my head didn't fall off. "I'm so sorry. I hate that we hurt you. I hate it took me so long to tell you what I've known in my heart since the day you put those locks on my bedroom door."

He wrapped his arms around me. "That was about an hour after we met. You didn't love me then."

Maybe I hadn't known it at the time, but in hindsight, I had. That was the moment I saw the depth of his kindness. He'd taken me into his home without a second thought. He'd made me feel safe and wanted at a time where I had no home, no family, and fear overwhelmed me.

I'd never be able to thank him enough for that.

He lowered his head, and I lifted up on my toes, closing the gap between us. He kissed me in a way he hadn't before, taking his time, licking over my lips, and exploring my mouth with his tongue like we had all the time in the world, and there weren't two other men in the room, watching us.

Kian made the world feel small. Like it was just him and me, and nothing else mattered as long as I was in his arms. The heat moved from my cheeks into other parts of my body, and I pressed against him, feeling the solid strength inside him. He held me tight, silently reassuring me this thing between us wasn't over.

It never could be. My heart would be missing a piece without him.

"Maybe we should give them a moment," Fang said softly to Vaughn.

Vaughn chuckled. "Fuck that, this is just getting good. I'm staying for the show."

I pulled away from Kian's lips in time to see Fang shaking his head. His fingers hovered over his gun. "You really make me want to use this sometimes, you know?"

Kian traced his thumb down the side of my face, ignoring Vaughn and Fang's bickering. "So, are you taking up poetry now or something? Don't get me wrong, I appreciate the sentiment..."

My shoulders slumped. "It was bad, I know."

"So bad," Vaughn choked out.

Kian frowned. "It's not about it being bad or good or

anything in between. It just doesn't exactly seem like it's something you'd normally do."

I had hoped this wouldn't come up, but I needed to be truthful with him. I'd realized something I wasn't proud of, and it needed to be aired. "You were right when you said I was self-centered and caught up in my own problems so much I was ignoring those around me who also had things going on. I didn't even know what to do to get you to forgive me. I knew a poem was a bad idea. But my only other thought was Jell-O wrestling in my underwear."

Kian glanced over my body and lifted one shoulder. "I could go for that."

I blinked at him. "I spent all afternoon writing you that poem and all I actually needed to do was get my tits out?"

"Maybe."

"Dammit! Fang! Get me some Jell-O!"

He looked between us, his eyes going squinty. "I don't know whether you're being serious or not right now."

Kian laughed and tugged me tight again. "I'd rather kiss you and tell you I love you too, Rebel Kemp. Almost as much as I love…hemp?"

Vaughn groaned. "Can we please stop with the rhyming already? You guys are terrible at it."

Kian shoved him. "Shut up, Vaughn, I'm still mad at you. Until you write me a poem, you're on my shit list."

I sniggered against Kian's chest, comforted by being back here.

Vaughn stood with a grin, and shoved his hands in his pockets. He cleared his throat dramatically. "An ode to

Kian's dick. It is totally lit. I'd like to suck it, and maybe fuck it."

And he called my poetry bad.

But Kian grinned. "Go on then."

Vaughn glanced at Fang. "You want to give us that privacy you were talking about earlier?"

Fang nodded and took a step backward, ready to leave the three of us alone. "I'll wait in the car."

"Stay," Kian said softly.

All of us stopped and stared at him. Shock punched through me at the idea of him wanting Fang involved in whatever was about to happen. It was quickly replaced by heat, and wet silky arousal between my legs.

Kian sniggered, taking in the three of us. "You should see yourselves. Fang is like a deer caught in headlights. Vaughn is pretty much green with jealousy. And Little Demon, you look like you're about to come at the very thought."

I huffed. "I can't help that the idea of the three of you together is hot."

If I happened to be in the middle of all the shirtless biceps and rippling abs and talented tongues and dicks that knew exactly what their job was, then who was I to complain?

Fang gazed down at me. "You want that, Pix? All of us?"

I breathed out a long breath, scared I'd hyperventilate and pass out if I panted like a slobbery dog, which was what I actually wanted to do.

They all seemed to take my inability to speak as consent. Which in this case, it absolutely was.

Fang knelt at my feet and pulled on the laces of my

boots, unravelling them so they loosened enough for me to step out of.

Kian lowered the zipper on the back of my skirt. The fake leather mini joined my boots on the floor.

"Hands up, Roach." Vaughn gathered up the hem of my long-sleeved Van Halen band shirt and lifted it over my head.

Kian kissed my bare shoulder from behind. "You'd look so hot Jell-O wrestling in nothing but what you're wearing."

I eyed the ring behind him. "Go on up there and lie down. Give me a head start."

He grinned and pushed himself up on the edge of the ring, then laid out to roll beneath the lowest rope. He didn't bother standing once he was in the ring, just sat back on his hands, with his chest bare, watching for what I was going to do.

"Need a lift?" Fang asked.

He put his hands on my hips and hoisted me into the ring. I gripped the ropes and slipped over the middle one.

Behind me, Vaughn and Fang climbed the ring stairs slowly, but I was focused on Kian.

I put one foot either side of his legs and walked up them, forcing him to lie back, while I stood over him.

He ran his hand up my leg. "I like you from this angle. Legs spread wide over me. A position of power, even when there's only lace covering you."

His fingers moved to the inside of my thigh, and he pushed my panties to one side, exposing my pussy. He let the elastic snap back, but the desire in his eyes was all too plain to see. "Take those panties off and ride my face, Little Demon. Get down here and let me taste you."

Doing exactly as he'd said, I put my fingers into the elastic lace at my hips and dragged it down. I stepped out of them and then dropped to my knees, one either side of his face.

In an instant, he had me in his grip, his fingertips pressing tight into the flesh of my hips and ass.

His tongue licked straight through my center, starting at my opening and finishing on my clit.

I shuddered in pleasure at the warm, wet feel of him in my most intimate of places. But he'd said to ride him, and I wasn't one for being a starfish in the bedroom.

Or in the boxing ring, as it were.

I rocked my hips over his face, taking everything he gave me gratefully, the flat planes of his tongue pressing against my clit and sending pleasure through my entire body. My nipples beaded beneath my bra, hard and needy.

Behind me, Vaughn made a noise, and I twisted to look over my shoulder. His gaze locked on mine as he pulled Kian's drawstring loose. It took some tugging because Kian was too focused on making me come to help, but Vaughn got his shorts off, leaving him naked beneath me.

And hard.

His erection jutted from his body, long and thick and proud.

Vaughn's ode to Kian's cock suddenly didn't seem all that funny. I wanted to suck and fuck it too.

Vaughn beat me to it. He palmed Kian's cock and put his mouth over the blunt head of him.

Below me, Kian moaned, but I had no idea if it was

because of what Vaughn was doing or because he was getting off on thrusting his tongue into my pussy.

I was definitely getting off on it. I ached inside, the prodding of his tongue only increasing the desperate need I had to have him inside me. I gripped his hair and increased the pace, rocking over him faster and faster, chasing down an orgasm until he put the brakes on, holding my hips still and refusing to lick me until I settled down and went slow.

The man was hell-bent on torturing me.

But I kind of loved it.

Fang watched on from the side of the ring, as stoic and silent as ever. His fingers strangled the ropes, like he was holding himself back.

"Fang." My voice came out deep and throaty. Needy. "Come here."

He crossed the ring to stop in front of me. With me low on my knees, the man truly was the size of a giant. One I wanted to get naked with so very badly.

Like he had with me, I started at his feet, undoing his biker boots and waiting for him to step out of them. I reached up for the fly on his jeans, and once that was undone, it was nothing to tug them down his legs and watch him step out of them. He kicked them aside, and a second later, he shrugged out of his jacket, and then his T-shirt too.

He was beautiful all the time, at least to me. But he took my breath away when he was naked and hard and looking at me with that expression in his eyes that told me I was his entire fucking world.

And he was mine. I loved him in a way that was different than how I loved Kian and Vaughn. It wasn't more or less, just a special something that seemed to be reserved only for him. "I can't reach you. Get down on your knees."

He did, his cock now a much better height for my tongue. I leaned forward, so I was on all fours, and took Fang's dick in my mouth.

His groans mingled with Kian's.

I slid down the length of him, tasting his skin and his arousal.

He ran his hands through the short lengths of my hair, his touch featherlight. I worked him up, licking and sucking him until he pulled.

My scalp sent pleasure sparking through my body, and I let out a moan that echoed around the empty gym.

Fang chuckled. "You like that?"

I so fucking did, but I wasn't about to take my mouth off his cock to tell him. I was pretty sure my answer was obvious from the way I doubled down on grinding over Kian's face. Pleasure spiraled, starting at both my hair and my clit and torpedoing through me so hot and fast I could hardly breathe.

Kian knew exactly what I needed. He trailed his fingers up my thigh and through my folds to push up inside me. First one, then two, then three until I was riding his fingers with an orgasm barreling down on me.

I took Fang's cock deeper with every moan, letting him hit the back of my throat because it turned me on as much as it did him.

I stared up, his gaze locked on mine, his abs tensing while I sucked him.

The orgasm took hold, right as the first spurts of Fang's cum hit the back of my tongue.

We came together, me swallowing him down while he held the back of my head and told me how beautiful I was with his dick deep past my lips.

I was sure I was flooding Kian's mouth with how wet I was. My legs trembled, threatening to collapse, but he held me tight, licking me into a sensitive mess.

I blissed out, taking everything they gave me until Fang pulled from my mouth. He reached around my back and undid my bra, freeing my aching breasts that begged for attention.

Kian shifted beneath me, holding me still and moving himself up the mat. "Want you on my cock, Little Demon. Want to feel you pulse and shake around my dick, not just my fingers. Come again for me."

I moaned as his wet dick slid inside me. He was so thick and hard and worked up from Vaughn's mouth that he stretched me deliciously. I arched my back, rising and falling on his dick, using the muscles in my thighs to maneuver myself so his tip hit me just right. My G-spot sang out his praises, while Fang played and tweaked my nipples.

He knew I liked it hard, and his fingers mimicked the clamps he'd once used on me so sweetly.

I could have let him do that for hours. My gaze rolled over his beautiful body, his dick wet from my mouth and his cum.

I turned my head, searching for Vaughn.

"I'm here, Roach."

He knelt behind me, his fingers wandering up and down my back, lingering on my ass. He took two handfuls and squeezed. He kissed a trail along my neck, up to my ear. "I want to fuck you while he fucks you." His hand dipped between my ass cheeks and nudged at my entrance. "I want to feel his dick inside you when I take you here."

I shivered in anticipation and nodded.

With one hand between my shoulder blades, he guided me forward so I was on all fours again. I rocked over Kian, taking him deep inside my pussy. Vaughn stopped me when just the tip of Kian's cock was inside. I looked down between my legs, and Vaughn had his fingers around Kian's cock, coating his palm in my slick arousal.

He used it to lube up his own cock, his free hand guiding me back into a rhythm over Kian.

When Vaughn's dick pressed against my rear entrance, he was wet and slippery.

I wanted him there. Wanted to feel them move together inside me.

He pushed inside me, giving me ample time to adjust to the stretch of taking them both.

It only heightened the need to come again.

Slowly, I set a pace on Kian, and Vaughn set one on me. We moved fluidly, making sure there was a rhythm all of us were enjoying.

But I was sure it was only me whose pending orgasm felt like this.

Like it was too big for my body. Like it could swallow me whole.

Like I wanted to drown in it and never come up for air.

As if they knew exactly what was going on inside my body, Kian's and Vaughn's movements became exactly what I needed them to be. Where I got sloppy and uncoordinated, lost in the feelings, they took over, their thrusts from above and below synchronized, faster and harder, until I couldn't take it another second. The sensations balled low in my belly and had nowhere to go but explode their way through the rest of my body.

I cried out when I came, not any of their names, because I couldn't even remember my own. But it was a cry of relief. Of a pleasure that neared on pain it was so hot.

Below me, Kian groaned, his abs rippling as he came buried deep inside me. A moment later, Vaughn put his arm around my middle and reached up to grab my tit, pinching my nipple while he came in my ass.

I cried out again, another orgasm catching me by surprise. I was too sensitive to move, and yet Vaughn worked me slowly and surely, wringing out every inch of pleasure that I thought would be too much.

It wasn't.

Vaughn pulled out, and I flopped down on Kian's chest, so completely and utterly spent I didn't even have the energy to hold myself there. I rolled off him, onto the mat beside him, and lay staring at the high industrial ceiling, crisscrossed with support beams and other structures I couldn't name. I breathed heavily, my chest rising and falling, my skin wet with sweat.

My legs were pushed open, and a tongue hit me right on my clit.

I shouted and grabbed Vaughn's hair, lifting his face up. "Are you trying to kill me?"

His gaze flicked to Kian, who was watching on intensely. Something flared in Vaughn's eyes, and tension crackled between them.

"His cum is dripping out of you, Roach. Wrap your legs around my neck. I want it in my mouth."

Kian groaned deeply and shifted onto his side, stroking his limp cock. "Kiss me first."

Vaughn didn't wait. He leaned over and put his lips to Kian's, pressing his tongue in with deep, plunging strokes.

Kian made a noise when Vaughn pulled away and put his mouth back to my core, licking Kian's cum and my pussy until I was ready to orgasm again.

"Pix," Fang bit out, his voice hoarse.

I looked over at where he leaned against the ropes, running his big fingers up and down his length. He was hard again. Thick. The look on his face said he was desperate for me.

Vaughn bit the inside of my thigh, a sharp pain so quickly turning into pleasure it shocked me.

He let me go with a slap on the ass. "Go to him. I've still got some making up to do with Kian."

Kian groaned from his spot on his side, his dick hard again in his hand. "You just licked my cum from her pussy. I've never seen anything that hot. We're good."

Vaughn rolled him onto his back and fit himself between Kian's legs. Supporting his weight on one hand, he took over stroking Kian with the other, while his dick moved between Kian's ass cheeks. "We're good when I've fucked you and made you come again."

Their mouths joined in a clash of tongues and teeth and guttural groans.

But my eyes were fixed on Fang. I flipped over onto all fours again, crawling across the mat until I was straddling his thighs and sinking down on his cock.

I couldn't come again. I didn't even want to, but I rode

Fang, taking his cock, lifting myself up and down and drawing out the same sorts of pleasure he'd spent weeks giving me. It was all about him, and that was exactly how I wanted it after being between Kian and Vaughn.

I needed that slower pace with Fang. That connection of his eyes on mine as we ground together.

I needed his 'I love you' when he came quietly inside me.

Because damn, I loved him too.

He wrapped his arms around me tight and came deep inside me with a single uttered sentence. "I want babies with you, Pix."

I shifted back to look at him, waiting for the rush of panic at the idea.

It didn't come.

I kissed him instead. There'd be time to talk about that later. The real world was just outside, Caleb a threatening part of it.

I couldn't think about babies right now.

Not while Kian and Vaughn were moaning through their orgasms. Not while my sister's daughter was missing.

But I smiled softly at the thought of a little blond-haired baby with Fang's eyes.

And I didn't say no.

13

BLISS

"Okay, so what are we *not* going to do when we get to the clubhouse?" Nash spun the steering wheel, making the turn that would lead us down the track to the clubhouse, rather than the one we often took to War's old cabin. He hadn't lived there since he'd moved in with the rest of us, but as prez of the club, it was there for whenever we wanted to use it.

Which was fun for a change of scenery. At home we had an entire house to have sex in. But War's cabin was cozy and sweet and held a lot of memories, both good and bad.

Plus it was surrounded by woods, which were always fun for a bit of 'might get caught' sex.

Not that anything like that would be happening today.

Because the man had gone and gotten himself shot. I picked at the sleeve of my hoodie, absentmindedly stressing out that a bullet had passed through his skin, even though Fang had assured me he was okay.

I couldn't even think about it. Just the thought alone made me want to vomit. This baby might have three dads...or four if you counted Vincent and Scythe as two people, which I generally did because they couldn't be more different...but he or she needed every single one of them.

"We're not going to slowly and painfully gut War, then pull out his intestines to feed to Little Dog," Vincent said quietly.

But his death grip on his knife didn't exactly give off the vibe he was planning to gently nurse War back to health either.

Nash shot him a look. "Seriously, V. I want to kill him right now too, but Bliss wouldn't like that."

Bliss was pretty angry herself and tempted to let Vincent have at it for at least a couple of minutes, but giving a psychopath free rein was never a particularly good idea. "No stabbing anyone, V."

He finally lifted his gaze to me. "You're upset because he's hurt. He should have thought about that before he put himself in danger."

I suspected Vincent was harboring some additional feelings on the subject, courtesy of his alter ego, Scythe, who was as much in love with War as I was. The divide between the two of them wasn't as rock-solid as it had once been. Scythe's feelings sometimes filtered through, and I could only imagine the racket he was making in Vincent's head. I reached over and squeezed his hand reassuringly instead. "He's okay."

Vincent just nodded, staring out the window.

Nash pulled the Jeep up outside the clubhouse, and

we all got out, slamming doors behind us. I strode inside the building, Vincent and Nash flanking me.

"Where is he?" I asked the first person I saw as we walked through the doors.

Ice pointed down the hallway. "Infirmary."

"They have an infirmary?" Nash squinted. "Where?"

I hadn't ever seen it either, but then War had been lucky enough not to be seriously injured since we'd gotten together. That luck had clearly run out.

I rubbed my hand over my baby bump, the sick feeling returning. I didn't want to think about raising this baby without him.

Ice came out from behind the bar. "I'll show you."

I thanked him and followed him down the hall, to the very end, and a door I'd never been through before. I'd never even thought to question what was behind it, assuming it was one of the brothers' rooms.

Ice opened it for me and reached around for a light switch on the wall. "He'll be glad to see you, Bliss."

He wouldn't. At least not by the time I was through yelling at him for scaring me half to death. It was a miracle I hadn't gone into early labor when Fang had uttered the words, "Bliss. War's been shot."

I shuddered, but thanked Ice, and made my way down the stairs, following the low tone of voices.

The closer I got, the more a lump lodged in my throat. War's voice came from behind a curtain, talking softly to someone, and I pulled it aside, tears already rolling down my face.

War and Hawk stopped talking and looked over.

Instantly, War's expression went soft. "Ah fuck, baby girl. Don't cry over me."

I'd planned on throwing myself at him and telling him I loved him.

Instead, I punched his arm as hard as I could. I needed somewhere for the fear to go, and apparently it was into physical violence.

Scythe would have been proud.

War flinched, wincing in pain, which only made me cry harder. I leaned over him, pressing my face into his neck and inhaling the familiar scent. I cried into his shoulder, reveling in the slow strokes he made up and down my back, comforting me when it should have been me comforting him.

"If you die…" I warned him.

He put his fingers beneath my chin and lifted it so our eyes met. "It's part of the job. You know that, Bliss. This life ain't glamorous."

Anger lit up inside me. "I know, and yet I still picked it. I picked you."

"Maybe not your smartest move," Nash mused. "Really not sure he's worth it." He chuckled when War flipped him the bird.

Vincent still ran his fingers up and down his blade. It was what he did when he was stressed, I knew that now, but it didn't make it any less creepy.

War eyed him warily, then turned his focus back on me. "I know. I lost it for a minute there. But those women in that house. And Caleb taking that baby…"

My gut clenched. "I haven't stopped thinking about them."

"Me neither," War replied quietly.

"Ditto," Nash agreed, while Vincent just nodded.

War shifted on the bed with a wince of pain, even

though he was babying his hurt shoulder. "I'll get the guys back out there in a couple of days."

I stared at him. A couple of days wasn't good enough. Caleb could do anything to them in that time. Plus we had no idea who was in charge at the Sinners anymore. And that poor woman, Kara... She needed her baby back.

"We send out a search party tonight. That house where they were keeping them backs onto the woods, right? So does the clubhouse. We might be miles away from them, but that doesn't mean we can't go in on foot. Plus, I want someone to go through Caleb's offices, as well as his house, and I've got a few other places we can check. His friends. His parents. There's no way he's taking care of that baby himself. She's either with someone he knows..." I didn't want to voice the alternative. It was too bleak.

Hawk frowned at me. "You might be his woman, but that don't mean we take orders from you, Bliss."

War silenced him with a murderous glare.

Hawk shrugged. "Okay, seems we do take orders from you. Fucking hell, asshole. What good is being your VP if your woman ends up running the show when you're down? You might as well patch her in."

He grabbed my hand and squeezed it. "She looks good in leather, so don't fucking tempt me." He turned to his vice prez. "She runs the search. She knows Caleb better than anyone. Do you know where his parents live or the code to his offices?"

"No," Hawk admitted.

"Then you're her VP for as long as she needs you."

Vincent put his blade back in his pocket, apparently satisfied War wasn't going to die or try to come with us.

I nodded, a little buzz working its way through me. "Call everyone into church. The women too."

Hawk and War both gaped at me.

"She can't do that!" Hawk yelped, his voice going high. "Come on, War! It's one thing for her to coordinate a search, but this is going too far."

War frowned. "Bliss, that room is a sacred space. No nonmembers. No women. Fuck, we don't even let prospects in there until they've been with us a year."

I didn't care. "We need the women out there searching too, War. All of us. Not as a club, but as a family."

"We'll get the other charters in to help," he offered as an alternative.

I shook my head. "That'll take too long. Even if they leave now, some of them are hours away. That baby could be dead by then." I grabbed War's hand and put it to my belly.

Our baby kicked at the weight.

His eyes went big. "She's moving."

"She could have so easily been Kara's baby, War. You weren't wrong in wanting them found."

His gaze searched mine, and I knew what he was looking for. A resurgence of the old Bliss. The timid mouse who'd let Caleb abuse her. The woman who would crumble under pressure.

He wasn't going to find her here.

He crooked his finger at me. "Come 'ere."

I leaned down, and he used the arm that wasn't currently in a sling to reach up and run his fingers into the hair at the nape of my neck. He pulled me in so my lips were just above his.

"Gonna marry you one day, baby girl. Because fuck, I love you."

I grinned and closed the gap between us. His lips were warm and familiar, and when he kissed me, my heart flooded with happiness.

I didn't imagine I'd ever get a down-on-one-knee proposal from this man, and I didn't need it. That was more Nash's style.

Scythe and Vincent would probably slaughter something and leave it as a marital offering if they ever asked me.

This was all I needed from War. A promise that I was his forever.

But there was work to be done first.

I was going to make sure it got done.

14

VAUGHN

Sitting on the edge of the bed, I winced as I eased my boots off. Blood from my blisters had seeped through my socks, staining the thick white fabric with red splotches.

Kian glanced over at me from where he was quietly putting on his new work pants. "Ouch. You want a couple of Band-Aids?"

I held up the little packages I'd swiped earlier from downstairs. "Already got some."

Kian leaned over to study my wounds more closely. "Keep them clean. The Slayers don't need another person down in their infirmary. Maybe you should take today off."

I ripped the top off the Band-Aid and stuck it over the worst of my blisters. "No. Rebel is still out there searching. So are Fang and all the others. I'm not going to sit around here and cry because I'm not used to traipsing through the woods and my shoes hurt."

Kian took my chin between his fingers and lifted it so

he could kiss my mouth. "I love your delicate rich-boy skin."

I shoved him away but then thought better of it and dragged him back for a proper kiss. One with tongue and moans and pulling him down on top of me so I could feel how hard I got him with just my lips on his.

He rolled off me all too soon. "Can't do this. Gotta go to work."

I let him go, knowing he was right. "I hope your third day of work is as good as the first two."

He grinned. "It will be. I hate I can't be out there helping you all look for Kara's baby and the women, but I'm loving this job."

I crinkled my nose. "You seriously love digging holes and nailing stuff?"

"Not as much as I love nailing you, but yeah. I know you don't get it, but then I don't get how you can sit in an office all day, pushing papers around."

I shrugged. "I don't do much of that anymore."

I missed it. I'd made mistakes with my business. Big ones that had resulted in filing for bankruptcy. But I'd been floating along aimlessly for too long. I needed to work out what I wanted to do with my life. Work out who the hell I was.

Fang had the MC. Rebel loved Psychos. Kian seemed content with his new job. It was just me without anything to fill my days. It was partially why I'd thrown myself into searching. Other people had jobs they had to go to.

Not me.

I said goodbye to Kian and finished up with my wound tending. I needed to get back over to the clubhouse, which was Bliss's central command for operations. We had to get a break soon. We'd had nothing for days, which was disheartening, but I had to see it through.

My phone buzzed, and my heart dropped when the screen told me it was Brooke. I opened the text message.

My father is on his way to the hospital. Can you please come down here? I know you're with someone else now and you probably don't care about me anymore. I get it. But I can't face him alone. You know how he is. I hate this.

I bit my lip. My instinct was to say no, but for once, Brooke wasn't overexaggerating. Her father was a mean son of a bitch, and she had always been scared of him. Or maybe scared of his disapproval. Which he made no secret of, even when she didn't deserve it. The hospital wasn't far from the clubhouse. I could stop in on my way over and not be much later than I'd planned to be.

The hospital reeked with a combo of disinfectant and something that just smelled of sick. I couldn't put my finger on it, but it wasn't somewhere I wanted to be. I picked up pace, making my way to Brooke's room.

Gordon Santry stood at the end of Brooke's bed with his arms crossed. Like almost every other time I'd seen him, he wore fitted suit pants and a business shirt. His jacket was placed neatly over the back of the chair.

Brooke stared up at him hopefully, suddenly seeming about ten years old again.

I cleared my throat.

Gordon glanced over in my direction. "Weston."

He held his hand out, and I shook it, but it was a lackluster effort by both of us.

"Daddy just got here, Vaughn. I'm so glad you came."

I wasn't sure which of us she was talking to, but since

she had her hero worship gaze trained on her father, I assumed it probably wasn't me.

He didn't return the same sort of energy. His scowl seemed fixed on the bandages wrapped around her hand. "What on earth have you got yourself into?"

Brooke glanced nervously at me and then back at her father. She promptly burst into tears. "I'm so sorry. I don't know how this happened. One minute it was just some fun gambling, and then I couldn't stop. I didn't want to tell Vaughn I'd spent all his money, so I just kept going on the credit they allowed me..."

Her father's face screwed up. "Are you stupid?"

She fell silent, dropping her gaze to the bed without a word.

She reminded me too much of myself. It hadn't been my dad who'd made me feel like that. I'd been lucky enough to have one of the good ones. But Harold Coker was cut from the same cloth as Brooke's dad. He'd once stared at me with that same expression, determined to make me feel as small as Brooke appeared right now.

Irritation prickled the back of my neck. "Don't call her stupid."

Gordon looked over at me. "What would you call her actions then?" It was a barely held-back sneer.

"Desperate. Confused. It doesn't mean she's stupid."

Brooke lifted her head. She mouthed "Thank you" silently.

I nodded and turned back to Gordon. "She needs your help. I can't get money out of my dad's business. I have none of my own. We need to pay these guys off or they're just going to keep coming after her."

"What makes you think these 'guys' she talks of are

even real?"

I frowned, getting annoyed by his dismissive, 'I know better than you' tone. "What does that mean? Look at your daughter's hair. Most of it was sent to me in an envelope. As was her finger, for Christ's sakes. You think she did that to herself?"

Gordon just stared at me.

I blinked.

No. There was no way. "She didn't cut off her own finger, Gordon! Are you insane?"

He sighed heavily. "No. But I believe my daughter might be."

Brooke sucked in a gasp. "Daddy!"

"What, Brooke? You know your mother's history. She's...unwell, too."

Her mouth hung open in shock at his accusations. "I'm not unwell. And I'm not making this up."

He cocked his head to one side. "No? You aren't just trying to extort money out of the husband leaving you because you know that without him, you haven't got a cent to your name?"

She swallowed hard and darted a glance at me. "You don't believe this, do you?"

I suddenly had no idea what to believe.

Gordon put his hands on the edge of the bed rail. "She's an elaborate liar, Vaughn. You know this. How did you not even consider she was behind this all along?"

The woman's finger was in my rubbish bin at home. It didn't seem even remotely possible she could have done that to herself. "Because that would be literally crazy."

Gordon looked over at his daughter. "You need to start telling us the truth, Brooke. I promised your mother

I would offer you help, instead of just cutting you off completely, which frankly, was my preferred option. So this is me offering it. I'm not giving you or any"—he made air quotes with his fingers—"'men' any money. I've done that for you your entire life, and look where that's gotten you."

His disappointment was thick. "If this was you all along, then now is your chance to confess, consequence-free. I'll pay Vaughn back for the trust fund you blew through, and I've already called White Dove Rehabilitation Facility in Bibury."

Her brow furrowed. "Where on earth is Bibury?"

"In the UK. And far outside any major city where you might be tempted to start gambling again. No one needs to know you're there. We'll just tell people you've gone to find yourself after your breakup with Vaughn. But stop this nonsense now."

Brooke's eyes watered with unshed tears. "No one would know where I was? You can promise me that?"

He nodded. "No one but the three of us here. I won't even tell your mother."

"It's true. All of it," she said in a rush, words spilling in my direction. "There were never any other men. It was me all along. I cut my hair. And my finger."

I blanched at the idea she was so desperate to get money out of me that she would mutilate herself on purpose. "Please tell me you're joking."

She wouldn't look at me. "Daddy, I need that hospital. I'm so sorry. Please, can you make the call? I can go tonight. I don't need anything. There's nothing left for me at home anyway."

Gordon gave a curt nod and pulled his phone from

the suit pocket of his pants. But before he made the call, he focused on me. "I'll transfer the money she took from you if you keep this quiet."

I didn't even know what to say. But a deep, sad, pity-filled feeling came over me. This all felt like a cry for help. Clearly, Brooke had been desperate and spiraling for a lot longer than I'd realized.

I hadn't seen it.

I should have.

When I looked at her now, all the anger I'd been harboring for her for the longest of times faded away. All that was left was pity. What else was there to feel for a woman who would cut off her own finger to continue the ploy?

"I won't say anything," I said stiffly. I shook my head at my ex-wife. "I hope you get the help you need."

"I'll call you later," she promised, reaching out for me.

I dodged her attempts to touch me.

Her father walked me toward the door. "Go. I'll be sure she doesn't contact you. The hospital won't let her have a phone anyway. You've done your part, Vaughn. I shouldn't have let this go on as long as it did, but I was trying the tough-love thing. I'm sorry it impacted you. I appreciate your discretion with this matter. I'm sure you understand this sort of thing is frowned upon in our line of work, and how it could damage a man's reputation if it got out. Not just mine, but also yours."

I swallowed thickly with a final glance over my shoulder at Brooke. "I don't care about my reputation. I just want her to get the help she needs."

I walked away from Brooke and Gordon and left that part of my life behind.

15

CALEB

Without Chaos, the Sinners were about as useless as my fat bitch of an ex-fiancée. I stared at the stringy-haired, rat-faced man who probably shot drugs for breakfast. "What do you mean you lost the women?"

He scrubbed a shaking hand through his hair. "The Slayers came snooping around again. So we left the house to flush 'em out—"

I gaped at him. "Flush them out? What do you think this is? The Wild fucking West?"

The man shrugged. "We got one of them though. Shot him right in the chest."

Like I fucking cared about that. I snapped my fingers in front of the man's face. "Focus. The women. What happened to them?"

He shrugged. "Guess they kicked the door down? I dunno. They were already running by the time we got back. Lost 'em in the woods."

I blinked at the sheer stupidity. Normally that sort of

behavior was reserved for women. I hadn't expected it from a team of men. "And you're only just telling me this now?"

"We searched for them..."

"Where? For how long?"

He shrugged. "I dunno. Me and Turbo got lost a couple times, and then we got hungry..."

Killing Chaos might have been the stupidest thing I'd ever done. At least he was smart enough to keep his men in line. Which clearly wasn't an easy task when there wasn't a brain cell shared between them. Killing him had been impulsive. A mistake I wouldn't make again.

I couldn't even look at this guy. "Go stand over there in the corner."

The man cocked his head. "What?"

I leaned in closer. "I said, go stand in the corner like the stupid child you are. You want to act like an imbecile? I'll treat you like one."

The man didn't move.

I snapped my teeth at him.

He scuttled to the corner and stood there, exactly like I'd told him.

A rush of power coursed through me. I breathed in the feeling, letting it sink deep inside me and fill the wounds across my chest. They'd healed now, but they were a constant reminder of what my ex and her friends had done to me. Every time I saw her name carved in my chest, every time I remembered hiding beneath my bed, pissing myself in fear, a hole opened up inside me. It was deep and dark and disgusting. A feeling that had started with my mother. I could never fully get it to leave, but power helped.

Power reminded me I wasn't that pathetic, sniveling mess who had cowered in fear. Power reminded me who I really was.

Watching this fool stand with his nose pressed to the wall made my dick hard.

I stared at his back, rubbing my cock through my pants while I pulled out my phone. This wasn't a call I wanted to make. It wasn't going to go well.

Luca picked up on the third ring. "Why are you calling me? It's not the fifteenth of the month."

I grabbed my dick, squeezing it hard. I needed to focus on the pain so my voice didn't tremble. "We have a problem."

The sounds of fists hitting a punching bag came from Luca's end of the phone. The man chuckled. "I ain't got no problems, Cal. Not a one. If you got a problem, it's not mine."

I fucking hated being called Cal.

But I didn't dare tell Luca Guerra that.

"The women I had for you. They're gone."

Luca didn't say anything.

"Did you hear me?" I eventually asked.

"I heard you, but like I said, your problems aren't my problems. You have a contract for five women. I don't care which five. Just deliver them on time."

"I told you; I don't know where they are. It's not that easy to just find five new ones."

"Get your hands up, O'Malley!" Guerra shouted at someone in the background.

I waited until he was done.

Eventually Luca's voice lowered. "Five, Caleb. On the fifteenth. I don't care who or how, just get them."

I ground my teeth. It had been hard enough finding someone to get the first four. It had taken months of negotiation with the Slayers' prez, using his connections at other chapters of his club. But I'd already had him killed after he pussied out and changed his mind, so I couldn't go back there again. It had been necessary. He was a loose end who needed to be taken care of so I couldn't be tied back to any of this. But now it left me in fucking predicament, didn't it?

I undid my fly and stroked my cock, staring at the back of the Sinner who was so fucking stupid he'd left my cargo unattended. He was making me look as stupid as he was.

That wasn't okay. He'd find those women or I'd put a bullet in him, just like I had his leader.

But now I had to do one better if I wanted to save face with Luca. Instead of four women, I'd deliver him more.

I could get to Kara and Rebel. That was an extra two.

And Bethany-Melissa...

She'd make a third.

I stroked my cock faster, thinking about how deep my hate ran for her. "I can fix this. I'll get you more than four women. There's another three I can get to."

Luca thumped something. "Fists up!"

Irritation prickled at the back of my neck. Here I was, doing my damn best to impress him and his family, doing everything they'd asked of me, and yet he was ignoring me in favor of watching some meatheads punch each other? It was fucking insulting. I needed something to get his attention.

"What about a baby?" I spoke up.

Luca paused. "Boy or girl?"

Interest filled his voice.

"Girl," I told him eagerly. "Young one. You could sell her to someone who wants a kid."

Luca thought on that for a moment. "She'd make more money if we held her for a while. Waited until she'd matured a bit..."

"Whatever you want."

"Don't promise me something you can't deliver, Caleb."

"I'm not. I can do it," I bluffed.

"See you on the fifteenth then, with seven women and a baby."

I ended the call.

I stroked my dick some more.

The man coughed. "Dude, are you jacking off?"

"Shut the fuck up or I'll jack off into your mouth."

He fell silent. I pumped my cock until my balls drew up and white cum spilled from the tip of my dick in arcs, landing on the scratched wood floor of the derelict house.

Soft again, I pulled my underwear up and did up my fly. "Find those women," I warned him. "You have two days. I don't care what you do or how you do it. They can't have gone too far. You search those woods until you find them. I've got a date with a trio of women who I'm sure are just dying to see me again."

I walked out of the house without bothering to clean up my cum.

16

WINNIE

We traipsed through the woods for hours. The thick undergrowth scratched up my arms and legs, but I kept the blanket pulled tight around the baby, shielding her from being injured. My stomach growled. We'd found a creek with fresh water and had followed it until it disappeared through trees and shrubs too thick for us to continue. But as day turned into night again, I knew we couldn't keep doing this. Something had to change. The baby was sleeping too much. She couldn't survive on just water, and neither could we. We needed food.

Georgia sat down heavily on a log as the sun dipped low in the sky. "This is hopeless. We've been wandering around here for hours. Look at that." She pointed to a gnarled tree that bent hard to the left. "We've definitely already been past this. We're walking in circles."

I'd known it for the past fifteen minutes but had been too scared to say anything. Spirits were already at rock bottom.

Nova shoved her hands onto her hips and cocked her head. "Shit. You're right." She sat next to Georgia, her head drooping.

That wasn't good. Nova was the one who had kept us going. She'd refused to let us give up, determined to get us into town and find us a way out of this place. She'd filled our walking hours with chatter about going home, seeing friends and family, and never thinking about the past few horrific months again.

Like it would be that easy to forget.

If we ever got out of here, I'd spend the rest of my life in therapy, I was sure.

But better a lifetime of therapy than a lifetime in that house with those men. I grabbed Nova's arm. "Come on. Get up. We aren't stopping here."

She shook me off. "What's the point? We're lost in the middle of the woods. We need to make some sort of camp before it gets dark."

My shoulders slumped. She was right. But I couldn't fathom the thought of sleeping on the cold, hard ground for another night.

I pushed the baby at Georgia. "Here. Take her. I'm going to go search for firewood."

"We have no matches." Georgia sounded completely exhausted.

I knew. But I had to try. I couldn't just give up.

I left the others staring into space and looked around, getting my bearings. We'd definitely passed that gnarled tree. I could see the path we'd taken, our footsteps flattening the grass. I picked a different route, turning to my left instead. Maybe there'd be another creek, though that seemed doubtful since I couldn't hear any water. But at least it would make starting again in the morning easier if I knew there was a way through in this direction.

My legs ached, but I dragged myself on, picking up sticks and twigs dry enough to catch alight. "The dryer, the better," I murmured to myself, pushing up a hill, despite the threatening exhaustion. "If I'm rubbing two sticks together, they're going to need to be as dry as the Sahara."

It would be a miracle if I could get a fire going, but the thought of warmth kept me trudging up that hill, collecting more and more twigs along the way until my arms were full.

The hill flattened out, and I gazed down into the valley on the other side.

The sticks all fell from my arms.

"There's a house," I whispered. I took a few steps toward it, expecting it to disappear into a shimmering mist at any moment, because surely, I was hallucinating.

But it didn't.

"Oh my God, there's a house!" I wanted to roll down the hill like I had when I was a kid, tumbling over and over again, getting dizzy and grinning from ear to ear. It would have been a terrible idea now, not only because I'd probably puke but because this wasn't exactly a lush, green grass hill like they had at parks. I'd get about twenty feet before I wrapped myself around a tree.

Footsteps came from behind me, and I spun around, my smile beaming at the others who struggled up the hill. I was sure none of them quite believed me. Hell, I had been talking to myself just before, so their skepticism probably wasn't unwarranted.

But when they got to the top there were hugs and

tears and excited chatter all around. Even though it was nearly dark, there was no talk of staying out here another night. I didn't care if I broke my damn ankle walking down there as the light disappeared, I was sleeping in that cabin tonight.

Maybe there'd be a phone. I could call my sister.

Tears welled in the backs of my eyes at the thought of hearing a familiar voice after so long.

The other women's smiles returned as we hiked to our safe haven. Georgia talked about all the things we were going to find in that cabin. If her manifesting came true, we'd be eating caviar and champagne in no time.

I would eat anything in the cupboards. Literally anything. I only prayed there'd be something we could give to the little one, because she needed it the most.

It wasn't smart, I knew, but I didn't have the heart to tell the other girls not to rush straight out of the woods and up the cabin's porch steps. The building was dark. The odds of anyone being inside it seemed small.

Nova was the first to reach the dirty windows. "No one inside." She tried the handle, but it didn't give. "Surely there's a key here somewhere..."

She ran her fingers along the doorframe, while the rest of us searched the garden for one of those fake rocks that hid keys in the bottom.

"Anything?" Vivienne kicked at a clump of dirt with the toe of her shoe.

"Nothing," I admitted.

She pouted. "Now what?"

Vivienne might have been an inner-city princess, but I wasn't. I crouched and collected a heavy rock, passing it between my hands, testing the weight.

Then threw it straight through the window.

The baby gave a squawk, and all of us looked over at her in marvel. She'd become so quiet, her crying felt like the second miracle of the day.

Nova reached through the broken window and around to open the door from the inside. She tested the lights, and we all cheered when there was working electricity. It lit up the single-room cabin, which was bleak by normal standards, probably used as a fishing or hunting sleepover spot by the owners.

But it may as well have been a mansion to us.

We all went straight for the kitchen, opening and closing cupboard doors.

"Doritos!" Nova shouted, clutching the bag and holding them in the air like she'd just been given a gold medal in the Olympics.

I pulled things out of my cupboard. "Granola bars! Ooh, Cap'n Crunch!"

Vivienne laughed, throwing food onto the round table in the middle of the kitchenette. "This place has gotta be owned by a sad single loser, right? This is total bachelor food. Oh my God, there's shelf-stable milk. Probably for that sugar overload they call cereal. Can the baby drink that?"

They all turned to me.

"I don't know. Probably not, but she has to drink something other than water, and that milk has gotta be better than trying to feed her a granola bar. Hopefully one night of it won't hurt her. Tomorrow we'll follow the road back into town, and then she can have all the formula her tiny heart desires. Can't you, little one?"

The baby gurgled at me.

For the first time since Caleb had thrown her back in with us, I thought maybe she was happy. Even if she was too little to smile.

We shoved Doritos in our faces while I warmed up the milk in a saucepan on the gas stove. Nova found some matches and got a fire going in the small wood-burning fireplace. Vivienne and Georgia wrapped themselves in blankets and sat on the couch chatting with more animation than I'd seen from any of them since we'd been shoved together.

I whistled as the milk heated, but I stood over it, stirring slowly with a spoon, not wanting it to burn.

A dark shadow moved outside.

I froze, searching for it through the darkness.

Nothing.

I shook it off and went back to stirring, but the next time I stared out the window, it wasn't with quite as carefree a glance as earlier. I didn't want to scare the others when it was probably nothing.

Everything was still.

Until the shadow moved again.

A man stepped out.

Then another.

And another.

They surrounded the house, approaching from all angles.

I wanted to scream. Wanted to warn the others. But it was too late. When four men stormed the cabin, all I could do was let them take me.

This was my life now. My reality.

I'd been stupid to think it could be anything else.

17

REBEL

Kara hadn't left Fang's room since I'd tucked her into his bed the first night she'd arrived here. She'd gotten up to use the bathroom but hadn't showered. She'd flat-out refused to go out into the common rooms, cowering whenever one of the guys got too loud or too close to her door.

I had spent hours watching over her, whenever I wasn't out searching for the other women and the baby. I'd brought her food and drinks, and if I wasn't there, I'd had Queenie take my place because she was the next best thing to a mother.

But the food all sat untouched on the bedside table, and Queenie had been forced to take it away again.

"You have to eat, Kara," I warned her again, wondering if this was how Vaughn and Kian and Fang had felt when I'd been so low I'd stopped eating too. If it was, I should apologize, because it wasn't a pleasant feeling. Worry gnawed away at my insides, making me not want to eat either.

Trying to set a good example, I picked up half the chicken sandwich Queenie had brought her for dinner.

"It's nice," I told the back of Kara's head, since she refused to roll over and face me. "Queenie makes the best chicken. Her Southern fried stuff is my favorite. But she makes all sorts of food. Ice cooks too, but his meals are more like steak and burgers."

She didn't acknowledge that I'd spoken. I sighed. Clearly, the way through to her wasn't with mindless food chatter. I chewed the sandwich and decided to just play my ace card. Beating around the bush had never got me anywhere. "Tell me about your daughter."

Kara tensed up. "Why would you ask me that? It's cruel."

Maybe it was, but she was scaring me. I was truly beginning to think she was just going to lie in bed until she died. The worst part was, I knew how that felt. I'd never been anyone's big sister. I didn't know what that role was supposed to be, but if it had been Bliss lying in that bed, this was what I would have done for her. So it was what I did for Kara.

"What does she look like? She's my niece. I want to know."

Kara flipped over to glare at me.

I gave her a small smile. Just her facing me was better than her lying there, staring at the wall. "Please? I've never had a niece before."

Kara bit her lip, tears filling her brown eyes. But she slowly sat up, leaning back against the headboard with a pillow shoved behind her. Her bottom lip trembled. "She's so beautiful. She has these big eyes that just stared into mine all the time. They're kind of a murky color at the moment, not blue or green but not really brown either. My mama used to say my eyes were like that until I was a few months old, and then they went brown. I hope hers are the same as mine. Not like…his."

"Caleb's?"

She nodded.

I reached out for her hand and squeezed it. "Even if they aren't the same shade as yours, those eyes are hers. Not his. Does she have hair?"

Kara stroked her fingers absently over the quilt, rubbing it like it was her daughter's head. "A little bit. It's blond." She glanced at me curiously. "My hair was blond when I was a baby, and then it went dark as I got older. Was yours the same?"

My heart squeezed. She was searching for a connection between us. "Yes. My mom loved it because hers was bottle blond and she used to say we were twins. Mine got dark by the time I was about ten, though. I dyed it blond once in my twenties, assuming I could pull it off because I had as a kid…yeah, not so much."

Kara smiled at that. "I was never allowed to dye my hair."

I cocked my head to one side. "So you never put green streaks through your hair during your emo phase?"

Kara screwed up her face. "My what?"

I chuckled. "You never had an emo phase? My God, you're such a baby. Maybe your emo phase is still yet to come. Don't worry, little sister. I can guide you through it. You can borrow all my black, ripped-up band T-shirts, and I have new eyeliner sent to my house monthly. I'm never in short supply."

She cast a glance down at my early 2000s Fall Out Boy concert tee. "I've never heard of that band."

I gaped at her. "What about Paramore? All Time Low? Good Charlotte?"

"Are they all singers too?"

"Oh my God. What music do you like then?"

Kara lifted a shoulder. "There's some church hymns we sing, but other than that, I never really listened to music when I was back at the farm. I've been listening to the radio since I left, but I don't know any of the singers yet."

I bounced excitedly on the bed. "That's okay! I can introduce you to all my favorites."

Kara smiled softly. "I wanted my daughter to grow up with music. All different types. I wanted to play her all of it, so she could choose which one was her favorite."

I stared her dead in the eye. "You will, Kara. We'll teach her everything from The Beatles to Metallica."

"Your bands have odd names."

I grinned at her. "Just wait until you get to know Kian. He loves the big belt-it-out female singers of the nineties." I smiled just thinking about his little quirks.

"Kian is your boyfriend? Husband? Who is Fang then?"

I cringed. "Not husband. Maybe boyfriend? I don't really know what to class him as. Because there's also Fang... And Vaughn. I think I'm kind of dating all of them."

Kara gaped at me. "Seriously?"

I bit my lip. "Do you think I'm a slut?"

She recoiled at the word. "What? No! Never. I think

that's...maybe actually really lovely. If you're all open and honest about it, why would having more love be a bad thing?"

It was so simple when she said it like that.

But then she continued, "It's the other way around where I come from, though. It's the man who has multiple wives or girlfriends."

A weird feeling twisted my stomach, and Vaughn's and Kian's accusations that my father and his family were part of a cult came rushing back. I wanted to blurt out a bunch of questions, but I didn't want to push her too hard and too fast either.

So I let the comment pass.

For now.

I wound the sheet around my fingers and changed the subject. "You and your sisters all have two names. Are you going to do the same for the baby?"

Kara looked down again.

I pinched myself. I'd just gotten her talking, and now she was clamming up again. "It's okay. You don't have to talk about it."

"I've been thinking about naming her Hayley."

I blinked. "That's a beautiful name. Does it have a special meaning to you, or do you just like it?"

"You're going to think it's stupid."

I frowned. "Try me."

She took a deep breath and blew it out slowly before she responded. "When Caleb left me in that house with the Sinners, Hayden took care of me."

I clapped a hand over my mouth, instantly making the connection. "Oh my God. You're naming her after him?"

She twisted her fingers round and round themselves and choked on a sob. "It's my fault he's dead. It seems the least I can do."

I needed to wipe that idea from her brain immediately. "What happened with Hayden is absolutely not your fault. It's his fault. His and Caleb's. They're as bad as each other. That man does not deserve a place in your baby's name, Kara."

Her eyes blazed hot at the insult. "You don't know him. He's nothing like Caleb. Nothing!"

Kara had so far been such a quiet, timid little mouse that I hadn't expected the sudden outburst of passion. I sat back and took in her fierce expression. I actually liked it. It was a thousand times better than her barely daring to whisper. I could see in her eyes she truly believed what she was saying.

I was willing to hear her side of the story. "Tell me why, then. Make me believe that everything I know about him isn't true."

She answered so quickly it was clear she'd already extensively thought this through. "He didn't like that we were being held there. He made sure we had everything we needed and we were as comfortable as we could be."

I shook my head. "Kara, you have Stockholm Syndrome."

She glared at me. "I don't know what that is, but I don't have it. You weren't there, Rebel. He's the only reason Hayley didn't die during her birth. I was ready to give up. It was him who coached me through it. It was him who went out and bought everything I needed for a baby. He took a bullet because of me, and now he's dead."

Her final word seemed to hang in the silence.

Even if she did have a case of Stockholm Syndrome, it didn't matter now, with Hayden gone. He couldn't hurt her anymore. "Hayley is a beautiful name," I assured her.

"Hayley Jade," Kara added on. "I've just always loved that name."

"Me too."

She stared at me worriedly. "Am I stealing your baby's name? I know that's a thing, and it's like some cardinal sin, right? One of the women I was held captive with told me about it."

I laughed and shook my head. "I love that name, but no. You use whatever name makes you happiest. I don't know I'll ever have kids. I'm already thirty."

Kara eyed me. "With three men, I dare say your odds are pretty good."

I snorted. "That's true." Fang's whispered words in the gym, his confession he wanted babies, echoed around in my head, replaying on a loop. "Fang would like it if that were to happen."

"Your other men wouldn't?"

On instinct, I went to say no, but then when I really thought about it, I wasn't sure that was accurate. "I don't know, to be honest. We haven't talked about it."

Kara studied me quietly. "Maybe you should."

I laughed it off. "It would be crazy. How would that even work, having a baby with three men?"

But Bliss was doing it. She had friends in the same situation, and they'd all made it work.

I was a wild child at heart. If I'd finished high school, I was sure I would have been voted 'least likely to settle down.'

I was still that girl who wanted to live life to the fullest, dance in the fucking moonlight, and drive my car too fast just for the thrill of it.

But I also wanted to be loved. I wanted family. Losing my mom had only reminded me we didn't get an endless amount of time on this earth. And maybe I should be using it more wisely.

My heart still hurt for the baby my mom had lost.

Bliss's baby bump was so sweet.

And I was desperate to get my niece back. I craved the feel of her in my arms. I wanted to hold her close and whisper she'd never be in danger again, because I was her aunty and I'd never let the bad stuff in.

My experience wouldn't be hers.

But giving that to a niece or my bestie's child was one thing. I wasn't ready for a baby of my own.

Shouts from out in the common room sent Kara scuttling closer to me. I took a chance, hoping we'd bridged the gap enough that I could put my arm around her and offer her some comfort.

She didn't pull away.

"They won't hurt you," I promised. "I swear that to you. No one here will ever lay a finger on you."

"I don't want to be here," she whispered.

"We can move you into my place. I live there with Kian and Vaughn, and Fang is there a lot too, but it's still a lot quieter than this place is." I smiled hopefully at her. "I'd really like to get to know you better."

More shouts came from outside, as well as the rumble of the two club vans. Kara flinched, sinking down into the bed.

I wanted to yell for them all to shut up. They were scaring her again, just as I'd started to coax her out of her shell.

Her eyes were wide. "I don't want to be here at all. In Saint View, I mean. Bad things happen here."

It crushed me to hear her say that. She would probably go back to her parents, and I'd never get to see her. That sucked, but if it was what was best for her, what she needed to mend her heart, then I would have to deal. "You can go wherever you want to, Kara. The world is your oyster."

I couldn't blame her for wanting to be anywhere but here.

But it was my home, and it was all I knew. Saint View was in my blood.

Fast footsteps came from the hallway, and then a thumping on the door. "Rebel! Kara!"

"Don't let them take me!" Kara whispered frantically.

Oh, my freaking, beat-to-shit heart. I wanted to kill Caleb all over again for ever laying a finger on someone like her. I was already all sharp edges. But he'd taken Kara's softness and trampled her into the dirt.

"It's Fang. He won't hurt you. Ever. Can I let him in?"

He thumped on the door again.

She gazed up at me with big eyes that made her seem about five years old. "I don't want to be sold."

Fucking Caleb.

Assuring Kara that would never happen, I unlocked the door and opened it.

Fang stood on the other side, grinning from ear to ear.

It was wholly unsettling. He never smiled like that. "What's happened?"

His eyes sparkled, and he stepped aside to reveal Vaughn, standing behind him, with a baby in his arms.

18

REBEL

I closed the hospital door quietly and left Kara nursing her baby. I'd insisted on bringing them both here to be checked over. It would have been a lot easier to have Hayley Jade treated at the clubhouse, but there was no way I was letting Hawk try to insert a needle into that child's tiny veins. She'd already suffered enough without him butchering her arm too.

I wouldn't leave them tonight. I'd sit right here, outside their door and keep watch. My knuckle-dusters were in my back pocket should I need them.

Though I knew at least one of the guys would be wandering around here somewhere, even though I'd told them we'd be fine.

I wasn't mad about that.

But I was mad about something else.

I scrolled through the numbers on my phone until I found the one that had previously been labeled Torrence. After our trip to his homestead, I'd secretly changed it to Dad.

Now I felt foolish. This was the man who'd refused to accept his daughter's baby. Who'd gone as far as saying she was dead because she'd dared to go out on her own. I'd spent hours today, staring at Hayley Jade's tiny, innocent face. I just couldn't fathom how someone could say something like that about their own child.

I hit the call button, and it rang a few times before he answered. "Bel? What's going on?"

The sound of his voice only made me angrier. "Why did you tell the girls Kara was dead?"

"Kara?"

"Louisa Kara. You do remember your own daughter, don't you?"

There was a sound of ruffled bedclothes, sheets and quilts shifting and moving around him. I'd clearly woken him up, but I didn't care.

He cleared his throat. "Why are you calling at two in the morning, asking about your sister?"

"Because she's here with me. And so is your granddaughter."

The sounds of his breathing stopped. "Granddaughter?"

"Remember, the one you didn't want because it would look bad on you?"

"I never said that—"

"Bullshit! I might be a liar, but Kara isn't. She said you told her not to come back while she was pregnant. To get rid of it. Yeah, well, she didn't do that, *Dad*."

"Could you...could I talk to her?"

I bit down on my tongue. "She's busy taking care of her child. You know, what parents do?"

Irritation spiked in his voice. "It's not that simple for

me, Rebel. You don't understand our core values and beliefs. We believe a baby born out of wedlock is from the Devil."

My mouth dropped open. "I was a baby born out of wedlock! So what am I? Satan's spawn? Please explain to me how that makes sense? I wasn't the one who asked to be born. If you weren't so busy sticking your dick into women—and I use that term lightly, considering my mother was all of thirteen when you knocked her up—you wouldn't have had an illegitimate child. Why am I punished for your sins?"

He sighed impatiently, like the answer was one-hundred-percent obvious. "That's why I asked you to come out here. You're right! You're right about everything. Your birth was caused by my sins. But you can be baptized. You can choose to walk in the light like I did. Josiah is willing to perform the ritual—"

"Josiah—what?" I remembered the man. Creepy, middle-aged dude who'd hung around when we'd been out at the homestead. I hadn't liked the way he'd looked at my younger sister, but he hadn't said anything as crazy as the rubbish spewing from my father's mouth right now. "I'm not coming out there to be baptized into your damn cult, Torrence!"

"I'm your father, Rebel."

"Yeah, that only works in the movies. Not on thirty-year-old women who have been on their own for more than half their life because their father was a dead-shit who ran off to join the fucking circus."

Torrence's words were tight and clipped. "The homestead is not a circus. It's a community of like-minded people. Your mind has been polluted by everything. TV.

Radio. The news. Social media. All of it is the Devil's work."

Wow. It was like he was reading out of the cult life manual. "You've been brainwashed. I know you weren't like this when I was a kid."

"You're right, I wasn't. I lived in the dark. I didn't know the light until I came here. And there's room for you here too. Always. If you ever change your mind, we'll hold your baptism in the creek, with the running water washing away your sins."

The door behind me opened a crack.

I spun around.

"Is that my father?" Kara asked softly, Hayley Jade asleep in her arms.

"Yes," I admitted. "Though he doesn't deserve the respectful title."

"Let me talk to him."

I hesitated, not wanting him to hurt her with his cruel words when he'd already hurt her so much she'd gone running to Caleb for money.

In a way, I blamed him for everything that came after it.

But she held her hand out, more insistent this time. "Please."

Reluctantly, I handed it over.

I could already see her decision in her eyes, and it broke my heart.

She was going to go back to them.

19

REBEL

I walked from one end of the bar to the other, pausing in front of each man and waiting for them to flash me their phone screens. "Fang? Tell me you got through?"

He held his phone up which still showed the same concert ticket loading screen he'd been stuck on for the past two hours.

I refrained from pouting because the last time I'd done that, he'd looked utterly crushed. It wasn't his fault the damn concert was so popular we couldn't even get on the website to try for tickets.

"Kian?" I asked hopefully.

"No dice, Little Demon. Should we give up?"

I gave him a look.

"Right. Gotcha. No quitting when Paramore pop-up concert tickets are at stake. I'll keep staring at this never-ending refresh screen."

Damn right. When your favorite band ever announced a pop-up show for that weekend as a surprise for their superfans, you didn't just give up on getting tickets. "Nash?" I called to my boss in his office behind me. "Gimme some good news!"

"Already told you a dozen times; I'll yell if I get on. Would you at least do some work out there while we're all trying to get these tickets for you?"

I stared dismally down at my phone. The loading screen changed to one that announced: *Paramore Concert Tickets are now sold out. Enjoy your day.*

"No!" I wailed. "How am I supposed to enjoy my day when I have no tickets! You all got the same message?"

Kian nodded, showing me an identical message.

Fang closed out of his and put the phone down on the bar top. "Sorry, Pix. I know how much you wanted to go."

If it had just been about me, I wouldn't have been so disappointed, even though I really did freaking love Paramore. But I really wanted to take Kara. Queenie had promised to babysit Hayley Jade, and Kara had eventually agreed to come to the concert, I think only because she knew it would be one of our last chances to hang out. She and Hayley Jade would be moving out soon, going back home to her parents' place in the middle of nowhere.

I wasn't happy about that. Sally-Ann's words kept ringing over and over in my head. That shame would be brought upon Kara's head for having a baby before she was married. I didn't want that life for my sister. I wanted her to stay here with me.

But she was an adult. One with no job. No money. And no support. It was my place or back home. I couldn't blame her for wanting to put a hundred thousand miles between her and the nightmare Caleb had put her through here.

Even if what she was going home to didn't seem much better. It was what she knew though, and I knew there was a comfort in the familiar. I didn't blame her for seeking that out after everything she'd been through.

My phone buzzed with an incoming text, and I opened it. I'd given Kara an old phone of mine with a new SIM card.

Kara: So? Did you get the tickets?

I sent back a sad face emoji.

Kara: It's not as good as concert tickets, but here's some Hayley Jade spam to cheer you up.

I opened the photos as quick as I could, squealing at how many there were. But quickly wrote back to my sister before going through them properly.

Rebel: Nothing is better than Hayley Jade spam. I miss her so much.

Kara: You saw her about three hours ago.

Rebel: Too long!

Kara just sent back a laughing emoji, well used to how obsessive I'd become about my niece in the past week or so since she'd been brought home. She'd only spent a single night in the hospital for some fluids, but she was a strong little girl, just like her mama, and the two of them had been flourishing since they'd been reunited.

I stared down at my phone, grinning like a loon. "Kian, look at this. No, wait, wait. Look at this one." I thumbed across the screen to a photo of Hayley Jade poking her tongue out. "Isn't this cute? She does that when she's hungry, I think. And ohhhh, this is a good one. Kara had just bathed her, and she was all snug and warm in her new onesie pajamas."

Kian squinted at the phone. "Does that onesie say 'Auntie's Girl' on it?"

I nodded proudly. "I bought it. 'Cause it's true. She's definitely auntie's girl."

Vaughn pulled up a seat at the bar and tossed a peanut into his mouth. I hadn't even seen him come in. I was so busy trying to get tickets and cooing over my niece. He'd conveniently been unavailable for the loading page party I'd had with the others. I suspected he just hadn't wanted to stare at a screen and listen to me wail about concert injustices.

He leaned back on the barstool. "How would you even know if you're her favorite? She's like what? A month old? It's not like she can shout, 'Aunty Rebel, you're the best aunty I have.' I saw her stare at a wall for a good twenty minutes the other day. Pretty sure that wall is more her favorite than you are."

I threw a peanut at his face. "Shut up or I'm blacklisting you from this place. I know the guy on the door, you know."

Vaughn glanced over at Vincent standing guard by the entranceway. "Nah, Scythe and I go way back. He'd let me in, right, bro?"

I hid a smile. Vaughn hadn't been around long enough to be able to tell Vincent and his alter ego apart. I wasn't even sure when I'd started noticing the subtle difference between them. It was always obvious once they opened their mouths, but I could tell before that now, just from the way they stood.

Scythe would never just stand silently at the door the way Vincent was.

He looked over now at Vaughn, and then at me. "Just

say the word and he's gone. In whichever way you want the word gone to mean."

Vincent always had my back. I smiled smugly at my stepbrother.

Kian elbowed Vaughn. "Don't go getting us blacklisted please." He glanced at Vincent warily. "Or cut up into little pieces. I still haven't even been to one of the Psychos parties. Not to actually...partake anyway."

I raised an eyebrow at him while I scrubbed out the inside of a beer glass. "You loser. How have you lived in Saint View your entire life and never been?"

He shrugged. "You need an invite. I didn't know anyone to give me one. But since I have an in with their sexy-as-fuck bartender, maybe I could get one now?" He gave me his most charming smile.

I winked at him. "I dunno. We don't just give them out to any old riffraff."

Nash came out of his office and tossed a card at Kian. "There. You're invited. Lord, anyone who put up with that loading screen for as long as we did deserves to get laid."

Kian looked down and then back up, his eyes wide. "Fuck! Seriously? I feel like the kid from *Charlie and the Chocolate Factory*. You just handed me a golden ticket."

Fang raised his beer bottle to his mouth. "That would have been a whole different sort of movie if Charlie's ticket had been to a Psychos party."

We all stared at him.

"That was so wrong," I told him. "So, so wrong. How dare you defile a classic like that."

He just shrugged and took a sip of his drink.

Kian was still waving the invite around. "Hey, can Rebel get the night off so we can...uh...you know?"

Nash squinted at him over the pile of papers in his arms. "Don't push your luck."

Vaughn leaned over the bar and caught the sleeve of Nash's flannel shirt. "Actually, Rebel needs Saturday night off. I know you need her for the party on Friday night, but I really need her for the night after."

Nash went to answer, his frown set into his forehead.

But Vaughn held up a hand, cutting off Nash's complaints. "Before you make a decision, can I add it's because I bought box seats at the Paramore concert.

I gaped at him. "You what?"

Vaughn carried on talking to Nash like I hadn't spoken at all. "I knew she'd want Bliss to go, too, but we're all feeling a bit...overprotective since everything went down, and that you guys wouldn't want her going solo, so I just went ahead and bought thirteen box seat tickets. One each for the four of us. One each for Kara, and her friends. And one for Bliss and the three of you..." He glanced over at Vincent. "Sorry, V. Only one of your alter egos can come."

Vincent just looked at him.

Vaughn quickly turned away.

I couldn't help but laugh, but I also really wanted to kiss him. So I leaned across the bar with wet, soapy hands, and hauled him in by his collar. Suds coated his cheeks. "Did you seriously? We just spent hours refreshing and couldn't even get on the site before they sold out."

He grinned. "I did. It pays to have old business connections and a newly topped-up trust fund that had more than enough to cover the cost."

"Brooke's dad actually paid you back?"

Vaughn brushed his lips over mine. "He did. I'm surprised too."

Kian groaned. "Watch him go all Mr. Moneybags on us again. Should we start calling you sir? Or Your Lordship?"

Vaughn leaned over to kiss him. "Only in the bedroom."

Nash rolled his eyes and went back to leafing through his papers. "Spare me the details of the kinky shit the four of you get up to. Rebel, there's mail here for you."

He tossed a white envelope onto the bar in my direction. It landed just short of in the sudsy water.

I wiped my hands on the backs of my jeans and turned the envelope over. My name was in the center, but there was no postmark.

My stomach twisted in a knot.

This was all too familiar.

I took the card out from inside, already knowing it would be white with plain black text.

"That better not be what I think it is," Fang growled low beneath his breath.

It caught Kian's and Vaughn's attention.

"Not possible," Vaughn said.

But when I turned the card over, I knew it was very possible.

You've been warned and warned again, and yet nothing changes. Time's up. Boom.

The card fluttered from my fingers.

Vaughn picked it up and read it, Fang and Kian reading over his shoulders.

"How is this possible?" Kian asked. "I thought Brooke was the one delivering notes. Isn't she off in Barbados or something, locked up in a mental institution? Or a 'health retreat' as the rich probably call it."

Vaughn tapped the card on the bar top. "She is. She's not even in the country. Her father told me that again when he called to tell me he'd transferred the money."

"Then how the hell did she hand-deliver this?" Kian took the note from Vaughn's fingers and studied every inch of it, like the back or one of the corners might give us some sort of new information we hadn't noticed yet.

"She didn't," I said quietly. "She might have sent the notes to Vaughn, but the ones I got were addressed to me."

"Same white cards though." Kian's fingers crumpled the thick paper. "That can't be a coincidence. She had to have sent all of them. She isn't exactly your biggest fan. And she's clearly lost it if she's chopping off her own fingers to blackmail Vaughn. She's definitely capable of throwing a few death threats your way for good measure."

I thought that over for a minute. "Or she didn't. If the sender already knew we were getting threats from someone else, a smart way to throw us off the track would be to just blend in. Make their threats look like the same ones Brooke sent. Pretty easy to just copy the 'white card, plain black text' format. Hardly creative."

"I always thought it was Hugh," Fang said quietly. "Or Leonn. Or even Caleb."

"Leonn's in a prison awaiting his trial. Hugh is dead." I shook my head. "This card can't be from either of them. It's gotta be Caleb."

Nash squinted at the card, his dad face firmly in place, even though he wasn't actually a dad yet. But he'd been playing that role with me ever since I'd first started working here. "He sent notes to Bliss once. Tricking her into meeting him. This is in his wheelhouse."

I sighed and plucked the card from Kian's hand and tossed it in the trash. "Then we don't pay it another second of attention. We can't live our lives in fear of what he might do. We have Kara and Hayley Jade back. The women are all safe and fed and making plans for returning to their old lives or new ones of their choosing. We're done with Caleb."

But even as I said the words so hopefully, I knew they weren't true.

We'd never be done with Caleb. He'd wormed his way into every aspect of not only my life, but Bliss's, Kara's and, in turn, all the men's.

We'd never be free of him.

Not until he was six feet under.

20

FANG

I'd never in a million years thought I would like babies. I knew nothing about them. I had siblings but couldn't remember them below the age of five or six. Nobody at the club had kids. I didn't even know how to hold one.

The first time Rebel had put Hayley Jade in my arms, I'd been terrified I was going to break her. She was so tiny and fragile I didn't dare breathe.

But then she'd snuggled into my chest and stared up at me with big eyes that slowly fluttered with exhaustion. And eventually, she'd fallen asleep.

When Kara had noticed, she'd offered to take her, but I'd said it was okay.

Then I'd sat there with Hayley Jade in my arms for three hours until she woke up again.

I was still thinking about it that night when I got ready for the Psychos party. I thought about holding her in my arms the entire ride to the club and was still thinking about it when I bumped fists with Kian, who arrived at the same time in his truck.

Kian was like an overexcited puppy, bouncing on the balls of his feet.

I eyed him. "Dude. Be cool."

"Can't. Too excited."

"You have had sex before."

He elbowed me. "You'd know. Since you were there watching."

A warm heat crept up the back of my neck at the reminder of him and Vaughn double-teaming Rebel. Fuck, that had been hot. I'd have never picked myself as the type of man who could watch his woman with someone else.

And yet, I kinda got off on it.

I looked over Kian's outfit. Black jeans. White T-shirt. Black boots. Black jacket. "We match."

Kian stared down at himself and then at me with a frown. "Yeah, I guess we do. But what else are you supposed to wear to a black-and-white party? Does it even matter? Won't we all be naked and writhing around on the floor in a few minutes?"

I squinted at him. "Is that seriously what you think goes on here?"

His expression turned sheepish. "Maybe? I didn't exactly get a good look last time; I was too busy freaking out about Rebel and those notes."

I didn't like the reminder of the notes. I didn't want to think about whoever might have sent them still being out there, watching and waiting for their moment with her.

Scythe met us at the door.

"Rebel wants to see you both." He pointed toward the

darkened doorway that led inside the sex club. "She told me if I saw any of you, you had to be immediately sent to the locker rooms."

"Is she okay?" Kian stepped forward.

"That was the only information I was given. I didn't inquire as to her physical health."

I cocked my head, realizing I'd mixed up the alter egos. "Vincent, right?"

He nodded.

So fucking weird how they swapped back and forth so easily.

I thanked him and ducked beneath the doorway.

The lights were dim on the other side, but the room was mostly empty. We were early, as Rebel had asked us to be. The party wasn't set to start for another forty-five minutes.

I lifted a hand in greeting to Bliss and Nash, who were busily setting up champagne glasses, and said hello to two of the couples who performed in the gilded gold cages scattered around the huge room.

Kian walked beside me, quietly taking it all in. "Those cages…"

I grinned at him. "You'll want to watch those later. You'll like it."

"Does Rebel get in them?"

I groaned at the very thought of her up in one of those, on display for every man in the room to watch. I wasn't sure I liked it. I'd liked seeing her with Kian and Vaughn, but that was because they were touching her the way I would. Making sure she was the one who was enjoying it most.

I didn't think that courtesy would extend to other men who had their hands down their pants.

Unless, of course, she wanted to perform for them.

Because I was never going to be able to say no to that woman. I never wanted to.

I caught Bliss's eye and called out to her. "Rebel apparently wants us down in the locker room. That okay?"

She waved me off. "She's the only one left in there." Her smile was wide.

Knowing.

I didn't trust it at all. It was too similar to the one Rebel gave me when she was up to no good. "Spill it, Bliss. What's going on?"

She shrugged, full of fake innocence that really spiked my suspicion. "All I know is she needs help with her outfit for tonight."

Kian frowned. "You couldn't have done her zipper up?"

She made a face at him. "Read the room, Kian. She isn't wearing a dress."

It might have been my imagination, but I was pretty sure Kian and I both moved at a slightly quicker pace.

The corridor was filled with doors, small, private rooms to accommodate different kinks on the other side. I'd never been in one. Never wanted to unless I was going into one with Rebel. But I'd heard from War all about the peepholes, the windows into other rooms, toy collections, tie-downs, and who knew what else. These rooms were all for private hire, and they were always booked out.

Kian gawked, catching a glimpse inside one with the door slightly open. "Was that a sex swing in that room?"

I shrugged. "Probably."

If Kian had any further thought on that particular room, he didn't voice it, maybe because we'd reached the end of the corridor where the staff locker rooms were.

I knocked cautiously and opened the door just a crack so I could call out. "Rebel? You in there?"

"Fang! Thank God. Get in here."

I pushed open the door to find Rebel standing in front of the mirrors, bare-ass naked. In front of her, a bench held multiple pots with what seemed to be paint brushes sticking out of them.

Kian groaned beside me. "I don't know what we're doing in here, but I love that you're naked already."

She flashed him a smile that did things to my insides. She was so fucking beautiful, especially when she was as carefree and confident as she was right now.

I eyed the pots. "What's going on?"

"I need an outfit for the party."

Kian hadn't stopped staring at her. "The one you're wearing will do the trick, if you ask me."

She winked at him but continued her explanation, "I was feeling myself when I decided on this costume, but now I'm having second thoughts."

I had no idea what she was talking about. There wasn't a stitch of clothing to be seen, in any color.

She pointed at the pots. "Body paint. I need you guys to paint me."

My dick went hard in an instant, but I ignored it, because that wasn't exactly uncommon in this place. I peered into the pots, picking up a brush and swirling the mixture around with it. One was black and one was white. "Why do these smell so good? They don't smell like paint at all."

She pushed her finger into the black pot and then lifted it back out. Black paint coated her finger before she popped it into her mouth, licking it clean. "Edible. They're chocolate flavored. Not bad either."

Fuck. My dick got the better of me, and I leaned down to kiss her mouth, tasting the chocolate paint still lingering on her tongue.

She was breathless when she pulled away. "Is that a yes to helping me? I can't reach my back."

Fuck her back. I was painting every damn part of her.

Then licking the entire thing off before I let her go out there.

I nudged the white paint toward Kian and picked up the black for myself. Watching her face, I circled the cold, wet paint around her nipple.

She raised an eyebrow. "Of course, that's where you'd start."

"You don't like my choice?" I ducked my head, leaning toward her. "No problem. I'll remove it."

I put my mouth to her breast and followed the circle of body paint with my tongue. It was as sweet as she was.

She shivered beneath my touch. "On second thought, that seems like the perfect place to start."

I shifted back, recoated the brush, then painted her other breast, this time covering the taut tip as well. I kept going, painting circles around her tits, then licking it off with my tongue.

I dropped to my knees and sucked her nipple deep into my mouth, flicking at it and sucking until she let out a gasp.

I painted a line down her belly and over her bare mound, not stopping. She cried out when I painted right between her folds and over her sweet clit.

I couldn't help myself. I immediately licked it off, flicking the little bud with my tongue to clean her off.

She moaned so loudly I painted her again and started over.

Kian moved behind her. He painted a line down her neck with thick white, chocolate-flavored paint, then removed it with open-mouthed kisses along her skin. She tilted her head to one side, giving him better access, but Kian was no more patient than I'd been. He ignored her offered neck and painted a line down her spine, the paint brush disappearing between her cheeks to coat her asshole.

"You want me to tongue fuck you there, Little Demon? While he tongue fucks your sweet, wet pussy?" Kian didn't wait for her permission.

He mirrored my position, getting down on his knees, and grabbed her ass. He spread her there and buried his tongue.

"Oh!"

Her cries were so hot. She rolled her hips, thrusting them first toward me, then back at Kian, like she couldn't decide who to give the best access to. She needn't have worried; I was so determined to get her off I would lick her in any position she wanted.

I slid two fingers up inside her, crooking them to find her G-spot, and knowing I'd hit it when her movements became frantic and her noises grew louder. She grabbed at my hair, holding me where she needed me most.

Her release came with a shout from her perfect lips. She flooded my hand with a new wave of arousal.

I just licked it right up, loving that she tasted even better than the chocolate.

After a few more slow licks, she pushed us both away, then reached for my jeans, undoing the button and drawing down the fly. She did the same to Kian, helping us drag down our jeans enough that she could get to our dicks.

On her knees, she painted our matching erections with her fingers and held us by our bases.

"Fuck, you look beautiful on your knees like that," I whispered. I thrust my fingers into her hair and guided her mouth to my cock. "Suck."

She opened her mouth and obeyed, tonguing the head and the length, taking me deep into her mouth to clean me off, before I pulled back and guided her to Kian. He took over, his fingers sliding down to her neck while she blew him.

I needed more. More of me inside her. I knelt behind her, reaching around to rub slow circles on her clit.

She licked Kian's dick. She moaned around his length and spread her thighs for me, grinding against my dick that prodded her back. I was too tall to penetrate her like this, so I just worked on her clit and bringing her closer to orgasm.

Kian leaned back from her mouth, breathing hard, his chest rising and falling and his cock quivering with the effort of not coming.

I took my chance to pull her back to me, wrapping my arms around her and lowering her onto the mats at our feet. It wasn't particularly comfortable or glamorous, but fuck if I cared. I just wanted her body. I wanted her heart.

I wanted to feel connected to my woman.

I fit myself behind her, spooning her so I alternated between squeezing her nipples and playing with her clit. She writhed in my arms, getting wetter and wetter when I fingered her.

I spread some of that arousal back to her sweet, tight little hole, and then pressed my dick to it.

Black spots appeared behind my eyes as I sank inside her. She took me there like I'd been made for her, and I fucked her slowly, grinding against her ass while she moaned my name.

Kian joined us on the floor, lifting her leg and drawing it over his hip. He kissed her mouth, smothering her moans, and creating new ones at the same time.

The pressure increased as he drove his dick inside her slit.

"I need to come," I groaned.

Kian picked up the pace, thrusting inside her easier now that she was used to us. She kissed him hard, with her other hand reached backward for me, holding my ass and encouraging me to fuck her just as fast.

Kian and I thrust in unison, Rebel's cries of pleasure the one and only goal.

We didn't come until her entire body shook, and she clamped down on us both, throbbing and pulsing while she shouted. "Oh! Oh!"

I came hard, my vision blacking out entirely; all that was left was the sweet agony of coming inside her. My shouts mingled with hers and Kian's, none of us trying to be quiet when there was no reason to be.

This hadn't been what I was expecting. But this was what we'd come here for.

I rode it out, focusing on her, making sure she was still loving it as much as we were.

Her moans and trembles of ecstasy said she was.

When I pulled from her body, she rolled over onto her back, staring up at me.

"Hey you." Her expression was nothing but blissed-out perfection. "Kiss me."

She didn't have to tell me twice. I kissed her mouth softly, whispering sweet words that reminded her how good she was, how proud I was, and how fucking sexy she looked pressed in between us.

She smiled at that last one, then looked over at the clock on the wall. "Shit. I have exactly three minutes to get out there."

"You want us to paint you real quick?" It would be torture, but I'd maybe be able to do it now my dick had had its fill of her.

She shook her head. "Not sure this was the best idea." She went to her locker and put on a lacy black pair of panties that barely covered anything. I was sure our cum would soak through in minutes, but she didn't seem to mind. In fact, her cheeks were so pink, I wondered if she was thinking the same thing and liking it.

She was a firecracker, and damn, I loved her. I put my mouth to hers, and my fingers between her legs, feeling that yes, indeed, they were already wet. "Just how I want you. All night. If you need a top-up later, we can do this again on your break."

"I'll come find you. But first, I need a shirt." She tugged at the hem of the one I was wearing.

It would be a million times too big, but I pulled it off in a second and drew it over her head. She put her arms through the designated holes and then gathered up all the extra fabric and tied it in a knot at the small of her back.

Kian made a choking sound as her dark nipples pressed against the fabric, which was definitely not thick enough to conceal them entirely. "You can't go out there like that. Every man is going to want to fuck your brains out."

Walking out, she blew him a kiss. "Welcome to party night as Psychos, Kian. That's exactly what's supposed to happen."

21

WAR

Even with an iPad for company, our infirmary was boring as hell. Gray cinderblock walls. Gray concrete floors. Not even a window low enough to look out.

It was real fucking hard to stay put. Hawk was being a prick and wouldn't even let me move to my cabin. He was convinced my damn gunshot wound was infected and was insistently shoving pills down my throat and cleaning the fucking thing every few hours.

I could have just gotten up and walked out, but truth was, I didn't actually feel that hot, and I had a feeling I wouldn't even make it up the stairs.

He might have been right about the infection. Pretty sure I had a fever. Not that I was going to tell anyone that. The antibiotics would knock it on its head anyway.

Exhaustion gripped me tightly, squeezing the energy out of my muscles, and I was sure I'd had more naps in the last few days than Hayley Jade had.

My eyelids were always heavy. I put on a good front

when Bliss or Scythe was here, because I didn't want either of them worrying about me.

"You look like shit," a voice croaked from beside me.

I jumped a fucking mile. The metal frame on the bed protested beneath me with a jangling rattle.

Hayden's blue eyes watched me quietly.

"Like you can fucking talk. Thought you were a goner for sure." I ground my teeth. This wasn't exactly the scenario I'd imagined when I'd told Hawk and Fang to peel Hayden off that road and bring him back here. At the time, the plan had been to nurse him back to health, at least enough that he could speak, then make him hurt until he told us everything he knew.

I'd imagined killing him with my own two hands for being responsible for my father's death.

Now all I wanted to know was what my father had been doing behind my back.

All of a sudden, Hayden Chaos Whitling didn't seem like the enemy.

Maybe my father had deserved everything he'd gotten.

I opened my mouth to ask if my dad had been involved in the trafficking, and yet, now that I had the opportunity, I didn't have the guts to ask.

"You in pain?" I asked instead. "Hawk's been taking care of you. Said we had to keep up your pain meds or you wouldn't heal."

"I'm fine." He struggled to sit up, but he didn't get far. He groaned, slumping down onto his back again.

I cocked my head to one side, watching him. "You've been in and out of consciousness for over a week. I wouldn't try moving around too much."

Suddenly, his eyes went wide. "Kara. Caleb has Kara. In the ambulance..." He stared down at his chest and ripped off a few heart monitor leads.

I tried reaching for him. "Hey. Relax."

He grabbed the IV stuck in his arm and yanked it out viciously. "You fucking relax. I need to find her. He'll hurt her."

"I said lay your ass back down." I didn't have the energy to physically restrain him, so I pulled the gun from beneath my pillow and pointed it at him. I'd have to give Fang and Hawk a pat on the back when I saw them next. They'd left it there for me in case of this exact situation, even though I'd scoffed at their concerns Hayden might wake up. I thought for sure the guy would be dead before the end of the week.

Hayden looked so panicked I actually felt bad for the asshole. He stared down the barrel of my gun, that *'I don't take orders from no one'* expression on his face I knew all too well.

Because I saw it in the mirror.

I dropped the safety on the gun.

Hayden sat his ass back down, just like I'd fucking told him to. But I threw the guy a bone, 'cause he was pretty pathetic. "Kara's fine. Now, at least."

The fight went straight of him. He lay back down. "The baby?"

I frowned. This was interesting. Why the hell did Hayden 'Chaos' Whitling even give a shit about that woman's child?

"Why do you even care? You were ready to sell the both of them to the highest bidder, right? That is what you and Caleb were doing, holding those women against their will. Wasn't it?"

He shook his head slowly. "No. I mean, fuck, yes. But I didn't know what I was getting into. I thought it was just a protection gig. That's what I was told. I didn't know until they were already in the house that they'd been stolen from the streets."

I ground my teeth. "Then why not let them go?"

He swallowed thickly. "I know you've got a family."

Despite how average I felt, I was off that bed and pushing the gun into Hayden's forehead quicker than you could blink. "Don't fucking talk about my family."

But Hayden clearly didn't know what was good for him. "You got a woman, right? Bethany-Melissa? Caleb loved to run his mouth about how she was such a whore she fell into bed with you and some other guys."

I snorted. "Is that how he told the story? Cowardly piece of shit." I pressed the gun against his head harder. "Also, if you ever say the word whore and my girl's name in the same sentence again, I'll pull this."

Hayden raised his hands in surrender. "Got it, got it. I'm not trying to piss you off. My point is, we're the fucking same. Caleb threatened my brother, Liam, and his partner, Mae. They have a baby, just like you do."

I blinked at the familiar names. Liam and Mae were friends of Vincent's. We'd gone to their older kid's birthday party not that long ago. I hadn't even made the connection between Liam and Hayden. Their last names were different, so why would I?

I mashed my lips into a tight line. Well, that fucking complicated shit, didn't it? I couldn't shoot him in the head, knowing I'd be hurting people we cared about.

Son of a bitch.

I put the gun down. "He threatened them if you didn't do what he wanted?"

Hayden nodded. "You would have done the same thing and you know it."

I wasn't sure I would have. I probably would have just shot Caleb on sight. But then I understood why Hayden hadn't. An oddly small number of problems were solved by shooting someone. There was always someone further up the chain who took their place. Or some other new problem that arose.

It had taken me years to realize that.

Maybe Hayden had gotten there sooner than I had.

I put the gun back under my pillow and painfully sat back on my bed. The room was spinning in lazy circles, but I wasn't going to let Hayden know that.

Silence fell over us. I wouldn't have said it was a respectful one exactly, but there wasn't quite as much animosity between us either. I understood the need to protect your family above anything else.

"I wanted to join your club when I was younger, you know." Hayden coughed and winced.

I'd bet he had a couple broken ribs that were giving him hell right now. "You like bikes?"

He nodded. "Always have. Couldn't ever afford one, though. Not even a shit one. That's partly why I fell in with the Sinners. The old leader, Nitro, he promised me things."

"And didn't deliver on any of it, I'm sure." I remembered him. A few years older than my dad. He'd disappeared a while back and never been heard of since. Mean old asshole. I was sure someone had taken him out into the woods and put a bullet through his head. I hoped they'd made it painful. No good had ever come from anything he'd been involved with.

It seemed to me that Hayden had followed in his footsteps.

"Promised me money. Somewhere to live. Respect." He scoffed. "I was only supposed to stay long enough to get a bike so I could join the Slayers."

"But then you stayed so long you became the Sinners' leader."

He shrugged. "It's not like we took a vote after Nitro fucked off. Just none of them were smart enough to organize their way out of a brown paper bag. Someone had to find us something to do so we could eat. By that point, I doubt you would have taken me anyway."

I stroked a hand over my beard. "Probably not."

He nodded, then gave me a half-smile. "That still kinda hurts to hear, even now."

Ah fuck. I almost felt bad.

Bliss probably would have had tears running down her face, listening to his story. She was still sweet and soft like that.

Apparently, it was rubbing off on me.

"I know you don't owe me shit, but can you please tell me if Kara's baby is okay? I know you think I don't care, and I know we aren't friends, just because I told you my little wannabe biker sob story, but I really need to know if that kid is okay. I delivered her."

I peered at him. "Hayley Jade? You delivered her?"

He blinked. "That's her name? Hayley?"

I suddenly made the connection between Hayley and Hayden. I didn't fucking like it. Had Rebel's sister seriously seen so much good in this prick she'd named her damn baby after him?

One of us was a poor judge of character.

And to be honest, I was beginning to think it was me.

I let Hayden have his little smile and bask in the glory of his moment.

When Hawk got back, we'd be busting his bubble.

Right after we worked out exactly what we were going to do with him.

22

VAUGHN

Things I knew for sure.
I loved Rebel.
I loved Kian.
And Fang was okay.

But I also knew I was restless. I couldn't continue to just hang around the house with Kara and the baby or follow Rebel and Kian to work if I wanted the numb feeling inside me to go away.

The money in my bank account felt like the answer, but it also seemed dirty. Tainted. I didn't feel good about Brooke being shipped off to who knows where, and the money her father had transferred to me didn't feel like mine.

I'd failed at business once, but I'd learned from those mistakes.

This money could be a fresh start.

I could take over my father's company.

But I sure as hell didn't want to run it with Harold Coker looking over my shoulder.

The money could buy him out, and if he was as broke as he made out, maybe he'd even agree to it.

I could already hear my accountant screaming about this being a terrible idea. But I didn't want all those people in my father's office to have to go home and tell their loved ones they no longer had a job to go to.

I wanted to rebuild with my father's dreams in mind. I wanted a company where everyone was welcomed and included. Where everyone had a finger in the pie and felt useful and needed.

I wanted the complete opposite of how Harold had made me feel and what he'd turned that company into.

I couldn't do any of that with him still at the helm.

Harold needed to go.

So when I was called—summoned, really—into his office, I went with my buyout offer in hand.

That afternoon, for the first time in a long time, I'd been able to look myself in the mirror and not feel shame.

I drove into the city, following the ever-present traffic lines to the office. I was so in my head about what I was about to do, I didn't even notice my mother's car in front of me until we were both parked and she was stepping out of it.

She blinked as our eyes met. "Vaughn! What are you doing here?"

I pointed up at the building with my family name on it. "Got some business things to discuss with Harold." I took in her smart work suit and low heels that matched her handbag. "What are you doing here? Do you have an appointment nearby or something?"

"Harold called me in."

My hackles instantly rose.

"That's weird, isn't it?" Mom asked, following my gaze up to the offices. "Him calling us both in? What do you think it's about?"

I had no idea, but it probably wasn't going to be good. "Let's just get this over with."

She tucked her hand into my arm and smiled up at me. "Despite the slightly suspicious circumstances, it's nice to have a moment with you. What's going on at your place? Is Rebel okay after the funeral? You all left so early, I didn't even get a chance to talk to any of you."

Because we'd been too busy burying a body at the bottom of my father's grave.

I couldn't tell her that. So I told her something I could. "I'm in love with her."

She stopped, which forced me to as well since she was holding my arm. I braced myself for her excitement and an avalanche of questions, like she'd done when I'd first brought Brooke home.

But her mouth gaped open in surprise, and she slowly shook her head. "Oh, Vaughn. No. Honey, I saw her at the funeral. That woman isn't the sort you fall in love with. She has that big blond biker man. He's always around, and I've seen the way he looks at her. That's not just a friendship."

I was about to blow my mother's mind, but frankly, it had to happen at some point. I was all in with Rebel, and she came as a package deal with Fang. "I know. She loves him. I'm okay with that."

She blinked. "What does that mean?"

I chuckled softly at her confusion. "It means she can love more than one person, Mom. I do too."

My mother gawked at me. "You love the big blond biker man too? Oh, Vaughn. I know you and Kian had an...experimental phase in high school, but that biker? You couldn't possibly!"

I fought back the urge to belly laugh. "Kian, Mom. I'm in love with Kian. Rebel is too. We're all with her, and Kian and I are together too."

She opened and closed her mouth a few times, but eventually it pulled into a line. "I don't understand this. She can't be with all of you."

"Says who?"

My mother threw up her hands. "Says everyone! I'm very open-minded, Vaughn. You know that. But I don't know what's gotten into you since your father died. When you were walking around the funeral holding hands with the two of them, I had to tell my friends they were just supporting you through your grief. That alone caused a lot of gossip to swirl. I can't continue to protect you if you aren't going to protect yourself. What you do behind closed doors needs to stay there. Don't bring it out into the open."

She dug her fingers into my arm and towed me toward the elevator, effectively ending the conversation.

But I wasn't done with it. As she hit the button for Harold's offices, I stared at her. "I didn't expect this from you, after all the marches you've protested in and the causes you've fought for. Does that not apply when the person affected is your son? Did you hear me say I love them? Rebel *and* Kian? We aren't hurting anyone. We're all consenting adults, and I'm sorry if your friends don't understand. But I like what I have here. I like who I am when I'm with them."

The elevator rocketed to the upper levels. She glared at me. "Vaughn. Think logically. You've only just broken up with your wife. You can't suddenly be dating multiple people at once. You're supposed to take over your father's business, for goodness sakes!"

"What does that have to do with who I'm in a relationship with?"

She shook her head. "You truly are as naïve as Harold says you are. I swear, Vaughn. I've always fought for you when he would say you needed training and guiding because you didn't get it. I never believed that. I always thought you were capable of making good decisions. You showed that when you married Brooke."

My irritation with her bubbled over. "I never loved Brooke! I only did that because Harold practically arranged our marriage!"

"And he was right to do so. Because look who you choose when you're left to your own devices? The riffraff from Saint View?"

The elevator doors binged open, as loud as a mic drop in the frosty silence between us. Neither of us made a move.

I just glared at her. "You sound exactly like Harold."

She glanced over at the workers at their desks. She plastered on a fake smile and spoke under her breath, through gritted teeth. "I don't like the man any more than you do. But this business is your father's legacy. I just want it and you to succeed. I'm sorry, but you cannot do that if the entire business world is gossiping about your sex life. We don't always get everything we want, Vaughn. Stop acting like a spoiled child."

She walked out of the elevator.

I ground my back molars.

It was so fucking tempting to hit the button for the ground floor and leave her here with Harold, since the two of them were apparently two peas in a fucking pod.

But fuck running away. This company was fifty-one percent owned by Rebel and me. I wasn't giving it up without a fight. If no one would do business with a man who just so happened to consensually love more than one person, then I didn't want to do business with them.

I strode across the floor to where my father's receptionist sat behind her desk, smiling pleasantly at me.

"Mr. Coker is expecting you, Vaughn. Please go right on through. Everyone else is already inside."

I nodded curtly and moved around her to Harold's office door. I knocked once but didn't bother waiting for the old codger to call me in.

The door opened into the spacious, modern office. Harold and my mother were all big smiles for each other, him shaking her hand and holding it while they talked animatedly.

Another man hovered behind, waiting for his turn to greet them.

Caleb fucking Black.

I swung my fist back and then plowed it straight into his nose.

"Vaughn!" Mom yelped as Caleb stumbled back, slamming into a heavy metal filing cabinet.

He blinked in surprise, blood dripping from his nose.

"What on earth, Weston!" Harold rushed to Caleb.

But I wasn't done.

I shoved the older man out of the way and barged

Caleb, smashing him back against the filing cabinet so hard it cracked the wall behind it.

He let out a groan before I cut it off with my fingers around his throat.

All I could see was Rebel at the bottom of that pool. The fear in Bliss's eyes when she spoke about him. The panic in Kara's when he'd taken her baby.

I loved Rebel, and Rebel loved them.

Which meant they were mine to protect too.

Caleb had done nothing but hurt them over and over.

He slapped his palms against my arms, his eyes wide. "You're crazy," he croaked out. "Call the cops."

Someone's hand clamped down on my shoulder, trying to drag us apart, but I refused to be budged.

"You piece of fucking shit," I hissed in his ear, then looked over at Harold, whose face was purple as he shouted for security. "This is who you want me to work with? This is who you care about impressing? Do you know he tied my girl to a chair and then threw her into the deep end of a pool? Do you know he stole a woman's baby? That he held women captive, intending to sell them, until they escaped, running to us for help? Do you even know about half the despicable things he's done, either in the name of furthering his own fucking career, or in jealousy because women see through his snakelike skin to the black heart beyond it? You don't see that, do you, Harold? Because you're just as fucking bad as he is."

Security finally rushed the room, two burly men, plus a worker in a suit hauled me to the other side of the office.

My face blazed hot, the backs of my eyes burning with rage.

Caleb choked and spluttered, clutching his throat. "You're insane. I'm suing."

I snorted. "You won't. Because I know all your secrets, Caleb. Every. Single. One." I grinned, completely out of control on adrenaline. His taunts I was crazy probably weren't far off.

I shrugged off the men holding me and then pinned Harold with a glare. "How much further do I have to dig before I find proof of your sins?"

"You're way off base, Weston." Harold's eyes were dangerous. "I've been nothing but a mentor to you—"

I snorted. "If you sleep with dogs, you wake up with fleas, Harry." I knew he hated the nickname, so I slung it at him like mud. "I know exactly what he's done to further his business connections and line his own pockets with dirty money. I'll bet I don't have far to poke before I find the skeletons in your closet too."

I could tell from the look in his eye I was right. There was anger and aggression in his expression, sure. But behind it, a tinge of fear.

I took a piece of paper from the pocket of my jacket and passed it to Harold. "That was my offer to buy you out. But now my offer is half. Take it and go retire on a beach somewhere. Or stay and I'll keep digging."

The security guards escorted me all the way down the elevator and out to my car. I stopped fighting once we were outside, and I was calm by the time I sat behind the wheel.

Before I even drove away, I had a text on my phone from Harold Coker, agreeing to accept my offer.

I smiled all the way back to Saint View.

23

CALEB

Vaughn's mother gaped at me and Harold, her gaze darting between the two of us. "Is any of that true? I mean, even one word of it?"

Harold shook his head. "Of course not. Clearly, he gets the hysterical from you."

I was less polite. "Your son is a cunt."

She stared at me for a long second, and then at Harold, before she shook her head in disgust and then ran after the men hauling Vaughn away. "Vaughn! Wait!"

Harold kicked the door closed and turned on me. "What the hell, Black?"

I stared at him. "What? You're hardly an angel here. It was you who introduced me to Luca Guerra and his family. I'm pretty sure you're well aware they have initiation processes so they can work out who to trust. Since he trusts you, I know you already went through all of this. How many women did you get for him? Was five the deal for you too?"

Harold grabbed my arm and dragged me away from

the door. His expression was pure fury. "Keep your voice down, you foolish child. Your father would be so embarrassed by you right now."

Rage coursed through me at the reminder of the man who'd raised me. The term 'father' seemed overly generous. It wasn't like he'd ever done anything fatherly, unless it was a public event where I made him look good. When I'd graduated as valedictorian, he'd proudly showed me off to all of his friends, Harold Coker included.

It had been the best day of my life, finally earning my dad's approval.

But he'd gone right back to ignoring me straight after. My mother had made a fuss for days, but it had only pissed me off. I didn't care what she thought, just like my father never had. "Don't speak to me about my father."

"Then tell me how Vaughn knows about the women?"

I shrugged, even though I knew full well how he knew. It was because of that bitch, Kara, who I'd let go. Fuck her. She was as bad as Bethany-Melissa, making demands on me, thinking I owed her something. They were as painful as my mother. I shook my head. "Who cares?"

Harold got up in my face. "I care, you little shit. Vaughn isn't like us. He doesn't see business as business. He doesn't have that drive to succeed like we do. He lets his heart get involved."

It was hardly the only reason Vaughn was such a joke. But it was one of them.

Harold's shoulders were stiff as boards, his eyes wide with panic. "He's going to go to the cops, Caleb. This place will be swarming with them in no time."

I rolled my eyes. "You're as dramatic as he is. You

think I don't have just as much dirt on him as he has on me? He's not talking to anyone."

Harold paced the floor. "If he knows about the trafficking then other people do too." He picked up the paper with Vaughn's offer.

I peered over the older man's shoulder and scoffed at the figure Vaughn had offered. "I'm embarrassed for you, Vaughn, if that's all you can afford."

The paper crumpled beneath Harold's trembling grasp. "I'm going to take it."

I snapped my head to the bumbling fool. "What? That's ridiculous. That figure is lousy."

He shoved it into my chest. "Yeah, well, it's a hell of a lot better than spending the next twenty years in jail. I'm taking the offer."

He took out his phone, his fat fingers moving rapidly over the screen. It made a whistling noise as a text was sent. He shook his head and then went to his desk, yanking out drawers and pulling things off shelves.

I just stared at him. "You are not seriously that scared?"

He raised his gaze to mine. "You have no idea who you're in bed with, Black. You should be scared. The Guerras are not to be messed with. If they know there's a weak link in their chain—and believe me, someone on the outside knowing about the women is most definitely a fucking weak link—it won't be the cops you need to worry about. The Guerras will take care of the problem themselves." He put a photo frame of him and his beautiful young wife into a box.

My throat still throbbed from where Vaughn had squeezed it, and my nose ached from the punch. I put my hands on the edge of Harold's desk and leaned toward him. "I'm not scared of anyone."

It was the mantra I had chanted to myself for years, every time my father beat the shit out of me for coming second in a race or for getting less-than-perfect marks on a math quiz.

My mother had tried to coddle me back then too, comfort me and tell me I was so smart. I'd shoved her away so many times, until any warmth in her eyes faded. I didn't want her softness.

So I made her hard with constant rejection.

She should fucking thank me. Soft people like her and Vaughn Weston were what was wrong with the world.

I wasn't going to be like them. I wasn't going to be a pussy like Harold Coker either, running away to fucking Bermuda or something with his tail tucked between his legs.

I couldn't believe I'd ever sought that coward's approval.

Luca Guerra and his family were where it was at all along. Young. Attractive. Ruthless.

That was where my focus needed to be. They would open doors for me that Harold Coker and his old boys' club could never even dream of.

While Harold ran away, I'd be Luca's right-hand man, sticking it out, making sure he got what he needed.

Which was those fucking women who Vaughn apparently had.

I pulled out Harold's throne-like chair and lowered myself into it.

It was right where I belonged.

24

REBEL

"It's so weird to be putting make up on again." Kara swiped a pale-pink gloss over her lips. "It's only been a month or two since I last did this, but it feels like a whole different lifetime ago."

I rubbed my sister's arm gently. "After everything you've been through in the last few weeks, that's understandable."

In the reflection of the mirror beside us, Nova, Winnie, Georgia, and Vivienne all crowded around the bathroom vanity, plucking from the large makeup bag I'd brought over to the clubhouse.

They were all roughly Kara's age, and the big sister inside me who had emerged in Kara's presence, also extended to the women she'd been held captive with.

They'd been through so much. After what Caleb had done to me, and to Bliss, it had bonded the seven of us enough the women had agreed to stay for the concert before they headed back to their hometowns.

It was odd. Though they'd all eagerly called their families, letting them know they were safe, none of them had seemed in a rush to get home. They were sleeping together, the four of them all in a spare room at the clubhouse, even though they'd been offered separate spaces. If they came out of their room, they were always huddled in a group. I'd never once seen any of them alone.

It would be hard to say goodbye. I was glad to have a reason for them to stay a little longer, in a place where they were safe and fed and free to come and go as they wanted. Even if they chose not to.

I brushed a mascara wand over my eyelashes and touched up the thick liner I was fond of.

Bliss nudged me. "Scale of one to ten, how excited are you about tonight?"

I couldn't help the grin that spread across my face. "About eleven billionty. I've loved this band since I was like, fourteen. I know their songs so well I could be *in* the damn band." Something occurred to me, and I widened my eyes at Bliss, grabbing her arm, digging my fingertips in. "What if I'm picked from the crowd to sing with them?"

She winced. "Then the entire stadium will go deaf because your singing is like nails down a chalkboard. But hey! At least you can say you got up on stage."

I hugged her anyway, because I needed somewhere for the pent-up energy to go. Her belly prodded mine, and I patted the top of her baby bump.

"You need to be careful in that crowd tonight," I warned her. "No one can squish Mini-Disney but me."

She pulled away and smiled down at the bump between us. "Don't worry, the guys have already decided they're covering me in bubble wrap. I'm surprised you can't hear Scythe popping it from back here."

I sniggered. "People are going to think you're rich and famous, with a group of us surrounding you, making sure no one bumps you." I held up my old, trusty knuckledusters, the ones I usually kept at Psychos for when people got too drunk and mouthy. "The dusters are making a comeback for the concert." I slipped them into my back pocket, liking the way they felt.

Though with all my guys, as well as Bliss's in tow, the dusters would get about as much of a workout as I did when Kian tried to drag me out for 5:00 a.m. runs.

In other words, none.

But I liked having them there anyway. They'd always made me feel like a badass. As did the music we'd hear tonight. I walked out of the bathroom, proud as hell I'd found my way back to the woman I'd been before.

I was moving on.

Healing.

Vaughn, Kian, and Fang were a huge part of it. So were Kara and Bliss and the world's sweetest baby, who stared up at me when I peered over Queenie's shoulder at Hayley Jade's pretty little face. "Bye, baby girl."

Then I glanced over at War, who was sitting awkwardly on the edge of a couch, looking paler than normal and totally uncomfortable.

"Do I need to pay for some sort of license to use that nickname for her? You do have copyright on the 'baby girl' nickname, right?" I couldn't help the tease. It seriously was pretty much all he called Bliss. She might as well have not even had a legal name.

He winced at me. "You can use it."

I frowned back, not liking he was in pain. "You aren't even going to fight for it?"

"I'm not really up for verbal sparring with you tonight, Rebel."

My gaze traveled to his gunshot wound, and I gasped, storming across to rip aside his jacket. "That's bleeding, War!"

He yanked the jacket back into place and waved his good arm around, motioning for me to be quiet. "It's fine. Don't tell Bliss."

Bliss wandered out of the bathroom, fixing an earring in her lobe. "Don't tell Bliss what?"

"War's wound is bleeding," I announced loudly.

War shot me a murderous look. "I could have you killed right here, Rebel. There's plenty of people here with guns. For fuck's sake."

We both knew he couldn't. Fang, Vaughn, and Kian were all in the other room.

Bliss stormed over and ripped aside his jacket. "You are! You said you were fine!"

"I am!"

She glared at him. "Hawk!"

War rolled his eyes. "Seriously with tattling. All of you are as bad as each other. I'm fine. Let's go."

But he was only halfway to standing before he sank back down on the couch.

Hawk raised an eyebrow from the pool table, pausing with the cue in his hand before he took his shot. "I told you; you can't be out of bed yet. You aren't strong enough. If you'd gone to the hospital like I'd told you, you probably would have been fine by now, but since you're a stubborn asshole, it's taking longer for you to heal. You can't go to that concert."

War sighed. "Fine. I'll go back down to the dungeon and go back to bed."

It was pretty obvious to me, even though he was complaining, that was exactly what he wanted to do.

Bliss stood, putting her arm around his middle. "I'll stay here with you tonight."

War put his fingers beneath her chin and tilted it up, dropping his mouth down on top of hers. "No, baby girl. You won't. You're not coming down there. You're going out, and you're going to have fun, because it won't be long before we're elbows-deep in diapers and bottles." He brushed his thumb over her mouth, cutting off her complaints. "This is Rebel's night, and you're her best friend. I know you want to go."

Bliss looked at me.

I loved War, but he'd be just fine without his girl tonight. She was my girl too.

I gave her the pouty, puppy-dog-eyes face. "Please? Stage diving won't be nearly as fun if you aren't there to catch me."

Fang rubbed a hand over his face wearily. "Please don't do that, Pix. I don't have it in me to kill all the men who'd be touching you."

I blew him a kiss for his pain.

Bliss laughed. "Okay, I'll come. If Hawk promises to watch War. And to call me if anything changes."

Hawk didn't answer.

Bliss prodded him again. "Hawk?"

I glanced over at him. His gaze was pinned on my

sister who had emerged from the bathroom with the others. She had her hair down, covering the stitches Hawk had put in her head. Her hair was long and dark and glossy. We'd gone shopping that morning, and I'd made her buy the little black dress that hugged her curvy figure to perfection. It plunged in the front, showing off a healthy amount of cleavage.

But it was not for Hawk's eyes.

Ew.

I stepped in front of her and scowled at him.

That snapped him out of his stupor, and he smirked, turning back to Bliss and War. "Yeah, yeah. I'll make sure he doesn't die. Go relive Rebel's emo youth."

I gave him the middle finger as everyone else found beers for the trip, except for Nash and Fang and Vaughn, who were all driving.

I had no such qualms. I grabbed a beer and Bliss's hand and tugged her out of the clubhouse toward the waiting cars.

She eyed my drink longingly. "I miss beer."

I squinted at her. "You don't even like beer."

She sighed. "I know! It's so weird. Ever since I got pregnant, it's all I've felt like drinking. Of course, I haven't. But just crack it open and let me smell it."

I giggled, waving the open can beneath her nose.

She inhaled deeply, then opened one eye. "Don't laugh. This will be you one day."

I shook my head. "You just reminded me I can't have beer while pregnant. So that's now put any pregnancy ideas firmly back in the 'no' category."

She narrowed her eyes at me. "*Back* in the 'no' category? Does that mean it was ever out of the 'no' category?"

I sipped my drink and leaned on the car, waiting for the others to follow us outside. "No. Not really. Shit. I don't know. Fang is baby obsessed since Hayley Jade and Kara came to stay with us. You know he just holds her for hours and hours while she sleeps? He changes diapers and everything."

"I noticed. His position is clear. But what's yours?"

"I really love Hayley Jade."

"That's not the same as wanting one of your own."

I nodded. "I know. I don't even know how that would work with Kian and Vaughn in the picture as well. It's a nice thought for one day."

Bliss looked a tad disappointed. "I get it. As much as I would love for Mini-Disney to have a tiny Rebel playmate, it's smart to be safe until you're all ready. I give you guys credit for not getting carried away." She rubbed her belly fondly. "Since that's how we got into this situation."

It was said with so much love I knew that situation was the best thing to have ever happened to Bliss.

I bit my lip. "Yep. Careful. That's totally us. Soooooo careful..."

Bliss glanced at me with one eyebrow raised. "Seriously?"

I huffed out a sigh. "Well, you try thinking about contraception when you've got three men all hell-bent on giving you multiple orgasms! It's hard, Dis!"

We both burst into laughter, and she slung her arm around my shoulders, taking the beer can with her other hand.

"Yeah, okay. No more drinking for you."

"I'm not pregnant."

"Not yet. Get on some birth control, and I'll give this back."

The thought squeezed my heart uncomfortably. "I know we're playing with fire, but…"

"You don't want to stop."

I grimaced. "I want a family. I never really thought about it until you went and got yourself knocked up, but shit, Dis. I really freaking don't want to be alone."

She hugged me close. "You lost your mom. Maybe now isn't the best time to be making big decisions like that."

I nodded. She was right. "Someday, though…"

She leaned back against the car. "Someday we'll have a swing set and a slide installed in that corner of the clubhouse right there. And War will push our kids too high."

I grinned at the idea. "And Fang will stand on the other side, ready to catch them if they go flying off."

She squeezed my fingers. "I can't wait for that. But it doesn't have to be now."

"I know. You're right. There're so many other things we need to sort out first."

Fang and Kian and Vaughn walked toward us in a line, the three of them happily chatting about something. I didn't hear what, but it didn't matter.

Happiness settled over me at the sight of the men I loved.

Vaughn screwed his face up at me as he approached. "Why are you gazing at us like the emoji with the love hearts for eyes?"

I could always count on him to ruin the moment.

"Anyone want to go flash their tits at the guitarist?" I asked chirpily in retaliation.

Bliss was apparently the only one who found that funny.

25

REBEL

The venue attendant opened the door to the box that sat in prime position to the side of the stage. I pushed past the others and ran to the glass doors, letting myself out onto the balcony beyond. "Holy fucking shit. When Kara flashes her tits at the guitarist, we're so close she might even squirt milk on his head!"

Kara went tomato red. "I already told you. I'm not doing that."

But her mouth turned up a little at the corner, and I shot her a wink.

Nova strode by her more conservative friend and joined me on the balcony. She yanked her shirt up and shook her ta-tas toward the stage. There was no band on it yet, but there were a few catcalls from some other concertgoers who were early like we were.

Nova and I collapsed into laughter, leaning on each other as we stumbled back inside the box.

"I love your sister, Kara." Nova flopped down onto a couch.

Nova had been drinking, but not so many she was drunk. When Kara smiled, I knew she was thinking the same thing I was. It was nice to see Nova and the other women letting loose. They deserved it after everything they'd been through.

Music played through the speakers in our box, and we all homed in on the food heaped on a side table, while our own private bartender poured us beer and wine and cocktails that Vivienne was busily sucking down like they were juice.

I had the bartender make me one too, and took a gulping sip from my straw, closing my eyes in pleasure when the fruity flavor exploded across my tongue. Even still, there was a distinct kick of alcohol too, and I eyed the bartender. "How many shots in this?"

"Four."

Yep, I'd be nicely tipsy by the time the band came on. Which, frankly, was the best way to take in a concert in my humble opinion. I gave the bartender a high five for his good work.

"Keep 'em coming," Vaughn told him, sidling up beside me. "That goes for everyone. Open bar." He pushed his credit card over to the bartender.

He put it inside his register. "You got it."

The lights dimmed and I kissed Vaughn's cheek. I ran for the balcony, joining the others who were already out there, waiting in anticipation for the band to come out.

"Rebel! Get up here!" Bliss yanked me forward so I could lean on the railing with her and all the other women surrounding me.

Below us, the stadium was now packed, every seat filled. The excitement was palpable, and it thrummed through me, swirling around with the little buzz I had going from the alcohol and the security of having the most important people in my life by my side.

I stamped my feet on the floor, joining in the building anticipation, and glanced over my shoulder.

The guys all stood shoulder to shoulder, Nash and Vincent with their eyes glued to Bliss.

Vaughn, Fang, and Kian with their eyes glued on me.

"Love you," I mouthed.

The band burst out onto the stage in a cacophony of sound and lights, guitars and drums, and the lead singer's powerful voice filling the stadium.

The scream I let out was one of pure joy. I'd almost forgotten what that felt like. It was sweet and pure, and I did it again when I recognized their biggest hit, "Misery Business."

I jumped up and down like a crazy person, singing every lyric, shouting them back at the lead singer when she looked up in our direction and waved.

I danced like no one was watching. I sang at the top of my lungs, feeling every word to my very core and connecting with the music like I never had when it was just playing through my headphones.

The bartender kept up the drinks, just like Vaughn had told him to, and I felt like a complete and utter VIP.

Halfway through their set, with a pounding heart, I caught a glimpse of Vaughn.

He had his sleeves rolled up, the neck of his shirt open. His gaze trained down on the band below us, until he noticed me watching him.

"You having fun, Roach?"

Fun didn't even begin to describe what I was feeling. I

suspected I wouldn't even be able to articulate with words how I felt to be here and see this band live after loving them for so long. This was my happy place.

And he'd given it to me.

With one of my favorite songs belting out on the stage below me, I grabbed Vaughn's hand and towed him back inside the box.

He followed after me, his steps shortened to match my strides. "Where are we going?"

I tugged him into the box's private bathroom and slammed the door shut.

I was on him in a second, going straight for his pants, undoing the button on his fly, and shoving the fabric down his legs.

He caught my wrists. "Whoa, whoa. What are you doing? You're going to miss the show!"

I shook my head with a wicked grin. I could hear plenty. The music was so loud, they probably could have heard it blocks away. I pulled his head down so his lips were barely above mine. "This is my favorite song. I want you inside me while it's playing."

He groaned and sank his lips down on mine. His tongue pushed its way inside my mouth, and I put my arms around his neck. He picked me up easily with one arm, helped along by the fact I was ready to climb him like a tree. He carried me to the bathroom vanity, sitting my ass on the edge of it.

I reached beneath my short skirt and lifted my ass, wiggling out of my underwear, letting them drop on the floor.

He shoved his down, freeing his thickening erection.

He flipped my skirt up and gripped my thighs, his fingertips pressing into my flesh as he spread me.

"Fuck," he groaned. "I could just look at you all day."

I didn't have all day. The music pounding in my ears demanded more than just him looking at me. It demanded action. Release.

I grasped his collar and yanked him closer. "Hurry. Before it ends."

He ran his hand down my back to my ass, drawing me closer, right onto the edge.

And then he slammed his way inside me.

"Oh!" The stretch was instant and satisfying. I didn't need any foreplay. Just being here, knowing he wanted me, was all I needed to get me wet. He slid out then pushed back in.

I grabbed his ass, encouraging him to fuck me fast. Hard. I locked my ankles behind his back, moaning with every deep thrust that filled me to the brim.

I leaned back on the mirror, and he yanked my shirt up, exposing my belly and my tits.

He gazed down at me. "Look at you." He shook his head, his eyes full of awe.

He tweaked my nipple, and I clenched around his cock.

His fingers lowered to my clit, rubbing at the tight bud while he thrust in and out of me. "Look at you needing my cock in the middle of a concert." He groaned, leaning over to lick my nipple. "I fucking love you. You're everything I ever wanted, Roach. You know that?"

The pace he set on my clit had me so close to orgasm I could barely answer. I moaned, short little 'ohs' that came out stilted because he was driving into me so hard I had to hold on to the edge of the vanity to keep from being thrust right into the mirror behind me.

It was exactly what I wanted. The band's magic in my ears. Vaughn working his own on my body. I let it all combine, closed my eyes, and let go.

The orgasm was as sweet as floating. It washed over me in a wave, sending my core into happy little pulses that sent Vaughn spiraling into an orgasm of his own.

He kissed me, and it was all need and desire, but when I kissed him back, and he slowed his movements, I felt the love in it too. I sat up straighter, putting my arms around his neck so I could whisper in his ear, "I love you too."

Breathing hard, completely spent, we stayed there as one song led into another, him still inside me.

I didn't want it to end. Him. This night. Any of it.

A knock came from the door. "Ah, guys? If you're done, I got a baby pressing on my bladder and I really need to go."

Vaughn smiled softly against my mouth. He pulled out and cleaned up, tucking his dick back inside his pants. He crouched to retrieve my panties and knelt at my feet, sliding them up into place for me. His fingers lingered there between my legs, nudging my clit one last time before he opened the door.

"I'll leave you two to it," he said to Bliss, passing her by with a sated smile.

She rolled her eyes at him but rushed into the bathroom, not bothered by the fact I was still trying to get myself together.

She stared at the toilet paper roll holder. Then turned to me, eyes wide with horror. "Oh my God, no! Please tell me there's more paper. I really need to go."

I searched around with her, opening the vanity door and finding nothing.

Kara came in behind us and stopped abruptly. "Uh, hi? What's going on in here?"

"No toilet paper," I told her.

She cringed. "My bladder is about to burst. Those cocktails are huge."

I couldn't have that. I stepped out of the bathroom. Everyone else was outside on the balcony, dancing and singing and having a good time. Only the bartender remained inside, moving around the room, cleaning up the mess we'd made.

I gripped his arm. "Is there more toilet paper somewhere?"

He glanced over toward the bathroom. "There's none?"

I shook my head. "And I have one pregnant lady, and one recently pregnant lady, both needing to go. As do I, come to think of it. Can we get some more please?"

He frowned. "I can call the cleaners to come in here, but it might take a while, they'll be busy taking care of the bathrooms on the main floors. You'd probably be better off just going down there if you're all really desperate."

I nodded eagerly, pretty turned off to the idea of getting an infection because I didn't go after having sex. "That'll do."

Bliss and Kara came up behind me to see what was going on, and the bartender grimaced. Probably because Bliss looked ready to cry and Kara was standing with her legs half crossed.

He pointed to the door behind the bar. "I'm really sorry about this. Go down via the staff corridors. That'll lead you out right to a bathroom."

Bliss didn't need telling twice. She grabbed my hand and towed me to the door, Kara following right behind.

"I'm sorry," Bliss babbled as we hurried down a long, steep flight of stairs that would presumably let us out on the ground floor. "You just have no idea what it's like. One minute I'm fine, then the baby shifts positions and I feel like I'm going to make a puddle on the floor."

"Been there," Kara called from behind us. "It's the worst. It's not much better after you have the baby either, to be honest. That cocktail was a mistake."

We got to the bottom of the stairs right when the doors opened and people spilled out, all heading toward the exits.

"Oh damn, that must have been the last song," I complained.

Bliss quickened her pace. "All the more reason for us to get to the bathrooms now before there's a huge line. Let's go!"

She strode toward the signs marked bathrooms like a woman on a mission. "I'll text the guys and tell them to meet us down here somewhere. No point us going back up there when they'll be down soon."

The three of us managed to get to the bathrooms before the masses, but the crowds were worse when we got out. There were too many people, all trying to get out of a handful of narrow exits, and a lot of them were drunk and boisterous. I shot a worried look at Kara as the crowd closed in around us, and the two of us fought to keep people away from Bliss and her bump.

The closer we got to the exit, the worse the crush became. People around us started complaining, and an argument broke out to our left.

"I don't like this," Bliss murmured to me.

Neither did I. There was an anxious feeling in the pit of my stomach that warned shit was about to get out of hand. I had no idea where the guys were, but even if they were nearby, they weren't going to be able to do anything when they couldn't get to us.

An emergency exit sign lit up a door just ahead, and I was amazed no one had opened it yet. But maybe they weren't trying to protect their best friend's baby from crush injuries or accidentally ending up in the middle of a fight.

Fuck waiting for some underpaid official to decide there was a danger here.

I herded Kara and Bliss in that direction, fighting the flow of people who tried to force us deeper into the crowd.

Kara's eyes were wide, and she gripped my fingers tightly. "There's too many people!"

There wouldn't be when I got that door open.

I fell hard onto the handle and nearly cried in relief when it opened into the cold night air.

The crowd behind us decided they were all taking this newfound exit too, and we were shoved out the door, people cheering behind us.

I breathed hard, the imminent danger passing, but I

was still eager to get back to our group. Bliss, Kara, and I walked fast, the three of us clutching each other tight while my heart hammered.

"That was not how I anticipated this night ending."

"Me neither." Bliss gazed around as we walked along the road that seemed to ring the stadium. "Do you guys know where we are? This isn't the side we came in on, is it?"

I didn't recognize it either. "I think we came in a different entrance altogether."

My phone buzzed in my pocket, and Fang's number showed on the screen. I answered it. "Hey, you."

"Where are you?" Fang practically growled into the phone.

Kara giggled, obviously able to hear him even from next to me. "You're in trouble."

I grinned. "I actually don't know," I told Fang. "Somewhere outside the stadium. I think we're walking in the direction of the parking lot though, so just meet us there. Damn, there's people everywhere. Did you enjoy the show?"

"I enjoyed watching you enjoy it. Kian is tracking your phone. Keep going. You'll hit the parking garage in about another five minutes." He paused. "Maybe six, if you're walking at Bliss's waddle rate."

"I heard that," she complained. Though she was indeed walking very slowly and had her hands supporting her bump.

I didn't like her pained expression. Cars whizzed by to her right, but there was a seat just a little up ahead. "Do you want to sit for a mom—"

A plain white van screeched around the corner,

bumping up onto the sidewalk. On instinct, I dropped my phone to grab Bliss, hauling her out of the way of the out-of-control vehicle.

It stopped mere inches from her, the sliding door opening, revealing a man dressed in all black.

Including a mask.

Terror hit me hard, freezing me to the spot.

"Get in the van!" His fingers gripped Bliss by the arm, tightly yanking her toward him.

I didn't think. I couldn't breathe.

Everything slowed down, and I went into autopilot, shoving Kara out of the way and screaming for her to run.

Before pulling out my knuckle-dusters, ready for the fight.

26

HAYDEN

The infirmary steps creaked and groaned, a sure signal someone was coming down them.

I froze in my search of the small facility beneath the Slayers' clubhouse. Two sets of boots clomped down the stairs.

"Shit," I whispered to myself, so softly it was barely audible beneath the racket they were making. I darted back to my bed and got beneath the covers, closing my eyes and faking sleep, even though my heart hammered behind my chest.

I'd been here for days. Hours of nothingness had passed, my only entertainment the voices that floated down from the floor above.

The Slayers hadn't killed me yet, but I was well aware they were just waiting for the right moment. I had nothing to do, except plan a way to get out that didn't involve a body bag.

My ideas all sucked though. The best I could come up with was to make out like my injuries were worse than they actually were. Like I was too riddled with pain to be of use to them yet. So far, that seemed to be working. I was still alive anyway.

My injuries were bad, there was no denying that. I was sure every single one of my ribs was broken. My gunshot wound didn't seem infected, thanks to whatever that Hawk guy had hooked me up to, but it sure as shit didn't feel good either.

I was hardly about to jump out of bed and run a half marathon. Hell, a stagger to the bathroom was about the best I could hope for.

But I wasn't as unwell as I was letting the Slayers believe. Every time anyone came down here, I put on the show of my life, either feigning sleep or moaning like I was in agony until they passed me a couple of pills I pretended to swallow.

I didn't.

I didn't need anything making me slow or foggy, though the pain relief would have been nice.

I needed every brain cell functioning if I was getting out of here with my life.

"You have a fucking fever, War. I can feel it through my shirt. You're like an inferno."

War and Hawk made it to the bottom of the stairs, War's arm slung across Hawk's shoulders. Hawk was definitely doing most of the heavy lifting there. He pretty much carried War to the bed beside me, dumping him on it unceremoniously while I watched on through my eyelashes.

War groaned, lying back on the pillow that was almost the same shade of white as his face. "Give me the good drugs, would you? I don't know what I was thinking, trying to go to that concert."

Hawk sucked up something in a syringe and jabbed it into War's bicep. "Don't get excited. That's an antibiotic, not a painkiller. I think I'm gonna let you suffer a little bit, just to keep it fresh in your head what a dumbass you are."

War glared at him. "You'd have done the same if it was your girl out there, needing protecting."

Hawk scoffed. "No, I would not. I ain't made for just one woman. That's why I got club hos. I get my dick sucked whenever I want, but no commitment. When I get bored of one, I can go right on over to the next, and nobody makes a fuss." He shoved War's good shoulder, pushing him down farther on the bed. "See how nice and simple that is? It also means that if I'm shot, I stay in my fucking bed and heal instead of chasing around a woman. See how that might have helped you here?"

War twisted uncomfortably and pulled his gun out from the small of his back, leaving it to the side of the mattress.

If anyone had been watching me, I was sure they would have seen my eyes light up. The gun was right fucking there, and the two of them were so preoccupied with their argument there was a chance I could take it before either of them noticed.

It was a ridiculous plan. One that would never work. But desperate times called for desperate measures. I probably wasn't going to get another chance.

One quick lunge, and it would be in my hands.

It would hurt like fucking hell.

My ribs were already screaming this was the worst idea ever.

And yet, I was going to do it anyway.

"You're so full of shit," War told Hawk. "I've seen the way you stare at Kara. You have the hots so fucking bad."

I froze at the mention of Kara's name.

So did Hawk.

War smirked. "Told you."

Hawk shook his head. "Fine. She's gorgeous. All ass and tits." He groaned. "What I wouldn't give to have her down on her knees, fingering her sweet pussy while she sucks my cock—"

They both turned in my direction.

It was only then that I became aware of the deep growl I was making and the rage coursing through my blood at the thought of another man looking at her. "Don't fucking talk about her like that."

The words were low. Guttural. Full of violence.

Hawk raised an eyebrow. "Excuse me?"

"You fucking heard me. Don't talk about her like that."

Hawk laughed, sauntering from his worktable to stand in the middle of the two beds War and I lay on. He peered down at me, crossing his arms over his broad chest. "Gotta crush on our new club girl, do we there, Chaos? Little bit jealous she was up there, showing me all those pretty curves, making me think about her riding my fat cock with her tits bouncing in my face?"

I couldn't stand it. I sat up, slowly swinging my legs over the edge of the bed. It was about all the energy I had, but it brought us closer to eye height. "I said, don't fucking talk about her like that."

Hawk got in my face. "Or what, Sinner? What are you going to do? You're nothing but a wannabe gangbanger who wanted to be a Slayer but knew you weren't good enough."

I shot a look at War. I don't know why I was surprised he'd told him my story. But it pissed me off anyway.

Hawk chuckled. "Yeah, he told me your sob story, how you wanted to be one of us, but life led you down the wrong path, blah, blah, blah."

He slapped the side of my face twice, both times condescendingly. "Sorry you couldn't cut it, little boy. Don't worry, I'll make sure Kara is very well taken care of for you."

There was so much anger coiled inside me I was sure I was vibrating with it. If someone had asked, I couldn't have even explained why. I barely knew Kara. I'd spent a matter of days in her company.

Yet, something deep inside me had already claimed her. It had claimed her from the minute I'd laid eyes on her. And again when she'd stared at me with big, vulnerable eyes that begged me to help her deliver her baby safely into the world.

There was a bond there that was instant and binding. It had a grip on me I couldn't shake. She'd been so vulnerable, and all I wanted was to protect her.

Hawk so much as muttering her name made me want to murder him.

War cleared his throat, obviously tired of this conversation. "Knock it off, the both of you."

But Hawk was on a roll, enjoying his mini power trip. He trailed his fingers along the edge of my bed. "Should have seen her tonight, Chaos." He made the 'chef's kiss' motion, touching his fingers to his lips then flicking them open to the air. "The dress swung around her hips, and fuck me, they're so grabbable. Front of it was all low-cut, tits spilling over, perfect fucking handfuls plus some." He groaned.

I couldn't bear it. In my mind's eye, I saw everything he described. Kara in a long dress that accentuated every curve, her hair brushed out and glossy, nothing like it had been the last time I'd seen her.

I fucking hated he'd seen her like that. Hated that I hadn't.

Hawk turned to War. "Get a load of this guy, fucking thrumming so hard I could use him as a vibrator."

Hawk had his Slayers cut on, the leather vest embroidered with their logo, but it was caught up at the back.

Hooked on his gun.

I pulled the weapon from the back of his jeans and pressed it to the middle of his back.

Hawk froze.

There was a long silence where nobody moved.

Hawk was the one who broke it. "You'd better fucking kill me, prick. Or I *will* kill you."

War reached for his gun.

"Don't," I snapped at him. "After all the fucking shit that just spewed from his mouth, I have no problem pressing the trigger."

War nodded slowly, backing his fingers away from the weapon.

I didn't move, just stood there, my brain racing.

"Go," War said before I could come to any sort of conclusion.

I looked at him sharply.

So did Hawk. "You didn't just say what I think you said, did you?"

War nodded toward the door. "I said go, Hayden."

Hawk stared at his best friend.

War sighed. "What am I gonna fucking do? He's Liam's brother. He and his partners are our friends. Plus, Hayden isn't even the one who ordered the hit on my old man."

"Bullshit!"

"It's true," I spoke up. "I gave Caleb the contact. It's one our old prez had used, and I knew they were good. But it was Caleb who wanted Army gone. He knew too much about what Caleb was doing. When he tried to back out of the deal, Caleb saw him as a loose end that needed dealing with." I shook my head. "Same thing he did to me. Just collateral fucking damage because we were both stupid enough to get in with some rich, white businessman who promised the world and delivered shit on a platter."

"Save me the fucking sob story for when you don't have a gun pressed between my shoulders," Hawk spat out through gritted teeth.

I stared at War. "I'm telling the truth."

I was. Every word of it.

He nodded. "I believe you. Go."

I couldn't see Hawk's face, but from the way he stood, he was anything but happy.

I backed away slowly, waiting for the other shoe to drop. For War to point his gun at me. For the door at the top of the stairs to be locked. My gaze never left War's, the two of us staring each other down.

But there was something that felt almost like mutual respect in the standoff.

At least for now.

I wasn't stupid enough to think it would extend past this moment.

But it was enough. I'd take it.

I walked backward up the stairs, and when I hit the door, reached behind me to open it.

"I'll fuck your girl real nice and sweet tonight, Chaos. Deep and slow, until she's crying out my name, coming on my cock, tits trembling as she orgasms."

Hawk was a stupidly attractive man, and Kara was beautiful. I could hardly blame either of them.

But jealousy surged through my blood.

I blamed that for the petty way I lowered the gun, aiming it at Hawk's calf.

I pulled the trigger.

I was out the door and halfway down the hall before I heard his howl of pain.

Mixed in with War's hysterical laughter.

"What the fuck is going on?" a big guy shouted from the common rooms. He stepped in front of me, seemingly not bothered by the fact I had a gun in my hand that I was clearly not afraid to use. They would have all heard the shot.

"Let him go, Aloha," War called from down below. "He's free to leave." The laughter was still fresh in his voice.

Aloha frowned but edged around me, giving me and the gun a wide berth. He planted himself right between me and a woman holding a tiny baby.

My heart stopped. "Is that Kara's baby?"

Rebel Heart

The woman glanced up at me so sharply, I knew instantly that it was. She didn't need to confirm it. I inched closer, but Aloha glared at me.

I was clearly losing my mind. But I offered him the gun. "I won't hurt her, I swear. Please. Just let me see her."

Aloha looked back at the woman who shook her head, shielding the little girl with her body.

But it was enough.

Enough for something deep inside to whisper, *mine*.

27

KIAN

Nova spun Winnie in a circle, the two of them laughing and singing the lyrics of a song we'd heard earlier in the night. I danced with them, doing my best 'running man' as we walked toward the parking station where we'd left the cars.

Vaughn shook his head at me, but his step was light too.

I caught his fingers, pressing mine between his. "Thanks for tonight. It was fun. Not as good as Britney would have been, but I give them props for trying. Where did you and Rebel disappear to at the end there?"

He grinned at me. "I'll ask her if she's up for a replay when we get home."

"With me watching?"

"What do you think?"

I glanced at Fang, getting kind of hot at the idea of a repeat of what had happened at the gym that night.

But Fang was already on his phone, his face as dark as

a thundercloud. He'd been like that ever since we'd realized Rebel, Bliss, and Kara weren't in the box when it had been time to leave. He'd been like a kettle about to burst its top at the fact he hadn't been able to get a call through to Rebel until just now, thanks to hundreds of thousands of other people all trying to make arrangements to get home at the same time.

"Where are you?" Fang practically growled into the phone.

He paused for a moment, and I watched him, wanting to know what was going on.

He dropped the phone away from his mouth. "Can you track her? They came out a different exit. I want to know where she is."

I nodded, opening the app on my phone that showed a Rebel avatar, traveling along a map. "She's not far. Five-minute walk, tops. Tell her it'd be quicker if she ran."

Nash pinned me with a glare. "Do not try to make them do cardio right now, O'Malley. Bliss is about as fast as a snail these days, and that's exactly how it should be when she's growing a baby. I do not want her trying to run because you have an exercise obsession."

I looked up from the little symbol on the screen that was indeed moving very slowly. I tapped Nash on the belly. "Anytime you want to train with me, I'd be up for it. I can get you those six-pack abs everyone wants."

He frowned at me. "I have abs."

Vincent or Scythe, I wasn't ever sure which, scoffed, "Yeah, sure you do. They're just hidden beneath the dad bod."

Truthfully, I could tell from just one tap of Nash's

midsection that the guy was ripped. But Scythe seemed delighted to have a reason to tease him, so I kept quiet with a smirk.

I went back to watching the tracker on the screen, with Fang staring over my shoulder.

A small amount of fight went out of him, seeing how close they were. His voice went deeper, softer, replying to something she'd said. "I enjoyed watching you enjoy it. Kian is tracking your phone. Keep going. You'll hit the parking garage in about another five minutes." He paused. "Maybe six, if you're walking at Bliss's waddle rate."

There was a small smile on his face.

So when it fell a moment later, I wasn't sure what to make of it.

His hand dropped away from his ear, and suddenly he was running. His long legs ate up the pavement, his boots heavy, arms swinging.

"Fang!"

"Something's happened," he shouted back. "Something bad."

I stared down at the tracker.

It wasn't moving.

They'd stopped walking.

I didn't need to know why. If Fang thought it was bad enough to run, then so did I.

Vaughn, Nash, and Scythe all had the same idea.

But I was faster and more agile thanks to decades of team sports and years of fight practice. I darted my way through the thinning crowd, catching Fang and then outpacing him. I searched every face in the crowd, praying Fang had misunderstood and the three women would appear in front of me, their arms linked, wide smiles on their happy faces, laughing at us for misreading the circumstances.

Instead, it was Kara's face that came into view, her eyes wide in terror, tears mixing with her mascara and running down her face in tracks. "Kian!"

I grabbed her by the shoulders, quickly checking her for injuries, but she didn't seem hurt. Just terrified. "Rebel...Bliss..."

"Where?" I shouted at her.

All she could do was point as her bottom lip shook violently.

She was here, safe. I couldn't stay to comfort her when Rebel and Bliss might not be.

I left her and ran, rounding the corner of the stadium, heading for the screams I could suddenly hear now that I was in sight of a masked man hauling Bliss toward a van.

And Rebel putting herself in between so he couldn't.

Metal knuckle-dusters glinting on her hands, she laid quick, sharp punches into the man's midsection, taking him by surprise enough he let Bliss go.

She stumbled away with a cry of terror, clutching her belly.

But that left the man with his hands free to focus on my girl. She was giving it all she had, a tiny terror, letting go of every bit of anger on a man a foot taller than she was.

But she was doing everything right. She was low. Quick. Even from here, I could see the expression in her eye that told me this was her fight.

This was the one she'd been waiting for, ever since that night Caleb and his friends had attacked her. This was her moment to prove to herself she could still be the woman she'd thought she was.

And she was kicking ass.

The low punch to the guy's junk had me groaning internally but mentally high-fiving her. She stomped his foot, dodged his swings.

She moved like a fighter.

She'd never needed me to teach her how to fight. She hadn't needed runs or boxing bags or fancy techniques.

The girl had worked at Psychos long enough to know a thing or two. She might have lost her confidence for a minute there, but Rebel was back, kicking ass and taking names.

Until the guy caught her around the waist, lifting her off the ground.

She kicked and scratched and fought, twisting in his arms, screaming insults at him at the top of her lungs.

My heart stopped, watching him toss her into that van, her back hitting the metal with a bone-jarring thud.

"Get in! Get in!" the driver yelled. "One will do!"

My stomach turned, nauseated. I was sure I recognized Caleb's voice, even though I couldn't see the driver behind his mask.

How the fuck did he know where they were? Had he been watching us this entire time?

But there was no time for questions. I was nearly there. Nearly within arm's reach. I pushed my body to the limit, a roar bellowing from somewhere deep within me.

I was going to be too late. I wasn't going to freaking get there.

Bliss ran in, grabbing the man's jacket, hauling him back as he tried to get in the van.

Rebel launched herself at him at the same time like some pro wrestler jumping off the corner buckles, using her body weight, and the fact Bliss already had him off balance, to send the man backward onto the grass at the edge of the road.

I was on him a second later, red haze covering my eyes. I ripped his mask off and held him down so Rebel could do her worst.

With a squeal of tires and the sliding door still open, the van sped away, Caleb leaving his friend for dead.

Dead he was going to be if I let Rebel keep going. The guy's face was a mess thanks to those knuckle-dusters and her vicious fury. He was barely moving beneath me.

"Hey, Little Demon. You won. He's tapped out."

She just kept going, her fists slamming against his skin until Fang pulled her off him.

On instinct, she went to punch him too, the fury inside her evident from the wild, unfocused expression in her eye.

I knew that look. It came from fighting for your life.

The gleam of victory as Fang held her and talked her down came next. She stared at the bloodied man, breathing hard, taking in what she'd done.

"I won?" she asked.

I cringed at the guy's face while sirens wailed nearby. "You definitely won. He ain't getting up anytime soon."

Rebel broke free of Fang's hold, her entire body vibrating, likely thanks to the adrenaline.

I grinned at her. I knew exactly what it felt like when you won the fight you didn't think possible.

It was hot and heady and exciting. Addicting.

I could see her feeling all those things too. And more.

A couple of beat cops arrived in a wail of sirens. They sent for backup and an ambulance when we explained what had happened. There were dozens of witnesses, and the guy Rebel had taken down was loaded and driven away while the cops finished up the last of the statements.

We stood in a huddle, watching them leave. Nash and Scythe had Bliss sandwiched between them, and the women stood around Kara in the same way Vaughn, Fang, and I circled Rebel.

"That guy was one of the Sinners," Fang said quietly. The last of the crowd of onlookers disappeared, leaving just our group. "I recognized him."

"And that was Caleb in the front," Bliss said in a wobbly voice. "I know his voice." She turned her face into Nash's chest.

He put his arm around her, rubbing her back softly. Over her head he said to the rest of us, "We're taking her to the hospital to get checked out. Can you get them all back to the clubhouse?"

We had my truck and Vaughn's car, so I nodded. We all walked slowly back to the parking garage, Rebel shooting worried glances at her best friend, who assured her she and the baby were both fine.

But even I could see the worry in Bliss's eyes. Scythe and Nash put her into his Jeep, and the three of them took off for the hospital.

Vaughn unlocked his car, and most of the women piled in there, quieter than I'd ever seen them, demons in their eyes.

Fang got into the truck beside me. "They don't look good. Do they?"

They looked like women who had been through too much, too many times. I already knew they'd be gone by the end of the week. Too much had happened here, and this was just the straw that would break the camel's back.

Rebel got into the back seat of my truck and put her arm around Kara, who burst into tears, crying on her sister's shoulder. "I'm so sorry. I'm so sorry."

Rebel shushed her. "Why are you apologizing? None of this was your fault."

"Of course it is! I just ran away! I left you!"

Rebel hugged her sister tight. "You didn't. I pushed you away. Told you to run. You did exactly what I wanted you to do. You kept yourself out of danger. You were amazing."

Kara sniffed. "You were the one who pulverized that guy's face!"

"Yeah. I did."

I glanced into the rearview mirror, and she was grinning from ear to ear.

We drove back to the clubhouse mostly in silence, all of us lost to our own thoughts. Fang reached a hand back for Rebel's, the two of them driving home like that, even though it had to be killing his shoulder.

We drove through the clubhouse gates, and I slowed when Ice waved us down.

"What's going on?" Fang asked him.

"So...Hawk kinda got shot."

Fang blinked. "What? Here? By who?"

"Long story." Ice turned to Kara. "Hay Jay is fine, though. Queenie told me to make sure I told you.

Queenie has her, and she's been fed, and she's had a nap, and I dunno, other good baby shit. Burped and farted or whatever." He turned back to Fang, switching topics. "It really wasn't that big a deal. But Aloha took War to the hospital because he was threatening to ride there himself after Nash called him about Bliss. And you saw him, he needs a fucking hospital himself. Couldn't have him falling off his damn bike halfway. He said to tell you to deal with Hawk."

Fang groaned. "That'll be fun. Thanks for the update, though."

Ice saluted him and closed the gates behind us after we rolled on through.

Kara got out the second I got to the clubhouse door, running into the building, searching for her baby. I was pretty sure she was never going to leave that kid's side again.

Fang got out too, pausing before he closed the door. "I gotta go deal with whatever the hell this situation is. You two coming in?"

I went to say yes, but Rebel climbed between the two front seats, which probably would have been impossible for anyone else but a short-ass like her to manage. "Can you take me somewhere first?" she asked me.

"Anywhere."

She leaned out the window and kissed Fang. "We'll be back. I just can't be in there right now. I need a minute. Or an hour, I guess. We'll be back."

He didn't question her. He never did. He just gave her whatever she needed, and right now, that seemed to be me, and this car, and maybe an open road.

I got it because it was exactly what I needed too.

Somewhere for the energy to flow. For it to be released. It was too big and raw and powerful for it to be contained.

"Whatever you need." He stared at me. "Keep her safe."

"Always."

He shut the door, and I turned the car around, thanking Ice when he let us back out onto the road that ran through the woods. I put my foot down and cracked the windows open, letting the cold night air pour in.

She watched me quietly. "You know this feeling, don't you?"

"Why do you think I like fighting?"

She leaned back on her seat, her hands tucked behind her head. "I get it. It feels fucking good."

"Where do you want to go?"

"I don't know. Anywhere? Nowhere? Take me somewhere I've never been." Then she glanced at me. "But not too far away, because I don't want to leave Kara alone too long."

I screwed up my face. "Somewhere you've never been, but inside Saint View…"

"Yeah. That. Take me there."

"You've lived here all your life. Where wouldn't you have been?"

She shrugged. "There's gotta be somewhere."

An idea popped into my head. It was late enough no one else would be there. "Ever been on a construction site?"

Her head whipped over to me. "We're going to your work? Can I drive one of those huge-ass digging machines?"

I raised an eyebrow. "Do you have any idea how?"

"Nope! But damn, that's some big-dick energy sorta thing. And right now, that's my vibe. I wanna drive it."

I shook my head but then took a leaf out of Fang's book.

And gave my girl whatever the hell she wanted.

28

REBEL

I wasn't going to think about the fact Caleb had very nearly captured my best friend.

Or that his voice still sent shards of fear spearing straight through my heart.

What I was going to concentrate on was I'd won.

For the first time since he'd sat at the end of a bar, flirting with me, and calling himself by a different name, I'd beaten Caleb at his own game.

If I'd done it once, I could do it again.

I could end him for good.

The power in that single idea had me so hot and wired and just bursting out of my own skin, I could barely stand it.

The truck cab felt too small. Claustrophobic. I had to have the windows down. The music loud.

When we parked at the darkened construction site, Kian turned off the truck, and we both got out. I gazed around. There wasn't exactly a lot to see. The site was huge, with multiple buildings being constructed all at once and all in various stages of development. Some had frames up that made it clear what sort of structure was to be built there, but others hadn't even had the slabs poured.

There were some lights around the perimeter fence, presumably to keep trespassers at bay, but Kian scoffed when I asked if there were security cameras. "None anyone checks. They're just for show. Why? You worried about getting caught?" He linked his fingers through mine and tugged me toward the gate. It was padlocked, but there was a little key on his keyring that had it undone in seconds. He pulled the chain from the gate and motioned me through. "After you."

I slipped past him and then spun in a circle beneath the moonlight. "So. Give me the tour."

He picked up my fingers again and led me into the darkness. "Well, this whole area is going to be a shopping village. So, see here, this is where shop fronts will be." He waved his arms in the opposite direction. "It's hard to imagine it right now, but this is where a multi-story parking garage will be erected. Careful of those reinforcement bars, they can have barbs."

I edged toward a deep, dug-out hole, but Kian grabbed my arm.

"Don't get too close to that either. They're holes we dug for the supports. The edges are crumbly, and if you fall down there, there's no easy way of getting back out. I watched one of the other guys do it just the other day."

I peered down into the hole. It was at least fifteen feet down and pitch black at the bottom. "Damn. Was he hurt?"

Kian grinned and shook his head. "Nah, but it was

pretty funny listening to him shout for help and jump up and down, trying to get out. We left him there for a bit before sending a ladder down for him."

I rolled my eyes. "Super mature."

He shrugged. "Hey, that's what you get for getting too close. He should have known better."

I paid attention to the warning, and watched where I walked, using the flashlight on my phone the farther we got away from the perimeter lights.

I tapped the side of a cement mixer. "Do you ever use this?" A memory jogged loose in my brain. "I think my dad worked on a construction site once when I was a kid. I remember watching the cement mixers turn around and around. They were kind of mesmerizing. At least to my four- or five-year-old brain." I cocked my head, studying the machine. "How do you even get the cement all up in there?"

"Pretty simple. Cement powder and water go there. Press the button here, and the machine does the work for you." Kian pointed out all the various parts as he explained. "But cement work is boring if you ask me. Excavators are where it's at."

I tugged him toward one. "Is this like the jock table versus the nerd table at high school?"

He laughed. "Pretty much. The excavator table is definitely the popular clique."

"And you're the star quarterback already, aren't you? Mr. Popularity." It was easy to imagine. Kian was so outgoing and funny, I doubted he ever wasn't the most popular person in the room. Or the worksite, as the case may be here. Even though he hadn't worked here that long.

He winked at me as he drew the ladder down from the biggest excavator I think I'd ever seen in my life. I wasn't even close to as tall as just one of its wheels.

"Whoa. Is this yours?"

He put a foot on the bottom rung. "Yep. Follow me up. You said you wanted to drive it."

"Hell yes, I do." The thing was a beast, and I was already imagining the rumble of power when it started.

I followed him up, sticking close behind him, and pausing when he got to the top and settled in at the controls.

I surveyed the tiny cabin. "Where am I supposed to sit?"

He pointed to his lap. "Right here."

I had to admit, it was the best seat in the house. I sank down onto his thighs, and he immediately put one arm around me, his hand flattening on my belly. His lips came to my neck and sucked gently.

Pleasure shot through me, and I let my eyes drift closed, enjoying the touch of his lips at my neck and his warm hand wandering up my torso toward my breasts.

He took a handful and squeezed me there. "Mmm. You feel good. You should come to work with me every day. Would make the day go a whole lot quicker if this was my reward."

I turned my head and kissed him but then pulled away, sitting up straight. "Come on. You promised I could drive this thing. Quit trying to distract me with your wicked ways.

I put my hands on the controls, wincing a little at the ache in my knuckles that had taken a bit of a beating beneath the knuckle-dusters.

Kian covered my hands with his big ones, his thumbs smoothing over my injuries. "I'm sorry I didn't get there quicker."

I shook my head. "I'm glad you didn't. I needed that win."

He lifted one of my hands to his lips, kissing my beat-up fingers, but then put them back on the controls. "Okay, this is how you start it."

The huge machine rumbled to life beneath us.

My eyes went wide. "Holy shit!" I shouted at him above the roar of the engine. "This is insane!"

He laughed and switched our hands on the controls. "This one goes forward and back. This one lowers or raises the bucket. Got it?" He demonstrated, and the arm of the machine pivoted around smoothly.

Seemed fairly straightforward.

But when he took his hands off mine, and I tried to do it myself, the bucket moved in jerks, hitting the ground but not scooping up the dirt like it had when he'd been at the controls.

Kian laughed. "Be gentle with my Petunia. Stroke her slow and easy. She doesn't like being manhandled."

"Petunia? That's what you call her?"

"Pet for short."

I glanced over my shoulder at him. "Ew."

He just laughed. "Come on, dig some dirt."

But no matter how hard I tried; I just could not get the hang of it. I suddenly had a newfound respect for Kian's job. "This is harder than it looks."

"It takes practice." He moved the controls around a bit, making it seem way easier than it actually was. "But it gives you good depth perception. For example, if I stop it here..." He paused the arm of the machine. "I bet you that would be right on your head height."

I squinted down. "No way. That's so close to the ground. Not a chance I'm walking under that."

He raised an eyebrow. "Want to bet? Go down there and test my mad skills."

I snorted, getting up off his lap. "Your mad skills, huh?"

I climbed down the ladder and walked out to where the bucket hung in the air.

To my surprise, it was only a few inches above my head. Low enough for me to reach up and wrap my fingers around the prongs. "Okay, I eat my words. You were right. You have mad skills. And I'm super short. Damn. I really thought you were way off."

He climbed down and sauntered over, cocky as shit.

I rolled my eyes. "Don't let one little compliment go to your head, Kian."

He covered my hands on the bucket with his and leaned down, planting his lips on mine. "I'm not. But you are fucking hot standing there like that."

I pressed my tits against his chest and kissed him back, turned on by both the display of competence as well as the fact he had me pinned.

He murmured something against my lips.

"What was that?" I asked.

"Can I fuck you right now?"

I blinked. "Seriously? Here? At your worksite?"

He tightened his grip on my hands, and his lips trailed down my neck, sucking and licking a path toward my collarbone. "Yeah, Little Demon." He let my hands drop and stooped to pick up a loose tie-down from the dirt. With a wicked gleam in his eyes, he made a loop and fit it around one of my wrists. In a second, a matching one was fit to my other arm, and then they were both raised above my head again. He hooked them over the prong, and the restraints tightened pleasurably against my skin.

"You kinky fuck." I laughed at him.

He gave me his most innocent expression. "What? It's not my fault I've been hard for you all night. Do you know how torturous it was watching you at that concert?"

I grinned. "How torturous?"

He leaned down and toyed with the hem of my cropped T-shirt. "Off the scale."

"I got so horny I had Vaughn fuck me in the bathroom," I admitted.

"I noticed. That didn't help the situation any. Then I was just thinking about the two of you in there... His cock inside your sweet little pussy..." He lifted my shirt to expose my bra, and the shirt was tight enough that it clung, not rolling down. He flipped the cups of my bra down, exposing my nipples to the cold night air. My arms and back were still warm in my jacket, but Kian seemed very intent on getting me as naked as the position allowed.

I let him, not caring about the chill. It only emphasized the heat of his mouth when he ducked his head to taste my nipple.

Pleasure sparked inside me, only to increase when he used his hand to tweak the other side.

He rolled and sucked and licked me there until I begged him for more. I wanted to touch him. To free my hands of the restraints and run my fingers through his hair. Or down his back. Or around his cock. But every time I tried, he covered the restraints and went back to making it all about me.

He found the zipper on the back of my skirt and lowered it. With one sharp tug, the skirt was around my ankles, leaving me with my tits exposed and just a tiny pair of panties covering my mound.

Kian stood back and soaked in the scene, his dick thickening behind his fly.

"Get your cock out."

He raised one eyebrow. "I'm supposed to be the one in control here."

"You are. I'm not moving."

"Not moving anything but your lips." He smirked.

"You could give me something else to do with them."

He stepped in and lowered his mouth so it hovered over mine. "Like what?"

I kissed my way along his stubbled jaw. "Make me scream."

He groaned and dropped to his knees, fitting his fingers to the lace straps at the sides of my hips. Torturously slowly, he lowered them and put his face between my legs.

I moaned softly at the first touch of his tongue to my clit. He flicked the little bud slowly at first, letting me warm up to the sensation, but as my moans became louder, his licks became more insistent. He flattened his tongue between my folds and tortured me with it until I was so wet it was probably dripping.

I spread my legs for him, desperate to be filled with something. His fingers. His cock. I didn't care. I just needed more.

He slid two fingers inside me, and I moaned at the intrusion, but knowing I could take more. A third slid inside me effortlessly, and I rocked on my feet, trying to get him in exactly the right spot.

He crooked his fingers perfectly, and a gasp fell from my lips. I looked up at the restraints and twisted my hands so I was gripping them, then used that to take some of my weight.

With the restraints to balance me, I put one leg over Kian's shoulder, shamelessly opening myself up to him.

"You taste like him," he groaned into my inner thigh. "Fuck, that's hot. Knowing he fucked you hard. Knowing his cock was right here where my tongue is." He speared it up inside me, pushing in as far as he could before replacing it with his fingers again.

I held the restraints tighter, leaning back and letting my head drop, grinding my hips over his face.

"That's it. Take what you need," he encouraged, tongue fucking me faster.

So, I did. I hoisted myself up by the restraints and put my other leg around his neck, locking my ankles behind his back.

He caught me, supporting my weight with his hands on my ass while he ate me out like I was dessert, and he was never going to get it again.

It was the most intense oral I'd ever had, Kian's tongue relentless, his sucking and fingering so perfect, I fell over the edge into an earth-shattering orgasm I hadn't even realized I was so close to.

He rode it out, until my screams died down, but he wasn't close to done.

Thank fuck, because neither was I.

He untangled my legs from around his neck and stood again. This time, I needed the restraints to help hold me up because my knees were so wobbly.

My entire body flushed hot, despite the cold night air. He lifted me onto his cock, sinking it in deep.

I groaned, taking every thick inch of him, feeling the slide of his cock and the fresh round of tingles it lit up inside me. With one thrust, I was on the verge of another orgasm, but he slowed the pace, lifting me off the hook but not undoing the restraints.

I put them over his head and rested them behind his neck, the two of us staring at each other while he was buried deep inside me.

"I love you so fucking much," he murmured. "Everything about you."

I brushed my lips over his. "You're only saying that because I let you fuck me on a construction site."

He laughed but then he shook his head. "I'm saying it because it's true. You surprise me, Rebel Kemp. In all the best ways, do you know that? I never know what I'm going to get with you."

"Some men wouldn't like that," I said quietly. "Common consensus, at least before the three of you came along, was that I'm 'too much.'"

His face clouded over, anger igniting in his eyes. "Fuck any man who ever said that to you. Fuck any person who ever thought it. You are never too much, Rebel. You're wild, and you're crazy, and apparently, I am too when I'm with you. No other woman has ever made me want to fuck them while they're restrained to an excavator bucket. But I don't care. I like who I am when I'm with you. I like who Vaughn and I are when you're in our lives."

I voiced one of the tiny worries that had plagued the space at the back of my mind ever since that night the four of us had had sex at the boxing club. "I don't want to be your third wheel. You guys have a history that goes well beyond the last few months."

He shook his head. "We tried and we failed. Then we spent a decade avoiding each other because we couldn't work it out alone." He smiled against my lips. "We were waiting for you, Little Demon. You were the missing piece."

My heart squeezed, that tiny fear put to rest once and for all thanks to the honesty and surety in his voice.

"Make love to me," I whispered, shifting on his dick. "You asked if you could fuck me, but I'm asking for more."

Something flickered in his eyes, but he nodded, carrying me to the side of the worksite shed and pressing me into the side of it. "It's not candlelight and roses," he admitted on a slow slide into my body.

"I don't need that. Where we are doesn't matter. I just need you."

And that's what he gave me. His mouth. His tongue. His fingers. His dick.

His heart.

We came together, softly and slowly, achingly sweet while he whispered I love yous across my lips.

I said them right back, cementing the feeling in my heart.

It was a long time before we let go of each other. We

stayed there, connected in the moonlight, the setting not romantic, but our feelings all that mattered.

When I finally put my feet to the earth once more, I was sure we'd lost hours, just being together in the moment.

The sun was beginning to rise, casting a soft orange glow across the darkness of the night. I slipped my fingers between Kian's. "The sun coming up feels like our cue to leave."

"Especially because the weekend crew will probably be here in the next thirty minutes." He tugged my skirt down. "As much as I enjoy fucking you with an audience, I don't really want it to be my new colleagues. I should maybe at least go out for a beer with them before I let them watch you come."

"Deal."

I got my underwear back into place and watched the sun creep higher over the horizon while Kian pulled up the zipper on his fly. I leaned back against the tin work shed, fingers brushing over something cold and solid, not made from the same corrugated material as the rest of the shed. I glanced down at it.

"Kian?" I asked quietly. "Were you aware you worked for Caleb's company?"

Kian's head snapped up, his fingers pausing on the button of his pants. "What?"

I pointed at the plaque that had Black Industries and their various license numbers etched into the brass metal.

Kian frowned. "Doesn't he have some consulting business in the city?"

"Yes, but if you Google him, all his businesses come under the umbrella of Black Industries."

Kian squinted at it, then swore low under his breath. "I had no idea. I was hired through a recruitment company, all my paperwork has their company name on it, not Black Industries. He must have outsourced." He shook his head, then grabbed my hand. "I'm so sorry. I'll quit as soon as someone gets here to open the site office."

"Do you think he realizes you work for him?"

Kian rubbed a hand over the back of his neck slowly while he pondered that. "I don't think so. The hiring of grunt staff like me is a minion job. I doubt he'd lower himself."

"Then stay. It might help us to have someone on the inside."

Kian seemed doubtful. "I didn't even know I worked for him, so I doubt anyone is going to be spilling company secrets here."

"Probably not. But you like this job, right?"

He seemed reluctant to admit it, but eventually, he said, "I do."

"Are we really going to let Caleb take yet another thing away from us?"

He sighed. "What's the worst that could happen?"

I looked at him sharply, and he chuckled.

"Okay, yeah, I heard it. We probably can't even imagine the worst that Caleb could come up with, can we?"

Unfortunately, I knew all too well how true that was.

29

VAUGHN

When my bedroom door opened at the ass crack of dawn, I rolled over, expecting Kian or Rebel, preferably both, to be sneaking into my room.

It was a rude awakening when it was a six-foot-six biker leaning on my doorframe with a scowl on his face. "Where's Pix?"

"Good morning to you too. She's out with Kian somewhere. They haven't come home yet."

Fang scowled some more.

"Jealous?" I asked him.

He actually pondered the question for a minute but still came out with, "No."

"I am a bit." I shifted onto my back and put my hands behind my head, sinking a little deeper into the softness of the pillow. "I was hoping you were them."

Fang folded his arms over his chest and shrugged. "I don't want to be jealous over her spending time with people she loves. And who love her. For as long as I've known her, she's always seemed a little...I dunno. Lost, I guess. I think it's what drew me to her in the first place, because fuck knows I was too. I have no family I talk to anymore. No friends until I came here and joined the Slayers. I think Rebel was the same."

"She had her mom."

Fang shook his head. "But she didn't. Not really. I know she loved her mom, and she misses her, but her mom wasn't really her family in anything but blood. Just like her dad isn't."

I didn't like the way that made me feel. I hated the idea of her on her own. "She has Bliss."

Fang nodded. "And Nash. They're as close to a true family as anyone could ever hope for. But I don't think it was enough for her. You know how she is. She needs people around her. People to love on. People who love her in return. I used to hate the idea of her with anyone else. But now, I don't know. I see her with the two of you, and I'm just happy you love her too. I want her to have a family. And maybe I..."

He turned away.

I frowned at him, then let out a snort of laughter. "What the hell, Fang? Are you blushing right now?"

He scowled at me again and stuck his middle finger up in my direction. "Fuck off."

"Finish what you were saying."

He shoved off the doorway. "Doesn't matter."

He stalked away, down the stairs.

Something made me get up and follow him into to the kitchen. "No, come on. Seriously. Tell me."

Fang just put on a pot of coffee, refusing to say anything.

"Maybe you want a family too," I finished for him.

Fang didn't respond.

But his silence was telling.

I walked past him and clapped him on the shoulder. If he could admit his truth, then I could too. I'd taken for granted the family I'd had. My dad had died, and I'd never even told him how much I admired the man he was.

I wouldn't do that again. Not with the family I was creating for myself. "Me too, bro. Me too."

He glanced at me. An understanding passed between us in the early morning light. He poured two mugs of steaming dark coffee and handed one of them to me.

We were completely silent when a noise came from the front door and both of us looked over to see a white card fall through the mail slot.

"No fucking way." Fang slammed his mug down on the kitchen counter, not even wincing when hot coffee sloshed over the brim and onto his hand.

I dropped mine into the sink, not giving a shit when the telltale sound of broken ceramic echoed back at me.

In unison, Fang and I bolted for the door.

Anger raced through me. A complete and utter rage at the person on the other side who dared to threaten my family.

Because that's what we'd become. That's what Rebel had made us. The discussion with Fang had just confirmed it.

This shit with the cards and the threats ended here. Whoever it was could balls up and face us like men.

Fang's legs were longer, and he beat me to it, yanking

the door open wide, simultaneously taking his gun from the back of his jeans. "Hey!"

Both of us blinked in astonishment at the face on the other side.

A kid of maybe ten or eleven strolled back to a bicycle that had been modified to tow a small trailer of newspapers. He glanced back at us chasing after him, his eyes wide. He quickly raised his hands in the air. "I'm sorry! I didn't mean it!"

I didn't even know what to make of that. I glanced both ways down the street but didn't see anything out of the ordinary. "Didn't mean what?"

The boy stared at Fang with pure terror in his gaze.

I glanced over and elbowed him. "Fuck, man, wanna put the gun down? He's like, ten."

"Oh." Fang lowered the weapon.

The kid didn't look any less likely to piss his pants, though. He focused on me, probably because I was clearly the less intimidating of the two of us. "I didn't mean to throw your paper in the bushes. My mom said I needed to be more careful and bring the papers to the doorstep, but it's so much quicker to just throw them."

I shook my head. "We don't care about the paper. But that card you just put through the door. Where did you get that?"

Understanding dawned on the boy's face. "Oh, that man down the road gives them to me."

Fang and I both turned in the direction the boy pointed. There was no one there.

Fang cleared his throat, his voice low so only I could hear. "Your mom and stepdad live down there, don't they?"

They did, but this kid could not mean Karmichael was behind those notes. I refused to believe that.

I bent so we were eye to eye. "What does he look like? The man."

He shrugged. "I don't know. He had brown hair. His car is nice though. Don't know what it is, but it was black and shiny with gold wheels. He gives me fifty bucks to just put the card through your mail slot."

I stared at Fang. "Karmichael doesn't drive a car like that."

He nodded tightly.

The kid glanced at both of us. "Can I go now? I'll get in trouble if I haven't delivered all these papers by six."

I waved him off, and the kid got back on his bike, peddling away down the street as Rebel and Kian pulled into the driveway in Kian's truck.

They both got out with big smiles on their faces, which slowly faded when they took in our expressions.

"What's happened?" Kian asked. "What are the two of you even doing out here?"

I held up the white card. "We got another note. That kid delivered it. Said a man paid him to put it through our mail slot."

Rebel stared at the card warily. "Just open it."

Brooke isn't the only one I can chop into pieces. The debt still stands.

Fang, Kian, and I all stared at Rebel.

She laughed uncomfortably. "It's Brooke. She's just messing with us. Right? She must have people she's working with..."

I picked up my phone.

Kian stared at me. "Who are you calling?"

"Brooke's damn rehab facility."

Kian covered the hand on my phone with his. "You already tried that. They wouldn't put you through."

I jerked away, covering the tremble in my hand. Finding Brooke's finger on my front step still sat fresh in my mind, just as horrifying now as it had been at the time.

I wouldn't let that be Rebel. "I'll continue calling until someone puts me through. I'll threaten to call the cops and demand they do a welfare check if they won't. They can't fucking keep me from her. I'm still legally her husband."

But the first dozen times I called, no one picked up the phone. Rebel searched the web for other lines to try, but all of them rang out as well. With each one, I grew more and more worried.

Something wasn't right.

After standing around watching me hit redial over and over, Rebel and Fang gave up and went upstairs to get some sleep. But Kian paced up and down the kitchen while I made call after call until he couldn't take it anymore.

"I'm going to the gym. I promised Luca I'd meet him for another training session. Apparently, he didn't get enough of torturing me when I went to his facility the other day. Are you going to be okay?"

I waved off his concerns. "Go. I'm just going to be here, calling this number over and over, *until someone fucking answers*." I slammed the phone down on the countertop when it went to the resort's answering machine once again.

Kian paused. "Brooke will be okay. She's locked up in a secure facility where no one can get to her."

"What about Rebel?" I croaked out, voicing my biggest fear. "Do I need to send her off too, just to keep her safe? This isn't fair on her. Fuck." I stared into Kian's hazel-green eyes. "Am I being selfish by staying here? I put her in danger coming here in the first place. Falling in love with her. Maybe I should have gone back to Cali. Kept my problems with Brooke to myself."

Kian grabbed me by the shirt and hauled me in, his usually easygoing expression fierce. "Don't fucking say that! We aren't better off without you, Vaughn."

I stared up the stairs where she'd disappeared into her room with Fang. "You can't speak for her. You aren't the one in danger."

He shook me a little. "But I am the one who was left behind. You left me when shit hit the wall with us, so I know exactly how she'd feel if you left now."

I stared at him. "I just don't want her to be hurt."

His voice was a low growl. "Then stay and fucking fight for her. Because walking away is guaranteed to hurt her. I promise you that." He picked up the phone and shoved it at me. "Keep calling. Don't stop until you get through to Brooke."

His hands moved to grip my face, his fingers tight on my jaw so I couldn't turn away. "We aren't better off without you, Vaughn. So get it through your thick skull that this is it. We're your family. You don't get to run anymore. You only get to stay."

His lips pressed to mine urgently, and I kissed him back, needing every ounce of his reassurances.

"Okay?" he asked, finally pulling away.

"Okay," I agreed. "Go punch things. Have fun. Say hi to Luca."

His lips brushed mine once more. "Will do. Good luck. I'll be back in a few hours, tops."

I watched him walk out, and then I went back to dialing every number on the list Rebel had made for me.

Over and over, I called each one, with no success other than draining my phone battery.

But I kept going. Refusing to give up.

When a masculine voice eventually answered with a, "Uh, hello?" I almost hung up on them because I was so in the habit of hitting redial.

I snatched up the phone, switching off the loudspeaker function. "Hello! Is this White Dove Rehabilitation Center?"

There was a crackle of static before the man answered. "Oh, um, yes. I'm sorry. I should have said that. I don't actually work on reception, but the phone just kept ringing and ringing, and it was driving me mad."

"Sorry about that," I murmured. But hope had lit me up inside. I had gotten nowhere with the regular telephone operators at that place. They were all clearly well trained to not let calls in or out. But with this man, maybe I had a chance. "I'm Brooke Weston's husband. I urgently need to speak to her."

"Oh, I can't do that. Patients in the intake wing aren't allowed calls."

I ground my teeth at the roadblock, but I wasn't giving up that easy, when this was further than I'd managed to get any other time. I also wasn't above lying to get my way. "Sir, are you close with your mother? Because Brooke is very close with hers, and the woman is on her deathbed.

They need one last chance to speak with each other. Please, don't take that away from them. There must be allowances for such situations, isn't there?"

"I really don't know. Can you call back?"

"There won't be time. Please, sir. It needs to be now."

I probably would have felt like an asshole for playing the dying mother card, but then I looked over at the card that threatened to chop up Rebel, and any lie felt warranted.

"Hold on, please. I'll see if I can find her. I really am sorry about your mother-in-law."

I muted the phone and fist pumped the air. "Yes!"

Rebel came running down the stairs. "You got through?"

Fang was close on her heels, and I waved them over, putting the phone on speaker again so they could hear.

Brooke's voice was the next one down the line. "Vaughn? What's going on with my mom? Oh my God."

I quickly unmuted the call. "Your mom is fine. I'm sorry I lied, but it was the only way I could get through to you. They have you locked tighter than Fort Knox."

She breathed a heavy sigh. "Tell me about it. I've been trying to call you ever since I got here, but there's no phones in the intake wing. It's zero contact with the outside world for the first thirty days."

I squinted, trying to make sense of her words. "Wait, why were you trying to call me?"

Rebel's and Fang's faces were equally confused.

Brooke breathed heavily into the phone and lowered her voice. "Because I lied, and I wanted to warn you. It wasn't me who cut my hair or my finger. I'm not the one blackmailing you. I never was."

I gripped the kitchen counter tighter. "What do you mean? Why would you say you did then?"

"Because I needed to get out of there, Vaughn! The Guerra family is dangerous. They don't just give up on debts, and it was becoming abundantly clear no one was paying mine. I didn't exactly fancy losing any more body parts."

I blinked at the phone. "So what? You just ran off and hid?"

"Yes! That's exactly what I did. You should too. Take Rebel and run, because if they can't get to me, they'll just find another way to torture you."

There were muffled sounds of Brooke talking to someone else in the background, and then she came back on the line. "The nurses just came on shift. I gotta go. If they bust me with the phone they might kick me out, and that's the last thing I want. It's not safe out there."

"Brooke!"

"Get out now, Vaughn. Rebel isn't safe, and neither are you. They won't stop until you pay."

The line cut out before I could say another word.

Rebel's face was white with terror when I looked up.

Guilt swamped me as I reached for her, trying to pull her close. But she wouldn't budge.

"It'll be fine," I promised her. I had no idea how, but I would make sure it was. "No one is gonna hurt you, Roach. I won't fucking let them. You don't need to be worried."

She shook her head. "It's not me I'm worried about." She gripped my arm. "Vaughn, she said the Guerra family."

"Does that mean something to you?"

Fang quietly spoke up. "At the gym the other night, Kian's friend's name was Luca Guerra."

Silence fell.

"Vaughn," Rebel asked slowly. "Where is Kian right now?"

My blood ran cold.

The note had said they'd cut up someone I loved.

They'd never said it would be a woman.

30

KARA

I couldn't stop shaking. My entire body trembled from head to toe, and no matter how much people reminded me I was safe in the Slayers' clubhouse, with my daughter in my arms, I no longer believed it.

I wasn't safe anywhere in Saint View.

None of us were. Not while Caleb was out there, still hunting us down.

Which meant it was time to leave. I needed to go back to my family, accept whatever punishment they had in store for me, and take the ridicule and shame that would no doubt be cast upon me for having a baby out of wedlock.

I'd sworn to myself when I left I would never return. I'd never go back to their way of life.

But what choice did I have? I couldn't make it in the real world. That much was clear. I needed the safety and security of the commune.

I could breathe there. I could watch my daughter

grow up without fearing white vans and men in balaclavas.

I would love her enough that she never missed having a father.

Winnie stroked my hair. Georgia had wedged herself tightly beside me on the couch, her arm around me.

Nova and Vivienne sat on the coffee table in front of us, both staring off into space. Vivienne's expression was calm as always, though tension held her rigid.

Nova's was a storm cloud, though. Her fingers clenched. "I'm so sorry, Kara."

I didn't understand. "What for?"

She shook her head. "I shouldn't have let us get separated. I should have been there to help you."

I leaned forward and squeezed her knee. "There was nothing you could have done."

But it was clear my words did nothing to ease her guilt. I wasn't sure when she'd decided it was her job to protect us, but I could see now it was eating her alive that she hadn't been able to.

"We need to leave this town," Winnie said quietly. "We can't stay here."

It was the same conclusion I'd already come to. "Where will you go?"

She lifted a shoulder. "Home, I guess. Though that doesn't seem any safer, since that's where they took me from in the first place."

I blanched at the idea of her going somewhere Caleb could get to her. "You can't go back there." I looked around at all the women who'd all been snatched from their hometowns. "None of you can."

"I've got friends in New York," Nova said eventually. "I can go there."

"I've got a sister in Idaho," Georgia admitted. "Maybe she'll take me in."

A little relief settled over me as the women all worked out places they could shelter, even if only temporarily. For a moment, I'd been scared one of them might ask to come home with me. Even though I knew I had no other options, I didn't want that life for them.

I stared down at Hayley Jade's sweet face. I didn't want it for her either, but there was no alternative for us. Not anymore.

Winnie cleared her throat and lifted my hand, squeezing it comfortingly. "I just want the four of you to know that although I would never wish this experience on anyone, I am grateful to have met the four of you."

"Ditto." Georgia picked up my free hand and linked her fingers between mine. She held her other hand out to Vivienne.

Vivienne took it, holding on tightly. "I've never had sisters I actually like," she said with a laugh. "But that's what you are to me now."

Nova nodded fiercely, completing the circle, holding hands with Vivienne and Winnie. "I know I can be a bitch, but I'd be a dead bitch without the four of you." Her eyes went glossy with tears. "So thank you for saving my life and not letting Caleb kill me that night." She swallowed thickly. "If any of you ever need me, anytime, even if it's just to get you hemorrhoid cream for your ass, Kara, I'll get on a plane."

We all burst out in giggles, and I wiped away the tear

rolling down my face with the back of my hand. "You wait 'til you're pregnant. You'll get them too."

Nova groaned. "Don't wish that curse on me, please." She gazed down at Hayley Jade, sleeping on my legs. "That one is worth a sore butt, though."

She really was. And so much more.

I'd go through everything with Caleb all over again if I had to, because without it, I wouldn't have my daughter.

31

KIAN

Sweat trickled down the back of my neck, dripping its way down my spine.

"Harder," Luca barked at me from the other side of the punching bag.

My muscles ached, and I desperately wanted some water, but I didn't want to seem weak or like I couldn't keep up with the other fighters in his gym.

Which was state of the art and located in downtown Providence, rather than a couple of dusty weights in the Saint View slums like Gino's place was.

I still couldn't believe Luca was letting me train here and not charging me a cent. The fight club was clean and well equipped, and nobody was asking me to throw any matches for money.

"Thanks again for letting me train here." I was using conversation to buy myself some breathing room, but I meant it.

"I told you you'd like it here. You've outgrown Gino's place. You need to be somewhere like this."

I knew he was right. I hadn't felt the same about Gino's place since I'd realized what they were doing there, setting up the fights. It had dulled the spark I'd once felt being there.

But Luca's place was a whole different ball game. These guys were pros, and the fighters they trained weren't out on the streets like all of us at Gino's.

Luca ran a professional tournament, and I wanted in. Not for the money. My construction job was more money than I'd made as the Weston's houseboy. I just wanted to fight for the love of the sport.

I slammed my fists into the bag a few more times in rapid succession.

Luca pushed it away, letting it swing. "That's enough for today."

I nodded, relieved because I was truly exhausted after not sleeping all night and then coming straight here. I was well and truly ready to sink onto my bed and maybe even stay there until I had to go back to work on Monday.

Luca and I headed to the locker rooms, both of us dumping our gym bags on the low dressing bench.

He looked over at me as I pulled off my sweat-soaked tank top. "You showering?"

I opened my mouth to say yes, but then his gaze wandered down my body quickly before rising back to my eyes.

Instantly, the vibe between us felt different. And not in a way I wanted.

Maybe I'd imagined it. I took a fresh shirt from my bag and shook my head. "Nah, I'll grab one at home. Thanks for today, though."

Luca cocked his head to one side, pulling off a sweaty

pair of shorts that left him completely naked. "You sure? Room for two in those showers." His hand slid over his thigh toward his cock.

Fuck. There was no imagining that.

Not all that long ago, I would have joined Luca in that shower in a heartbeat. With his dark hair and tanned skin, he was exactly my type.

But my tastes had narrowed to only one dark-haired, bronzed-up man, and it wasn't the one in front of me. "Gotta get home. My family is waiting for me."

Luca shrugged and grabbed a towel. "You're with that guy I saw you with at Gino's?"

I shoved my gloves into my bag. "Vaughn. Yeah. The woman and the other man too."

It felt a bit strange to say that out loud to someone. Except, we were. We were some weird little foursome that shouldn't have worked. Except it really kind of did, if what we'd done at Gino's that night was anything to go by.

I wasn't going to fuck it up. Not with Luca.

Not with anyone.

Luca nodded. "Say hello to Vaughn for me."

I paused in the doorway, finding that statement a bit odd. But Luca was already turning on the shower, and I didn't want to stand there any longer when the man had made his position clear and I'd rejected it. No need to make it more awkward than it already was.

I waved to a few of the other guys as I passed through the gym and headed back out into the weekend sunshine. I unlocked the truck and threw my bag over to the passenger-side seat before turning the key in the ignition.

The engine gave a pathetic chug, and that was about it.

I groaned, slamming the heel of my hand down on the steering wheel. "Not again. Come on!"

I was so over this damn truck breaking down on me. I'd only just fixed the stupid thing. I tried it a couple more times, but it was in vain. It wasn't going anywhere, and apparently, neither was I.

I got out and popped the hood, wrinkling my nose at the smell. Something was definitely not right if the burning odor was anything to go by. At least I had some tools with me and might be able to get it going enough to not have to call a tow truck.

I was elbow-deep in grease when Luca stopped beside me. "That doesn't look good."

"It's not." I dropped my wrench down onto the portable toolbox I carried around, exactly for situations like this. "It's been on its last legs for a while, so I knew this was coming. I'm going to have to get it towed. I'm really sorry. I'm going to have to leave it sitting here for a bit until I can find someone to come get it."

Luca shook his head. "I've got a guy. Leave me the key. I'll get it home for you."

"I can't ask you to do that."

"Why? Because I hit you up for a good time in the showers and you turned me down?" A small smile tugged at the corner of his mouth.

I laughed awkwardly. "Yeah, something like that."

"My ego isn't that easily dented. Come on, get in the car. I'll drive you home."

I could have called home for someone to get me, but Vaughn was busy trying to reach Brooke, and Fang and

Rebel were hopefully getting some sleep. So I took Luca up on his offer. "That would be good. Thanks. I owe you one."

To Luca's credit, he didn't try coming on to me again during the short drive across Providence. We talked about an upcoming fight and a possible training schedule, then my phone rang, Vaughn's face on the screen.

"Hey," I answered. "Did you get through to Brooke's rehab—"

"Are you with Luca?"

I frowned at the panicked tone. "Yeah. My car broke down, so he's driving me home. Why?"

"What? Fuck!"

I winced at the volume of the shout. "What's going on? Are you okay? Is Rebel? Has Fang got another concussion? Fuck, that man really needs to learn how to protect his head better."

"Kian, shut up and listen to me for a second. School your face so it looks neutral or something."

I opened my mouth to ask what the hell he meant by that, but he didn't give me a chance to respond.

"Luca isn't who you think he is. He's not just some fighter you met at the gym. He's part of a very long line of crime families."

I glanced over at the man on the seat beside me. True, he'd been wearing an expensive suit the first time I'd met him, but that hardly meant he was some crime lord. He seemed pretty fucking regular, just sitting over there in a T-shirt and jeans. "I think you have the wrong—"

"Kian! I don't. Brooke named him as part of the group blackmailing her."

Which would make Luca the one putting white notes through our mail slot.

And the one who cut off Brooke's finger.

I glanced at him again and then back at the road just as quickly.

I didn't recognize it. I hadn't noticed we'd actually missed the turnoff to my place and were now somewhere on the other side of Providence, the woods looming up ahead of us.

There were millions of acres of trees and thick undergrowth within those woods.

It would be real easy to lose a person in them if a crime lord so chose.

Fuck.

"Kian? Did you hear me?" Vaughn asked.

I didn't answer him, instead forcing my voice to try to remain calm. "I just realized I never told you my address, Luca. It's—"

"Don't need it," he said calmly. "You aren't going home."

For the first time since Vaughn had called, true fear lit up inside me, but I tried to stay calm. I laughed it off, though I was sure it didn't sound natural. "Come on, man. I told you my family is waiting for me. Got no time for a stop off."

"Then tell Vaughn to meet us at my place. I think we both know we have some unfinished business to take care of. That is what he's telling you about, right?"

Vaughn had gone silent on the other end of the phone, no doubt listening to everything Luca was saying.

I didn't know about him, but I'd suddenly just realized the extent of the danger I was in. If Luca's family truly was as connected as Vaughn claimed, then going to their home didn't seem like something I wanted to do.

"And if I refuse?" I asked Luca quietly.

He stared over at me and patted me on the thigh. "That wouldn't be smart of you. I really wouldn't want to have to threaten your cute little girlfriend."

I pressed my lips into a tight line.

"That's what I thought. Tell Vaughn to meet me at my house. You can text him the address. Leave the biker boyfriend and the woman at home."

He pinned me with a cold stare. "This is a private chat, just for the three of us."

32

VAUGHN

"I'm going with you."

I wasn't even surprised at Rebel's announcement.

But I also wasn't surprised when Fang picked her up and started up the stairs with her.

"Fang!" She twisted and hit his arms, banded tight around her middle. "Stop!"

"Not a fucking chance, Pix." He looked over his shoulder at me. "Go. I've got her. I'll call a couple of the guys from the club to go after you and wait out in front. You got thirty minutes to get Kian back before they come in, guns blazing. Crime family or not, no one is taking either one of you from us."

Rebel stopped kicking and punching, though Fang still didn't let her go.

Her eyes were big and scared when she stared down at me. "Just give Luca whatever he wants, Vaughn. If it's money to pay out Brooke's debt, give him the house. Or money. Or the business. I don't need any of it. I just need us."

It was the same conclusion I'd already come to. Nothing was worth more than getting Kian back safely. I just hoped he knew that. Had I told him? That I'd fucked us up in the past, but that nothing was worth more than it now? I'd clean toilets for the rest of my life to make ends meet if I had to. I didn't care, as long as he wasn't hurt.

I picked up my keys and with a nod at the two of them, went out to my car.

The address Kian gave me was deep in the Providence woods, miles from the main road. I drove my car toward the sprawling mansion that overlooked the river, my palms clammy. I checked the rearview mirror a few times, but if Fang's guys were following me out there, I couldn't see them. At least not yet.

I parked in front of the house and slowly got out of the car, half expecting to be shot down in a hail of bullets at any minute.

But nothing happened. And when I knocked, a polite blond man in a suit opened the door. "Vaughn Weston?"

I blinked. "Uh, yes?"

"Please do come through. Mr. Guerra and Mr. O'Malley are downstairs playing pool."

"Excuse me?" Was that code for locked in the basement being tortured? Was it just some sort of ploy to get me down there so he could do the same to me?

"Would you like a drink? Bourbon, perhaps? Or something to eat? We have a lovely array of cheeses I could bring down to you. They go nicely with our estate's wine if you prefer?"

Was this Luca's game? Feed up his victims before he threatened and hacked them into little pieces? What kind of crime family had a butler who politely asked their victims if they wanted some cheese? Was this just what he did when he wasn't typing up threatening white card notes on his boss's computer? Or did Luca prefer to do the dirty work himself?

I declined all offers of food and drink. After what had happened to my dad, they could very well be poisoned, and I wasn't taking any chances. I followed the man downstairs to a rec room that did indeed have a pool table in the middle of it.

Luca looked up with a cue in his hand and waved me in. "Hey, Vaughn. Come on in. Do you play? I'm afraid I'm not much of a match for Kian. He kicked my ass on round one."

I stared at Kian, taking in the fact he was leaning on the edge of the pool table, seemingly as cool as a cucumber. It was only that I knew him so well that I noticed the way he gripped the table hard enough his knuckles were white. Or the muscle that ticked in his jaw, giving away the fact he was anxious. He shot a wary glance at Luca, but when he turned back to me, he just shrugged. "I wasn't going to go easy on him, since he didn't exactly give me a choice about coming over here."

Yeah, because that's what I was concerned about. Whether Kian let the crime lord win at pool.

Jesus Christ.

Luca sent the white ball rolling across the table. It bounced into several colored balls which went scattering in all directions, but none of them actually landed in a pocket. "See? No good."

I wasn't about to stand here and discuss his pool technique. "Why am I here?"

Luca stood the cue on its end and leaned on it. "Getting right down to business, huh? I can appreciate that. Do you want to sit?"

"I'd rather not be here long enough to make myself comfortable, if it's all the same to you."

Luca put the cue back on the rack and went to sit on an expensive leather couch. It was the same color as the one in the Slayers' common room, but where the Slayers' couch was cracked and ripped, Luca's was pristine. He sank into the cushions and studied the cheese platter in front of him, picking up a small square of cheese and tossing it into his mouth before he answered me. "Fair enough. We need to talk about the money you owe me."

"Brooke owes you money, not me."

Luca waved a hand around. "You're married to her, so it's the same thing."

"You do realize her father has more money than I do, right? Why don't you blackmail him?"

Luca leaned forward, resting his elbows on his knees. "It's not him I'm interested in working with. It was always you."

"I wouldn't exactly call chopping up my ex-wife and sending me her body parts working together, but you do you."

Luca's smile widened. "Funny."

"It wasn't meant to be."

He grabbed another piece of cheese, this time placing it on top of a cracker. "You're a straight shooter, I get it. We're both businessmen, so here's the deal. You owe me a considerable sum of money. I'm going to go out on a limb and assume you don't have it to just pay me back, otherwise you probably would have done it already, am I right?"

After I paid out Harold Coker for his part of the business, I wouldn't be dead broke, but there wouldn't be enough to pay out the situation Brooke had created either. I stayed silent, letting Luca continue.

"That's what I thought. So here's my proposition. I have a little…exchange program running, and I need more people involved. You can pay out your debt that way."

I was rapidly losing patience. "Just spit it out, Luca. What do you want?"

"I need women. We've got associates outside the U.S. waiting on us to provide them. Bring me five women, and I'll consider your debt cleared."

I narrowed my eyes at him, bile churning in my gut. "Call it what it really is, Luca. You're trafficking women."

Kian stalked around from behind the pool table. "This is what you're into? Who the hell does that?"

Luca shrugged. "Take the emotion out of it, and it's just a business transaction like any other. You'd do well at this, Vaughn. It could be very profitable for you if you want to make it an ongoing arrangement. Rich, young, businessmen like yourself who want to get ahead are exactly who we want to be in bed with. You have the face to pull women in, or the contacts and money to hire people to do it for you if you prefer. We have a very generous remuneration package for a successful transfer. Enough to pay out all your business debts and set yourself up for life." He chewed his cheese. "This is a good deal for a go-getter like yourself. Don't get all up in your feelings about it and throw away an opportunity that could change your life."

My skin crawled just listening to the way he spoke about selling women. Like they were nothing more than cattle. There was no emotion in his voice at all. It was as passionless as pushing paper around a desk. A simple business transaction.

This had to be who Caleb was working for. Kara and the others would have been sold to Luca and smuggled out of America if they hadn't escaped.

If Caleb had a quota to fill, he wouldn't stop until it was complete.

I leaned across the table, so Luca and I were eye to eye. "I would rather chop myself into little pieces than traffic women for you. I own one-hundred-percent of my father's business. Give me some time, and I'll make the money you're owed."

Luca's eyebrows furrowed together. "Wait. You bought out Harold Coker?"

I bristled. "I did."

He snorted on a laugh. "Even better. Because Harold and I already have a contract for several women a year, and we paid him in advance. That contract is now yours too."

I stared at him in horror. "No."

"I can get it out and show you if you want. You buy the business; you buy the debt." Without waiting for me to answer, he strode to a filing cabinet in the corner and pulled out a file. He pushed the cheese and bourbons to one side of the coffee table and spread out the paperwork on the other end. "Ted Dutrow, Garrison Elliot, James Lusk..."

I stared in horror at the names on the papers in front of me. I recognized them all as men who did business with my father's company. Hell, there were photos of them together in Harold's office. I'd seen them the last time I was there.

Luca carried on like he hadn't just rocked my world. "Caleb Black... and oh, here it is. Harold Coker." He pushed the paperwork across the table to me. "Honestly, Vaughn. This is actually great. Here I was, thinking I had to use your wife and her little gambling habit to get you to work for me, but turns out all I had to do was wait for you to buy in." He stabbed a finger at a date on the bottom of the contract. "You have a shipment due to me by the end of the year, by the way. Might want to get on that."

Kian stared at me in horror. "What the fuck did you do, Vaughn?"

I had no idea.

All I knew was I didn't want any of it. Not my father's business. Not his house. Not a single thing his money had ever paid for. I didn't believe for a second that he'd known about any of this, but it didn't matter.

It was all tainted anyway.

"Take the business," I said quietly. "And the house. Have your lawyers draw something up. It's all yours. That's more than enough to pay you out, am I right?"

Luca raised an eyebrow. "Don't be stupid. That business and the house are worth more than the debt and delivering a couple of Saint View whores a couple times a year. There's a reason your father's friends are all involved. You think they're making anywhere near this sort of money trading stocks and bonds or whatever the hell it is they're doing in those offices?"

I didn't care. I pinned him with a glare. "You just said it yourself. The business and the house are worth more than the debt. So we have a deal. Right?"

"Vaughn," Kian said quietly. "Are you sure? We can find another way."

I shook my head. I'd never been surer of anything in my life. I'd been riding my father's coattails for years, letting his business rule my life. I'd married a woman I didn't love because it was good for the company. I'd started my own with funds he'd given me, because I was spoiled and privileged. I'd fucked that all up because I had never learned what true hard work was or how to make smart business decisions.

But I was making one now.

I was standing on my own two feet and being the man my father would have wanted me to be.

And I was walking away.

"Send me the paperwork, Luca. The business and the house are yours."

I turned and moved toward the exit, Kian following close behind me.

I stopped at the door. "Just to be clear, my debt is cleared. You don't send any more of those white cards threatening my girl."

Luca shrugged. "No need to threaten Brooke when I have everything I want."

"Rebel." My voice was cold as ice. "You don't threaten her anymore either."

Luca's eyebrows furrowed. "The little dark-haired

woman you were with the other night? I never threatened her."

I lost my patience. "Bullshit, Luca. We've been getting those fucking white cards for weeks. It ends now. No fucking more."

Luca held his hands up. "Whoa. I accept your deal and I'll have paperwork sent for it. The debt is cleared. But I never threatened Rebel. I had Kian to use as leverage." He glanced at Kian. "Sorry, bro. Don't take it personal. It was just business. But yeah, I didn't need your girl."

I paused.

As much as Luca Guerra was a scumbag of a human for what he did to women, I had the odd impression the man didn't lie. Hell, he'd laid it all out on the table for me. Literally. He hadn't thought twice about sharing the names and details of what he and his business partners were doing.

I brought up the photos I'd taken of the notes and spun the phone around. "You're telling me you didn't send all of these?"

Luca took the phone from my fingers and studied the screen. "The first couple, yeah. And this one, that's mine. The rest, not me." He passed the phone back. "Should I be flattered that there's a copycat out there? Or should I sue for imitation? Is that a thing?"

I walked out of the room without answering, Kian behind me.

"We considered the possibility there was more than one person sending the notes…" Kian said softly.

We had, but I hadn't wanted to believe it. I didn't even want to believe it now.

I'd lost my house. My business.

And there was still someone out there who wanted Rebel dead.

33

KARA

Winnie, Nova, Vivienne, and Georgia stood on the front porch of my sister's house, their suitcases at their feet.

I instantly burst into tears at the sight of them. I'd been trying to hold it at bay all day, but seeing those suitcases made it all too real. I had a matching one packed upstairs, not that there was much in it. Only the handful of clothes and baby items I'd been gifted from my sister and her friends since they'd taken us in.

Winnie dropped her purse and wrapped her arms around me, and a moment later, the other three surrounded us in a group hug.

This was the last night we'd probably ever see each other. We were all flying out later, Vaughn booking our flights for similar times so none of us would be left behind.

Vivienne waved her hand around, pushing cool night air across her tear-streaked cheeks. "Come on. We'll have time for crying at the airport later. Party first."

I let her lead the way back inside the house, where music thumped from speakers and the kitchen table was practically heaving with more types of alcohol than I'd known existed.

Rebel twirled by on her way to the drink table but stopped abruptly when she caught a glimpse of the five of us. "What happened? Which of these assholes made you cry?"

She pulled her favorite set of knuckle-dusters from her back pocket and fit them over her fingers, glaring at Hawk who was pouring drinks.

He raised one eyebrow at her. "Why are you looking at me? Damn, shorty. What happened to innocent until proven guilty?"

"Doesn't apply when you're always guilty." She ran her knuckle-dusters over the edge of the table. "You're well known for making women cry."

He scowled at her and then at me. "Please tell your sister to back down."

I squeezed Rebel's arm. "It wasn't him. We were just having a moment because this is our last night together."

Her shoulders fell. "Oh. I see."

"Can I get an apology?" Hawk asked.

"No," Rebel and I both told him in unison.

She smiled softly at me. "I'm rubbing off on you."

"Maybe a little bit." I would never be as bold or outgoing as her. But she was also brave, and strong, and those were qualities I wanted my daughter to have.

Which meant I needed to find them within myself so I could be a good example for her.

Even though we were going back to the commune where I would be expected to follow the rules, I really hoped Rebel's influence stuck around. "Please tell me you'll come visit me."

Rebel rolled her eyes. "I'm going to visit so much you'll get sick of me."

"Not humanly possible," I told her, and it was the truth. Horrible events had brought me to Rebel's door, but finding out I had another sister was the light in the dark. Watching her be aunty to Hayley Jade was another. The baby was currently strapped to her chest, her head nestled over Rebel's heart. I already knew I was going to have problems retrieving her to go to the airport later.

Rebel shifted her weight, rocking Hayley Jade from side to side. "I don't know. I'm not sure how I feel about living at the Slayers' compound until we find somewhere else to live. I might be searching for any excuse to get away."

I glanced around my sister's almost empty house. There were still a couple of couches to be moved out, and the table, but other than that, it was mostly bare, the removal company putting all the furniture into storage. "I can't believe you don't get to live here anymore."

She lifted one shoulder, gazing around. "It's a beautiful house. I would have happily lived here for the rest of my life," she admitted. "But everything I really need is coming with me." She looked over at Vaughn, Kian, and Fang playing beer pong on the back deck with some of the guys from the MC.

I didn't understand her relationship, but I didn't need to. All I needed to know was clear for everyone to see.

Those three men loved Rebel.

They made her happy.

That was all anyone needed to care about.

Rebel picked up a tray of cupcakes from the table and offered me one. I took one of the little cakes with blue frosting, peeling off the wrapper and taking a bite.

The delicious butter and sugar exploded on my tongue, and I enjoyed every bite a tiny bit more because it would be the last one I got to eat for a while. I was sure that once I got back to the commune, there'd be talk of my weight and losing it so I could attract a suitable husband.

My mother had already alluded to as much when I'd called to tell her I was coming home. She'd gone on a twenty-minute rant about how I'd need to be picture perfect for any of the men to consider taking on both me and my child.

I knew she was right, but I took a second cupcake anyway. I didn't want a husband. I just wanted safety for me and my daughter. That would always be enough.

A dark-haired woman a few inches taller than my sister and I wandered over, and Rebel offered up the platter of cakes in her direction.

"Sasha! You made it! Here, have a cupcake."

Sasha wrinkled her delicate nose. "Oh, no thanks. I can't. Not after...you know."

Rebel frowned. "Not after I made them so painstakingly from scratch with my own bare hands?" She glanced at me. "Well, Kara did, but I watched."

Sasha glanced at me. "I'm sorry. I don't mean to be rude. I'm sure they're delicious. I'm just kind of weird about cupcakes after what happened to Bart and Miranda."

I glanced at my sister and then back at Sasha. "I'm not following."

"Neither am I." Rebel put the tray of cakes down on the table again. "What are you talking about?"

Sasha grabbed a bottle of gin and poured a healthy dose into the bottom of a red Solo cup. "I thought I told you? Some of my crime investigation group got it in their heads that it was cake that poisoned your mom and Bart. Specifically, cupcakes."

Rebel screwed up her face. "What made them think that? There was nothing in the autopsy report that said that, was there?"

Sasha took out her phone from the purse slung over her shoulder. "Well, no, but see here." She pulled up a photo on her screen while Rebel and I peered over her shoulders.

I squinted at the grainy photo. "What is that? A hotel room?"

"Yep," Sasha confirmed. "Specifically, the honeymoon suite at the hotel Bart and Miranda stayed in the night before the wedding."

"They didn't sleep apart the night before?"

Sasha shook her head. "Probably should have, because it really did turn out to be bad luck to see the bride before the ceremony, huh?"

I elbowed her subtly, and she bit her lip.

"Sorry, Rebel. I didn't mean to be insensitive."

Rebel waved off the comment. "Just tell me about the cupcakes."

"It's just a theory, but you see here?" She zoomed in on the photo. "This photo came from the police database, as far as I can tell. At least that's what the metadata marked it as, though that can be altered. But assuming it hasn't, some of the people in my group think these…" She pointed to something blue on the screen. "...are cupcake wrappers. We know Bart and Miranda were poisoned. We're working on the assumption they weren't injected with it, since an injection would be fast-acting. I believe they ate something that was laced with a concentrate."

"Wouldn't they have been able to taste that?" I asked.

Sasha pointed at the cupcakes on the table. "What better way to hide a poison than beneath a ton of sugar and butter?"

She had a point. The cupcakes I'd made were so sweet it would have been hard to taste much else. Plus, I'd just eaten an entire cupcake in three bites. It had taken less than thirty seconds. If there'd been poison in that thing, I probably would have swallowed it before I even noticed anything was amiss.

Rebel stared at the cakes I'd made and then at Sasha's photo. "Did the cops investigate this theory?"

Sasha shook her head slowly. "I honestly don't know. It was one of my group who came up with it as far as we know. I didn't see it reported on any of the official channels. The police don't ever listen to any of our suggestions."

Rebel nodded. "Okay. Thanks. I'll check with the cops and see what they say. They've been awfully quiet on the subject lately, unless they're threatening me with false accusations, which also hasn't gotten them anywhere."

Sasha gave her a tight smile. "I'm sorry they've been so useless. They always are."

"I know."

Sasha walked away, and I put an arm around my sister's shoulders.

"Are you okay?"

She shook her head. "No, not really."

"Do you think she could be right?"

Rebel shrugged. "It's not even that. It's just that she reminded me I've been so caught up in everything else, I haven't even been searching for my mom's killer."

I was part of the 'everything else.' "I'm really sorry."

Her eyes went wide, and she grasped my fingers. "No! Kara, oh my God, no. That's not what I meant at all. I've loved having you and Hayley Jade here. I just meant I feel guilty that I haven't been doing more."

"It's not your responsibility to do that, you know? It never was. You aren't the police. Maybe you were searching for the killer more because you didn't want to face the fact she was gone."

She didn't say anything.

"Nobody likes grief," I said softly.

I had my own weird form of grief to deal with too. I remembered what Hayden had done for me every time I looked at Hayley Jade. But that was also wrapped up in confusion, because how could I feel grief over losing a man who had never been mine? How could I feel grief over a man who had aligned himself with someone like Caleb and who had kept me and the other women hostage? No matter how sweet and kind he'd been, Hayden wasn't a good guy.

Maybe trying to believe that was the only way I stopped my own grief from swallowing me alive.

I drew my shoulders back and picked up a third cupcake, shoving it in my mouth, because eating my feelings was better than feeling them.

"Louisa Kara Churchill," a man called from the back yard. "Are any of you Louisa Kara Churchill?"

I went to call out, but Rebel grabbed my arm, shaking her head. "Do you know who that is?"

"No," I admitted.

"Then until we do, you say nothing."

My heart rate picked up, thumping a little harder. My mind raced through the options, quickly discarding them all.

I didn't know the man. But he certainly seemed to know me.

His gaze caught mine, but then he lowered his head to study some paperwork in his hands. "Louisa Kara Churchill?" he asked again.

Through the window, I watched Rebel's men straighten, staring at the newcomer with scowls on their faces.

"Who wants to know?" Fang asked with a growl.

The shorter man cleared his throat nervously. "Hey. I'm just the messenger. I can see her inside. That's good enough." He thrust the paperwork into Fang's hands. "Louisa Kara Churchill, you've been served."

He skedaddled back the way he'd come from around the side of the house.

Fang, Kian, and Vaughn turned to stare at me, and Fang opened the sliding door. Silently, he passed me the paperwork.

"Are you being sued?" Rebel peered over my shoulder at the official-looking envelope with my name and photo on the front.

My fingers trembled as I slipped one along the sealed section of the envelope. "I have no idea. Who would want to sue me?"

I put my hand inside the envelope and took out a

sheaf of cream-colored papers. Quickly, I scanned the small text, my gaze centering on a bolded title about a quarter of the way down the page.

The papers slipped from my fingers, falling onto the floor at my feet.

"Kara! What is it?"

I could only shake my head and stare at my older sister in horror.

She crouched, picking up the papers, and shuffled through them.

But I found my voice at the same time. "It's a summons to attend a hearing in court." I swallowed thickly. "Caleb wants full custody of his daughter, Hayley Jade."

34

REBEL

"Read faster, Liam," I murmured, shifting my weight from foot to foot impatiently.

Fang picked up my hand and squeezed it. "He's reading as fast as he can, Pix."

Vaughn was less sympathetic. "You interrupting every two minutes isn't making this go any faster. Chill out."

I flipped him the bird, which he accepted as easily as if he'd been expecting it. "I can't chill when Caleb wants my niece, Vaughn! You chill!"

But although I was taking out my frustrations on him, we were both aware I wasn't actually angry at him and none of this was his fault.

Kara sat with Hayley Jade in her arms. Kara's eyes were red from crying, but a fierce expression morphed on her face as she quietly waited for Liam to finish going over the paperwork.

Liam ignored us all huddled around him, impatiently waiting for his legal opinion. It didn't seem to be making him read any faster, though I was incredibly grateful for him coming over here the moment I'd called him in panic.

Eventually, Liam put the papers down and removed his reading glasses. He focused on Kara, directing his words to her, even though we were all desperate to know if Caleb truly had a claim on the baby.

"He has a case."

My heart sank. "No! That scumbag piece of shit cannot have any sort of legal standing—"

Fang squeezed my hand.

I shut up.

Liam went on talking to Kara like I hadn't just had an impulsive, emotional outburst in front of everyone.

"He's her biological father. He has a home, a very good income—"

"That he gets at least in part from trafficking women," Vaughn muttered under his breath.

Liam looked over at him. "I don't think we can prove that unless that Luca guy wants to provide some evidence. I can't see that happening, since he'd have to implicate himself too."

"Considering Luca happily took our house and Vaughn's business; I don't think I'd count on any favors from him." Kian protectively rubbed his big hand over Hayley Jade's mostly bald head.

"I'll testify," Kara said eagerly.

"We will too." Nova's voice was strong and clear, full of determination.

Liam grimaced. "But do you have any actual proof of what happened? Photos? Paperwork? Video? Anything that we can take to a judge?"

Kara and Nova both fell quiet.

Liam sighed. "The system is messed up, I know. If Caleb was less well connected, we might have been able to make something stick on just your word. But this paperwork came from one of the most powerful law firms, not just in the state, but in the country. They're going to dredge up every skeleton in your closets and use it against you. They're going to use the fact you never went to the police as proof you're making it up. They're going to find every tiny thing you've ever done wrong in your life and spin it to drag your names through the mud and discredit anything you say."

"All while making Caleb look squeaky clean," Vaughn added in.

Liam nodded. "I'm not saying it's hopeless. But I am warning you this isn't good."

This was my fault. I hadn't gone to the police either, knowing they wouldn't do anything. I'd never expected there to be a lawsuit where a police report, even if they'd never acted on it, might have helped. "I'm so stupid."

Kara reached out a hand for me. "Don't say that. You're not. None of this is on you. You don't take the blame for his evil."

I nodded sadly, staring at the tiny baby girl in my sister's arms. "Liam, she cannot go to Caleb. The things he'd do... We'd never see her again, I'm sure of it."

"I know." His mouth pressed into a grim line. "Kara, I can't officially say this to you in any legal capacity, but take Hayley Jade and go. From what you've told me, your family farm is off grid? If Caleb's lawyers can't find you, even if it's just for a little while, that'll buy you some time. I'll do what I can from here, and we'll bring in our sister firm who more often deals with this sort of case. But for now, just go on with your plans to return home. Get Hayley Jade as far away from Caleb and Saint View as you can."

"Kian and I can drive you all to the airport," Vaughn offered, checking his watch. "You can still make your flights if we get moving now."

But Winnie shook her head. "We already have a shuttle booked. They've been outside for the past fifteen minutes. I asked them to wait because I didn't want to leave without Kara." She gave Kara a sad smile. "Are you ready to go?"

Kara's bottom lip trembled, and she flew into my arms, the baby safely nestled between us. It was right where I wanted to keep both of them forever, even though I knew it wasn't safe here for either of them. I wrapped my arms around her tightly. "It'll be okay, I promise. He won't ever lay a finger on her. I won't let that happen."

She nodded into my shoulder. "I would rather die than give her up to him."

Her voice was so solid and fierce, I knew without a doubt she meant every word. "I know. Me, too. But it won't come to that. You go home and raise that little girl surrounded by green grass and wildflowers and ponies. All you need to worry about is giving her the best life possible. Let the lawyers take care of the rest."

She pulled back. "Thank you for everything. This has all been…"

"A horrible, horrific, traumatizing shit show?" I asked with a teary smile.

She laughed. "Yes. But it brought me you. And my daughter. So I'd do it all over again."

I swelled with pride at how brave and determined she'd had to be. Going home wasn't going to be any easier for her. I knew that. But I also knew Kara had a hidden strength inside her soft outside. As long as I kept the wolf away from her door, then she'd be okay.

The wolf needed to die.

There was no way around that. There never had been. He needed to join his friend six feet under in a graveyard.

We walked Kara and the women and Liam outside, waving goodbye as their cars all drove away. The four of us, me, Fang, Vaughn, and Kian, all stood there in the darkness, our half-empty house behind us, glowing with warm lights.

"We need to finish packing," Kian said eventually.

Vaughn stared up at the building. "I can't believe that from tomorrow someone else will own it."

I put my hands in my pockets, digging them in deep. "And then we'll all live at the Slayers' compound. Won't that be fun?"

Everyone stared at me, and I laughed.

"Okay, it probably won't be fun. But at least we have a roof over our heads. If our cars break down, there'll always be someone around to help fix them..."

Kian lifted a shoulder. "That will be handy since my truck is a useless piece of shit."

Fang elbowed him. "I'll help you with it."

Kian elbowed him back. "I know."

Their growing friendship made me happy.

Fang was hell-bent on convincing us of the club's positives. "Other pros of moving into the clubhouse for a while. The prospects make almost all the meals. And there's always someone to talk to. You'll never be lonely."

"We'll also never be alone," Vaughn complained. He eyed me, his gaze warming as it skated over the cropped T-shirt that showed off my belly. "Am I ever going to get to see you naked again?"

He reached out for me and drew me in, his mouth skimming over mine until he got greedy and kissed me deeply.

It spun my head. "I think that can be arranged," I whispered against his lips, our earlier bickering forgotten, because that's just what we did.

"We should have sex in every room tonight," Kian mused out loud. "Just so we can laugh about it when Luca takes possession. I like the idea of knowing that even though he took our home, I fucked my girl on the kitchen counter he's eating off of."

Fang groaned quietly.

I looked up at him. "You like that idea?"

"Fuck yes, I do."

"Of fucking me on the counter, or watching Kian do it?"

They all groaned in unison.

"Both," Fang said quietly. "So much both."

Warmth swept through me at the heat in their eyes. They were nearly identical, and all focused on me. I walked backward toward the half-packed-up house, grinning when the three of them followed me.

"Run, Little Demon," Kian warned.

With a laugh, I turned and ran into the house, grateful I had them tonight when everything else felt dark. They were the opposite. They were the light in a stormy sea.

They were the reason I knew everything would be okay.

So I ran.

Because I knew they'd catch me.

"You better be naked when I get in there," Fang growled.

"What if I'm not?" I called back.

Fang strode into the kitchen with the other two at his back. My breath caught at the sight of them, all staring at me, eyes hot with lust.

I put a hand up in a stop motion, pleased when they all froze.

I might have been half their size, but the three of them respected me. They let me call the shots when I needed to.

"Naked, Pix. Now. Then turn around and hold on to the kitchen counter."

But I didn't mind taking their directions sometimes either. I shivered at Fang's demand.

I bent over and undid the laces on my boots and slipped them off my feet. My tights and skirt followed, my jacket hitting the floor next. I shivered a little as I took my T-shirt off, leaving me naked except for my panties.

Fang stopped me when I went to pull them off. His fingers traced over the pink lace.

"Leave them. This reminds me of the pair you were wearing the last time I punished you." He spun me around and put my hands on the edge of the counter. "Do you remember that?"

"I remember you snapping my panties in half and spanking me until I was on the verge of coming in front of all your friends."

He glanced over his shoulder at Vaughn and Kian. "Different friends here tonight, but I still want to see your sweet pussy poking out between your thighs while I make your ass cheeks pink."

I breathed a little quicker.

Fang smiled into my neck. "I love how turned on you get with an audience."

His dick hard against my ass gave away that he liked it just as much.

"I never thought I'd want to share you," he murmured. "But now it's all I think about. You taking me, then taking their cocks, coming so many times you can't even count them." He kissed my neck, rubbing against me from behind.

"Yes." My nipples beaded tight, an ache starting up there that begged for his touch.

"But tonight you weren't naked when I told you to be."

I laughed. "You gave me all of three seconds."

He nipped at my neck. "Don't care." He ran his palm down my naked spine and tucked his fingers beneath the lace of my thong. He tugged up on it, so the material pressed on my pussy and rubbed over my asshole. "These panties barely cover you, Pix. I want them soaking wet for me." He took a handful of my ass and massaged, digging his fingers deep into the muscle before smoothing over my skin with a lighter touch.

He nudged my knees wider apart with his own and pushed me over farther, so my back was almost as flat as the countertop I held. My tits dangled, but he was all about getting me wet.

His palm cracked across my backside, sending sweet tingles straight to my core.

It was the sort of spank clearly designed for pleasure rather than punishment, and I moaned for more.

He did it again, the sharp sting to my other ass cheek just as pleasurable as the first.

"Take his cock in your mouth."

Kian moved in closer and twisted my face to one side so I could watch him stroke himself.

When he was hard, I dropped one arm, giving Kian room to give me his dick.

He was warm and thick in my mouth, and I closed my eyes, jolting a little at Fang's palm on my ass, while Kian slowly thrust past my lips.

"Vaughn," Kian said roughly.

Vaughn moved in, standing shoulder to shoulder between Kian and Fang, his dick bulging behind his pants.

Kian flipped the button on his fly, and I lowered the zipper, setting Vaughn's cock free.

Kian got his hand to it before I could, stroking him in the same tempo he fucked my mouth.

Fang ran his hands between my thighs, rubbing the lace panties over my clit. "So wet for us."

He pinched the bundle of nerves like it was a reward.

My panties were pulled away a second later, and Fang's fingers dug into my hair, tilting my head and arching my back. "Up on the counter so he can fuck you like he promised."

I whimpered at the way he wanted Kian to have me. I wanted it too. I straightened, and Fang gripped my hips, lifting me onto the kitchen counter. My ass perched on the edge, he and Kian swapped positions, Kian taking up the spot between my widespread legs.

His gaze narrowed in on my slit, wet and needy for him. For them.

I lay back on my elbows, letting him take his fill.

"Look at you," he murmured, leaning over to kiss me. "So beautiful."

"Thank you." I didn't know what else to say.

The way he looked at me was everything. He took in every inch of my body, noting the scars other men had left behind and accepting they were a part of my past that would never be repeated. He kissed me slowly as he pushed inside, his dick filling me so completely.

"Oh," I moaned and pulled away from his mouth to clutch at his shoulders. "You feel so good."

Vaughn reached over to the kitchen table still laden with various bottles of alcohol. While Kian thrust in and out of me, Vaughn poured tequila across my tits.

I shouted at the cold liquid hitting my nipples, beading them up, but then a second later, they were warm and wet, surrounded by his mouth, his tongue licking off the alcohol.

I dug my fingers into the short lengths of Vaughn's hair, scraping my fingernails along his scalp and holding him to me until he moaned and reached down to stroke his cock.

Fang was tall enough to quiet my moans with his dick, pressing it to my lips.

"Good girl," he growled when I opened for him.

He was so big, but I worked hard to take him as deep as I could, focusing on giving him pleasure so the building orgasm inside me stayed at bay.

I didn't want to come yet. I wanted this to last forever. To stay here between the three of them where I was warm, and safe, and well taken care of in absolutely every way.

Kian had other ideas. He didn't change his speed, fucking me at his leisure, but each thrust got harder, his pubic bone grinding against my pussy, hitting my clit each time until the tingles inside me became so insistent I couldn't fight them.

My core clenched. "I'm going to come."

Vaughn sucked my nipples harder. Fang's precum hit the back of my tongue.

Kian sent me over the edge with a pinch to my clit and well-angled thrust that lit me up inside.

I orgasmed hard, spiraling from deep inside, clamping down on Kian's cock. He groaned and pulled out.

They didn't even give me a second to recover before Vaughn was in Kian's place, sliding inside me.

He picked up the pace, and so did Fang, filling my mouth, pushing in deeper, all while watching me carefully, making sure this was what I wanted.

It was. Fuck, I wanted them all so bad I ached. I wanted to bring them as much pleasure as they brought me.

When Fang asked if it was too much, I shook my head, because it never would be.

I wanted their pleasure. I wanted their groans when they came.

I wanted everything. Friendship. Sex. Love. Family.

Babies.

Fuck. Now was not the time to be thinking about that.

Fang slipped out of my mouth. "Need to come on you, Pix. Need to see my cum on your pussy."

Oh, fuck me. He was so hot when he talked like that.

The three of them stroked their cocks in unison, Vaughn between my legs, Kian and Fang moving either side of my hips.

"Need her to come again first." Kian reached between my legs and rubbed fast fingers over my clit.

Vaughn stroked his cock with one hand but used his other to press two fingers inside me and find my G-spot.

I gasped at how good it felt. How his fingers hit me in exactly the right spot. Already sensitive from my first orgasm, I barreled into my second with a heady shout of pleasure. "Oh my God!"

Warm cum hit my clit.

Still in the grips of my orgasm, I forced my eyes open, clenching down on Vaughn's fingers while he drowned my pussy.

Kian groaned, falling over the edge into his release, rubbing the liquid into my clit as it fell from his tip in hot bursts.

Fang was the last to give in, but he came with a moan, joining the other two in marking me and making me theirs.

Their noises of pleasure mingled with mine, taking my breath away. Their abs flexed, their biceps rippled, their full concentration all on me.

Kian looked down at the beautiful mess they'd made of me and scooped me up, carrying me toward the stairs. "Sex in the bathroom next, then. Anyone else coming?"

I touched my lips to his neck to hide the smile when

Fang and Vaughn ran after us without a second of hesitation.

We had sex in every room that night. For hours and hours on end.

Never getting tired of each other.

Never wanting to be anywhere else.

Because for that night, and many more to come, the four of us were all that mattered.

35

VAUGHN

The men from the removal company loaded the last lamp into the back of the truck and slammed the doors shut, locking the bolts in place to stop them flying open on their way to the storage facility I'd rented.

It stung a bit, knowing this was the last time I'd be here.

But there was an odd sense of freedom in it too. I still had half the money left in my trust fund. That was enough to set us up in a new, if not somewhat smaller house, when we were ready to do that.

A house we chose.

The same went for my career. I didn't have the business, but I felt such little sorrow over it now I knew what it really was, that I wondered why it had ever seemed like such a big deal.

Luca had done me a favor.

He'd shown me the sort of man I would have become if I'd tried to hold on to it. Greedy. Desperate.

Unscrupulous.

I looked over at Rebel and her sweet smile as she play fought with Kian. I didn't want to be that man. She'd had enough of men who only cared about money and wealth and status and power. That sort of man had nearly destroyed her.

Letting go of the business and the house meant I would never hurt her like that.

My mom was probably going to hurt me when she found out what I'd done though.

"See ya, Providence. Been nice living in you, even if it was only for a little while." Rebel saluted the house and the surrounding neighborhood.

I grabbed her fingers and linked mine through them. "Don't get too eager. We still have lunch at my mom's before we head back to Saint View."

Kian had already started walking in that direction. "Thank God, because I am starving. Is she making those little quiche things I like? I freaking hope so."

I shrugged. "No idea. Probably. She knows you will inhale about a dozen of them."

Rebel and I followed after him, our shoes crunching over the dry, winter grass.

Fang held back, hovering around his motorcycle.

I glanced back at him when I realized he wasn't following. "You coming?"

He shrugged. "Wasn't sure if I was invited."

I stopped and frowned at him. "Of course you're fucking invited. Do you need a gold-foil invitation for a family barbecue?"

He flipped me the bird. "I just...fuck off. Whatever."

I raised an eyebrow. "Good words, Fang. Super eloquent."

He just glared at me.

I let go of Rebel and went back to where he stood, the two of us going eye to eye. I needed to make sure he knew something. "I don't have a gold-foil invite. But what I do have is a friend who will do anything for someone I love. That makes him family. Capiche?"

Kian snorted. "Also super eloquent, Vaughn. Jesus fuck. You went to a private school. You don't have anything better than that?"

I glared at him. "Do you?"

He cleared his throat. "Hey, bro," he called to Fang. "We love ya."

I rolled my eyes. "Would you please just come to lunch?"

A small smile flickered at the edges of his mouth. "You could call me Milo, you know. Since we're family and all."

Me, Kian, and Rebel all stared at him.

I squinted, trying the name on for size. "Yeah, I don't think I can do that."

"Me neither." Kian mouthed the name silently. "Nope. You sure that's the name on your birth certificate? You sure it's not…Gunner, or…I don't know, I really do think it should be Fang."

Rebel ignored him and turned her head into Fang's arm to press a kiss on top of his jacket. "Sorry, babe. You're always going to be Fang to us."

He brushed his lips over the top of her head. "Lucky I like it then." He glanced my way and silently mouthed, "Thank you."

All I did was nod.

The four of us strode down the street, leaving our first home together behind.

I wished the walk was longer. I coughed uncomfortably as we got to the front door of my mom's place. My hand hovered over the doorknob. "One quick thing I should probably tell you all before we go in."

The three of them looked at me expectantly.

"I haven't told my mom and Karmichael about the house yet."

Rebel's mouth dropped open, and she slapped my chest. "Are you serious? She's going to kill you!"

Kian groaned. "At least you told her about the business."

He eyed me when I didn't say anything.

"You did tell her about the business, didn't you?"

I shrugged.

"Is it too late to remove myself from the family?" Fang asked quietly. "I don't do scenes, and I think there's about to be a big one."

He wasn't wrong.

"Do it fast, Vaughn," Rebel warned as we let ourselves into the house. "Don't let the afternoon drag on without telling her."

She was right. I just had to rip it off like a Band-Aid and tell my mother that I'd lost everything my father had worked for.

Fuck.

As confident as I was in the decision, it didn't sound great when I thought about it like that.

We all traipsed into the kitchen where Mom was busy flittering around, mountains of food on trays covering the kitchen counter. She jumped a mile when she noticed us. "Oh my word, the four of you snuck in like you were robbing the joint. What's wrong with you?" She laughed and came around the counter to kiss me. "Hi, sweetie."

"Where's Karmichael?" I snagged a cookie from a tray of them that were cooling on top of the oven, making polite conversation as an ease into what I really needed to say.

She batted it out of my fingers. "Stop. You'll spoil your appetite. Your stepfather is out with his brother, cleaning pools again. He's been gone most of the week. It seems ridiculous to me that they're still so busy when it's winter, but apparently everyone has pool heaters these days, and winter spas are all the rage."

"Vaughn gave the house and the business to a sex trafficker," Rebel blurted out.

Everybody froze.

My mom's mouth dropped open. "Excuse me, I think I just had a stroke. I thought you just said Vaughn gave the house and business to a sex trafficker."

I widened my eyes at Rebel. "Seriously, Roach? You're fucking killing me."

She frowned at me. "Don't swear in front of your mother."

I threw my hands up. "That's what you're worried about after what you just said?"

"I think I need to sit down." Mom slumped backward toward the kitchen chairs.

Fang and Kian both caught her by the arm, helping her to sit.

Eventually, she looked up at me with watery eyes. "I don't understand. Is that true?"

I sighed. "It's not the full story, but yes, that's basically what it boils down to."

"Vaughn, your father worked so hard for that business!"

"I know. But he didn't know any of what Harold Coker was doing behind his back. I couldn't be involved in any of that, Mom."

"Sex trafficking?" Her eyes were huge. "That's what Harold is involved with?"

"Him as well as a lot of their associates. Ted. James. Caleb Black."

She rubbed a hand over her face. "I can't believe that. Harold has daughters. A wife. Sisters even! How could he?"

I honestly had no idea. "Letting go of the house and the business wiped clear the debt Brooke owed and got us out of any further involvement with those men. I couldn't run a business if that's the sort of thing they do to get ahead."

Rebel took Mom's hand and rubbed the back of it. "I'm so sorry, Riva. I shouldn't have just blurted it out like that. I've had some time to get used to it. Are you okay?"

Mom drew in a deep breath, her gaze bouncing around between each of us. "Where are you all going to live?"

"I have a little money left," I assured her.

"And in the meantime, they can come stay with me at the MC clubhouse," Fang's voice was so polite it almost verged on sweet.

Mom screwed up her face. "What? No. Oh my goodness, you'll all come stay here. We have so many spare rooms."

I shook my head. "We'll be fine at the clubhouse."

She eyed me. "What, on Fang's couch?"

"We have a bed, Mom."

Fang cleared his throat. "Actually, it's a pull-out couch. You and Kian will have to share it."

I stared at him. "Seriously, bro?"

He lifted a shoulder. "We were going to give you the room the women were sharing, but War's mom already claimed it for one of her friends who's in town visiting."

"Couldn't War have just told her no?"

Fang shook his head quickly. "Nobody tells Fancy no. But the pull-out is good. I've slept on it before."

Rebel cringed. "Maybe we could just stay here a few nights."

"You think?" I asked her sarcastically.

Mom smiled. "Now that that's settled, eat. I don't know when Karmichael will be home, so we aren't waiting for him." She pushed us toward the platters of food and smiled at the four of us. "It'll be lovely to have a full house again."

I took the guest room farthest away from my mother and Karmichael's room. Kian took the one next door, and even Fang was persuaded to stay, bribed with promises of a quiet night, and took the room across the hallway.

Mom cleared her throat when Rebel followed me into my room, wheeling her suitcase full of clothes to the corner beside mine.

"Vaughn, can I speak to you for a moment, please?"

Mom walked away without giving me the chance to say yes or no.

Rebel lowered her voice to a whisper. "Uh-oh. Is there a no-sex-before-marriage rule in your mom's house? Does she think I'm a virgin?"

I stared down at her. "You're dating three men, Roach. I think she might have an idea you aren't the Virgin Mary."

"Dammit!" she swore, then called out to my mom in the hallway. "Sorry for the bad language, Riva!" She dropped her voice again. "And for letting your son come all over my pussy."

I widened my eyes at her, trying not to laugh. "What is wrong with you? Go to bed and get naked. I'll deal with you later."

She laughed and shoved me toward the door, but it was nice to see her happy. I knew she was scared about the court case and what might happen to Hayley Jade. But she wasn't letting Caleb win. She was clearly choosing happiness, even in the midst of the multiple disasters around us.

It was all we could do if we didn't want to drown in it.

I stepped out into the hallway and closed the door behind me, already imagining her sweet body naked and wrapped in sheets, just waiting for me to come back in.

"Mom?" I called, not finding her in the hallway. I wandered along it and down the stairs, snagging a cupcake from the kitchen counter as I went. "Mom?"

"In here."

I poked my head around the door of Karmichael's study. "Did you want to talk to me?"

She looked up from the computer and took off her

reading glasses. Her mouth pressed into a tight line, and she let out a heavy sigh. "I didn't want to ask in front of your friends but, Vaughn, what on earth are you going to do with your life?"

I raised an eyebrow. "Rather broad question, don't you think, Mom?"

She gave me an exasperated look and stood from behind the desk, coming around to perch on the edge of it in front of me. "You know what I mean. I understand you can't do the same sort of work as your father. We both wanted you to take over the company and follow in his footsteps, but that clearly isn't going to work out." She wrung her hands. "All that matters is that you're happy, of course," she added in a rush. "That's all your dad truly ever cared about."

I eyed her twisting her fingers around in knots. "I miss him."

She nodded. "I do too."

I sucked in a deep breath, mulling over my words. "To answer your question, honestly, Mom? I don't know what I'm doing tomorrow, let alone with the rest of my life. I need to find what makes me happy, instead of just blindly doing what others expect of me."

She winced. "I'm sorry if we made you feel like this was the path you had to take. I never meant that you had no say in it."

I shook my head. "It was Harold more than either of you. He fed me a load of bullshit that I was stupid enough to believe."

She gave me a weak smile and reached over the desk, picking up a piece of blue paper with writing on it and crumpled it. She tossed it toward the rubbish can.

"What was that?" I asked her.

"Me trying to force you down a path of my choosing. I just spent an hour writing out job options for you, but I realize now that's what I've done your entire life. Trying to control every aspect of your career when those decisions aren't mine to make. I'm sorry."

I put the cupcake down on the desk and put an arm around her shoulders, squeezing her in a hug. "Show me the list."

She leaned back and gazed up at me hopefully. "Really? I do think there's some very good options on there for you."

I laughed and walked over to the rubbish. "Like what?"

"Well, you could be a swimming coach or teacher? You're so good, you could definitely teach others."

I screwed up my nose. "In that pee-infested pool? Hell no. What else you got?"

I reached into the rubbish bin and picked up the balled-up list.

My eye snagged on the sheet of white cardstock beneath it.

It was eerily familiar.

With a rising sense of dread, I took out the sheet and straightened it.

From the top-right-hand corner, a perfect rectangle was cut.

Exactly the same size as the threatening notes Rebel had received.

The ones pushed through our mail slot, with no postage mark.

Because someone local was the one threatening her.

Mom took the list and smoothed it out. "Okay, so if you don't want to be a swim teacher, I was thinking you could work at a menswear store? You know a good suit when you see one, right?" She frowned at me when I didn't answer. "What?"

"What's this?" I held up the cut-out piece of cardstock.

She glanced at it. "Scrap paper?"

"Did you suddenly take up arts and crafts?"

Her eyebrows pulled into a frown. "No?"

I sat heavily at the desk. "What's Karmichael's password?"

I waited for her to tell me no. For her to clam up and get protective of the computer.

"Seven-three-eight-one."

I typed it in, and the screen switched to Karmichael's home screen.

It was a photo of him, my mom, and my dad. "What the hell is this?"

Mom looked over my shoulder. "What? The photo? We took it when we went on vacation about a year ago. Right before your father met Miranda."

"You don't think it's weird that this is the home screen on your computer?"

She paused. "No? Why would I?"

I stared at her. "Because you're standing in the middle of your ex and your new husband!"

She narrowed her eyes at me. "Vaughn Weston, if you're insinuating there was something more than friendship going on between us, then you can go wash your mouth out with soap. You of all people know better than that."

Maybe I did, but I couldn't stop staring at that cut-out piece of cardstock.

Something didn't add up here.

I opened the print queue and found the printer history, scrolling back through the list of already printed documents. They were all clearly labeled, most of them work documents.

I paused on one that was just called 'Untitled.'

I hit reprint and then held my fucking breath, praying I was wrong.

The printer spat out a piece of paper with the duplicate of a file that had been printed the day before we'd received the last note threatening Rebel's life.

I knew even before it finished printing I was right.

My mom's sharp intake of breath when I handed her the paper only confirmed it.

I couldn't even look at her for fear of what I might do. Anger bubbled up inside me, so swiftly it quickly felt out of control. I gripped the table. "Why?"

"Why, what? What is this?"

I snapped my head around to stare at her. "Did you kill my father?"

She stared down at the paper in her hands, her fingers trembling. "I don't understand."

"Did you kill my father?" I asked again.

"Of course not! He was my best friend, Vaughn. I loved that man more than life itself."

It's like the same thought dawned on both of us at the same time. But I was the one who voiced it.

"Which Karmichael knew. Which we all knew! The three of you were always together! I remember my friends at school asking if the three of you were in some sort of three-way relationship because you always included Dad in everything the two of you did."

"Vaughn," she said quietly, reaching out for me. "Your father was my best friend. But that was why we broke up. You know that. I want to say we should have never gotten married, except then I wouldn't have you. But that aside, we should have just stayed friends. We should have never been more. When Karmichael came along, I had to call it off. He was the one I was always meant to be with. It didn't mean I didn't still love your father, though. He was always my best friend."

"Did you ever stop to ask your new husband how he felt about that?"

Her eyes filled with tears. "He never said he had a problem..."

"But did you ask?"

She fell silent.

I shoved the note in her face again. "If I go through these files, what's the bet I find more? The notes that threatened Rebel. I bet they're still in that print history."

She just shook her head silently.

"Say something! Do you even understand what I'm saying here? The person threatening Rebel is probably the person who killed Dad! One of the notes she received had a headline about the murders cut out of the newspaper. It warned she'd be next."

"No. He wouldn't..."

I slammed my fist down on the table. "Wouldn't he? Fucking hell, Mom. Did you know there's a theory Dad ate a cupcake poisoned with Oxyanedride? It's the active ingredient in pool cleaners. Where is your husband right now?"

"Cleaning pools with his brother," she whispered, her face white as a ghost.

Bile swirled in my stomach. Karmichael might not have been warm and fuzzy, but I'd thought he and my dad were friends. The sickly feeling of betrayal crept in as I stared at that photo on Karmichael's desktop. I picked up the cupcake I'd left there.

Mom knocked it out of my hand, sending it spinning across the room.

I stared at her.

"He made those," she said quietly. "He only ever bakes when he's stressed, but he made those. They're the same ones he made the day before your father's wedding. He said he was nervous about Miranda and whether Bart was doing the right thing. I didn't think anything of it." A tear dripped down her face. "I'm calling the police."

I swallowed thickly, focused on the cupcake frosting smeared across the carpet.

The fucking wrapper was even the same blue from the photo of the crime scene.

36

REBEL

I held Vaughn's hand as we watched from the second-story window of his mother's house while her husband was dragged out in handcuffs. Detective Richardson put one hand on Karmichael's head, pushing him down and guiding him onto the back seat of the police cruiser, flashing blue and red lights lighting up the entire neighborhood.

Another officer spoke with Riva, who stood with her arms tucked around her middle, as if she were trying to hold herself together.

"You should go down there," I told Vaughn. "She needs you."

"I can't, Roach. I'll fucking kill him with my own two hands for what he did to you. And to my dad. And to your mom."

Kian stood on Vaughn's other side, his face darkened by shadows. "Why would he do that? I thought they were friends. I never saw any sign of jealousy."

Fang leaned forward, clutching the edge of the windowsill. "When you love someone but think they don't love you back the same way, it can make you crazy." He looked down at me. "I was so fucking crazy in love with you I walked away that night at the bar and let Caleb take you home. I'll regret that every day for the rest of my life."

I swallowed hard. "That wasn't your fault."

Fang pressed his lips together. "Jealousy makes you stupid. And reckless."

Kian shook his head. "Why threaten Rebel though?"

Vaughn stepped away from the window. "She was too close. Too determined to find her mom's killer. Karmichael probably thought killing Miranda would be nice and simple. I doubt he even knew she had a daughter who would care enough to chase her mom's killer."

"You were searching too," I pointed out.

He looked at me. "I would have left it to the police if I weren't stupidly in love with you."

I gave him a half-smile, but it fell quickly. I couldn't stop watching Riva. She was so sad and broken. As completely and utterly devastated as if her soulmate had just died.

Karmichael would be going away for the rest of his life, and Bart was gone. She'd lost the two men she'd loved most in the world, and her grief was palpable, even from a distance.

I gazed up at Fang. "That's what you're trying to save me from, isn't it?"

He squinted at me. "What do you mean?"

I pointed down at Riva. "That sort of heartbreak. If

something happened to you, and you were all I had, that would be me standing down there."

A lump rose in my throat at the thought of losing him.

He pulled me into his arms, crushing me to his chest. "I can't tell you nothing is going to happen to me. But I can promise you won't ever be alone like that."

Kian sat on the edge of the bed. "Are you angling for a group hug there, bro?"

Fang stiffened. "Definitely not."

Kian stood, arms open wide. "Yeah, you are." He stepped in behind me and wrapped his arms around me from behind. He motioned over at Vaughn with a jerk of his head. "Come on, Weston. Get in here too."

"I'm not a hugger."

"Liar," I said from between the two big men.

Vaughn reluctantly got up and joined the hug.

I soaked in the feel of the three of them surrounding me, and the sweet knowledge that I would sleep better tonight, knowing my mother's killer had been found.

"I know we're having a moment and all, but I'm so uncomfortable right now," Fang said quietly.

The three men broke apart, laughing quietly.

Vaughn stared down at his mom again as the police drove Karmichael away. "I really should go down there."

But it was clear he still wasn't ready.

"I'll go," I volunteered.

Vaughn dug his teeth into his bottom lip. "Her husband tried to kill you."

I shook my head. "Caleb tried to kill me. Karmichael only made threats I don't think he ever intended to keep. I think he wanted me to stop poking around. Run me out of town, maybe. But he had no reason to kill me."

The three of them looked at me doubtfully, which was probably warranted, but it didn't matter now.

Riva was Vaughn's mom, and if Vaughn was holding a grudge, she had no one. I knew all too well how that felt and I didn't want it for her.

I went downstairs and put my arm around the woman who'd slept next to a murderer without even realizing it.

37

REBEL

"Getting the blankets ripped from your body in the middle of winter is a legitimate cause for murder," I grumbled at Kian while tucking myself into the fetal position, my hands wrapped around my legs, trying to conserve body heat.

"Losing fitness because it's cold is not going to be an excuse the next time you go up against Caleb. You think he's going to step back and say, 'Oh, sorry, Rebel. I won't try to drag you into a van today because I know it was a little chilly last week. So get up!'"

Vaughn reached over without opening his eyes and gave me a solid shove off the side of the bed.

I hit the floor with a thump and then popped my head back up over the mattress. "Seriously, Vaughn! After what I did to you last night!"

He grinned a sleepy smile. "That was really good. But for fuck's sake. Go running. He won't shut up until you do, and I want my blanket back."

"Traitor," I mumbled, taking Kian's offered hand and

letting him pull me up off the floor. I glared at them both, hating that my phone said it was only six in the morning. "I'm sleeping in Fang's room tonight."

Vaughn sniggered as he rolled over onto his stomach and tucked his hands beneath his pillow. "We'll see you in there for group activity time around eleven then?"

I hated that I had no comeback.

Because I wanted that.

"When I get back all sweaty and gross, I'm wiping it all over you," I promised him.

But he was already asleep again, his breathing deep and even.

Annoying man. Shame I loved his stupid handsome face.

Kian pushed me toward the closet I'd unpacked all my things into, and a few minutes later we were both decked out in running gear. Kian bounced down the hallway, already warming up with side-to-side steps and fast little runs on the spot.

I dragged my feet, feeling anything but chirpy. This hour of the day was never going to be my friend. Neither was exercise. But I'd been making more of an effort ever since the incident outside the concert. I'd won that day, but it had only reinforced that Caleb wasn't a man who gave up.

He would try again.

When he did, I'd be ready.

Right now, he seemed focused on getting custody of Hayley Jade. But I never left the house without my knuckle-dusters in my pocket. I'd asked Scythe to get rid of my gun, explaining I didn't want to have it on me if

Hugh's body was ever found. I wanted zero evidence that could be tied back to me.

Scythe, of course, had found that insulting, claiming his bodies were never found and neither would Hugh's.

I hated he was buried beneath my mother. But I had to hand it to Scythe, it did seem like the ideal place to get rid of a body.

"Five-minute warm-up jog, fifteen minutes of running, five-minute walk, then we go again for the last fifteen. Yeah? After that, we can do a weights session."

I raised an eyebrow at him. "You saying my muscles aren't huge already? We've been training for weeks."

He eyed my chicken legs and untoned arms. "I'm not saying that, but your muscle mass is about on par with Hayley Jade's."

I slapped his arm. "Hilarious. Come on. Let's get the torture over with."

For all my complaining and my dislike of the hour, these training sessions were helping. Each day we ran it felt a bit easier. Each time he made me lift heavy things; I felt a little stronger.

It was all I had while we waited for Caleb to show his slimy face again.

At the top of the stairs, I paused at Riva's bedroom door. It was open a crack, but no sound came from the other side.

Kian gave me a sad look. "I heard her crying again last night. It went on for hours."

"Again?"

He nodded.

My heart clenched for the woman who'd lost everything. Her partner. Her best friend. Vaughn was here, but he and Riva hadn't really talked much since Karmichael had been escorted from the house. I'd tried assuring her it wasn't her he was mad at. That he was finally processing his grief, so he was kind of just mad at the world.

But I could see the way he held her at bay was hurting her.

So I'd been doing everything I could to keep her busy. I'd asked her to teach me how to cook, and I'd made all sorts of things with her hovering over my shoulder, watching me measure out ingredients.

But there was really nothing more I could do, other than let time heal the wounds and try to be a good daughter-in-law. That was something I never thought I'd care about, but it was kind of an 'eff you' to Brooke, who I was still holding a grudge against for all the shit she'd brought on us.

It was kind of nice to have a mother figure in my life. Even before my mom had died, it was something I'd been severely lacking.

I tiptoed past Riva's bedroom, not wanting to wake her if she was finally getting some sleep. "She needs to get out of the house. Bliss and I are going baby shopping tomorrow. She can come with us."

Kian held the door open for me with a laughing smile on his face. "Please do not bring a baby home from the shops."

It took me a second to understand what he meant. I'd said baby shopping instead of baby clothes shopping. I forced a laugh. "No, no real live babies will be put into shopping bags and brought back here, I promise."

He broke into a slow jog, though he shortened his

strides so I could keep up. "Good. Shit, could you imagine bringing a baby into the middle of all this chaos? Us with no home. Riva crying all night. Watching over our shoulders constantly for Caleb…"

I didn't answer.

He glanced over at me. "Oh, I know Bliss and War and everyone are really excited. And I'm excited for them. But that's a lot with everything still going on."

I nodded. "Yeah, of course." But something about his words hit me deep in the gut. I knew we weren't there, where Bliss and her guys were. But it kind of hurt to have someone else confirm it.

"Let's run." Kian took a turn onto a track that led through the woods around Providence.

It was narrow and forced me to run behind him. Which was probably just as well, because I didn't want him to see the expression on my face.

Normally, the two of us talked a million miles an hour while we ran. Or at least, he did, and I tried to reply around my panting and wheezing. But today's run was mostly quiet, just our footsteps on the track, the inhale and exhale of our breaths, and the occasional encouragement from Kian.

He checked his watch as we were nearing the end. "Come on, last sprint home and you'll beat your personal best. Push it!"

I did. I ran hard, oddly keen to beat my best time, even though I would never admit it to Kian. Just to be a showoff, I ran around him and took the lead.

He playfully swatted my backside as I passed. "Go, girl."

We both pulled up hard at the end of the track, Kian hitting stop on his watch.

I grabbed his arm to see and gave him a beaming smile. "Smashed it."

He held a hand up for a high five, and I connected my palm to his.

He jerked his head toward the road home. "Come on, let's get back and hit the weights."

I nodded, but my body suddenly felt weak. I trudged along beside him.

His forehead furrowed with concern. "Are you okay?"

I went to nod yes, but suddenly, I wasn't so sure. I doubled over, hands to my knees. "Fuck, no. I don't think I am."

Without warning, I vomited up whatever was left of last night's dinner.

"Shit!" Kian pushed my hair off my face and rubbed my back.

I heaved some more, puking up the last of the contents of my stomach then finishing it off with some dry heaving for extra effect.

Kian cringed at my patheticness. "I'm so sorry, Little Demon. I shouldn't have pushed you so hard. I thought you were past the 'running so hard you puke' stage."

I took a swig from my water bottle and spat into a shrub at the side of the trail. "Me too."

I straightened, taking some deep breaths to clear the nauseous feeling that still had a grip on my stomach.

Kian put an arm around me gently. "Quit trying to beat me, and this will stop happening."

I glared at him. "That's like telling me not to breathe.

If you're dragging me out in the mornings, I need to at least win."

He plopped a kiss on the top of my head. "Have I told you today how much I love you?"

"Want to kiss me so I really feel it?"

"With your vomit breath, you're just going to have to take my word for it."

I elbowed him in the ribs. "Rude."

"Ready to run again yet?" He started off a slow, backward jog.

I shook my head, but I did pick up the pace. Because that competitive part of me was damn hard to switch off, even when it did end with me gagging.

The house was still quiet when we got home, everyone asleep. Kian went to the downstairs bathroom for a shower, and I collected my clothes from my closet. I slipped into the upstairs bathroom and showered, running soap all over my body.

Including the tiny swell of my belly.

My heartrate picked up and hadn't slowed by the time I turned the water off. I dried off, then wrapped myself in the thick, warm towel, tucking it in beneath my arms.

I stared at myself in the mirror. "Just fucking do it, Rebel. Quit being a chicken. Rip the damn Band-Aid off and do the test."

I knelt on the tiled floor and rummaged through the under-sink cupboard, searching for the pregnancy test I'd stashed there after the first morning puke I'd had while running with Kian.

It was definitely possible that I was just pushing myself to the limit with all the exercising. That was what

Kian kept telling me. It was completely normal when you were training. It was a sign of how hard I was working.

He'd almost sounded proud of me.

Which would have been really sweet if I had actually been trying as hard as I could.

I was getting better, no doubt. And I did like to win.

But I was also inherently unathletic. My gut instinct was that I wasn't actually running so hard I should be puking at the end.

"So pee on the fucking test already," I muttered.

My stomach twisted in a knot again, but I managed to keep the nausea at bay long enough to do what needed to be done.

I dropped the test on the counter and backed away from it like it was a ticking time bomb.

"It'll be negative," I whispered to myself, wringing my hands. "I'm the cool aunty. I'd be a terrible mom. That's definitely not in my future. There'll only be one line, and then I'll tell the guys about this, and we'll all laugh because won't that be fucking hilarious?"

I didn't know why it seemed anything but funny.

It actually seemed really fucking sad.

I looked at the test.

Then threw it in the bin.

38

REBEL

"These baby stores have changed so much since I was last inside one." Riva poked at a swinging baby chair, sending it rocking back and forth.

"Aren't they hideous?" Bliss asked. "The prices are absolutely insane. Completely taking advantage of women who are probably about to go on maternity leave and need every cent." She pulled out a tiny blue onesie with a puppy dog on it. "I totally need this thirty-dollar, handkerchief-sized piece of clothing though." She held it over her bump and gave it that lovestruck look she always got whenever she talked about the baby or one of her guys.

I smiled at my best friend who was so hopelessly in love. Once upon a time I might have given her a hard time for being such a sap, but I got it now.

I kinda wanted to make that face at Fang every time he held the door open for me, or at Vaughn when he made sure I'd eaten, or at Kian when he went running and left me sleeping soundly in my bed.

I pulled out a matching pink one and eyed it. "Do you think this will fit Hayley Jade?"

Bliss eyed it critically. "Seems about right. But babies grow so fast. Maybe go one bigger…"

But if it was too big, then it would be summer and too hot for her to wear it. "I'll call Kara and ask. It'll save me returning it if it's wrong, and spending more of my money, because I definitely need to buy Hay Jay at least a dozen of those plushie toys we saw on the way in."

Kara answered the FaceTime call, but it was Hayley Jade on the screen, dribbling milk from the corners of a wide, gummy smile.

"Oh my God! She's smiling! Hey, baby girl! You smiling for Aunty Rebel?"

I flashed the phone to Bliss and Riva, showing off the world's cutest niece. They both smiled and cooed appropriately until I turned the phone back to me.

"Kara, just need to know what size Hayley Jade is?"

"Do not buy her any more clothes, Rebel! She hasn't even worn all the ones from the last package you sent."

I waved my hand around dismissively. "Pfft. Aunties have rights, you know."

Kara shook her head with a wry smile. "Aunties need to come visit soon. We miss you."

I nodded happily. "As soon as I have a weekend off work, I'm there. Tell our daddy dearest to make up the couch for me."

She snorted. "You might have to do that one yourself. Pretty hard to ask him anything when he won't talk to me."

I frowned. "He's still being a dick about you bringing

the baby back there? He's not absolutely in love with her like the rest of us?"

Kara tried to smile, but it was clear she was forcing it. "He'll warm up in time, I'm sure. He organized for me to have this little cabin, so there's that."

I didn't like the sound of that, though she was clearly trying to paint it as a positive. "So you're all alone with the baby?"

"Yes, but at least we have privacy. She's good company."

It sounded more to me like she was tired and lonely, but just doing her usual Kara thing and trying to make the best of a bad situation.

I wanted to fix it for her, but there was really nothing I could do. I wanted her here with me, but with Caleb's whereabouts unknown, and him clearly switching his focus from trafficking women to trafficking his own damn child, we couldn't be too careful.

I swallowed thickly. "I'm sure you've made a beautiful home for her. That smile tells me she's a happy baby."

"I just want her to stay that way," Kara whispered.

"Me too."

We ended the call, and I made my way back to Bliss and Riva who were rifling through a bargain bin that was all still well overpriced in my opinion.

Riva glanced up. "Your niece is beautiful."

"She's the love of my life, that one."

Bliss tossed a teddy bear at me. "I'll be sure not to repeat that to the three men you have waiting at home for you."

"You know what I mean."

Bliss looked at me coyly. "I do. But I don't. Rebel, you

stare at that baby with a lot more than aunty love in your eyes."

I squinted at her. "What do you mean?"

"It's a motherly sort of love."

I shook my head quickly. "No. I don't want to be her mother. Kara is amazing with her."

"That's not what I meant, of course she is. I didn't mean you wanted to be Hayley Jade's mother. But I think maybe you do want to be someone's."

Riva's eyebrows furrowed up with interest. "Is that true?"

I had no idea what to say. I turned to Bliss for help, but that was a mistake. She knew me too well.

She clapped a hand over her mouth. "No!"

I shook my head frantically, but she clearly wasn't getting the message.

"You are, aren't you!"

I shook my head again.

Riva's gaze bounced between the two of us like she was at a tennis match. "You are what? Someone fill me in on what's going on here."

"Pregnant!" Bliss blurted out.

Riva's eyes widened and then dropped to my belly.

Her gaze seared, like she could see through my clothes to the tiny baby bump underneath.

Bliss threw her arms around me, squealing and jumping up and down, even though I hadn't actually confirmed anything. I'd wanted the guys to be the first to know, except I'd spent the last twenty-four hours trying to work up the nerve and it hadn't come. Kian's comments about us not being ready for a baby played loudly in my memory, drowning out Fang's whispered words that he wanted children with me.

I knew where I fell.

I'd fallen in love with this baby the moment I'd seen the positive symbol on the test. I was already so in love with his or her daddy, no matter which one of them it was. Nothing bad could come from that.

And yet I hadn't been able to tell them.

Bliss clutched my sleeve. "Do they know? I can't believe you didn't tell me immediately! Our babies are going to be besties! Or grow up to get married. We'll be in-laws!"

She danced me around in a circle, and I couldn't help it, her enthusiasm was infectious. "They don't know yet. I was thinking about maybe buying one of these onesies and wrapping it up or something cringey like that..."

"Is it Vaughn's?" Riva asked quietly.

Bliss and I stopped.

I couldn't read Riva's expression. It wasn't exactly one of joy, but then I couldn't really blame her. It was a lot for someone of her generation to try to process the relationship between me and her son and Kian and Fang. She'd been amazing so far, taking us all in, not commenting on the fact I didn't have a bedroom and just slept in whichever of the guy's beds I felt like.

We'd attempted to be discreet, but I was sure she realized that some nights, we were all in the one room, and when that happened, we weren't actually sleeping at all.

"It might be," I said to her truthfully. "I honestly don't know." I searched her face, hoping she would be understanding. "Please don't tell anyone yet. I need to do that myself."

That seemed to shake her out of her shock. She squeezed my fingers. "Of course, sweetheart. I wouldn't ever dream of stealing that from you." She gave me a wobbly smile. "I'm going to be a grandma. Maybe?"

I nodded fiercely. "It doesn't matter whose biological baby it is. Vaughn will still be this baby's father. I'm sure of it."

As I said the words, I realized I truly believed them. Kian and Fang would be the same. I didn't exactly know why I'd been so scared to tell them, when deep down, my heart knew it was true.

None of us had been careful about preventing this.

We were all grown adults. We knew this could happen.

Maybe some part of all of us had been searching for it. That little piece that would tie us together and cement us as a family.

Bliss smiled sweetly at me. "You're having that moment when you realize this is the best thing that ever could have happened to you, aren't you?"

I couldn't stop the smile that spread across my face. "I think so."

Bliss squealed again, which was so her thing, not mine, but it was kind of nice.

"Help me find something cute to wrap up for each of them," I told her. "I'm so clumsy with words. It'll be better if I just give them all a gift and then run away while they work it out."

She snorted on a laugh. "You chicken. They're going to be thrilled. You'll see."

I really hoped she was right. We rifled through racks of tiny clothes, and though it took forever to find the perfect items, I went to the register with a pink onesie, a blue pair of tiny shoes, and a soft, squeaky baby book. Hopefully that would make it obvious what was going on, even if I was too nervous to get the words out.

Bliss bought a few things too, and then we looked around the store.

"Where did Riva go?" I asked.

Bliss stepped back to peer around a display of diapers. "I've no idea. Maybe she's waiting in the car?"

We both headed to the exit, noting Ice and Aloha sitting on their bikes at the end of the parking lot. They'd been sent by Fang and War to babysit us, the two of them unwilling to let us out without chaperones after what had happened at the concert.

I peered into the late afternoon sunshine, shielding my eyes with my hand so I could see into Riva's car. "Yep, she's already here."

Bliss cringed. "I feel bad we took so long."

But I couldn't. I was too excited by the package in my arms. I nudged Bliss as we walked to Riva's car, giving an employee on a smoke break a wide berth. "I don't even know who I am right now. Am I seriously doing this?"

She gripped my hand. "*We're* doing it."

Tears welled in the backs of my eyes, which I totally blamed on the pregnancy hormones. But I said the words on the tip of my tongue anyway. "I never had a best friend until you came along."

"And you don't know how you lived without me?" She was smiling, her tone joking.

But it got me right in the feels. "Actually, yeah. I really don't."

She put her arm around me and squeezed me tight.

"Let's get you home so you can tell those men they're going to have a little mini-Rebel wild child on their hands in nine months' time."

I actually couldn't wait.

With a shout to Ice and Aloha that we were heading home, I opened the passenger-side door and slid in, Bliss maneuvering herself into the seat behind me.

Riva quickly finished a phone call and then glanced over at me. "You're back. Sorry, I had to take a call, so I came out here where it was quieter. What did you buy?"

I eagerly showed her the things in the bag, pleased when she made clucking sounds of approval. She eventually pulled her seat belt on and turned on the car, checked her blind spot, and then steered the car out onto the road.

Aloha and Ice gave us a questioning thumbs-up as they drew equal with us, and I shooed them on with a smile.

Aloha nodded once, and the two men peeled away, their job for the day done now that they'd seen us safely into Riva's vehicle and on our way home.

Nerves kicked up in my belly again, making me feel vaguely nauseated, though that might have been the morning sickness. Now that Bliss knew, I spent the drive back to the house twisted in my seat, peppering her with all the pregnancy questions I had.

I was so distracted with our conversation I didn't notice for a long time that we weren't heading back toward the house. In fact, we were driving in the exact opposite direction.

"Where are we going?" I asked Riva.

She put her blinker on and changed lanes. "Sorry,

sweetheart. I just have something to drop off on the other side of town. You two don't mind a little detour, right?"

Bliss shook her head politely. "Of course not. There's no rush."

She was right. There wasn't. Except for the fact I was about to go tell the three men I loved that I was carrying one of their babies.

Holy fucking shit.

It didn't matter how many times I thought about it, it just seemed to get more and more crazy.

I wildly seesawed between terrified and ecstatic. Maybe at some point I'd find a middle ground, but right now, it didn't feel like it.

I blamed the fact I was half delirious with hormones and emotions for not noticing Riva pull into a familiar parking lot. It was the bumping of the unpaved road that drew my attention and when I looked out the window and recognized my surroundings. "This is Kian's construction site."

Riva didn't say anything. The site was filled with trucks and heavy machinery, the same way it had been the night Kian and I had come out here. But there was only one other car in the lot, parked by the site shed.

I hid a smile at the memory of Kian taking me against the back of it. It might have even been the night this baby had been conceived, who knew?

"What were you dropping off again?" I asked Riva.

She swallowed thickly as we stopped next to the car and two men came out of the site office. I frowned when they walked to mine and Bliss's side of the car.

On autopilot, I reached for the door locks, instinctively realizing something was wrong.

They beat me to it. The doors jerked open, and I screamed as strong hands grabbed me, yanking me out of the car. I twisted and fought against the big man I didn't recognize, until one I did stepped out of the office.

Caleb.

My heart plummeted.

I stared back at Riva in helpless despair.

Riva's mouth pulled into a trembling line. "You, sweetheart. I'm delivering you."

39

REBEL

The betrayal hurt more than the binds around my ankles and wrists. They chaffed and scraped at my skin, too tight to budge.

Bliss whimpered beside me, her eyes so wide the whites showed the entire way around. I inched closer to her, quietly murmuring it was going to be okay.

Even though I didn't believe a word of it.

Caleb and his two goons watched us from the corner, the three of them in a muttered conversation I didn't like the sound of.

Words kept floating back to me. *Pickup. Auction. Exchange.*

Riva stood on the other side of the room, nervously watching on, not a part of their discussion but clearly not on our side either.

I wanted my heart to turn cold so I could hate her. Except I couldn't process what was going on quick enough to get there. All I felt was hurt.

She dragged her gaze away from me and stepped up

to Caleb. "Are those restraints really necessary? You promised you wouldn't hurt them."

He stopped his conversation to address her. "Does she look like she's going to willingly stay here until they pick her up for the auction?"

Riva glanced over at me.

I glared at her.

"No, I suppose not."

"Why?" I spat out at her, ignoring Caleb because his behavior wasn't out of the ordinary. But Riva had blindsided me. I'd thought we were friends. "Why would you do this?"

She bit down on her lip. "I'm sorry. I never meant for this to happen. It all got so out of control. I never even knew you existed until the wedding day."

I frowned, trying to make sense of her words. I couldn't. "I exist, Riva. I exist, and so does the baby I'm carrying. Your grandchild! And you deliver me to this monster? Do you even know what you've done?"

Caleb sniffed in my direction. "She knows. Don't buy her little sob story."

For once in his miserable life, I actually believed him.

Riva was guilty as fuck. "You're dragging him down, Rebel."

"Who? Vaughn?"

"Yes, Vaughn!" she snapped. "If you'd just walked away after the first card was delivered, none of this would have happened!"

I shook my head, none of this making sense. "You knew about the cards?"

"Of course, I did."

I narrowed my eyes at the tone in her voice. "You

knew because you wrote them yourself, didn't you? I knew it didn't all add up. Why would Karmichael care about me? He wouldn't. But you're Vaughn's mother..."

She didn't say anything, which was how I knew I was right.

Bliss lifted her head, her eyes red with tears. "Did Karmichael even know what you were doing? That you sent those vile threats to the woman your son loves? Or were you so cowardly you just let your husband go to jail for you?"

Riva stormed across the room and smacked her palm across Bliss's cheek.

I saw red at the sound of Bliss's shocked gasp. I struggled against my restraints, fingertips brushing over the knuckle-dusters, forever in my back pocket.

They weren't much good to me when my hands were tied, but I ached to have them on my fingers. "How dare you," I hissed at Riva. "She's pregnant."

"Another bastard baby for me to sell." Caleb laughed. He leaned down into my face. "How does it feel to know you and I are related by blood now, Rebel? Little Hayley Jade will make me a small fortune. If you were nicer to me, I might have made arrangements for the two of you to be sold off together."

My heart stopped.

He shrugged. "But, since you're a psychopathic little bitch, I decided not to."

I spat squarely in his face because it was all I had left. "You piece of fucking scum. You won't ever lay a finger on Hayley Jade. What kind of man sells his own daughter?"

Caleb slowly wiped my saliva off his face with a handkerchief from his pocket. His voice was low and deadly when he spoke again. "The kind who knows all too well that women are a fucking useless waste of space who only get in your way and hold you back. I never asked for a daughter. Nobody ever gave me a say in whether your slut sister had a child."

The anger inside me was so hot. If I could have, I would have thrown myself across the room and clawed his fucking eyes out with my bare fingernails. "Kara never had a say in that baby either, Caleb. You took that away when you forced yourself on her."

Bliss stared at the man she'd once loved. "I don't even recognize you anymore. You were never kind or good, but hell, you were never...this."

He turned his rage on her, grabbing a fistful of her auburn hair. "Shut up, you stupid fat bitch. Don't you know you were never more than a pity fuck? Your opinions mean nothing to me."

My anger soared. It was one thing for Caleb to call me names and get in my face, but it was a whole different ball game when he did it to Bliss. Despite everything she'd been through, she'd managed to keep her sweet softness. That was who she was at her core. I didn't want anyone taking that from her.

But there was none of that to be seen right now. Bliss looked him up and down and then smiled. It grew into a grin, and then a laugh. "Your obsession with me is an embarrassment. You went after my friend, just to get back at me. You can say I was a pity fuck all you want, but we both know the truth. I was always too good for you, and you were just trying to keep up. You were always a pathetic excuse for a man who could never keep me satisfied. But don't worry, I'm very fucking satisfied now. Every. Damn. Day."

Despite the situation, I smiled so wide to hear those cutting remarks spew from her lips. The woman never even swore, but damn, that sort of attitude was good on her.

Riva folded her arms over her chest and stared at the two of us. "You're as bad as your mother. Gutter trash Saint View whores, the lot of you."

I glared at Vaughn's mother, that hate finally seeping through to my shock and turning my heart to stone. "Is that why you killed her? Because she wasn't good enough for the man you threw away?"

She shook her head at me. "I never threw Bart away. He was the one who ended things. Not me."

Well, that made things a lot clearer. "And he was gentlemanly enough to let everyone think it was you who'd ended it? I barely met your husband, but I could tell he was one of the good ones. Shame the same can't be said about you."

She shook her head. "I never meant to kill them. It was just supposed to delay the wedding so I could talk some sense into the man! They moved so fast. She got her claws into him, and the next thing I knew they were talking weddings. He would have seen in time that she was so wrong for him, but your whore of a mother was so busy trying to get knocked up with his babies, she wasn't giving him a chance. He was a decent, honorable man, so of course he wanted to marry her before she got pregnant." She shook her head, staring at me. "I'm not letting my son fall into the same trap with a slut from Saint View who makes no secret of the fact she's sleeping with three men."

"He loves her, Riva," Bliss said sadly. "You've seen them together and you know that. You're too late to save him from anything. All you've done is break the only relationship you have left. Because when he finds out what you've done, he'll never speak to you again. I can assure you of that. You'll be as dead to him as if you were the one who was poisoned."

Riva's gaze turned nervous, darting between us, and then back to Caleb. "I need to go."

I shook my head. "Go on then. But every time you look at your son, just remember me and the fact you stole his happiness. Clearly, you think yours is worth more. I hope you're right."

Ghosts haunted Riva's eyes. Ghosts I'd put there. But I didn't feel an ounce of remorse.

I'd been a mother for less than twenty-four hours, and I already loved this baby enough to sacrifice anything for their happiness.

It was a pity Riva had never loved Vaughn like that.

I'd given him a hard time for not comforting her after Karmichael had gone away, but now I realized he just knew her better.

She hadn't deserved his sympathy.

My heart tore at the thought of Vaughn and Kian and Fang at home, wondering where I was, waiting up for me, panic setting in each minute I didn't return.

I fought against the restraints, but it was useless.

But I refused to panic.

It was there, simmering away below the surface, ready to consume me like it had in the past.

But this time, I would control it. I would think clearly, and I would fight.

I would fight right up until my last dying breath if that's what it took.

Caleb would die before the clock struck midnight.

Or I would.

40

FANG

"Admit it," Kian called over his shoulder. "You like living here with us better than living at the MC."

I leaned on the bathroom doorway, watching him down on his hands and knees, scrubbing the clawfoot bathtub. "I like that it's clean here, I'll give you that."

Vaughn paused beside me, overhearing the conversation. "Didn't the cleaner come yesterday? Why are you even doing that?"

Kian stood and rolled his eyes. "That woman needs to be fired. That tub was not clean. I think I just found your pubes in the drain."

I screwed up my face at Vaughn. "You take baths?"

He raised one eyebrow at me. "You don't?"

I gestured down at my long legs. "I don't exactly fit well." Though to be fair, Vaughn wasn't that much shorter than me, and the tub was huge.

I eyed it critically, trying to figure out if there was a way I could fit in there.

Preferably with Pix on my lap.

I had to swallow, just thinking about getting her sweet body naked, wet, and soapy. Gliding my hands up and down her spine, gripping her ass and guiding her onto my cock submerged beneath the warm water.

Kian threw a rubber glove at me. "Don't go getting any ideas. I don't need anyone else's body hair—or anything else—to clean out."

Vaughn stepped in and bent to kiss Kian on the mouth. "Get up off your knees before I start thinking about other things you can do while you're down there."

Kian looked around Vaughn's leg at me. "Fang is here."

"Fang has seen you suck me off before, you know."

"Not when Rebel isn't here. He might not be into it when it's just you and me."

They both turned to me with interest.

I thought about it for a second, then wrinkled my nose. "Nuh. You two are good together, don't get me wrong. If I was gonna go there…"

Kian seemed pleased by that.

I shook my head. "Now who's getting ideas?"

He chuckled. "Nah, I feel you. I'm kinda a one-guy man too. So, while I'm down here on my knees…"

Vaughn looked hopeful.

Kian grinned. "…Empty the trash."

I snorted at Vaughn's crestfallen face. It was pathetic. I held my hand out to Kian. "Give me the bin. I'll take it downstairs. Which will give the two of you time for other kneeling activities."

Kian passed it up to me.

I left the room to the sounds of him pushing aside cleaning supplies and Vaughn undoing his fly.

I'd wait for Pix to get home from her shopping trip with Riva and Bliss and then maybe we'd join them. I suddenly needed to test out that bathtub with her.

I grinned at the thought as I wandered downstairs and out the front door. The sun was right at eye height, just barely clinging to the horizon, with night determined to set in. I pulled my phone from my back pocket to check the time.

It was later than I'd thought. Rebel should have been back by now.

I rounded the corner of the house, stepping around the short privacy fence that hid the large bins from the road. I brought up Rebel's number and hit call, tucking the phone between my ear and my shoulder so I had both hands free to empty the trash.

Hey, it's Rebel! Why are you calling instead of texting? What sort of monster are you? But since you're here, do your thing and leave a message after the tone.

I shook the little can into the bigger bin. "Hey, it's just me. Just checking to see where you're at and when you'll be home. I want to make sure I've got some dinner ready for you. Then after, I want to try something I think you'll like..."

I stared down at the contents of the bin I'd just emptied and froze. "Uh, Pix? Why is there a pregnancy test in the bathroom trash?"

My heartbeat picked up. "Why does it have a plus sign and the word pregnant in the results screen?"

I just stared at the test in silence, until her voice

message beeped again, signaling the end of my time, and the line went dead.

As good as Riva looked for her age, there was no chance that pregnancy test was hers. Rebel was the only other woman in the house. It couldn't have been Kara's. She had a newborn baby. It could have been Bliss's, but the woman clearly already knew she was pregnant. Why would she take a test? And outside her own home?

I stabbed the call button and tried again to get a hold of Rebel. It rang for a while, but the result was the same. Her voicemail chirped in my ear. I tried Aloha and Ice, but neither answered. Which probably meant they were still out on the road with Rebel, and I was just going to have to be patient until they got back.

Not knowing what else to do, I fished the test out of the trash and went back into the house with it clutched in my hand. On autopilot, not thinking straight, I went up the stairs and walked back into the bathroom where I'd left Kian and Vaughn.

"Jesus!" Vaughn shouted. "A little privacy, please!"

I barely even took in the fact his cock was in Kian's mouth. It didn't even register. I just held up the pregnancy test.

Kian pulled away and stood, wiping his mouth with the back of his hand. "What the hell is that?"

"It was in the bin I took out."

Vaughn yanked up the zipper on his fly and peered over at me. He froze. "The bin you just took out from this bathroom?"

Kian looked over at him. "No, the bin he just took out from Kim Kardashian's house."

"Is it Rebel's?" Vaughn got out eventually.

"Pretty sure it isn't your mom's." My fingers shook as I set the test down on the counter. "Rebel didn't tell either of you?"

"No," they said in unison.

Kian linked his fingers and the back of his head and took a deep breath. But as he released it, a smile grew across his face. He leaned in, staring at the test again. "It's seriously positive. There's no mistaking it."

There wasn't.

Vaughn paced the length of the bathroom, his movements stiff and jerky. "I should call her."

"Already did." I slumped back against the wall. "It's going to voicemail."

"It might not be hers," Vaughn insisted.

I let him have his freak-out because I'd already eliminated all the other possibilities.

But they all came back to one thing.

One idea that was rapidly taking a hold on my heart, wrapping it up in a feeling I hadn't had until a little dark-haired siren had walked up to my table at Psychos and asked to go home with me.

She was having a baby.

A baby, who in a heartbeat, I'd already fallen in love with.

Kian's grin had become so wide it rivalled the Cheshire Cat. "Hey, boys. Guess what?"

Vaughn and I both looked at him.

"We're having a baby."

Vaughn choked. "We're? What do you mean we're? Four people can't have a baby, Kian!"

"Are you going to walk away from her?" I asked him quietly. "Because I'm not."

"Me neither," Kian said instantly, his gaze pinned on Vaughn.

Vaughn's eyes turned dark, like the thought of walking away from Rebel was abhorrent. "Never," he murmured. "I just...can't."

It was like the realization had only just hit him. How deep we all were. How bonded we'd become, not just to Rebel, but to each other as well. I might not have wanted to suck their dicks, but when Kian had gone missing, that had hit me like a ton of bricks. I hadn't breathed until he'd returned.

Somewhere along the way, Rebel's love for them had rubbed off on me. Though mine wasn't sexual, it was still strong.

At some point when I wasn't paying attention, we'd become a family.

And now Pix was cementing it with a baby in her belly.

Kian let out a laugh that was deep and full of humor. "Then like I said. I guess we're having a baby." But the color quickly drained from his face. "Fuck. I said some things to her yesterday... Things that might have made her think I wouldn't want this."

Vaughn and I both stared at him.

"What did you say?" I demanded.

He shook his head. "Fuck, I don't even remember. Something about it being a disaster if we were in the same situation as Bliss..."

Vaughn groaned. "Kian!"

"Yeah, I know, I know! It's bad. I don't even know why I said that, because now I know it's happening, it actually seems pretty cool to have a little mini-me."

Vaughn eyed him. "As if your swimmers would have been fastest. If they're anything like you, they probably stopped off at a karaoke bar on their way to the uterus."

I would have laughed at Vaughn's sarcastic sense of humor if I hadn't had other things on my mind. "It's getting late, and she's not answering her phone."

A door slammed downstairs, and we all hustled into the hallway to peer over the banister.

"Mom," Vaughn called. "Weren't you out with Rebel? Where is she?"

Riva startled, and with her hand over her heart, she gazed up at the three of us staring down at her. "I was. But she and Bliss left together."

I frowned. "Are Ice and Aloha still with them?"

Riva fiddled with the strap on her purse. "No, they rode off. I had some things to get at a different store, so we split up."

"Why didn't she call us to come pick her up?" Vaughn asked.

Riva threw her hands up, quickly frustrated by our questions. "I don't know, Vaughn! She's a grown woman, I'm not her keeper."

"I'm going to kill Aloha and Ice. Why the fuck didn't they stay with her?" I muttered.

Vaughn pressed his lips together, ignoring his mother's outburst and my grumbling. "Call me an overprotective asshole, but I don't like that her and Bliss are out somewhere on their own.

"I'm calling Bliss," Kian announced. "Someone call Rebel again."

I already had my phone out. Kian and I both made the calls. I watched Riva scurry out of sight, locking herself in her bedroom while the phone call went straight to Rebel's voicemail again.

I turned back to Kian and Vaughn. "Nothing." I cancelled the call.

Kian ended his as well. "She didn't answer either."

A sinking sense of dread filled my belly. My gaze kept drawing back to Riva's closed bedroom door. Something didn't feel right.

"Call War," Vaughn suggested. "They're probably over at their place. Quit panicking, the both of you."

I couldn't even deny it. That fear I'd felt when I'd lost track of her at the concert threatened to take over again. I ignored it and called War.

He answered on the first ring. "Fang. I was just about to call you. Is Bliss with you?"

That pit in the bottom of my stomach opened wide. "No, she's not. We don't know where either of them are. Vaughn's mom was with them, but she's saying they split up. Where are Ice and Aloha?"

War breathed into the phone. "No fucking idea. Let me see if they're outside. Shit. I shouldn't have let them go."

"They would have hated that," I reminded him. "Rebel would have punched me in the balls if I suggested she couldn't go somewhere."

"Yeah, yeah, I fucking know. Wait, Ice and Aloha are here." There were muffled words from his end, and then a clear curse when War came back on the line. "Shit! Aloha says the women were in Riva's car. They told them they were headed home, so they went in opposite directions. The boys coming back here while the women presumably went back to Providence with Riva."

I stared at Riva's bedroom door again.

Vaughn followed my line of sight and I ended the call. He looked at me. "You don't believe her, do you?"

I lifted one shoulder. "I don't know. Something feels off, but you know her better than I do."

Vaughn swore low under his breath. He stormed to his mother's room. He tried the handle, but it was locked. He thumped his fist on her bedroom door. "Mom!"

He didn't give her time to answer, just went right on bashing on the wood.

Eventually, the lock clicked, and Riva poked her head out. "Vaughn! Stop it. You'll break it."

"What happened with Rebel today? I know you didn't just leave her and Bliss there by themselves with no way of getting home."

She waved him off. "You're being ridiculous."

He stared at her.

She huffed out a sigh. "I left them at the baby store, Vaughn! They do have the Uber app, you know? You don't need to mollycoddle her the way you do. Honestly, it's embarrassing watching the way you carry on when she's around."

Vaughn narrowed his eyes. "The way I carry on? What the hell does that mean?"

Riva said nothing, but her gaze dropped to the floor, refusing to meet her son's.

That feeling in the pit of my stomach intensified. I'd tortured the truth out of enough men to know what it looked like when someone lied.

Riva had that expression in her eyes right now.

"My guys said they got in the car with you," I accused.

Riva shook her head. "They're lying." She turned to

Vaughn. "This is ridiculous. They aren't children. They'll be home when they want to be home."

I got out my phone again and searched for a number.

Kian watched me. "Who are you calling?"

The woman on the other end answered at the same time, and I held up one finger in Kian's direction, indicating for him to wait a moment.

I put the phone on loudspeaker. "Uh, hi. Listen, my girlfriend was in there earlier today. Short-ass with a pixie haircut? Super loud. She was with her best friend, Bliss. She's taller, kinda reddish-blonde hair. Really pregnant..."

"Oh, yes. I remember the two of them."

"Great. Did you by any chance see an older woman with them?"

Riva's mouth fell open in indignation, but Vaughn hushed her with a glare.

The store clerk cracked her gum. "Dark hair? Yep, I assumed she was your girlfriend's mom or mother-in-law."

"Did they all leave together?"

"No. They didn't. The older woman left before the younger two."

Riva shot me a triumphant look.

Well, fuck. That blew that idea out of the water then. Shit. I probably owed Riva an apology for not believing her. "Thanks for that," I said to the woman on the phone.

"I told you," Riva hissed. "We had separate things to do. I left them at the store, I haven't seen them since."

I nodded. "Sorry."

My thumb was headed for the end call button when the woman spoke up.

"Oh, I did see them drive away together though. I went outside for my smoke break as the younger two were leaving. The older woman was driving. I remember because the car was really nice."

We all stared at Riva.

"Hello?" the woman on the phone asked.

I ended the call.

Vaughn's gaze turned to ice. I'd known cold-blooded killers who had more warmth in their eyes than he did in that moment. "Where are they, Mom? I know you aren't telling the truth."

Riva shrugged. "She's remembering wrong. That woman probably saw five hundred short, dark-haired women with a taller pregnant friend today. It's hardly unusual." Her gaze darted away nervously.

Vaughn pushed past me, taking long steps down the hallway to the bathroom and then back to where we stood in the hallway. He thrust the positive pregnancy test in his mother's face. "She's pregnant, Mom! She's carrying your grandchild! Why are you lying to me? It's written all over your face."

Riva stared down at the positive pregnancy test, her bottom lip wavering. "She's actually pregnant?"

"Of course she fucking is!"

Riva shook her head. "Women like her...like her mother...they lie to trap men, Vaughn. She just wants your money."

"What money? I don't freaking have any!" Vaughn's eyes were wide. "She knows that, and she loves me anyway. And I love her. We all fucking do. I know I've always been a disappointment to you—"

Riva grabbed his hand. "You weren't! You aren't!"

He stared at her hard, pulling his fingers from her grip. "I was. I was the son who loved a man instead of my wife. I was the son who lost his own business and then his father's. I'm the one you never wanted here, embarrassing you in front of all your friends whose kids were walking in their parents' footsteps."

She shook her head, her eyes wet with tears. "I never..."

Except it was obvious she had. Maybe she was only just realizing it herself, but Vaughn had seen it all along. It was clear now why he'd stayed away for so many years.

He swallowed hard. "If you ever cared about me, even the tiniest bit, you'll tell me where she is. Because if she's in danger, Mom, it's real. You don't know the half of what is out there. What men like Harold Coker and Luca Guerra and Caleb Black are capable of."

"He said he wouldn't hurt her."

I stiffened. "Who?"

Riva never looked at me, her gaze was fixed on her son. "Caleb."

"Son of a bitch." I pushed past them, no longer able to stand the sight of her.

Kian was hot on my heels.

"Where, Mom?" Vaughn shouted.

"A worksite..."

"Mine," Kian spat out, voice clipped and tense. "Caleb owns it."

I didn't even have it in me to question him. It didn't matter anymore anyway. All that mattered was getting to her.

Vaughn thundered down the steps behind us.

"Don't go, Vaughn," Riva called after him. "I won't be here when you get back."

He paused at the bottom of the stairs, while all three of us were shoving our feet in boots. "After you delivered the woman I love to Caleb Black, it's probably better that you aren't."

Riva's mouth dropped open. "Vaughn!"

He shook his head. "I mean it, Mom. Go. Run away from whatever the hell you've done, because if you're still here when I get home, I'll be calling the cops myself."

If Riva said any more, I didn't hear it. We were in Vaughn's car, tires screeching out of the driveway, covering up the cries of Riva's betrayal.

41

REBEL

"It's pretty dark out there, boss." Goon One, as I'd nicknamed him, let the curtain fall back into place. "I thought these guys were coming at four?"

Caleb folded his arms over his chest and glared daggers at his hired help. "They were."

It was hours past that now. Bliss stared at me in panic.

I gave a tiny shake of my head, trying to tell her to stay calm.

I knew she was thinking about her baby. Because I was thinking about mine.

All I could think about was something I'd been taught a million years ago at school, when we'd been warned about stranger danger and personal safety.

Don't ever let them take you to a second location.

I wasn't well known for being smart, but fuck, I was scrappy when I needed to be.

And right now, it was needed.

I had a plan.

I just needed a moment to enact it.

I knew where we were. I'd walked around the site in the dark the night Kian had brought me here.

I just needed to get us out there.

Just needed one lucky break to set the wheels in motion.

A weird thrill of excitement buzzed through my veins. It wasn't quite enough to knock the fear away, but it kind of mixed with it, making me sharp.

"What are you smiling for?" Caleb complained, catching a glimpse of my face as he paced back and forth, checking his expensive watch. "You do realize you're about to be put on a truck with a bunch of other whores and sold like cattle?"

I didn't say anything.

"I cannot wait to cash in on the two of you and never see either of you again." He glanced over at Bliss. "Shame you won't get to tell your psychopath boyfriend all about it."

Though I saw the panic flare in her eyes, I gave Bliss credit for staring at Caleb like she was bored stupid.

"How's those letters he carved in your chest, Caleb? What did they spell again? Oh, that's right. My name." She laughed in a manner that was definitely Scythe-ish. "You'll never be rid of me, Caleb. You'll think of me every time you look in the mirror."

Caleb scowled at her as his phone rang, and he walked away to take the call.

I nudged her with my elbow. "I'm so fucking proud of you right now. I'd high-five you if my hands weren't tied behind my back."

She gazed at me with watery eyes. "I'm so scared I might pee myself."

Despite the situation, I grinned. "No, you won't. You're too badass for that."

She gave me a weak smile. "You see how badass your pelvic floor is when you're this pregnant."

I couldn't wait.

Caleb ended his call and barked orders at his goons. "There's another car bringing more women for pickup. Go get them and bring them in."

The two men nodded and hightailed it out of the room.

Caleb turned his smug gaze back on us. "I had a quota to deliver on. You two are just the cherries on top of the cake, hand-delivered to me by your boyfriend's mother. I mean, really, if you're going to blame anyone, it should be Vaughn. He blabbed all my secrets in front of his mom so she knew exactly who to call when she wanted her new daughter-in-law to disappear. 'Don't kill her,'" he mocked, in a posh, feminine voice. "She just can't be near my precious baby boy.'" Caleb sniggered. "Truly, that phone call was so embarrassing. I wish I'd recorded it so I could play it for Vaughn."

I raised an eyebrow at him. "Like he's the only one with mommy issues around here."

The look Caleb shot me was as cold as glass. It only made me want to needle him more. I was clearly getting under his skin.

But a walkie-talkie on Caleb's belt crackled to life, and Goon Two's voice came down the line. "Boss, we got a couple of fighters. Gonna need an extra set of hands to get 'em in."

Caleb stared at the ceiling. "For fuck's sake." He focused on me. "You try anything, and I'll go after every single one of your sisters. Including that sweet little eight-year-old. What was her name again? Bobbie? Brady?" He grabbed the hair on the top of my head and yanked it back. "That's right. I know every single one of your weaknesses, Rebel. You think I don't know your sister is hiding at your father's farm with her bastard baby? I know. I know fucking everything."

"Because you're bigger and better than everyone, Caleb. You are a god. Blah, blah, fucking blah." Bliss was still running with her boredom act.

I used it to my advantage, seeing an opening. "Bliss! Stop it. He's talking about my sisters! Just do as you're told."

Her brows furrowed in confusion because she knew me well enough to know something wasn't right.

I implored her with my eyes to go along with the act.

She glanced up at Caleb and swallowed. "She's right. I'm sorry. We'll be good."

He traced his hand slowly down the side of Bliss's face. "It could have been so different, you know. If you'd just learned your place."

She nodded obediently.

I wanted to vomit at the sight, but it was enough to get Caleb to believe exactly what he wanted to believe.

That he had the power.

And we were just stupid, useless women who didn't know anything.

The second the door closed behind him, I twisted my legs and got my feet beneath me so I could press up into a standing position. I bent my knees and stuck my ass out between my bound hands, sliding them down the backs of my thighs.

Bliss gaped at me. "I would never be able to do that. My ass would get in the way."

I grinned at her. "I know I always say I want your curves, but today, my flat, bony ass is coming in handy." I stepped one foot backward through my arms, and then the other, so my hands were in front of me. I couldn't do anything about the restraints, but at least I could use my hands. I turned to Bliss. "Come on, pregnant lady. Time to get you up. All you gotta do is get on your feet. We'll worry about your hands later."

"Easier said than done with a belly, Rebel!"

"I know. But you gotta do it for Mini-Disney, Bliss. Twist your legs to the side like I did then push while I pull."

I'd had the advantage of being short and maybe even a little bit fit since Kian kept making me run places. Bliss didn't have those advantages.

But she was strong in her own way, and that was going to be what got us out of here. I held her upper arms and helped as much as I could, but the urgency was all Bliss needed.

She got up on her feet, arms still behind her back, but with fire in her eyes. "Now what?"

"Now we run."

I slammed down the door handle, sending up a silent thank you when it wasn't blocked from the outside. I peered around, not seeing anyone in the darkness.

But in the distance, women screamed.

We both paused at the noise, my blood running cold.

"Those women. We can't just leave them," Bliss whispered.

I didn't want to, but staying here wasn't the answer either. "We can't help them until we help ourselves. Run."

Bliss took a step toward the gates that would lead to the road.

It was the way out. We'd be forced into the bushes at the side of the road to avoid Caleb and his guys, but it might have worked. We might have gotten free and escaped.

But just escaping was no longer an option.

I stopped.

Grabbed her arm. "No. Get my brass knuckles out."

"What?" But to her credit, she turned around, blindly groping my ass pocket for the weapons I always kept there, even though her hands were still tied behind her back and she couldn't see what she was doing other than by feel.

When she put them on my fingers, I nearly cried with relief. But it was quickly followed by a wave of sheer determination. "This way."

Bliss shook her head in panic. "That will lead farther into the construction site."

"I know. Do you trust me?"

She didn't even hesitate. "Always."

Together, we set off into the darkness, her a few steps behind me as I weaved my way through machinery. Last time I'd been here, we'd tried to stay in the light.

This time I chose darkness. In more than one way. I clenched my fingers around the brass knuckles so tight my fingers ached.

Behind us, the screams grew louder. I looked over my shoulder to see Caleb and two other men dragging women across the worksite while they fought and screamed and kicked with all their might, none of it to any avail.

Caleb's curse when he found us gone from the shed echoed through the night air.

"Stupid little hos," Caleb cooed loudly enough for us to hear from the shadows. "Not long to go now until you're off to the life you deserve, sold off as some rich man's dirty little sex slave secret."

Bile rose in my mouth. Bliss stepped closer to me.

"He can't find us." Her voice was choked with fear.

But he could. He would.

And when he did, we'd be ready.

42

CALEB

Minutes earlier...

The slut with the blond hair bit and kicked at me, fighting me with everything she had.

It only made me enjoy slamming her down on the hard laminate floor all the more. I circled my fingers around her throat and whispered in her ear, "Stop your fucking bitching or I'll keep you for myself. Trust me, sweetheart. You don't want that."

Something wild inside me settled at the fear in her eyes and the way her screams cut off into silence.

"Where's the others?" Frank asked.

I snapped my head up, searching the room now full of sniveling women I couldn't stand the sight of.

Two were missing.

Of course, they fucking were.

A scream bubbled up inside me, desperate to get loose, but I wouldn't let it. I wouldn't stoop to the level of pathetic in front of me. Instead, I let it swirl and build inside me.

They couldn't have gotten far.

I'd find them.

Then I'd make them pay for disobeying me.

That would be the fun part.

"Hold down the fort."

Frank looked at me. "What are we supposed to do with them? There's four of them and only two of us."

I passed him my gun. "Here."

He took it eagerly. "What about you?"

I rolled my eyes. "I can handle two bound women without having to shoot them."

"What are we supposed to do with these ones?"

I shrugged, hand on the doorknob. "Whatever the fuck you want until the truck gets here."

Heat flashed in Frank's eyes. "*Anything* we want?"

I chuckled. "Anything except kill them."

I slipped out of the door as the screams started up again.

It filled my ears. Stoked my blood. But it was Bethany-Melissa I wanted to hear scream the loudest.

My chest throbbed, the scars where her boyfriend had cut into my skin a reminder of what she'd done.

Hurting her friend wasn't enough.

I needed more. She was just giving me the opportunity to deliver.

"Come out, come out, wherever you are," I called into the darkness of the worksite. "Let's talk about this rationally, shall we?"

Nothing but silence and the sound of my boots crunching over dirt and gravel filtered back to me.

I walked carefully, scanning the darkness, my dick stiffening with the thrill of the hunt. My breath came in short pants, hard to control. Blood rushed in my ears.

Fucking stupid bitches.

Punishing them was going to be so sweet. Luca wasn't expecting the two of them. The Sinners had rounded up enough to meet my quota, and so they should have, after they lost the first lot.

Bethany-Melissa and her mouthy bestie were just a sweet bonus that got me hot under the collar.

Maybe I'd keep them for a little while.

Play with them the way their men had tried to play with me.

I rubbed my hand over my cock, knowing it needed this. Needed their fight, and then their submission when they realized who the fuck I was.

I wasn't just some dumb kid who didn't know what he was doing. I'd spent years now, aligning myself with powerful men who understood what it took to get to the top. I wasn't going to fail now, when I was this close to showing my father who I was.

That I was as capable as he was.

That I didn't need a woman to help me get there.

I ground my molars, feeling that familiar surge of uselessness I always felt when I thought about my father.

I fucking hated it.

I fucking hated him.

I switched on the flashlight function on my phone, shining it around, illuminating the work trucks and excavators. "Tick-tock. I'm getting annoyed, Rebel. I know this was your idea. Bethany-Melissa wouldn't have the balls."

I paused and listened.

Something moved in the darkness to my right, and I spun around.

A black cat ran for its life across the worksite. I followed it, my flashlight bouncing over another shape, hidden in the darkness

I chuckled to myself. "Run, pussycat. Run. Watch the holes. You wouldn't want to fall in there and snap your neck..."

The figure didn't move. I couldn't get over how stupid women were. "You aren't even going to run? Seriously? Come on, Rebel. At least make me work for it."

Headlights flashed in the parking lot, blinding me. I squinted through the bright lights, vaguely making out the shape of a truck. Luca had finally come through.

"That's your ride over there," I called to the women hiding in the dark. "Time to go."

A whimper floated across to me.

Fuck, I loved the sound of her fear. It soothed every ragged edge inside me.

I drew closer, her features becoming clearer as the light from my phone lit her up. She was folded in on herself, her cries full of pain and fear.

I stared down at her. "That's what you get for trying to run from me." I glanced around but didn't see any sign of Bethany-Melissa. "Your friend just left you for dead, huh? Great friend she is. Get up."

She didn't move. Just crouched there, shaking like a leaf between holes dug out for pylons and mountains of dirt. The excavators around her made her look even smaller and more pathetic than she already was, their size dwarfing her.

"I said, get up. Luca Guerra is not a man you want to keep waiting."

She disobeyed me again, refusing to move. My patience snapped, my anger boiling over.

"Are you deaf, bitch? Move!" I shoved my fingers into her hair and yanked her up.

She unraveled from her crouched position, straightening.

Metal glinted around her fingers.

I opened my mouth to shout something, but her fist hit my stomach, the metal knuckles stealing my breath. Pain splintered through my abdomen, and I let go of her hair to reach for my stomach.

She followed up with a second loaded punch before I could.

A howl escaped my lips at the burn of agony. I hunched over, trying to breathe but couldn't. I dropped my phone, the screen shattering when it hit the hard ground.

Rebel delivered another two strikes to my ribs, each one creating a cracking noise as the bones broke.

Spearing pain shattered through my entire body, radiating out from the sharp, unexpected hits I hadn't been able to protect myself against. "You stupid—"

"Now, Bliss!"

Something hard rammed me from behind and didn't let up. Already off balance, I stumbled forward, pain pounding through my injuries with every step.

Until the dirt gave way below me.

The edge of the pylon hole crumbled.

And I fell headfirst into a hole so deep I had no chance of getting out.

43

REBEL

My hands throbbed from the impact of the knuckle-dusters against Caleb's midsection.

My wrists ached from the open wounds I'd given myself getting the restraints off with a combo of my teeth and pure determination and the barbed reinforcement bars I'd seen the night Kian had brought me here.

But Caleb hitting the dirt at the bottom of the pit was music to my ears. It made all the pain and the fear and the waiting in the dark, completely exposed, worth it.

I peered over the edge at his crumpled body.

"Is he dead?" Bliss gasped, breathing hard from the exertion of running her ex into a pit.

Caleb groaned from the bottom of the hole.

Anger coursed through me. "Of course not. Because he's a fucking cockroach and will outlive us all."

Caleb's groans turned into cruel laughter. He rose to his feet, staring up at us with vile hate in his eyes. "What now, Rebel? Was this your big plan? Shove me into a hole so I'd break my neck?"

"One could only hope," Bliss muttered.

Caleb's gaze turned to her, the fury in his eyes visible even from where we stood. "You're dead, bitch. No matter where you run, when I get out of here, I'll find you."

He was right. He would.

We all knew it.

He laughed again, though it was tinged with pain. "Frank! Frank! Bring the fucking gun out here and put it to good use with a bullet through my blushing bride's head."

Bliss glanced over her shoulder nervously. "There's headlights in the parking lot. We aren't that far from it. They're going to hear him."

"Damn right, they are, bitch. Frank!"

I spun around, the headlights blinding me. Men climbed out of the truck; their figures dark as they ran from the vehicle to the worksite office where Frank was holding the other women hostage.

Bliss staggered backward, grabbing my arm and dragging me with her. "We can't do any more here tonight. We need to run. Report this to the police."

But I shook her off.

I recognized that truck.

Through the glare of headlights, I could barely make out the O'Malley's Handyman Service decal on the side of the vehicle.

I grinned. "It's Kian, Vaughn, and Fang."

In the next second though, I realized there were two armed men inside the work shed they were running straight into.

My blood ran cold.

"No!" I screamed, waving my arms, trying to catch their attention. "Don't go in there!"

I broke into a run, my ankle twisting on the loose gravel, but it didn't matter. I needed to warn them. Help them.

Two gunshots ripped through the night air, stopping me in my tracks.

A blood-curdling scream tore from my lungs and mingled with the screams coming from inside.

I couldn't move. I couldn't breathe.

Bliss's arms came around me, holding me up, preventing me from collapsing. "It's not them. It's not them."

I held on to her, knowing that the three pieces of my heart were inside that building.

And that maybe now, one of theirs no longer beat.

Caleb's laughter from the pit was the thing that pushed me forward. I stumbled, clutching Bliss's fingers.

The worksite door opened. Fang stumbled down the steps, his white T-shirt covered in blood.

"Oh God," Bliss whispered.

"Fang!" I pulled away from Bliss and sprinted across the lot. I grabbed him by the arm, my fingers coating in sticky, red blood. A sob burst from my chest, the aching pain of knowing he was hurt as sharp and painful as if I'd been shot myself.

I yanked up his shirt, searching for the bullet hole.

He grabbed my hands. "Pix. Pix, stop! It's not my blood."

I stared up at him in confusion. There was so much of it. "Vaughn? Kian?"

"Not ours either," Vaughn said from behind me.

I spun around, another round of sobs overcoming me when they were both standing tall, spattered with blood but clearly uninjured. I rushed up the stairs, and they both engulfed me in their arms, sandwiching me between them.

In the room beyond, the two Sinners' members lay on the floor, bullet wounds in their guts, the two of them bleeding out slowly and hopefully painfully after what they'd done to these women.

"These men won't hurt you," I assured the scared group.

They stared at me with big eyes. I wasn't sure if they believed me or not, but they had to know they were better than the two pieces-of-shit humans who lay bleeding out in front of them.

And the one still hollering from the hole.

I looked up at Kian and Vaughn. "Luca is coming with a truck to pick them up for trafficking."

Fang shook his head. "Listen."

Not too far away, a group of engines roared.

"War and the rest of the MC are only a few minutes behind us," Fang explained. "We called them as soon as Riva admitted what she'd done. If Luca knows what's good for him, he'll take one look at the crowd and keep on driving. He's not going to be prepared for all of this."

Fang was right. The headlights of a group of bikes were already turning onto the road up ahead, the engines growing louder with every mile they passed.

War rode at the front, and Bliss let out a sob when he dropped his bike in the gravel and caught her in his arms.

He cradled her to his chest, one hand to the back of

her head, his eyes wide with fear. "Are you okay? What the fuck happened?"

Fang shook his head. "Long story."

A shout from behind us had everyone turning in that direction.

"Is somebody out there?" Kian shielded his eyes from the brightness of the headlights and peered into the darkness.

"Is that Caleb?" Vaughn strode forward, his eyes darkening with anger.

I caught his arm. "Yes. It is. But he's not going anywhere."

"We shoved him into a pit." A tiny smile lifted Bliss's lips. "We thought he'd break his neck, but unfortunately that didn't happen. But there's no way for him to get out."

Fang raised an eyebrow at me. "Seriously?"

I was sure it was a mixture of giddy relief and adrenaline, but I jerked my head toward the pit, almost proudly. "Go see for yourself. Trapped him like a pig."

Vaughn frowned at me as we headed in the direction of the pit. "How long were you at your dad's farm to start talking like that?"

I shoved him. "Seriously? You couldn't even give me five minutes without reverting back to your regular, asshole self?"

His expression softened, and he slung his arm around my shoulders, pulling me in tight to kiss the top of my head. "I love you, Roach. Even if you did just sound like a redneck."

I elbowed him, but then the four of us were on the edge of Caleb's hole, and my heartrate picked up again.

He stared up at us, his eyes murderous, his lips pulled

into a scowl. "You want to fucking get me out now or what?"

None of the guys said a word.

Neither did I. What we did next wasn't a decision I could make alone.

I turned at footsteps on the gravel behind us.

Bliss was flanked by all three of her guys. Nash and Vincent must have arrived sometime after the MC. She gave me a wobbly smile. "He's still alive, I see? That's a pity."

Vincent peeked over the edge and then back at his woman. "Scythe says to tell you, you did good." He paused. "And...I'm not repeating that, Scythe. You can tell her yourself later."

We all knew Scythe well enough to have a pretty good guess at what he was probably saying in the back of Vincent's mind. I would have bet my money on it being kinky, sarcastic, or completely deranged.

That about summed him up.

"What do you want to do, Bliss?" I asked her quietly. "We can't just leave him in there."

Her white teeth dug into her bottom lip. "I don't know. I just want this to be over. I want to go home with my family and raise my child in a world where Caleb and his evil don't exist."

I put my hand over my belly. "So do I."

I stared down at Caleb. He looked small, so far below me. Weak even, clearly hurt though he was putting on a brave front. I was pretty sure his arm was broken.

I felt no sympathy.

I crouched on the edge of the hole. It was too deep for him to even get a fingertip to the top of it, though he wasn't even trying. The hate in his gaze was all-encompassing. It was pure evil. He was so far past being human, he actually resembled a rabid animal, trapped and fighting for his life.

"You hurt me," I said slowly. "You held me down, ripped my clothes, tore my skin. You took something from me that I'll never get back. And I'm not the only one. You took it from Bliss. From Kara. How many other women, Caleb? How many would it have taken to satisfy you?"

He spat on the ground at his feet. "You whores are all the same to me. Feel privileged I even remember your name. Now call the cops. Whatever. I don't fucking care. Just get on with it. We know you're all talk and no action."

"I killed your friend."

He smiled snidely. "You pulled the trigger in the heat of the moment, with hot blood. What are you going to do now, Rebel? You going to shoot me in cold blood? We both know you aren't."

Bliss cocked her head to one side. "You talk a lot of smack for someone well aware that even though Rebel and I might not do it, there are several other people here just waiting on us to give them the green light."

Fang stuck his head over the edge and pointed his gun down at the man in the bottom of the pit. "Hi, Caleb."

War put his arm around Fang and waved down. "Howdy."

Even that didn't quiet Caleb. He snarled up at the two men, one covered in blood. "Go on then. You've wanted to kill me for this long. Just fucking do it. Put a bullet through my brain."

Fang looked over at me.

I shook my head.

Vaughn gaped. "You are not fucking letting him live?"

Down in the pit, Caleb was smug as fuck. Like he had me all figured out. That Bliss and I were bleeding hearts who would let him go free again, because we'd tried to end this before and hadn't been able to follow through.

"You underestimate the hate I have for you, Caleb." I stared down at him, making sure he saw every ounce of it in my eyes. I lowered my voice. "Letting one of them shoot you is too kind. Too. Fucking. Easy." I laughed, surprised at the tone.

I sounded as crazy as he was.

But maybe I liked it.

"Kian. Can you get the cement mixer on, please. And bring it over here?"

Bliss gasped. "Rebel... What are you doing?"

Kian didn't ask me why. He just did it. Vaughn, Nash, Vincent, and Fang all silently moved to help him load cement mix and water into the swirling barrel of the truck.

War remained behind; his gun trained on Caleb.

He glared at me. "You wouldn't."

I cocked my head. "Wouldn't I? Thing is, you don't know me at all. You know the scared, weak woman you left on the side of the road. You assumed that's who I really was beneath it all." I toed the edge of the hole, sending dirt down into his helpless face. "I was *never* truly that woman."

He spluttered as the dirt hit his face. "You're a weak-willed slut."

His words washed over me like he was singing

nursery rhymes. So much vile, putrid hate spewed from his mouth.

"Is that the best you've got? Schoolyard taunts? You know why it's you in that hole right now and not them? Because they saw me, Caleb. They saw Bliss. They saw that we are more than some spoiled little boy who grew up with too much money and parents who didn't love him." I threw some more dirt down the hole callously. "We see you, Caleb. We see every damn thing you're scared of."

"I'm not fucking scared!" he screamed.

"Pix," Fang said quietly.

I glanced over my shoulder at him.

"Kian says it's ready."

I gazed down at Caleb and wriggled my eyebrows. "Hear that?"

Reversing beeps filled the air. Kian backed the truck up to the edge so the cement slide hovered above Caleb's head.

He stared up at the chute, and his face paled with realization. "Wait. No. Wait, I'm sorry. I didn't mean it—"

Kian guided me to the control. "Just push this button when you're ready."

I searched his eyes for judgment on what I was about to do. But there was none.

There was none when I checked with Fang and Vaughn either.

Lastly, I turned to Bliss.

I didn't even need to say anything. She stood well away from the edge, her arms wrapped around herself, protecting her baby.

I'd expected some hesitation. A whispered question, asking me if we were doing the right thing.

All she did was nod, giving me the okay.

I pushed the button.

Thick, heavy cement slid from the barrel, down the chute, and into the hole.

"No!" Caleb screamed. "What are you doing? No!"

But my finger didn't tremble. I held down the button, watching the cement fall like rain, coating Caleb's expensive shoes and then his ankles.

In seconds, the thick, sloppy cement covered his knees, and in a minute, it was up around his waist.

"Please!" Caleb screamed. "Stop! Someone help!"

Vincent had his hands in his pockets, watching the pit fill. "Did you know, when you swallow cement, it actually burns? Swallowing cement can cause burns of the lips, mouth, throat, and stomach. Drooling. Difficulty swallowing. Agonizing pain in the intestines." He shrugged. "Probably feels like being burned alive from the inside out. Unpleasant to say the least."

Vaughn folded his arms across his chest, his head bobbing in agreement. "Very interesting facts, Vincent. Thanks for sharing."

Vincent nodded like they were having a conversation about toast.

From the pit, Caleb fought desperately, clawing at the dirt walls, fighting in vain to somehow lift himself above the rising concrete.

It crept higher and higher, until it covered his chest and then his neck. He stared at me with huge eyes, the whites visible right around. "Please!" He gasped, begging me for his life.

I moved the chute a little so the cement hit him square in the face.

I hoped Vincent was right.

I hoped it burned like the flames of Hell. Because that was where he was going.

Caleb sank beneath the concrete, his gaping mouth the last thing to disappear, filled with fiery concrete.

44

VAUGHN

*I*t was a long moment before anybody spoke. The eight of us stood there, staring at the hole we'd used to suffocate a man.

"Do you think he's dead yet?" Kian asked.

I stared at the spot where Caleb had disappeared. "I hope not. I hope he's under there, suffering."

"Hear! Hear!" War shook his head. "That was long overdue."

Rebel stepped back from the edge of the pit and turned to Vincent. "Sorry you didn't get a chance to torture him some more first."

Vincent's eyes gleamed in the darkness, like a demon straight out of a horror movie. "You did a very thorough job of torturing him all by yourself. I've never thought of drowning someone in cement. I enjoyed that."

Mental note to self, never get on Vincent's bad side. Jesus fuck.

I tugged Rebel to my chest, smoothing my hand down her back. "You did good, Roach. It's done."

She nodded into my chest. A tremble worked its way through her body.

I lowered my voice to a whisper only she would hear. "It's okay if you're not okay."

She pulled away and looked up at me with watery eyes.

Fuck. Even though it was well deserved, it was still a lot to kill a man in the way she just had.

But then she turned to the pit and stuck her middle finger up. "Fuck you, you piece of shit. I hope you fucking rot in Hell."

Bliss let out a bitter laugh. "Ditto." She ran a hand over her belly and focused on Nash. "Can you take me home, please? I don't want to be here when…" She turned big eyes on Vincent.

He nodded, his expression serious and matter of fact. "All of you should leave. Let me handle the body. It's what I'm best at. War, I'll need one or two of your guys to stay behind and get this concrete out so there's no questions in the morning."

"I'll stay," Fang offered.

But War shook his head. "Not you, brother. You need to be with your family tonight."

Fang nodded and thanked him.

The two of us flanked Rebel, herding her toward Kian's truck. We had her halfway into the back seat before she lifted her head and looked over at the worksite shed.

"The other women…"

"Let the club deal with it, Pix. The women will all be returned to their homes. Tonight, you're the only one we need to worry about." He swallowed thickly. "You and the baby."

Her mouth dropped open. "You know?"

"We found your pregnancy test in the bathroom trash can." I pulled her seat belt on for her and clicked it into place, adjusting the bottom strap low over the tops of her thighs so it wasn't pressing on her belly. I traced my fingers absently over her abdomen.

She caught them. "Are you okay with it?"

"I haven't even had a minute to process it," I admitted.

"I can give you that. You don't have to say anything right now. None of you do. Let's just go home."

Kian drove us back to Providence, but I didn't move my fingers from Rebel's belly.

We turned into my mom's empty driveway, and Kian parked next to the spot where her car normally sat.

"She's gone, isn't she? For good, I mean." The words were hard to force out, but I knew they were the truth.

"I'd run too, if I was going to be spending the rest of my life in jail for murder," Rebel said quietly.

Kian just shook his head. "I never would have picked it. She loved Bart."

"Too much," I said gruffly. "Too fucking much. She should have just let him go." I rubbed a weary hand over my face, trying to make sense of the jumble of confusion inside my head. "I need to go have a shower, I think. And sleep."

I pulled away from the other three and let myself inside. I could feel their worried gazes on my back, but I needed a minute.

I couldn't get out of my head. The thoughts swirled around like a tornado, dark and stormy and confusing.

Caleb. My mom. Luca. The businesses I'd lost. The people I'd hurt and lost.

But as I stood beneath the spray of hot water, they all disintegrated until only one thought was left.

One that shook me to my core when I considered what it meant.

I snapped my head up when the bathroom door opened.

Rebel leaned on the doorframe, still dressed in blood and cement-spattered clothes, but her brown-eyed gaze solely filled with concern.

For me.

I didn't fucking deserve it.

"Is there room for one more in that shower?"

I was a weak asshole for saying yes, but my lips were moving before I could even think about denying her.

On the other side of the glass shower door, she took her clothes off, each item piling up on the floor. We'd burn them later, everything we'd worn tonight, but that could wait.

Her eyes were big when she stepped beneath the spray, and I turned up the hot water, knowing she liked it that way.

She didn't say anything, just watched me carefully.

I didn't know how to say the things that were on my mind, so I squirted soap onto my hands and then put them to her body.

She closed her eyes beneath my touch and the warm spray of the water. "That feels nice," she murmured as I massaged it into her back.

She moaned softly so I slipped my hands around to the front and coated her breasts. I shouldn't have, but I tucked myself in tight behind her, my dick against the top of her ass, my lips finding a spot on her neck that had been washed clear of suds.

She pressed her ass back on me and dropped her head to one side, giving me better access.

My fingers washed clean, I let one hand trail down to her mound, and then between her lips, searching for her sweet little bud.

She rocked with my fingers. "Talk to me, Vaughn. I know something's wrong. If it's the baby, you don't have to do anything you don't want to do. Even if it's biologically yours. I'd never force you—"

"It's not that," I mumbled into her neck, inhaling the clean scent of her skin. I rubbed her clit faster, hoping she'd let it drop just long enough that I could at least make her come. I kissed every inch of her I could reach, trying to imprint the taste and shape of her to memory in case this was the last night she let me do it.

She moaned again but pulled away.

I dropped my hands to my sides. "You liked that. Why did you make me stop?"

Water droplets fell down her face. "Because you're keeping something from me. I can't do that with you when you're only here in body, but your mind is somewhere else."

I lowered my gaze to the floor. "I love you. You know that, right?"

She put her palms to my chest and stared up at me. "I know. But you're scaring me right now."

I swallowed down the lump in my throat, feeling more vulnerable than I ever had in my life. "Is this where we end?"

She recoiled so far, her back hit the tiled wall and she flinched at the temperature of it. "What? No! Of course not."

"My mother killed yours, Roach. How do we move past that?"

The tension fell out of her shoulders. "She killed your father too. But that's beside the point. You aren't her. You aren't your dad. You aren't anyone but you." She smiled ruefully. "You're the man I fell in love with, even though you still insist on calling me Roach."

I couldn't help but smile at that. "Can't stop, won't stop."

She shook her head. "I wouldn't expect anything else." Her palms drifted up my neck to cup both sides of my face. "I love you, Vaughn Weston. I'm carrying a baby who is yours, no matter who its biological father is. You aren't your mother any more than I am. You aren't going to run away to California again. So if you were even considering that, remove the idea from your brain immediately."

"I wasn't," I promised. "Not unless you told me you didn't want me anymore. Even then, I probably couldn't have left." I held her tighter. "You're addictive, Roach. So fucking addictive it hurts."

She pushed up on her toes and brushed her lips over mine. "I want you. I think I've wanted you since the minute I met you. And I'll want you until the minute I die. I don't need time to know that. It's always been there between us. We both know it."

We really fucking did.

I pushed her up against the wall, ignoring the way she

squealed at the cold tiles, and then dropped to my knees to suck her pussy.

"Oh," she moaned, lifting one leg over my shoulder and grabbing my head to use for balance. "God, yes."

She rocked her hips over my face, and I tongued her deep and hard, spearing up inside her before licking her clit and then repeating. The moment I slid my fingers inside her she crumpled, shouting out my name as she came.

When she was done, I licked my fingers clean and stood.

Her eyes were half-mast, but a happy smile played around her mouth. "I'd return the favor, but Kian and Fang are organizing something, and we're expected."

I reached behind me and shut off the water. "It's a foursome, isn't it?"

She glanced over her shoulder at me as she pulled a towel from the rack. "Is there something you'd want more?"

There was only one thing I could think of. "You. Forever."

Her smile was the sweetest thing I'd ever seen. "You already have that."

45

REBEL

"Fang has agreed to let me try something," Kian announced as Vaughn and I stepped into Fang's bedroom.

Vaughn surveyed the two queen-sized mattresses on the floor. "Did he agree to let you disappear his bedframe?" He stuck his head out into the hallway. "Where the hell is it?"

Fang pointed at the walk-in closet. "It was held together by four bolts. Not exactly difficult to take apart. We just pulled your mattress off your bed."

Vaughn toed it. "If you'd wanted a trampoline, Kian, you could have just bought one, you know."

Kian flipped him the bird. "You'll thank me when I'm fucking you and you're bouncing up and down on a nice soft mattress rather than the floor. We couldn't all fit on the one bed, you know. Especially when your ego takes up half the room."

Vaughn sauntered across the room and kissed him

hard on the mouth. "My back thanks you in advance. Feel free to go hard to teach me a lesson."

Kian grinned but then shoved him away. "Back to me. Fang has agreed we should kiss."

I was sure my eyebrows were raised as high as Vaughn's. The two of us darted looks between Kian and Fang like Kian had just revealed the two of them had been picked for the next space shuttle to the moon.

Vaughn cleared his throat. "By we, do you mean me and you? Or...?"

I was pretty interested in hearing that answer too.

Kian shook his head. "I mean me and Fang." He squinted in Fang's direction. "If Vaughn is more your type, though..."

Vaughn and Fang both shook their heads quickly. "No," they said in unison.

"Are you having some sort of bi-awakening?" I asked Fang. "What's brought this on?"

He lifted a shoulder. "Kian asked if we should try it—"

"For group cohesion," Kian explained.

Vaughn snorted. "What the fuck, Kian? Just say you want to kiss him."

Kian shrugged. "He's hot. But I like brunettes." His gaze turned heated as it rolled down my body and then did the same over Vaughn's.

"I'm still in the room, you know," Fang said.

Kian clapped his hands together. "So come on, then. Lay one on me. See how it feels. Maybe it feels good, and we take it further." He glanced at me and Vaughn. "If the two of you don't mind us exploring this."

I hid my laughter. "Please, go ahead. This will be the

best entertainment I've had since Caleb went glug, glug, glug."

They all stared at me.

"What? Too soon?"

Vaughn put an arm around my neck and covered my mouth with his hand. "Kian, please hurry up and kiss Fang before Rebel can talk anymore."

I nipped at his palm, and it fell away so he could kiss my mouth.

Kian jumped up and down on the spot a few times, stretching his arms and cracking his neck by rolling his head side to side.

Fang stared at him like he'd lost his mind. "You aren't about to compete in the Olympics, Kian. Just fucking kiss me."

Kian stepped in and grabbed the back of Fang's neck, hauling him in and kissing him hard. He opened his mouth, tongue pressing in, which Fang accepted for all of three seconds until the two of them broke away.

They both grimaced at each other.

"That wasn't good," Kian admitted with a cringe. "Damn, that was not good at all."

"Nope. Definitely straight." Fang rubbed the back of his hand over his mouth before drawing me in. "So very fucking straight." He put his hands beneath my arms and lifted me right off the floor.

I wrapped my arms and legs around him and grinned. "I could have told you that."

"Then why didn't you?"

I chuckled. "Because it was kind of hot. At least until the two of you started gagging at each other."

He bent his knees, dropping me down onto the mattress and peeling away the towel I had on.

I was completely naked beneath, and I lay there in front of him, Kian, and Vaughn, without an ounce of shame.

Fang's lips found my neck and then slid down over my breasts and eventually to my belly. The kiss he placed there was tender rather than sensual.

He gazed up at me, his lips lingering on my skin. "I'm so fucking happy, Pix."

I stroked my fingers through the blond lengths of his hair. They were damp from the shower he must have taken while I was in with Vaughn. "I knew you would be. You're going to be the best dad."

He shook his head a tiny bit, then pressed his lips to mine. "I've wanted a family as long as I can remember. I never thought I'd get to have it." He kissed me sweetly, and there was absolutely nothing gross about it. He and I fit together perfectly.

We always had.

I knew without a doubt we always would.

He covered my body with his and yanked his sweats down over his hips, freeing his erection. "Need to take you now, Pix. I can't wait."

He didn't need to. I was already primed from Vaughn's tongue work in the shower and Fang saying he wanted this life we were building together.

I spread my legs beneath him, welcoming him home, where he'd always belonged.

He and I moved instinctively, his thrusts deep and hard, each one ending with a grind of his pubic bone to my clit that set me on fire. He stretched me perfectly, and we joined together easily, having done this many times before, but never with the knowledge that there was nothing better than this. That there was never going to be anyone else for me but the three of them.

There was no fear in the idea. Only happiness.

We came together, my cries muffled by his kisses. His groans, swallowed by mine.

"I love you," he whispered as we slowed into a barely rocking movement.

"Not as much as I love you." I meant it with every beat of my heart. He would never understand that I remembered every time he'd been there for me. I remembered every heated look. Every sweet word.

I would never forget the way he'd seen me when nobody else had. I would love him forever because of it.

He rolled me to the other side of the bed, where Kian and Vaughn were lying on their sides, their legs and arms as entwined as their tongues. Kian's hand was between their bodies, and I lay there with my hand propped up under my head, Fang spooning me from behind while we watched Kian get Vaughn off.

"Fuck," Vaughn moaned. "I need to come."

Fang's hand slid over my hip and between my folds again, working me up, playing with my clit.

Kian kissed Vaughn again, swallowing his groan of ecstasy when he came over Kian's hand, coating it with his cum.

Vaughn flopped onto his back, his eyes closed, a happy smile on his face. "Maybe you should try doing that to Fang. He might have a different reaction to your kisses."

"He's gonna have to wait if he wants a turn. I need my girl. Come here, Rebel."

I crawled across the bed and straddled his hips.

"Higher, Little Demon. Ride my face."

I whimpered as I took my spot, legs wide either side of his head. He put his arm around my thigh and pulled me down, tonguing me from top to bottom.

I arched my spine, leaning back and giving him full access to my most intimate places. He finger fucked me, using Vaughn's cum as lube, and the beginnings of another orgasm lit up inside me. My legs trembled with anticipation.

"Not yet." His voice was muffled from between my thighs, and he guided me back down to where his cock strained for my attention.

I sank down onto him, crying out at the sensation of being filled again when I was already so sensitive. I bounced on him, erratic and out of rhythm, desperately seeking the finale I knew was coming.

He was there to wrap his arms around me. To connect us with his gaze. To ground me until we were working together again, slowly joining.

I could barely breathe for wanting him.

"I'm sorry about what I said earlier," he murmured. "About it being a disaster if we were to have a baby."

I shook my head, cupping his face, kissing his mouth. "No. You were probably right. I'm probably going to be terrible—"

He put his thumb to my lips, drawing it down and then inside so I couldn't speak. "I was wrong. You are going to be the most amazing mother ever. And I'll do my best to keep up. That baby inside you deserves no less than a man who will step up for him. Or her. But I'm pretty sure it's a boy."

Happiness bubbled up inside me.

Kian took his thumb from my mouth and pushed it between us to rub my clit.

With a grin, I pushed him back onto the bed and took over, riding him fast and hard while he pinched the little bundle of nerves that made me want to scream in all the best ways.

"Come with me," he groaned. "Need to feel your pussy flutter around me. Fuck."

I was so close. I moaned, grinding over him, taking his cock completely, letting the sensations of knowing he loved me and this baby filter through until it was all I knew.

"Oh!" I came hard, drowning us both in my arousal, as well as his.

My eyes rolled back, fireworks of color exploding behind my eyelids.

We came together like we'd been born to do it.

Like nothing else mattered except the happiness these three men had brought me.

My hand drifted to my belly.

These three men, and the tiny gift they'd given me.

EPILOGUE
REBEL

One Month Later...

Christmas music played over the speakers when we left the OB/GYN's office. The waiting room was decorated with tinsel and colored lights, and a half-sized tree sat in the corner, traditionally decorated in red, green, and gold. The laughing, inflatable Santa wiggled about in the breeze created by the heating system.

I ignored all of it, too busy staring down at the black-and-white photos the doctor had given us.

Out on the street, Kian hurried us to his truck, and I pulled my jacket tight against the wind.

My belly poked out, though. I hadn't been able to do it up for a week now. A tiny baby bump getting in the way.

Settled on the back seat next to Vaughn, I passed him the photos.

He studied each one again and again, like something

might have changed since they'd been taken ten minutes earlier.

Kian got us on the road to home, but the car was deathly silent.

So silent I couldn't stand it.

"Somebody say something!" I begged.

Kian's gaze remained firmly on the road. He'd been like this ever since he'd found out I was pregnant. Driving everywhere at a snail's pace. It was maddening how long it now took us to get places, but it was pretty sweet too. He cleared his throat.

"Sorry, I'm just mentally planning out all the things I'm going to have to baby proof around the house. She gave us pamphlets, right? And a book recommendation list? Do you think they come in audiobook? I could get through more of them like that."

Fang reached a hand back to me, and I took it, letting him trail his fingers up and down my palm. "I liked what she said about cloth diapers. Do you think we could do that?"

I nodded. "Sure. If you want to." I grinned at him. "You can be the one to scrub them clean of poop, though."

His smile was wide. "I won't mind."

Gosh, I loved him. Who else would be so into his unborn child he actually wanted to scrub poop?

I glanced over at Vaughn again.

He hadn't said anything since the appointment. Butterflies took flight in my belly. He'd been as excited as the other two when we'd arrived, talking all about how he was going to teach the baby to swim and lecturing the rest of us about how we'd need new pool fences before he or she was born.

But now he was a little green.

Kian kept flicking glances back at him in the rearview mirror too. "Hey, Vaughn. You good?"

Vaughn eventually looked up. "What? Sorry. Yes. Fine. Yes. Good."

I cringed internally. It sounded like he was anything but. But there wasn't anything I could do about it right now. We were nearly home, and we weren't alone.

Our street was lined with cars on both sides, and Kian slowly maneuvered the truck in between them. "Damn, how many people did Bliss invite to this thing?"

"I've honestly no idea," I admitted. "I'm regretting giving her free rein over this gender reveal party."

"You couldn't plan one for yourself," Vaughn said finally. "You would have decorated in all black."

I looked over at him. "Of course you come out of your shell shock just to mock me."

"Did I lie?"

He had a point. The entire front of the house was covered in pink and blue streamers. It was like she'd TP-ed the place in the two hours we'd been gone. Bunches and bunches of balloons formed an archway we had to walk under to even get to the front door.

"I can't imagine what the inside is like. God, do you think she's going to make us play that baby shower game where they melt chocolate onto diapers and then you have to lick it to guess which flavor it is?"

Vaughn jerked away from me in horror. "You...what? You lick the shit?"

"It's obviously not actually shit." Kian shook his head. "It's chocolate shit."

"That's still disgusting." Vaughn's face was so screwed up it was comical.

Not that I disagreed. But when Bliss had found out my ultrasound was on a Saturday morning, she'd declared she'd throw me a gender reveal party straight after because, apparently, I had a big mouth and couldn't keep a secret long enough for it to be any other day.

I would have been happy to just send everyone a text, but then she'd given me the guilt trip over everything being so doom and gloom for the last few months, with Caleb's missing poster plastered all over town, and Riva awaiting trial after she'd been picked up on a highway just outside the state. Karmichael was out on bail, but he hadn't returned to the house, probably because the property had belonged to Riva. He was still being investigated to determine whether he had been her accomplice, or if he was actually innocent. I didn't know how to feel about that. It was something that would only be determined by a trial.

We'd been trying so hard to put all of that behind us. So Bliss was right when she said that this was something that needed to be celebrated.

Plus, as I was beginning to understand well, arguing with a pregnant woman wasn't a smart idea.

Especially when the woman was *very* pregnant and prone to irrational outbursts of tears that didn't seem to ever end. Just a few weeks ago she'd cried for an hour because a bee had stung her and subsequently died. She wasn't worried about the sting. She said she'd barely even felt it. But she couldn't stop crying over the fact the insect was dead.

Nash and I had to close Psychos just so he could take her home.

Kian eventually parked the truck in the driveway and opened the door for me, grabbing my hand to help me down.

I gave him a sidelong look. "We've talked about this. I am not going to fall out of the truck and land on my belly."

He didn't let up on my hand. "You don't know that. You're carrying precious cargo, you know."

I smiled up at him with what was very likely a stupidly lovesick expression.

Truthfully, my moods were as all over the place as Bliss's were. Less crying, but I was unusually sappy. I'd told Vaughn I loved him so many times this morning he'd asked me if I was having a stroke.

Rude. I'd tell Fang next time the mood struck me.

But we had a party to get through first. The moment we opened the door, the house full of people cheered.

Despite myself and the fact I hadn't really wanted any of this, I couldn't help but grin when I saw the sea of familiar faces.

Bliss rushed me, grabbing me in a hug. "You did find out the gender, didn't you? Tell me right now. No! Wait. Don't tell me. I want to be surprised too. I bought a blue and a pink popper thingo so we're all set for whenever you want to do it. Oh my God, I'm so excited."

I eyed her. "You do know you could have found out if yours was a boy or a girl, too, you know?"

She gripped my hand so hard I had to wonder for a second if she was having contractions. "I know, but I wanted a surprise. But that was also possibly the worst idea of my life, and now I'm in agony waiting to know, so please just let me live vicariously through you."

I laughed at the desperation in her expression. "Chill out. We found out the gender. The reveal can go ahead."

"Ah!" She spun me around in a circle. "It's a girl! I just know it."

She moved aside, tucking her arm into the crook of my elbow and dragging me around to say hello to everyone else. War, Nash, and Vincent were already talking to Fang. Sasha waved from where she was pouring drinks for her and Kian.

There were some of the performers who worked at Psychos on party nights, and the entire MC was here. Queenie waved from the back of the room, and I stood on my tiptoes to blow her a kiss above the sea of leather. There was more black clothing here today than any other baby party in history, I was sure.

I scanned the room, frowning when my gaze landed on Liam. "Bliss, why is my lawyer at my baby shower?"

She tugged me in that direction. "Because suddenly, the two of you have more in common than him getting you out of jail."

Liam grinned as we approached. "Good to see you under happier circumstances. Rebel, meet Mae, Rowe, and Heath. My partners."

I'd forgotten their similar lifestyles was how Bliss even knew Liam in the first place.

Mae smiled warmly at me. "I hope we're not crashing. Bliss was very insistent we come."

Bliss squeezed my fingers. "Mae has been receiving the brunt of my 'pregnancy with three daddies' freak-out calls. I thought it might be helpful for you to have someone to talk to as well."

"I'm here too, though it's been a while for me." Lacey stepped in with a smile, hefting her daughter on her hip. "Luna is getting big."

I remembered the younger woman from the fights Kian had taken me to. I'd stood with her and her partners when Kian and Fang had been punching the crap out of each other. "Oh my God, hi!" I hugged her. "I feel so bad for running off on you that night."

Lacey shook her head, dark curls that matched her daughter's ringlets bobbing around her face. "Don't even mention it. I could already see back then you were heading down the same path as the rest of us. Juggling multiple men. Kian was staring after you with hearts in his eyes, even as you walked off with someone else."

Heat tinged my cheeks, but I laughed. "You could have warned me."

She winked at me. "But where's the fun in that? Wasn't it more fun to work it out for yourself?"

If I took out all the Caleb shit, she was probably right.

Lacey started telling me about her birth with Luna, and Mae chimed in, explaining some complications she'd had with her own pregnancy.

I was sure I looked like a bobble head, nodding constantly while taking mental notes.

I had so much to learn, and I desperately wanted to do a good job at being a mom. I wanted more than what I'd had. I was probably never going to be the mom who baked cookies or volunteered for the PTA. That was more

Bliss's domain than mine. I'd have to get her to make a double batch when our kids had bake sales at school.

But I wanted a house filled with the love and support I hadn't had. I wanted to be the parent who showed up. I wanted to be the one to tuck them into bed and read them stories, even if they were twisted fairy tales where the bad boys on motorcycles were the ones who rescued the princess.

Mid conversation about the pros and cons of pacifiers, Bliss cut in with a groan of frustration. "Okay, I'm sorry, I love you all, and this conversation is truly noteworthy, but can we put a pin in it for a minute? Can we do the gender reveal? I can't concentrate!"

I sniggered at the exasperation on her face. She'd clearly been holding that in for the past twenty minutes. She was going to explode if I didn't agree to this.

"Okay, gimme the poppers and round up my men."

She clapped excitedly, and War put two fingers to his lips and blew out a short, sharp whistle that cut through the buzzing noise of the room. "Vaughn! Kian! Fang! Up front."

Bliss pressed the poppers into my hand. "This one is pink for a girl. This one is blue for a boy. Don't let anyone see the sticker colors before you pop them, though."

"You're taking this very seriously," I told her.

She shoved me toward the front of the room where the guys were gathering.

I held the poppers out to the men. "Anyone want to do the honors?"

Fang shook his head. "All you, Pix."

I checked the colored stickers on the handle and then

put one down on the table before turning back to the crowd. "Okay, so Bliss tells me you might all want to know if we're having a boy or a girl?"

A round of cheers went up as people raised their drinks in the air. Some of the guys from the MC stamped their feet on Riva's hardwood floors.

My hardwood floors, I corrected myself. We'd had a letter in the mail from a lawyer, giving Vaughn the title to the house.

We hadn't made a fuss about it, because the circumstances around him inheriting it weren't anything pleasant. It hadn't been enough for him to forgive his mother and stepfather for what they'd done.

But we had a home again. A place to raise our family. For that, I was grateful.

I shook the popper in the air. "You ready?"

"Five!" Bliss yelled. "Four! Three!"

The rest of the room joined in. "Two! One!"

I ripped the cord on the popper.

Blue confetti filled the air, bursting out over our friends who'd gathered.

A scream of excitement cut through the rest of the cheers, and Bliss threw herself at me.

"A boy! Oh my God, I was so sure it was a girl, but maybe that just means that's what I'm having. You're going to be a boy mom, Rebel!"

I glanced over at my men standing shoulder to shoulder behind me. The three of them looked proud as punch, even though this wasn't a surprise for them, since they'd been there in the OB's room when we'd been told. They were going to rock the boy-dad role, taking our little man to football games and teaching him to ride a bike. I was already imagining the mischief the four of them would get into.

I accepted hugs from multiple people before disentangling myself because there was something else I needed to say. "There was something else we found out at the OB's office this morning," I said loudly, trying to be heard above the din.

Bliss's eyes went wide, but there was worry behind them. "Is everything okay? I didn't even ask if he was healthy…"

I grinned at her and reached behind me for the other popper. In one quick pull, the pink confetti flew up in the air.

Bliss screamed so loud I could have sworn it pierced my eardrums. "Twins? Is it twins?"

I nodded.

She screamed again.

The people I loved most in the world surrounded us, every single one of them happy and safe and loved. Just like our babies would be.

Someone turned the music up, and the drinks flowed, at least for everyone but me and Bliss.

It was a party I'd never thought I'd have wanted, but in the moment, it was everything.

Vaughn tugged me aside after I got through the line of people waiting to pepper me with questions about how I was feeling and what the doctor had said. He towed me up the stairs until we were in his bedroom. Kian and Fang were on the other side.

I grinned at them happily. "Everyone was so surprised. That was actually pretty fun."

The three of them wore matching smirks.

My smile turned into suspicion. "What's going on?"

Vaugh let out a laugh. "I didn't have my head together enough to ask during our consultation, but something niggled at me all the way home."

I frowned at him. "Something about the babies?"

He nodded. "So I just got off the phone with Dr. Storley."

"And?" I prompted, waving him along so he would talk faster.

"Fraternal twins, like ours, are created by two eggs."

Fang shook his head, clearly not understanding where Vaughn was going. Couldn't blame him because I had no idea either.

"Yeah? So?"

"Two eggs. Two sperm," Vaughn announced.

I put a hand over my mouth. "No...you don't think..."

"Two baby daddies?" Kian asked, wide-eyed. "If our twins were conceived during one of the times we were all together, they could have different biological fathers?"

"What are the odds of that happening?" I gripped the edge of Vaughn's dresser.

Vaughn laughed. "Apparently we're all in with a shot, according to the doctor."

Holy shit.

Fang chuckled and caught my chin in his fingers. "You okay with that, Pix? Today has been a lot to take in."

It had. But as I looked around at the three men I loved, I knew I was exactly where I was supposed to be. No matter which of them had helped to make our babies, they would get the best of all three of the men who would raise them. Fang's kind heart. Kian's sense of humor. Vaughn's fierce loyalty.

I'd found the pieces of my heart amongst revenge and obsession, fear, and greed. I'd picked them up, sewn them together, and made them mine.

The only thing left to do was let it beat for eternity.

BONUS EPILOGUE
KARA

"Want to go for a little stroll in the moonlight?"

Hayley Jade's eyes shined, her smile wide just because I looked at her. She was so sweetly chubby now and the absolute bright spark in my otherwise quiet and lonely days.

"Everyone is probably inside having dinner with their families. The coast should be clear."

Ever since I'd returned home with Hayley Jade in my arms, the people I'd once called my friends and family had been cold and distant. They'd looked away when I'd passed them on my way to Sunday morning church and ignored Hayley Jade's happy gurgles as she'd tried to get their attention from the back pew.

I missed being seen. Becoming invisible had given me a lot of time to relive all the moments Hayden's quiet gaze had settled on me. What it felt like, and the reactions it set off inside.

I couldn't imagine I'd ever get to feel that again. Not

living here, in the middle of nowhere with my options limited to the handful of middle-aged men. That I was so disgraced was probably a good thing. It meant none of them had the chance to leer at me, or for their gazes to linger for an indecent amount of time when they thought no one else was watching.

But I was grateful to have been given a roof over my head. Even if I had become the commune leper and the subject of gossip. I was sure they were using me as a cautionary tale, warning the other young women of what would happen if they dared to leave and try to make it on their own.

They probably weren't wrong to do so.

It wasn't easy to endure though, and maybe it was cowardly of me, but I'd taken to staying indoors when a lot of people were around and only going out when I wouldn't be noticed.

I put Hayley Jade into her stroller with a beanie on her head that Rebel had sent for her, and then tucked blankets all around her to keep her warm against the chilly night air.

She gurgled happy baby sounds, which mingled with the quiet rustle of the breeze across the fields and the distant hooting of an owl.

I took the same, well-worn path I always did, guiding the stroller over the uneven ground to the commune's shared gardens. I'd always enjoyed working in them. There was something soothing about having my fingers in the earth and watching food grow from the tiny seeds I nurtured.

I pushed Hayley Jade right to the edge of the garden beds and put the brake on the stroller. Kneeling, I pulled a couple of weeds from around the plants. "This is cauliflower," I told Hayley Jade, even though she was much too young to comprehend anything I was saying. But some days, the only words I heard were the ones I spoke to her, and it had become habit. "And broccoli. They both grow well here, even in the winter." I looked around, making sure there was no one watching and then picked a stalk. "We can roast some of this for our dinner tomorrow."

"You don't have permission to do that," a voice said from the darkness.

I jolted, dropping the broccoli and standing quickly. "I... um..."

A man stepped from the darkness, coming close enough I could make out his features.

My heart sank. Of all people, of course it was him.

I bowed my head respectfully. "I'm sorry, Brother Josiah. You're right. I didn't have permission. It's just so lovely and delicious. Greed got the better of me."

He walked around me in a circle, slowly watching me. He was tall, his legs encased in dark denim jeans, a flannel jacket with a sheepskin collar covering his top half. He had to be around my dad's age, with crinkles at the sides of his eyes and faint lines across his forehead.

Many of the women here found our leader attractive, but I couldn't see it. While others took his attention as flattering, it had always made me nervous.

His gaze lingered too long.

And on parts of me I didn't want anyone noticing.

My breasts. The curve of my hips. The place between my legs.

I didn't dare breathe. I knew what I'd done was

wrong. We had rules that all food was to be shared. You didn't just get to go take whatever you wanted. A community couldn't run like that.

I just hadn't wanted to leave my cabin when the food rations were handed out. The entire commune came out on those days, and everyone would have stared. I didn't need much to eat, and Hayley Jade didn't need anything but my milk. I'd had enough to get by, especially by adding a few little bits and pieces to my supply when I was out on my nighttime walks.

"I haven't seen much of you since you returned," he said eventually. "Only at church."

I only went there because I knew not going would only make the rumors about me worse. "I've been busy, I guess. Taking care of my daughter."

He peered into the stroller, staring down at her.

Instinct told me to jerk her away. Cover her up. But I knew that would be rude, and I'd be admonished for my poor behavior. Instead, I clenched my fingers around the handle tighter and forced myself to remain still.

He was just looking at her.

He wasn't doing anything wrong.

His gaze drew back up to mine. "She's a lovely baby."

My response was barely more than a whisper. "Thank you."

He trailed his fingers along the fabric of the stroller. "And you're a lovely woman."

I gasped when his hand settled on mine, wanting to snatch it away. Instantly, I realized my daydreams of Hayden were ridiculous. This felt all wrong. My skin crawled. After what Caleb had done to me, I never wanted a man to touch me ever again. Definitely not this man, who was clearly twice my age.

But he was our leader. I'd already disrespected his authority once by leaving, and he'd been gracious in letting me return. I couldn't insult him by cringing away from his touch as well.

His fingers traced idly over the back of my hand, and he stepped in closer, his breath warm on my neck. "Did you like her father's touch, Louisa Kara?"

I widened my eyes at him, shock punching me in the stomach. "Excuse me? I don't understand."

He chuckled, brushing my long hair aside to expose my neck. "Sure you do. You laid with a man, did you not? He took your clothes off. Put himself inside you. Spilled his seed so that darling child could be brought into this world. I'm merely asking if you enjoyed it?"

My skin crawled. "This is inappropriate," I mumbled.

His hand skimmed down my back and over the curve of my ass. "Nothing wrong with asking if you enjoy sex, Louisa. I do."

Rude or not, him touching me there, in a place he clearly knew wasn't allowed, was the last straw. I turned away from him. "I need to leave. My daughter needs to go to bed."

To my relief, he let me. I hurried back down the path, the delicious green stem of broccoli forgotten in my haste to get away from him.

He didn't stop me.

For that, I was grateful.

I would go outside during the day tomorrow.

I didn't care if people stared and gossiped.

It was better than meeting Brother Josiah alone in the dark.

The knock on my cabin door came early and completely out of the blue.

I blinked a few times, the early morning sun creeping around the edges of the blackout blind in the bedroom I shared with my daughter. Hayley Jade was still sound asleep in her crib, her perfect rosebud lips parted slightly as she breathed. Her dark eyelashes fanned out across her rosy cheeks.

The knock came again, more insistent this time. "Louisa Kara! Open this door this instant."

"Mama?" I stumbled out of bed, leaving the little bedroom that opened into the rest of the cabin. It was cold, the fire I'd made the night before had gone out. I opened the door and rubbed briskly at my bare arms as my mother strode through the door, a dress hanging over her arm.

She thrust it in my direction. "Get dressed."

"For what?"

She glared at me. "Have you learned nothing? Stop questioning everyone and everything. Get dressed. There's a celebration happening today."

"I'm actually invited?"

She guided me to the tiny kitchen table and pushed me into one of the two hard, wooden seats. "Of course you are."

I didn't say anything, because it only would have annoyed her, but I thought I had a right to be surprised to be invited to anything happening on the commune.

Mama pulled out the tie from my hair, and the long lengths tumbled down my back.

She took to it viciously, brushing out my hair the way she had when I was a little girl, and then redoing the tight braid so it was neat and tidy, making sure she covered the scar from when Caleb had ripped my scalp.

She gave a satisfied nod after I stood and faced her, but then her gaze turned away, landing on the dress. "Hurry. I don't want to keep everyone waiting. You get dressed, and I'll change Hayley Jade."

I picked up the dress and stepped into the small bathroom to freshen up. The water was cold when I splashed it on my face, but it had the bonus of shifting the last of the sleepy feeling. I patted my face dry with a hand towel before rummaging through the top drawer in the vanity for my makeup.

"Not too much, Kara. No lipstick."

"I know, I know," I muttered. She would have died if she'd seen the bright-red lipstick I'd worn sometimes when I'd been living with Rebel.

My heart squeezed at the thought of my older sister. I missed her a lot, and FaceTime wasn't the same. I didn't even know how much longer I would have that. As it was, I'd been hiding the phone Rebel had given me from my parents, knowing full well they wouldn't approve. They didn't approve of technology in general, which had been part of the reason I'd left in the first place.

The outside world had seemed big and exciting, and though I was insignificant, I'd wanted to be a part of it.

The outside world scared me now I'd had a taste of it.

Though I missed my sister, the commune was safe. Even with Caleb dead, there were other dangers outside our fences.

Other men who would take advantage of a single mom with limited means and a lack of street smarts. It had taken barely any time for Caleb to set his sights on me. There would be others who would do the same.

It didn't matter how lonely I was here.

All that mattered was my daughter was happy and healthy and had a home where I could take care of her and shield her from the dangers I wished I'd never learned of.

I applied a tiny amount of natural-looking makeup, coating my long lashes with dark mascara and rubbing blusher onto the apples of my cheeks.

The church bells rang from our chapel across the field.

Mama appeared in the bathroom doorway with Hayley Jade on her hip and a frown on her face. "You aren't even dressed! Louisa!"

I sighed. "Mama, please. I've asked you so many times to call me Kara."

She pursed her lips together. "That's not the name I gave you."

"It's part of it."

But clearly the matter wasn't to be discussed any further. Sounds came from outside the main door, and Mama shot me a look that clearly said, 'Hurry it up or there'll be words about it.'

I put on the soft pink dress that gathered around my breasts and then flowed over my hips and behind. Smoothing my palms over the material, I actually felt pretty. Something that hadn't happened much since I'd returned and been forced to give up the majority of the clothes Rebel had sent me home with.

"Your father and sisters are here. It's time to go."

I nodded. "Thank you for the dress." I tried yet again to bridge the gap between us. We'd been close once, but any semblance of that relationship had been destroyed by my leaving.

Another regret I couldn't shake. Though my mama was sometimes sharp and to the point, I loved her. I hated that I'd disappointed her, even though I would have never swapped Hayley Jade for the world.

I just wished Mama could love her like I did and see past the fact I'd had a child out of wedlock.

I followed her down the stairs, meeting my father at the bottom.

He cast an eye over my outfit and makeup and then nodded. "Okay. Let's do this."

Mama said nothing.

Neither did any of my siblings as we walked across the field and past the gardens.

I tried to make conversation with my family anyway. I hadn't seen any of them for a few days. "How are your studies going, Samantha?"

"Fine, thank you."

She didn't elaborate, so I pushed further. "If you need any help with your homework, you can always bring it down to me—"

"No, thank you. I'm fine."

I pressed my lips together, trying to fight off the hurt at being cut out. After even my youngest sister gave me nothing but yes-or-no answers, I gave up trying to reconnect with them. It clearly wasn't going to happen today.

But it would eventually. I would keep trying until I was blue in the face. I missed them. I was sure that deep down, no matter what people within the community had said about me, they missed me, too.

More people arrived the closer we got to the chapel, but after the cold reception from my own family, I didn't dare try to speak with any of them. I cast my eyes down like a good, obedient daughter, and kept my mouth shut.

The chapel bells rang again as we entered.

My father nodded at my mother, his mouth tight. "I'll see you inside."

She nodded back and passed Hayley Jade to Samantha, who followed after my father.

I went to do the same, but Mama stopped me, grabbing me by the shoulders. "Not you, Louisa Kara."

I frowned. "What do you mean?"

"You need to wait here."

Irritation prickled inside me, even though I knew I'd brought this sort of treatment on myself by doing the things I'd done. I'd been happy to sit at the back of the church instead of toward the front with my family. But today had been different. They'd sought me out. Not the other way around. "Mama, you came to me. You told me I was invited."

Her gaze darted to the rest of the commune filing inside and taking seats. "You are."

"Then let's go inside. It's cold out here." I shook off her hold on me and stepped aside, getting my first glimpse at the chapel I'd spent so many of my days inside, praying I could be as good as my parents asked me to be.

The interior was filled with white decorations. There were flowers and ribbons everywhere, large bouquets on the altar, and streamers flapped at the ends of pews in the cool breeze we were letting in by standing in the doorway.

I'd only seen the church like this maybe a dozen times in my life, and I smiled now at seeing it like this again. The traditional wedding decorations were a sacred part of the ceremony, and they had been one of the rare, exciting occasions in an otherwise dull life.

My excitement dimmed when I took in the man standing at the altar, dressed in his finest clothes.

Brother Josiah.

Our gazes met, and instantly, my skin crawled with revulsion.

Everything about him reminded me of Caleb.

His blue eyes looked sweet and innocent, but behind them, there was a darkness I'd come to know all too well.

A shudder rolled down my spine even thinking about a woman standing up there, reciting the marriage vows that promised to love and serve a man who had evil in his eyes.

"Brother Josiah is getting married?" I asked in a hushed voice. "To who?"

My mother's grip on me tightened. "To you, Kara. He's chosen you to be his wife."

THE END.

Want to know who the baby daddy (or daddies!) is? It's

all in the free bonus scene on my website. Click this link or check the bonus content tab at www.ellethorpe.com

Forced into marriage by the dangerous leader of a cult, Kara's story is only just beginning. **The Saint View world continues in 2024 with Kara, Hayden (Chaos), Hawk, and a new mystery man. Click this link to preorder the series now!**

SAINT VIEW READING ORDER
EACH TRILOGY CAN STAND ALONE, BUT IF YOU WANT TO BINGE...

SAINT VIEW HIGH
REVERSE HAREM

SAINT VIEW PRISON
REVERSE HAREM

SAINT VIEW PSYCHOS
REVERSE HAREM

SAINT VIEW REBELS
REVERSE HAREM

SAINT VIEW STRIP
**MALE/FEMALE
(BEST READ ANY TIME AFTER PSYCHOS)**

PLUS SHORT STORIES AND BONUS SCENES AT
WWW.ELLETHORPE.COM

WANT SIGNED PAPERBACKS, SPECIAL EDITION COVERS, OR SAINT VIEW MERCH?

Check out Elle's new website store at
https://www.ellethorpe.com/store

ALSO BY ELLE THORPE

Saint View High series (Reverse Harem, Bully Romance. Complete)

*Devious Little Liars (Saint View High, #1)

*Dangerous Little Secrets (Saint View High, #2)

*Twisted Little Truths (Saint View High, #3)

Saint View Prison series (Reverse harem, romantic suspense. Complete.)

*Locked Up Liars (Saint View Prison, #1)

*Solitary Sinners (Saint View Prison, #2)

*Fatal Felons (Saint View Prison, #3)

Saint View Psychos series (Reverse harem, romantic suspense. Complete.)

*Start a War (Saint View Psychos, #1)

*Half the Battle (Saint View Psychos, #2)

*It Ends With Violence (Saint View Psychos, #3)

Saint View Rebels (Reverse harem, romantic suspense)

*Rebel Revenge (Saint View Rebels, #1)

*Rebel Obsession (Saint View Rebels, #2)

*Rebel Heart (Saint View Rebels, #3)

Saint View Strip (Male/Female, romantic suspense standalones. Ongoing.)

*Evil Enemy (Saint View Strip, #1)

*Unholy Sins (Saint View Strip, #2)

*Book 3 (Saint View Strip, #3)

Dirty Cowboy series (complete)

*Talk Dirty, Cowboy (Dirty Cowboy, #1)

*Ride Dirty, Cowboy (Dirty Cowboy, #2)

*Sexy Dirty Cowboy (Dirty Cowboy, #3)

*Dirty Cowboy boxset (books 1-3)

*25 Reasons to Hate Christmas and Cowboys (a Dirty Cowboy bonus novella, set before Talk Dirty, Cowboy but can be read as a standalone, holiday romance)

Buck Cowboys series (Spin off from the Dirty Cowboy series. Ongoing.)

*Buck Cowboys (Buck Cowboys, #1)

*Buck You! (Buck Cowboys, #2)

*Can't Bucking Wait (Buck Cowboys, #3)

*Mother Bucker (Buck Cowboys, $#4)

The Only You series (Contemporary romance. Complete)

*Only the Positive (Only You, #1) - Reese and Low.

*Only the Perfect (Only You, #2) - Jamison.

*Only the Truth - (Only You, bonus novella) - Bree.

*Only the Negatives (Only You, #3) - Gemma.

*Only the Beginning (Only You, #4) - Bianca and Riley.

*Only You boxset

Add your email address here to be the first to know when new books are available!

www.ellethorpe.com/newsletter

Join Elle Thorpe's readers group on Facebook!

www.facebook.com/groups/ellethorpesdramallamas

ACKNOWLEDGMENTS

Are we seriously at the end of another Saint View trilogy? It blows my mind that I've been writing these books for four years now, and with two new Saint View Strip books, plus Kara's story coming in 2024, that'll be five! I get lots of questions about how long Saint View will go for, and the answer is always 'as long as you guys want me to write it.'

I really hope Caleb's death was a satisfying one, after you waited six books for it. But of course, he's not the only bad guy in Saint View these days, is he? I can't wait to see where Kara's series takes us.

As always, there's an ever growing group of people who make these books possible.

Thank you to the Drama Llamas. You guys make my days fun. If you aren't already a member, it's a free reader group on Facebook where I share all sorts of stuff. Come join us, everyone is welcome. www.facebook.com/groups/ellethorpesdramallamas

Thank you to Montana Ash/Darcy Halifax for writing with me every day.

Thank you to Sara Massery, Jolie Vines, and Zoe Ashwood for the constant support, friendship, and book advice.

Thank you to my editing team:

Emmy at Studio ENP and Karen at Barren Acres Editing.

Dana, Louise, Sam, and Shellie for beta reading. Plus my ARC team for the early reviews.

Thank you to the audio team:

Denise and Troy at Dark Star Romance for producing this series in multicast audio! Thank you to Troy (again), Michelle, Michael, and Gregory for voicing Kian, Rebel, Vaughn, and Fang.

And of course, thank you to the team who organize me and the home front:

To Donna and Ari, for taking on all the jobs I don't have time for. Best PA's ever.

To my mum, for working for us one day a week, and always being willing to have our kids when we go to signings.

To Jira, for running the online store, doing all the accounting, and dealing with all the 'people-ing.' Not to mention, being the best stay at home dad ever.

To Flick and Heidi, for helping pack swag, and to Thomas, who refuses to work for us, but will proudly tell everyone he knows that his mum is an author.

From the bottom of my heart, thank you.

Elle x

ABOUT THE AUTHOR

Elle Thorpe lives in a small regional town of NSW, Australia. When she's not writing stories full of kissing, she's wife to Mr Thorpe who unexpectedly turned out to be a great plotting partner, and mummy to three tiny humans. She's also official ball thrower to one slobbery dog named Rollo. Yes, she named a female dog after a dirty hot character on Vikings. Don't judge her. Elle is a complete and utter fangirl at heart, obsessing over The Walking Dead and Outlander to an unhealthy degree. But she wouldn't change a thing.

You can find her on Facebook or Instagram(@ellethorpebooks or hit the links below!) or at her website www.ellethorpe.com. If you love Elle's work, please consider joining her Facebook fan group, Elle Thorpe's Drama Llamas or joining her newsletter here. www.ellethorpe.com/newsletter

- facebook.com/ellethorpebooks
- instagram.com/ellethorpebooks
- goodreads.com/ellethorpe
- pinterest.com/ellethorpebooks

Printed in Great Britain
by Amazon